Didn't You
Use to Be
Queenie B?

Also by Terri-Lynne DeFino

*The Bar Harbor Retirement Home for Famous Writers
(and Their Muses)*

Varina Palladino's Jersey Italian Love Story

Didn't You Use to Be Queenie B?

A Novel

Terri-Lynne DeFino

WM

WILLIAM MORROW

An Imprint of HarperCollins*Publishers*

HarperCollins books may be purchased for educational, business, or sales promotional use. For information, please email the Special Markets Department at SPsales@harpercollins.com.

FIRST EDITION

Designed by Nancy Singer

Library of Congress Cataloging-in-Publication Data

Names: DeFino, Terri-Lynne, author.
Title: Didn't you use to be Queenie B? : a novel / Terri-Lynne DeFino.
Description: First edition. | New York, NY : William Morrow, 2025. |
Identifiers: LCCN 2024008152 | ISBN 9780063393110 (hardcover) | ISBN 9780063393141 (ebk)
Subjects: LCGFT: Novels.
Classification: LCC PS3604.E33 D44 2025 | DDC 813/.6—dc23/eng/20240223
LC record available at https://lccn.loc.gov/2024008152

ISBN 978-0-06-339311-0

25 26 27 28 29 LBC 5 4 3 2 1

For Brian, Christofer, and Scott—
all present and accounted for

Didn't You
Use to Be
Queenie B?

1

Mise en place: French culinary phrase meaning "putting in place," referring to the organization and preparation of ingredients that a chef will require for the menu items to be prepared during a shift.

New Year's Eve 1999

It is too hot inside. Too noisy. Too much booze and too many drugs and more people than she ever imagined she'd know. But she knows them. Kind of. They certainly know her. The whole world does.

The balcony overlooking Times Square isn't any quieter. Only cooler. Cold. January in New York City. In a few minutes, anyway. New year. New decade. New millennium. But not really. That will be 2001, but, as always, facts don't matter. What's the big deal, anyway? The earth isn't keeping the same time humans do. Hell, not even all humans keep the same calendar. It's all a construct. All that Y2K nonsense. No way the world is going to end when midnight strikes because the computers get confused. If anyone is going to end her world, it's going to be Queenie B herself. She's been trying a long time, and . . . nothing.

Sipping her cocktail—something gin heavy and cranberry light—Queenie feels the numbers clapping—*Bam! 49. Bam! 48. Bam! 47.*—counting down on the giant Discover Card light board, kitty-corner to where she stands. Below, a giant Father Time puppet seems to float, accompanied by an equally colossal red dragon. The masses whoop, champagne corks pop from their bottles, everyone is ready for the crystal ball to slide down its pole into the year 2000.

Inside the apartment—can it be called an apartment when it's bigger than a mansion in the burbs?—Dick Clark is speaking. From the television. An eighty-inch monstrosity all those who's whos in New York gather around instead of watching it all unfold from the balcony.

Fifteen seconds. Ten.

Others crowd onto the balcony. Queenie presses up against the railing to make room. She even smiles at those crushing her, laughs with them. Someones she should know but can't remember. It's hard, when there's no telling whether she's actually met those someones acting as if they've been long acquainted or they simply recognize her signature black hair and red lips on sight. Queenie B. Goddess of the culinary world. Superstar. The who's whoest.

... three ... two ... one ...

Happy New Year. Happy 2000.

Cannons shoot literal tons of confetti into Times Square. Fireworks sparkle. Queenie slams back her gin-heavy drink, takes a flute of champagne offered and slams that back too. She kisses the men. She kisses the women. Everyone whoops and she kisses and kisses and kisses. Everyone. So many someones. None of whom matter to her. Where those who do went, she doesn't want to think about.

Queenie takes several kamikaze shots from a tray on the long, black-marble bar. Down. Down. Down the hatch. Two more. She throws back that heavy ink-black mane Osvaldo once claimed had sentience all its own, to do a line with the twentysomethings cheering her on. The world, blurred by way too much alcohol, comes into sudden and sharp focus before blurring again. Too much of one. Not enough of the other. Queenie B knows the balance. Too well. Hers is off. The world is fuzzy.

Someone is calling her name. A voice she knows. A face familiar. Her brain takes its sweet time catching up. Saskia. Sweet Saskia. The girl thought she'd landed her dream job when Queenie B herself pulled her out of a line of hopefuls to be her assistant. Her keeper. Her PR disaster fixer. Poor Saskia. Poor kid. She doesn't jibe with the "if money can fix it, it isn't a problem" mentality. Good thing Queenie B can afford to pay her well . . .

Queenie is in the elevator. She is pressed up into the corner, spandex and sparkle hitched up to her hips. There is a man thrusting between her thighs, his face buried in the luxury of her hair. She has no recollection of how she got here, or when, or who this someone who is no one truly is. His hair is black, like hers, and whatever he's doing inside her, he's doing it well. He's making her groan. He's lighting that fire, lighting her up. Queenie feels it in the roots of the hair he's buried in. And then he's done, and she's not. She pushes him down, onto his knees. He doesn't protest, but gets to it.

Ah, there it is. That glimmer. That roar. Dulled by alcohol, but still pretty damn good. Queenie pulls him up by his hair. She kisses him without opening her eyes, feeling for the elevator buttons that will send the car on its trajectory down.

Up.

It doesn't matter.

She's finished.

Time to go.

2

On the line: The "line" is the kitchen space where cooking is accomplished. Being "on the line" means one is a line cook, an essential foot soldier of any functioning restaurant brigade.

2015

February in Connecticut. The most boring month in the whole year, unless you skied, which, despite living in New England, Gale Carmichael did not. A New Haven boy, born and bred, where trips to the country were few and far between, even though the country could be found with a car and a few miles' worth of gas. February's only highlight was Valentine's Day wooing couples out to restaurants for that special dinner. One and done, like St. Patrick's Day for local pubs, Irish or not, though there were a bunch of those speckled throughout the city. The winter holidays, on the other hand, crammed too many parties into a little over a month, catered and in-house. Once the patio opened to outdoor dining, winter-month doldrums would burst into warm-weather festive. But in February it was never busy on random Friday nights. Typically. Tonight was an anomaly, and, of course, Gale was on the line. By himself, except for the new kid who couldn't pull his own weight yet.

Leaning against the brick wall, Gale didn't even shiver against the coarse cold seeping through his chef coat. Winter didn't make the kitchen any less a furnace. All he needed was five minutes to cool down, to uncurl the clench in his hands, ease the band of aching heat across his shoulders. Chopping, stirring, flipping, plating. He craved a cigarette, fantasized flicking the lighter, inhaling deeply, feeling the nicotine prickle into his toes. Only fantasized. He quit smoking when he quit everything else. His sponsor said, as long as he was having those cravings, it was better to have a cigarette than a relapse. Eighteen months, and Gale hadn't had a drink, a smoke, or a hit. It was all horseshit anyway; AA mentality chafed, but court ordered was court ordered. Gale had served his time for a full year, still had his year-sober medal thing. At least, his mother, Lucy, did. He hadn't been to a meeting in months.

"Hey, Gale!"

His shoulders tensed. "I'm on break."

"There are no breaks during dinner service. Hurry up, before Marco notices."

Frances, Marco's sous chef, took no breaks, so no one else was allowed to either. She'd left the line to chastise Gale. She wouldn't do it again. At least she called him out, and not Marco. She was right, of course. A line cook's job was grueling, often chaotic, and rarely appreciated. No glory; it all went to those higher on the culinary ladder—sous chef, executive chef.

Low pay, sharing tips with the waitstaff who couldn't be trusted to be honest when cash was concerned . . . such was the life of a line cook, and the price of getting to sous chef. Chef de cuisine. Executive chef/restaurant owner. Celebrity chef. At least he'd already done his time as busboy, food runner, dishwasher—the lowest forms of life in the kitchen. The better restaurants had fancier-sounding names for the brigade from front of the house to back. Gale had learned them all in culinary school, but he'd never worked in a restaurant fancy enough to call its line cooks *chefs de partie.*

"Back on the line," Frances barked.

"Heard, Chef."

Gale fell back into his place. Into the frenzied heat of a working kitchen. Marco's, an established fine-dining experience where New Haven locals—the ones who could afford a $45 steak—ate. Being near Wooster Street, they got a lot of overflow traffic when the more landmark waits were too long. He was still just a grunt in the brigade, but at least it was better than working the line over at the vegan restaurant by Yale.

"Fire two scallops, a calamari, and crab cakes for table twelve," Marco boomed from the pass. "Heard?"

"Heard that," the whole brigade called back.

Gale put the crab cakes on the flat top to sear with one hand, tapped a knob of butter into a hot skillet with the other. The butter foamed and sizzled, the taste and texture of perfectly sautéed and basted scallops phantom in his mouth. Tender, slightly caramelized to perfection. Two minutes, turned once, two more minutes. He flipped the crab cakes. Perfect. Now a squeeze of lemon, a sprinkle of fresh herbs, and, "Scallops and crab cakes walking. Risotto ready?"

"Risotto walking."

"Calamari walking!"

Marco waited at the pass. "Beautiful."

"Thanks, Chef."

And that was all. Back to his station. More orders called. More food prepared. An endless cycle of sizzle and aromas that somehow excited him every time.

Home sweet home, man.

The only place he ever wanted to be.

SERVICE WAS GRUELING, BUT IT WENT FAST. GALE WALKED HOME ONLY half aware of where he was going. His feet knew the way. His body. No brain activity required aside from that deepest deep within the medulla oblongata. Animal brain. Caveman, maybe. He remembered learning it was where the brain stored the most basic functions. There was breathing. There was fight or flight, a term he'd learned in those few college days he had before realizing his foodie heart was incompatible with the career as a biologist that his high school career test had recommended. Gale was an artist whose art lived on his tongue, in those tiny bumps—papillae— that differentiated sweet from sour, bitter from salty. And umami, a word learned only because he quit college and went to culinary school. With Sean. Where so many things started to make sense—and fall apart.

"There's no money in it," his mother said. "Restaurants open and close overnight. You'll end up in debt up to your eyeballs. Wait and see."

"No one ever trusts a skinny guy like you to feed them," Danny Carmichael said. "The Irish aren't known for their culinary prowess. Cooking is girlie stuff anyway. What're you? A homo?"

He loved his dad, but the man could be an idiot. The cooking world was still and unfairly male-dominated. Besides which, Gale wasn't gay, and was only half Irish. Kind of. His claim on Ireland being several generations behind his dad, intermixed with so many other nationalities, the cultural claim to the Carmichael name had overtaken the bloodlines long ago. Lucy was Italian, born and bred. Being Italian didn't make her a good cook any more than being Irish made Gale a bad one, only a delayed sort of food-woke. He was sixteen before he tasted food that was not fast, pizza, boxed, or from a jar.

The apartment was as cold as the kitchen was hot, evidenced by the cloud of breath accompanying his sigh as Gale let himself in. Thermostat said it was fifty-eight degrees, though it was set to sixty-eight. Kyle called the landlord days ago; apparently, no one had been sent to see what the deal was.

Gale yanked open the fridge; a crescendo of beer bottles clanking together made his mouth water a little. He shoved aside take-out containers, searching for his lone carton of chocolate milk, the kind he used to get in elementary school on Fridays, when his mom let him spend the extra nickel. Gone. He looked in the trash; there was the empty container, sitting right on top. At least he ate at work, but damn, he'd been looking forward to that chocolate milk.

"Dude." Kyle Sisto shuffled into the kitchen in his boxers, rubbing his eyes. Unlike Gale, Kyle wasn't a skinny chef no one would want cooking for them. He scratched his soft, hairy belly. "You just getting in?"

"Yeah. Did you drink my chocolate milk?"

"That was yours?"

"You knew it wasn't yours."

"Sorry, dude." Kyle shrugged. Fucker. If he had anything in the fridge besides beer, Gale would have consumed it out of spite.

"Supe stopped in this afternoon, said he was getting on the heat situation this week."

"Yeah, right. Jimmy here?"

"Nah. He and Nando went out someplace."

"Out? Neither one of them's contributed to the internet bill in months." Fuck, he was sounding like his dad. "Jimmy was supposed to pay me back that ten bucks I lent him."

"You don't lend Jimmy money." Kyle grunted. "You give it to him."

It's true. You know it is.

"What am I supposed to do for breakfast? I didn't get tipped out—"

"Again? You got to stop letting the waitstaff get away with that shit."

He's right.

"—and I don't go in until three tomorrow."

Kyle opened the fridge, pulled out a container. He opened it, sniffed, made a face. "This is his. Some kind of curry from the other night. I'd say you bought it off him."

"I wouldn't pay a dollar for that crap." Gale took the container anyway. Mold laced the edge of the topmost layer. If he had to, he could scrape it off. He handed it back.

"Yo, we should go to that soup kitchen I told you about," Kyle said. "Free food."

"No thanks."

Beggars can't be choosers, man.

"Dude, seriously. I heard it's good. Nice."

"A good, nice soup kitchen. In New Haven."

Kyle sniggered. "Yeah, I know. I haven't been there myself, but I got it from a good source. A few guys at work go there when the money runs low and the shifts don't align with the hunger pangs."

"I'll pass, thanks."

"Your call. If you change your mind, let me know. I'll go with you."

Leaving the kitchen—such as it was without a working stove, only a microwave and a hot plate to cook on—Gale gave a thumbs-up over his shoulder. He stepped into his room and out of his shoes, his clothes, grateful he'd obeyed his mother and changed the sheets yesterday. It felt good to get into a clean bed, even if he needed a shower, big-time.

You should go with him.

Gale closed his eyes. Mistake. Sean, pale and too thin, burned like an afterimage behind his eyes. Always this haggard specter he became, never the blond-haired, blue-eyed charmer he'd been. "Not now, okay?"

Whatever, man. I only wanted to say good on you. Encouragement, you know?

"I have no idea what you're talking about."

The beer. You didn't cave. Good on you.

"I wasn't even tempted."

If you say so, man. I'm still proud of you.

Gale rolled over onto his side, phone in hand. He found a text from his brother that he'd heard come in and forgotten about. Brian—the success-bound Carmichael brother in his second year of law school—would be home for their dad's birthday on the twentieth; would Gale be around? Gale sent him a thumbs-up. He wasn't getting out of joining the family festivities. Birthdays were sacrosanct. They'd even celebrated his own in rehab.

He scrolled. Twitter. Instagram. Facebook. His parents paid for the phone. Just so he had no excuse not to call. Check in. Let them know he was alive. Okay. Not wasted. Speaking of, he clicked into a text:

Hey, Mom. Just getting home. Beat to hell. I'll see you for Dad's birthday next week. Love you.

Eighteen months hadn't eased her insta-panic, because even at that hour, the little dots that said she was typing, that she had her alerts on through the night, appeared on his screen.

. . .

. . .

. . .

A full thirty seconds of dots.

Good to hear from you, buddy. See you soon. I love you, too.

Gale felt bad but grateful his mom had deleted whatever had taken so long to tap in. It was going to be a while, if ever, before her first instinct wasn't to gush relief, keep him talking, ascertaining his level of coherence by the speed and clarity of his response. Or lack of one. Maybe the longer Gale stayed clean, the more that whole catastrophic thinking would ease up. For her. For them both.

Leaving her message on the screen, Gale plugged in his charger. He set the phone beside him, illuminating a circle on the clean sheets. As if his mother were there, watching him sleep.

Night, man.

Gale sighed. "Night, Sean."

3

In the weeds: Phrase meaning a cook is overwhelmed by tickets, trying to do it all and not necessarily succeeding.

2015

Jimmy didn't pay Gale back, but he did get him a free Egg McMuffin and coffee the next day; there wasn't a fast-food place in town where Jimmy couldn't get free food. The superintendent fixed the heat that they weren't allowed to turn up higher than sixty-eight, but it was way the hell better than fifty-eight. Gale's dad's birthday came and went, punctuated by Brian blessing them all with his exalted presence for two days before heading back to Boston and the Harvard law degree—to complement his Yale undergrad—it was going to take even a lawyer half a lifetime to pay for. Danny Carmichael did that Dad thing he did, comparing his sons and finding one lacking in the most loving and humorous way, that being not at all funny but coming from a place of concern. Lucy told her husband and Brian to knock it off before she cracked some heads, as always and obviously worried that any adversity was going to send Gale off the deep end.

Stay the course, man. Don't prove them all right.

Gale stayed the course. He worked. February turned into March, bringing milder temps. Walking home from work wasn't quite as grueling, even after a Saturday night shift. March wasn't typically any busier than February, and this one didn't prove out of the ordinary. Gale couldn't blame the cold or exhaustion for his carelessness, his lack of street savvy. He could, however, blame the asshole who rolled him.

"I don't have any money!"

"Give me what you got."

It was dark. The street, deserted. And Gale had been scared shitless. He couldn't tell the police or the ER staff anything about his attacker, only that he—or a very deep-voiced she—had shoved him hard from behind, and then when he was on the ground had taken the three bucks and change in his pocket, a lighter, and a container of Tic Tacs. His attacker left him with his easily trackable cell phone.

Good thing you didn't have your knife kit, man. Or get tipped out. Again.

"That's a pretty bad wrist sprain," the ER doc told him.

"Do I need a cast?"

"No cast, but you need to keep it braced."

"Can I use it? I'm a line cook in a restaurant."

"Knives? Hot stoves and pans? I suggest you take a couple weeks off. For safety's sake."

Yeah. Right.

Gale refused the prescription for codeine, but accepted the one for superstrength ibuprofen. The thought of walking home after a full shift, half the night in the ER, and an extra couple miles to boot, wouldn't even form into a maybe. He called his dad, knowing what would result, but deemed worth it in the end. This would set everyone back on the comfort scale. Maybe his father wouldn't tell anyone else.

Wouldn't count on that, man.

Waiting outside, trying not to think about the throbbing in his wrist, Gale dry-swallowed the ibuprofen. It'd hopefully kick in by the time he crawled into bed. He spotted his dad's 2006 yellow Subaru Baja—hard to miss—pulling into the ER parking lot, waved over his head with the braced hand. Maybe seeing the brace would prove he hadn't been lying about what happened.

Gale got into the front seat. "Hey, Dad. Thanks for picking me up. I'm wiped."

"You look wiped."

Ire rose. Gale tamped it down. "I didn't—"

"I'm not accusing you of anything, son."

He sounded sincere. Gale let go of the lingering ire in a sigh so soft he barely felt it.

"What'd they get?"

"He. One guy. Nothing, really. Three bucks."

"Damn. Sure worth sending someone to the hospital for, am I right?"

For some, yes. "I landed on one hand when he shoved me down. Doc says it'll be a couple of weeks for my wrist to mend. She doesn't know kitchen life." Gale chuckled. His father did not.

"You need to take time off?"

"For this?" He held up his hand. "Pssh, no way. Seriously, I can't afford to."

"I can give you a little money to get by."

Again, sincere. "I'm thirty, Dad. Besides, it's not just the money. Two weeks out of the kitchen puts me back on the line. I'm working hard to get higher—"

Well, you can't get much lower, man.

"—on the ladder. Two weeks out isn't an option."

Danny Carmichael grunted appreciation of his show of toughness, even if he still didn't approve of his vocation. Lucy Carmichael would have kept arguing.

"What'd they give you for pain?"

Ah, there it was. "Codeine."

His father's knuckles whitened on the wheel.

"But I told them no thanks." Gale shook the bottle of ibuprofen. "Got this instead. It's just superstrength Advil."

"Good call, Gale."

The sincerity was going to make him cry if it didn't let up soon.

"What'd the bill set you back?"

"Nothing," Gale told him. "When you make as little as I do, you qualify for Husky D. Free insurance. Free everything, pretty much. It's one perk of being poor."

"Sounds like socialism to me."

"Not having this discussion, Dad."

Another grunt. More familiar ground. Gale actually smiled.

"Does Mom know?"

"About this?" His dad gestured to the brace. "Nah. I'll tell her when I get home."

Good call, Mr. Carmichael.

"Where does she think you went at this hour in the morning?"

"I don't have to report my comings and goings to your mother." Then, "I told her I had to go into the shop early."

Gale let it go. It was all sorts of fucked-up and his brain wasn't in the mood for the self-recriminations that would result if he didn't.

His father pulled up in front of Gale's apartment—the second floor of an old Victorian converted into four units. The house had once been beautiful. Home to wealthy New Havenites, back in the day. Now, like most of the area, it showed only paint-peeled shadows of its former grandeur. Danny didn't even take the car out of drive. "You going to be okay?"

"Yeah."

Pressing a twenty into his hand, his father only shook his head, eyes closed, when Gale tried to give it back.

"Thanks."

"Don't mention it."

Gale got out. "See you, Dad."

"See you, son. Call your mother!"

Walking backward, Gale saluted. His dad pulled away from the curb, waved. Barely seven in the morning, and Gale hadn't slept but for the doze he fell into while waiting to be treated. It's all he wanted. Bed. Sleep. Oblivion . . .

Too far, man. Too far.

"Sorry."

Slippery slope.

"I know. Sorry."

The other guys were still asleep. Restaurant work made them all night owls. Gale kept as quiet as he could, even though they all slept like logs. He opened the refrigerator door, more out of habit than desire, beer bottles, as always, clanking. There, right in front, sat a little carton of chocolate milk. A note attached. In Kyle's chicken-scratch writing. Gale's name, and a skull.

Taking it from the fridge, Gale closed the door carefully, so the beer bottles wouldn't clank. He opened the lip, tipped all eight ounces down his throat in a few satisfying gulps. Tears slipped from the corners of his eyes. Sad, when the kindness of a replaced chocolate milk could make a grown man weep.

Not sad, man. Appreciation is a noble thing.

Gale appreciated the sentiment. He appreciated Kyle's gesture. He appreciated the free insurance that got him fixed up in a world that generally disdained people too poor to insure themselves. He appreciated that he was alive, even though Sean was dead. Even though it was his fault that he was.

"YOU'RE GOING TO SLOW DOWN THE LINE." FRANCES, HANDS ON HIPS, shook her head. "I'm sorry, Gale."

"Please, I can't—"

"She's right." Marco blew a breath through his lips. "Sorry, kid, but you can't work the weekend shifts like that. It's a safety issue."

"I'll take the brace off. Come on. I can't afford not to work."

"I hear you. I do. But—"

"Trust me, okay? I won't slow down the line."

Bushy eyebrows raised, Marco looked to Frances. He'd cave before she would. Classically-trained-at-the-Sorbonne Frances was his right hand; Gale wasn't even his left. That would be Santos, sous during the services Frances didn't work, and who Gale had worked under until his recent promotion to weekends.

She's going to ice you, man. Think fast!

"What if I go back to Tuesday through Thursday, and Sunday?" Gale asked. "Kitchen's way slower."

"That's not a bad idea." Marco crossed beefy arms, knife tattoo barely visible under all the hair there. "Santos has been griping about losing you."

Frances groaned. "Who would you put in Gale's place?"

"Dai?"

Another groan. "I guess he's better than Gale with the brace. But his skill level is hardly up to the task."

Could that have been a compliment?

Gale tried not to fidget from foot to foot. Tips were a huge part of his pay, when the waitstaff got around to tipping him out. They always did. Eventually. They were a family. Dysfunctional, but a family. Everyone knew how important those tips were. Especially the Friday/Saturday shifts, the only time those tips amounted to anything. But lower pay was better than no pay.

"Only for two weeks," Gale burst. "The doc said I'd be out of the brace in two weeks."

Frances let go a long exhale. "Fine. Dai it is. But you better be back to fighting form in two weeks, Gale, got me?"

"Heard, Chef. I don't want to lose my place on the line. I worked hard to get there."

"You won't," Marco said. "I promise."

But Frances did not, and that was crucial. She just stood there, hands still on hips and lips pursed. How did a woman as small and slight as a hummingbird give off bird-of-prey vibes? An eagle, or a hawk. Some kind of raptor, for sure, able to spot prey, swoop down, and swallow it without mercy. Gale used to think it was her elite education in France that intimidated everyone. Until he started working in her brigade. Nothing got past her. No quarter given. Gale was more than a little afraid of her. He almost felt sorry for Dai, truly not up to the task. If the kid had any brains, he'd work extra hard to win Frances over and steal Gale's spot. It was nice for Marco to promise, but he'd been so long off the line, he probably forgot how cutthroat a kitchen could be, family or not.

Frances left them to finish prep. The air shifted. Marco uncrossed his arms, shaking them out as if released from a straitjacket. "You'd never know I stole her from a hole-in-the-wall Chinese takeout, huh?"

No freaking way.

"But . . ." Gale fought for words. "I thought . . . didn't she graduate from . . . ?"

"The Sorbonne," Marco finished for him. "Yup. Look, Gale, I know you're afraid of losing your spot, but I appreciate your talents. I'm not going to fuck with your place in the kitchen. In fact . . ." He put that beefy arm around Gale's shoulders, drawing him away. "Funny thing is, I was talking to Santos, just last night, about trying out that chicken thing you made last month, you know, as a special. Remember? The one with the portabella and smoked mozzarella."

After hours, two months ago, in fact. There'd been chicken that didn't sell—because it wasn't a very good dish—and needed to be used. Gale transformed what was left, taking what he found in the pantry and fridges, into one of the best chicken dishes he, personally, had ever eaten. Frances had plenty of critique—the chicken wasn't pounded thin enough, the cheese overpowered the delicacy of the sauce, which she found slightly too sweet because he used sweet vermouth instead of dry, it could have used a little acid—but she ate every bite.

"That'd be awesome. Do you think Frances'll know how to replicate it? Or should I—"

"Tell her how?" Marco boomed laughter, like he boomed everything; he had that kind of voice, that kind of presence. "It'd go over like a lead balloon. You know?" More quietly now. "With you going back to your old schedule—"

"Temporarily."

"Yeah, temporarily. That's what I meant. So maybe you could do that dish this week. You know, on a slower day. Wednesday, you think? Santos wouldn't mind you subbing in, unlike . . ." He jerked his head in Frances's direction.

Damn, dude. That's awesome.

Every hair follicle on Gale's body crackled. "Yeah?"

"You sure you'll be up to it?"

"Absolutely. Wow. Thanks, Marco."

"Don't mention it." He leaned in. "And I mean, don't mention it. Frances'll have my nuts in a vise if she finds out."

"I won't. Again, thanks."

Silver lining, man. Silver lining.

"I'll see you Tuesday then," Marco said. "Leave me a list of what you need and I'll add it to today's order."

His own dish. Cooked by him. It was every line cook's dream. And he'd missed working with Santos, those less frenzied services that afforded him downtime to create things like that chicken dish. If he hadn't sprained his wrist, it might not have happened.

Kismet, man. That's how shit gets done.

GALE ADDED THE ITEMS HE NEEDED TO THE MASTER LIST. MARCO WOULD figure out the quantities. He hadn't cooked regularly in a really long time, but he'd once been something of a celebrity in New Haven, back in the day. Several James Beard Award nominations, but no win. No Michelin Stars. He still had the mounted and framed articles, published in various Connecticut papers, touting Marco's as the "best food in New Haven," number two on the top ten list in Connecticut, among the fifty-best, off-the-beaten-track—New Haven wasn't by any means off any beaten track, but it wasn't on Wooster Street, so it counted—restaurants in New England. He had friends in high places. Famous friends. It was hard to imagine Marco rubbing elbows with the culinary elite. Gale was grateful, and a little humbled, that his boss liked his dish enough to give it a trial on a midweek dinner special. It was a start.

But money was going to be supertight for two weeks. An hour at his kitchen table trying to figure it all out came to the same conclusion; the weekends he didn't get tipped out on time meant the occasional missed meal, but two entire weeks of lower tips was going to make that more than occasional.

Go to your folks' place to eat.

"I'm thirty, Sean."

Lucky you.

"Cheap shot, dude."

I'm just saying.

"I know what you're saying. Fuck off."

"Hey! Whoa! What'd I do? I didn't say anything."

"Sorry, Kyle." Gale rubbed his forehead. He hadn't even heard his friend come in. "I wasn't talking to you."

Kyle pulled out a kitchen chair, sat. "How's the wrist?"

"Okay. Not too bad. Marco won't let me work the line on the weekend. I'm picking up my old shifts during the week."

"Sucks, dude."

Gale grinned. "Not entirely. He's letting me cook a special. That vermouth chicken I came up with back in January."

"The one with the portobellos and mozzarella? Damn, that was good."

"Midweek special, but it's something, right? Money's going to be tight though. Thanks for the chocolate milk, by the way."

Kyle waved him off. "I'd offer to spot you but . . ."

"Yeah, I know." Gale took a deep breath. Always broke; a cook's life. Even a lot of chefs complained of the same. There wasn't a huge amount of money in the food industry, especially not for people like him. Always tight. Always shoestrings. Always a bad review away from failing. He couldn't imagine being one of those Food Network celebrity chefs, who never seemed to cook a bad meal or run out of new ventures to add to their fame and fortune. He'd be happy being sous in a kitchen like Marco's, making food and feeding people, and earning enough to live on.

Someday.

Someday was not today.

He swallowed hard, pride and all. "How about you tell me about that soup kitchen again."

4

Reconstitute: To restore dried food to its original consistency; to change texture by letting it soak in warm water.

2015

Rock Landing was its own neighborhood within a neighborhood of New Haven. It was a forgotten, ignored neighborhood that used to be a little fishing town swallowed—and regurgitated—by history. Before they were condemned, New Haven's oyster beds fed a lot of people. Some of the beds came back. Others did not. Rock Landing, apparently, was built around one of the latter.

Getting there wasn't an issue; it was close enough to walk, but Kyle had a car—if his 1992 Corolla still qualified as a car—that mostly ran, and he was willing to drive.

"You sure this area is safe?" Gale held his wrist closer to his stomach. He still had fifteen of the twenty dollars his dad had pressed into his hand; he wanted to keep it. "Looks pretty sketchy."

"It's hard to say where it's safe in New Haven," Kyle said. "Nice today. Murder-town tomorrow. You're a New Haven boy. You know."

A New Haven boy who's never been truly poor. Until now.

"The kitchen feeds its local homeless," Kyle went on. "Many of them with some kind of mental or drug issues. Some are just poor people trying to get by. There isn't much housing around here that shouldn't be condemned, but some of the guys I work with make do. This"—he pointed—"is where they eat."

It was an incongruity, the building Kyle pointed to. Stone on the first floor, cedar shakes on the second. Very Old World New England. Likely an original home restored to some former glory, if former glory was homey and quaint. Opening the door treated Gale to the delicious aromas—mostly garlic, if his nose was on its game—that came close to overpowering the ever-rank odor of a waterfront too long neglected.

"Wow."

"Right? I told you it was good."

"You told me your friends told you it was good."

Kyle grimaced. "Okay, so I been here. Don't rag on me. We don't all have daddies slipping us cash."

"We grew up in the same neighborhood, Kyle."

"Yeah, well, my parents are divorced."

He never did make much sense, man.

"Why don't we just go in. I'm starving."

Exaggeration. Mostly. The hunger pangs had been near constant the last couple of days. If his parents knew he was at a soup kitchen, they'd be ashamed, but that twenty had to last until Wednesday.

Inside was everything Gale expected. Ratty banquet tables and folding chairs and the indigent. But it was also nothing he expected at all. The tables and chairs were clean. The floor wasn't sticky. A sign on the door read:

CLEAN ZONE! IF YOU'RE NOT, THERE'S A
WASH STATION OUT BACK. USE IT!

There were parents with their kids. Teenagers clustered in groups and older people in singles and odd pairs, the oddest being the elderly woman wearing a Burger King crown and talking to herself in a corner. All in all, there were about thirty eating bowls of what looked like *pasta e fagioli*. Good choice, nutritionally. Protein, veg, carbs. It smelled delicious.

A group of young men waved at Kyle. He waved back.

"What do we do now?" Gale asked.

"We go sit with my buds. Someone'll bring food to the table."

"A waitstaff?"

"Just a volunteer," Kyle said. "More hygienic."

More dignity. Nice.

"Who runs this place?" Gale asked. "It's definitely not state."

"You mean, who funds it?" Kyle shrugged. "Probably a church or something. I don't know. But the lady in back doing the cooking is Regina. I think she runs the day to day."

Kyle led Gale to the table of his work friends. Good guys. Few of them spoke more than get-by English but Gale had enough get-by Spanish to keep up. He had no idea where they were from, and he felt kind of lame for being clueless like that. A few minutes later, a man with the face of an old prizefighter brought two bowls and bamboo utensils to their table, set a plate of rolls between him and Kyle.

"You're new."

"I'm Gale. Gale Carmichael."

"Drugs?"

"Not anymore."

"You sure? Regina doesn't turn junkies away, but it's better for everyone if we know who they are."

Junkies. Man, that's harsh.

Gale was used to it. The derision. "Been clean for nineteen months. I'm just poor."

The man's smile took ten years from the face Gale would have put at seventy. "Sorry. We don't get many white boys in here. When we do, they're usually strung out." He held out his hand. "Troy."

Gale rose to take it. "Good to meet you."

"Same. Now, eat, before it gets cold. Welcome to Regina's Kitchen."

"Thanks."

Gale waited for the man to move on before shoveling a spoonful into his mouth. Zesty, garlicky, rich, smoky. His face stopped chewing in awed appreciation for the food in his mouth. Whoever Regina was, she knew how to balance flavor.

"Told you," Kyle said. "Right?"

"Not what I was expecting. How is this place not packed?"

"Location, dude. No one wants to come to this area. And the locals keep it on the down-low. They know a good thing when they taste one. So, yeah. Don't go blabbing. My guys told me. I told you. Needs to end there, you know?"

"Sure." Gale ate. Slowly. Savoring every mouthful. Picking out the herbs and spices as they rolled across his tongue. Marco put *pasta e fagioli* on the menu now and again; this was nothing like that. His—rather, Frances's—version was refined and delicate. Delicious in its own way. This was hearty. Served in a bowl with crusty rolls, not on a plate with tweezer-placed microgreens.

Gale could have eaten more, but he was grateful for what he'd gotten and didn't ask. Especially since he was one hundred percent certain this would not be his last visit. Spotting bus trays lined against one wall, he picked up his and Kyle's dirty dishes, deposited them there. The woman wearing the Burger King crown eyed him imperiously. He smiled, though she didn't, and bused her table of one, too. Through the doorway, door propped open, he spotted Troy talking to a woman who had to be Regina. All he could see of her was a long, thick, salt-and-pepper braid bisecting her white T-shirt, the comfortable roundness of a body that had never been lean, but didn't push too hard into plump, and the backs of what could only be Vans slip-ons, sparkly gold.

"Can I help you?" she asked over her shoulder.

"Sorry," Gale said. "I just wanted to say thank you. It was delicious."

Regina's brow furrowed, as if she couldn't see very well. She looked familiar, somehow, but Gale couldn't place her in that moment it took for her to look at him, nod, and go back to the pot she was washing.

"NICE BOY, HELPING CLEAN UP LIKE THAT."

Regina grunted, handing Troy a washed pot. "Another cook."

"How do you know?"

"I know one when I see one," she said. "And he had a chef-knife tattoo. They all do it these days. No originality."

"Maybe a rite of passage."

"Yeah, maybe." Regina had one, too, though she'd been one of the originators, and a woman. Women didn't get tattoos, back then. Most men didn't either. Now everyone had tattoos, and every chef had one of a knife. "Give him another few years and he'll end up moving back in with his parents, work at Home Depot or IKEA or some shit. But yes, nice. Polite. Drugs?"

"He says he's been clean for nineteen months."

Counting in months was dangerous. Just long enough to make a body feel like they'd beaten it. Not long enough to claim victory. Decades wasn't long enough. In her experience. The fall from grace was never an if, only a when. If you survived, you had a shot at regaining control. Until the next fall. She'd been waiting years for hers, and still it loomed, ever vigilant.

"Think he'll be back?" Troy asked.

"I imagine so. That brace on his wrist is probably going to be a problem for him in the kitchen."

"Yeah, I was thinking that. I wonder where he works."

Regina chuckled. "Since when do you take interest in polite white boys?"

"Since we don't get many like him in here." Troy sighed dramatically. "Not white. Responsible. Willing. I'm getting too old for this work."

Old. Not entirely dependable. One of the biggest reasons she didn't pay him more than a twenty after a "volunteer" shift. Troy lived in subsidized housing, the assistance he was due as a vet and as an elder. Never enough to live on, which was why he helped out in her kitchen. The twenty. The meals. She knew the twenty she handed him bought him a bottle, which was why he rarely volunteered more than a couple of days in a row. He also had to keep believing she was dirt-poor and running the kitchen on a well-intentioned shoestring.

Regina scrubbed another pot, handed it to Troy. Another, and a last. The kitchen, spotless. The dining room, same. Chairs tucked, tables wiped down with disinfectant. Regina insisted on the cleanliness of her clientele but there was no way some of them could really clean up in the provided wash station. Especially in the winter months.

Reaching for two teacups—the last two she'd kept, Bernardaud, A La Reine, for obvious reasons—Regina felt that twinge in her back. The one reminding her, always, of the past she could not escape. She refused the need to press a hand to it. As if that would do any good. Panaceas were like excuses; completely useless. Never to be indulged in.

She poured tea into the cups, and headed out to the dining room where Gladys—aka, the Burger Queen—waited. As always. Troy never joined them. He'd wait, like a gentleman, while her majesty held court. She and Regina sat together in the empty dining room. In the dark illuminated only by the battery-powered, flameless candles in the front windows Troy had put up at Christmas and she'd yet to take down.

"Another day done." Regina raised her cup.

Gladys sniffed in that imperious way she had. "I've had better."

Their habit, these words. This tea. Their ritual. That first sip always restorative in the way the rest of the cup couldn't replicate.

"Is the tea hot enough?" Regina asked.

"Very nice." Gladys sipped daintily, pinkie raised in some pantomime from those years she taught young ladies how to be married women.

"Did you speak to your landlord about the refrigerator in your apartment?"

"Troy is seeing to that for me."

Regina would have to ask him. "Did you enjoy dinner tonight?"

"Of course. You are a wonderful cook. I'd hire you myself, but Mother would never agree to an Italian. She only hires Irish. You understand."

"Sure."

So that was where they were; not those penniless teaching days after Mother and Daddy were taken from Gladys, leaving her penniless, but when she was still a young woman with a fine future and the promise of a vast inheritance, suitors lined up around the block. Regina had no idea how much of the old woman's past was real, and what was fantasy. Gladys was consistent in her delusion, if delusion it was.

Eight o'clock. Time to lock up. Regina finished the tea in her cup. Gladys knew her cue, as did Troy, who came out of the kitchen. She offered to drive them. They both said they needed the walk. Habit. Ritual. The three of them. It needed to be kept. Every part of it. Superstition, maybe, but Regina had a lot of those when it came to keeping life on an even keel. Even Troy's constant battle with alcohol—never conquered; never vanquished.

Standing there in the dark, staring at the flameless candle in the window, Regina let the quiet envelop her. Seep into her. She'd been all over the world, fed people in establishments where dinner for two cost thousands, and in shacks so ramshackle they could barely be called shacks. The former filled her and cost her everything. The latter drained everything she was and cost her what was left. Regina was nothing if not a survivor. This kitchen struck a balance—sustainable restitution. Good work that didn't fill her or drain her. Not in those dangerous ways.

Time to go home. Regina lifted the china cups and their saucers from the table. In the still-bright kitchen, she washed them carefully. Osvaldo had given her a service for twelve that first Christmas after money had become a disposable resource. It cost more than she'd once upon a time made in a year of working two kitchens at the same time, just to make ends meet. Like those young cooks at the table, including the polite white boy. A gift from the man she once loved, in a life no longer hers.

Ancient past, so hazy she never knew what she remembered and what she imagined any more than did the Burger Queen. Regina didn't even remember why she kept the teacups when she had no idea where the rest of the service had gone. Only that she found them in a box. Wrapped in expensive lingerie she had no use for. When she moved into the run-down little crapshack she turned into Regina's Kitchen. With the money from another life. Earned by another woman. She'd kept them as a reminder of what had been, of all she'd lost.

Regina locked up. All those dead bolts. She was pretty sure no one from the neighborhood would break in, but you just never knew. Desperation made people do desperate things. She unlocked the door leading to her apartment above, locked it again behind her. Up the stairs she went. Home. A bedroom and a spare. An office and a bathroom. A sitting room and a kitchen. A thousand square feet of well-appointed comfort and luxury no one who knew Regina Benuzzi, soup kitchen cook, would imagine her living in. Those who had known Queenie B? They'd only laugh.

5

Flambé: The process of cooking off alcohol that's been added to a hot pan by a burst of flames. The flame goes out when the alcohol has burned off.

2000

January is a black hole from which not a single memory can escape. Queenie stares up at the ceiling thinking the first coherent thoughts since her Christmas promise to Julian. The one she broke on New Year's Eve. He doesn't know; no nine-year-old should be aware just how badly his mother fucked up. Again. But Osvaldo does, and that's just as bad. Worse. Julian will forgive her, in that sweet way of little boys enamored of their mothers, even distant, distracted ones. Maybe especially those. Osvaldo, in the vindictive ways of husbands wronged, will not.

"You're awake." The nurse—or so Queenie assumes—is smiling way too brightly, given the circumstances. "Can I get you anything?"

"The key?" Queenie lifts one shackled wrist holding her down, trying hard not to panic. Not to remember. The locked doors. The small spaces. The punishment for being a kid in households that don't want you, only the money the system supplies.

"I'm very sorry, but I can't do that." The nurse checks the drip line, Queenie's blood pressure, the pulse ox. Writes on her chart. "There's an officer outside your room. We might ask her if it's okay."

"Might we?" Queenie smiles, saccharine sweet. "How about we do that? Thanks so much."

A little brightness leaches from the nurse's smile. She nods and leaves Queenie alone. In her private room. In a hospital not the local kind, but the obviously expensive kind. Where someone—probably Osvaldo—has had her taken instead. Queenie wishes she could remember. Any of it. As much as she wishes she could forget the panic worming through her pounding skull.

"Ms. Benuzzi?" The officer stepping into the room isn't young. She isn't old. Queenie met dozens of her kind when she was a kid getting passed around. The I've-seen-it-all kind of tough, hardened beyond the ability to bend.

"Balcazar. Ms. Balcazar. Thanks."

"Mr. Balcazar made it clear that here, you're Benuzzi." The officer nods. "Tabloids, you know?"

Queenie knows. Of course. In protecting her reputation, Osvaldo protects his own. This dance they do. It never seems to end. "Can we just take this off?" She lifts her hand. "I'm not going anywhere. I assume the security here is tight."

The officer approaches, pulling keys dangling from her belt. "Only cuffed you to keep you from getting out of bed on your own. Nothing's broken or anything, but the docs said not to let you get up without someone standing by."

Rubbing her freed wrist, the panic subsides enough to attempt sitting up. Mistake. The pain displaces memory. Her back. The room blurs and her head swims. "I'm not under arrest?"

"For?"

"Whatever landed me here."

"Last I checked, falling down two flights of stairs isn't an arrestable offense."

Queenie tries again to sit. Her back screams. The officer helps without being asked.

"Why are you stationed outside my door?"

"Just an added precaution. Those tabloids, remember? No one wants the publicity, especially your networks."

Ah. "My producers hired you."

"For your own protection."

"And Osvaldo?"

"Mr. Balcazar was here when you arrived. To oversee your admission."

"And how long ago was that?"

A slight intake of breath. An even slighter shake of her head. "Two, no, three days."

"And that means I have twenty-five days left, yes?"

"Twenty-seven," the officer corrects. "This is a thirty-day program."

Twenty-eight. Thirty. It doesn't matter. Rehab isn't for her benefit; it's for everyone else in her life. Those who need a break from worrying. About her. About ratings. About tabloids clamoring to get stories and photos concerning celebrities falling down two flights of stairs, high on said celebrity's drug of choice; tabloids that absolutely adore the rehab tales. The contrition. The redemption. Queenie will try to remember to thank her producers, and even Osvaldo. Maybe, just this once, she'll get through it without all the press. Maybe, just this once, rehab will actually rehabilitate her.

Because she wants to be rehabilitated. She always does, after a crash like this one. After twenty-eight or thirty days clean, she leaves whatever facility Osvaldo has found to take her, feeling like a new Queenie B. Or the old one. The younger one. The Queenie B who earned a James Beard award at the age of twenty-six; who owns restaurants boasting three Michelin Stars apiece. The woman who hosts two shows—one on the Food Network, and one on PBS—bearing her name, shows that got her a star on the Hollywood Walk of Fame.

She wants to be that woman again, not just for herself or her networks. Certainly not for Osvaldo. She wants to be that Queenie B for Julian. Maybe, if rehab finally sticks, she can make up for not being that woman while she carried him in her womb. For not being the mother he deserves. For not wanting him in the first place.

"Are we ready for something to eat?" The nurse again, her brightness back in place. "Just a little something?"

It will be disgusting. The food, no matter how expensive the "spa," is always bland. As if salt and garlic are yet another substance to be avoided at all costs.

Behave. Stick to the protocol. Get out of here with an A for effort.

Swallowing the venom that would singe the poor girl's gently curved, concerned eyebrows off, Queenie tells her, "That'd be great. Thanks."

6

Pickle: The process of preserving food in brine, a salt or vinegar solution.

2015

Gale closed the laptop on his application, his stomach already doing flips. Damn Kyle for his get-rich-quick schemes. *Cut!*, the culinary competition that was the aspiration of every young chef—and some pretty old ones—was so out of his league. He'd seen the show, seen the frenzy of it. He couldn't do it. His head would explode. Ten grand sure was a lot of money if he won, but not enough to embarrass himself on television, in front of some of the greatest chefs in the world. Because he'd be first to bomb on the appetizer course. At least before the dessert course.

You could totally win, man.

"I won't even get on."

Who says?

"You know how many thousands of chefs fill out applications? Never happen, Sean. Never happen."

Then what's the harm in sending it? You already filled it out.

"How about I get picked? I'd have a heart attack and die, trying to come up with something delicious with oddball ingredients and only half an hour to make it in."

You would not. Chicken.

"Stop."

Bok-bok, man.

"Bite me."

Taking the brace off his wrist always felt so good. For the first minute or so before the effort of using it kicked in. Working without it his first service back had been brutal, but his two weeks were up, and he had to pretend he could because, as promised, Marco put him back on the weekend shift. That his *pollo portobello* had been a tremendous hit with Marco's clientele didn't hurt, of course, though Frances was miffed. She insisted on that hit of lemon Gale gladly included; she was right, the dish needed some acid. It was about the food, not his ego. It just would have been nice if she hadn't been so obnoxious about it. Marco leaving it on the special's menu through the weekend might have contributed to that, though.

On Thursday, with a "Good to have you back" from Frances, he was on the line. In his place. Gale had to admit, he preferred his old shift, if not the lower tips. Working with Santos on Tuesday, Wednesday, and Sunday had lifted more than the workload. Marco's wasn't as booming on off nights. Or maybe it was working with the more relaxed, self-taught chef versus the rigid, Sorbonne-trained one. Santos was a genius with food, even if it was sort of hit or miss when he went off on a tangent. Where Frances had technique, Santos had creativity. Where she had schooling, he had instinct. What Gale strove for in himself was equal parts of both chefs; to that end, working under both of them had been invaluable.

"I'm heading out!" he called to no one in particular. Kyle, Jimmy, and Nando were probably gone already anyway. Gale put his brace back on, ignoring the closed laptop, the application page to be a contestant on *Cut!* still up, if sleeping. Waiting for him to hit send. Which he was no way in hell doing.

Smoothing the Velcro down, Gale pushed out of his chair. Out the door. Out to work his first Friday shift in two weeks.

MAYBE IT WAS HARDER BEING A FEMALE CHEF, BUT FRANCES WAS ALSO A straight-up narcissist. That was the only word for her. She had to have her hand in every pot, pan, and serving dish. Not even the saucier was trusted to make the sauces. He took the heat, though. Like everyone did.

Technically, Marco was the executive chef, but he expedited more than cooked, unless there were old friends, rivals, or VIPs in house. He created menus, approved by Frances. Ordered supplies, approved by Frances. Hired and fired and put on probation those chosen by Frances. Considering she pretty much handpicked everyone in her kitchen, it made no sense that she trusted no one to do their jobs without her hovering. Maybe it was worth the lower pay for Gale to permanently take back his old shifts.

Kyle, as always, wearing only boxers, was clicking around on the shared laptop when Gale practically collapsed onto the chair beside him.

"Do you even own clothes?"

"Clothes are for outside," Kyle told him. "You heading to bed?"

"I'm beat, man. Yeah."

"Wrist okay?"

Gale held up his hand. "Fucking hurts, but whatever. It'll get better."

"Yeah. Oh, hey." Kyle stopped him. "Your application hadn't sent. I did it for you, though. You're brave, dude! Maybe I'll send one in too."

"Appli . . ." Gale's stomach churned. "For *Cut!*?"

"Yeah."

Salivary glands kicked into overdrive. "Fuck me."

"You're not my type."

Gale had already turned the computer. He minimized the online game Kyle was obsessed with, opened the tab still showing—

Your application has been submitted.

Sinking back into the wobbly kitchen chair, Gale had to force the sick down.

"I don't get it. What's wrong?"

"I didn't send it on purpose, you idiot."

"But you filled the whole thing out." Kyle's voice rose an octave. "How was I supposed to know?"

"Maybe ask me?" Gale groaned, head in hands. "I'm totally fucked."

"Dude." Kyle slapped his shoulder, gave it a shake so Gale's head fell out of his hands. "If you get called, you don't have to do it. It's not like they'll put you in chef-jail or something."

His stomach roiled. Actually roiled. Gale not only felt it, but heard it clearly.

He's right, man. You'll probably never get called. You said it yourself.

"Sorry, Gale. Seriously. I thought I was doing you a favor."

"I'm going to bed." He pushed out of the chair, away from the table.

"Don't be like that."

"I'm not being like anything."

"How about I take you to Regina's for lunch tomorrow," Kyle called, winking when Gale turned. "My treat."

Come on. That was funny.

Gale did not laugh. He shouldn't be angry. Not at Kyle.

"Regina asked about you," Kyle coaxed. "Come on."

Dude. You could have clicked out of the application. You didn't. For a reason. Give the guy a break. Look at that face.

That face, as guileless as it had been when they were kids, only hairier. "Fine. Sure."

"Good. And really, I'm sorry."

"It's . . . whatever. Don't worry about it." Gale scrubbed his face with the palm of his hand. "G'night."

In his bedroom, Gale undid his brace. What was done was done. Why stress over something that wasn't going to happen, anyway? He repeated that in his head, until the sweaty stink wafting up from his brace wiped it out.

"Gross."

Yeah. Gross. You need to wash that thing.

Could he wash it? Just in the sink? Considering the condition it was in, it certainly couldn't hurt. Or maybe it was better to toss it, let his wrist get stronger, even if it hurt. The more he relied on the brace, the weaker he'd get.

No truer words, man. No truer words.

"Do you ever fucking stop?"

When you don't need me, I'll stop.

"I don't need you."

Sure thing.

"Stop being noble."

Would you rather I was an asshole?

"I'd rather you not haunt me."

Man, I'm not haunting you. You're the one haunting me.

Gale kicked off his shoes, shucked off his clothes, got in the shower. He sang a song in his head to distract himself from the voice in there, and his sent application

Toweling off, he heard Jimmy and Nando in the kitchen with Kyle. Talking, hushed but excitedly. Probably about how Kyle sent his application. He couldn't help smiling, just a little, for the briefest moment getting excited at the prospect. Only the briefest.

He walked naked across the hall, got into bed. Staring up at the ceiling, he tried like hell to ignore Sean's haggard afterimage hanging out like a ghost up there. Gale's exhaustion didn't equate to sleepy. His brain went everywhere at once. Star brain, Sean used to call it. Thoughts shooting out of his head like the arms of those stars they used to draw—start with an A—in grade school. It was like that, when he had time on his hands. Always had been, but worse, since Sean. Working long hours exhausted Gale, but it succeeded where nothing else did. Almost nothing.

Idle hands are the devil's playground, man.

"Workshop."

Same difference.

Breathing deeply in, slowly out, Gale tried every meditation technique he had learned in rehab. He picked off each thought—work; *Cut!*; Regina's; Lucy, he hadn't told her he was home—putting them gently to sleep with a promise or a thought. He messaged his mother. Leaving him, at last, with Sean.

Nearly two years.

The anniversary was coming up.

That afternoon. That horrible afternoon.

Images. Behind his eyelids, even though he still stared at the ceiling. The echo there convulsed.

Don't, man.

Lips frothed. Eyes rolling.

Seriously, Gale. Let it go.

He'd been unable to move. Unable to help. Just drifting. Sweet oblivion.

Gale. Come on.

Tears, hot and silent, rolled down the sides of his face. His text chime *gabba-gabba*ed robotically.

Sleep well, sweetheart. I love you.

No echo now. Just the glow of the lit-up reply from his mother. Gale wanted to call her. To hear her voice. To tell her he was sorry. For all of it. But she'd only worry. He plugged his charger in, and texted back—

Love you too

Gale set the phone on the mattress beside him, watching the glow fade.

7

Blanch: To briefly plunge into boiling water, then into iced water to halt the cooking process.

2015

Working late nights gave good reason for sleeping until noon. At least, it was the reason Gale gave. Getting up at ten o'clock would give him a solid eight hours. And then there were those nights he didn't work, when he still slept until noon. Bad habit. But his sponsor used to say routine was a good thing, and bed at two, up at noon was Gale's routine.

You do you, man.

"I fucking hate that expression."

"Huh?" Kyle kept his eyes on the road. Driving in New Haven was treacherous.

"Nothing. Sorry."

"You okay?"

"I'm fine. Wrist hurts." It did. A little. "I'm starving."

"Me too. I'm trying to limit my meals at Regina's."

Gale shifted in his seat, adjusted the always-locking-up seat belt. "Why? How often do you go?"

"Once a day, tops."

"Once a day? Really?"

"That too many?"

"Depends on how broke you are." No response. "Kyle?"

"Pretty broke, dude."

"Why?"

Kyle glanced his way. "Cut pay. Gogi caved to the waitstaff. They only tip us out fifteen percent now. And you know some of them are never honest about it all anyway."

No one at Marco's did that, thank goodness. Gale had worked in places, though . . . "Damn."

"I get it. We all work for the tips. Sure as shit isn't worth working for minimum." Kyle grinned, slightly lopsided. Maybe a little cynically. "We can't all have sweet gigs in high end like you."

Culinary school wasn't guaranteed success in their world, but it did open up access to better jobs. Gale and Sean had tried to convince Kyle of that, back when they were roommates watching *Top Chef* and *Hell's Kitchen*, boys with dreams of culinary stardom.

"I barely make enough to get by," Gale said.

"But you do get by. With one four-shift job a week. You can go to Regina's because you want to, not because you have to."

"I did have to."

"For two weeks."

Not even. Gale liked the soup kitchen. The food was good, and he liked the people there. Regina. Troy. The strange old lady who wore the Burger King crown like a Sunday church hat. He still couldn't get his dad's voice out of his head. That disappointed voice wondering why they spent all that money on culinary school if his son depended upon charity to eat.

He has a point, man.

SOUP. IN A SOUP KITCHEN. NOT ORIGINAL, BUT DELICIOUS. REGINA WAS also handing out sandwiches by the trayful, standing at the door of the kitchen looking harried and worn-out. It wasn't even two in the afternoon.

"You think she's alone today?" Gale asked Kyle.

"Don't know," he answered despite the mouthful he chewed. "That old guy usually helps her."

"Troy. Yeah." Gale tried to get a peek into the kitchen. "I don't think he showed up." He pushed away from the table. "Come on. Let's go see."

Kyle followed, slightly flustered and a little behind. Regina was indeed alone.

"You need some help with that?" Gale asked.

"I can manage."

"I'm sure you can, but an extra set of hands would probably be better."

She frowned but said, "I'll pay twenty bucks after service. That work for you?"

"Free food and twenty bucks." Kyle rubbed his hands together. "Works for me."

Regina's eyes narrowed. She handed the tray to Kyle. To Gale she said, "You, come with me."

Regina's kitchen was nothing Gale would have anticipated, didn't know he'd anticipated anything at all, but the reality was not this. State-of-the-art everything from the industrial Wolf ovens to the Matfer Bourgeat pots and pans. Not even Marco's had such nice stuff to work with.

"Close your mouth. You'll catch a fly."

Gale shut his mouth so fast, his teeth clacked. "Sorry. Nice kitchen."

"Rich benefactor with a guilty conscience." Regina grunted. "You buy good, you buy once. Service is nearly finished, but if you could grill a few cheese sandwiches, that'd be a huge help. I have to get started on dinner."

Something Gale knew from experience should have been done yesterday. At least, this morning. He put together cheese sandwiches, grilled them to golden, gooey perfection on the flat top, and handed them to Kyle, who passed them to those still lingering in the dining room. Then Gale got right to work beside Regina chopping veg, butchering chicken into pieces, peeling potatoes. He sautéed the mirepoix in a giant pot, added the chicken pieces and the bouquet garni Regina handed him.

"Stir in a little chicken base too," she told him. "Just go easy on the salt."

When Kyle finished busing the dining room, he jumped in to help with dinner prep. Somehow, they all worked together as if they always had, and Gale never even worked with Kyle before. In the lull after lunch and before dinner service began, they sat together eating what was left of the vegetable soup.

"Troy's not exactly dependable." Regina dipped a heel of stale bread in her soup. "But when he says he'll be here, he usually shows up. It's been a few days now." She was silent a moment, chewing absently, then, "I could use the help tonight, if you're available."

Gale and Kyle spoke over each other.

"I'll stay."

"Sorry, working."

"It's Saturday night, dude," Kyle said. "Your first in two weeks."

"I'll call Dai. He'll cover for me one more week. He'll be happy for the extra cash."

"No," Regina told him. "You take your shift. Thanks for all your help. It's mostly done. I'll manage service by myself, but if you could drop off a box to a shut-in for me, I'll give you an extra ten."

"Sure," Kyle said. "No problem."

Gale felt bad, but she'd refused his offer to stay, and Regina didn't seem the kind to be argued with. Rising, both young men cleared away dishes while she dug into her pockets for the crumbled bills. Kyle pocketed his, plus the extra ten she'd promised.

"Here's the address." She also handed him a slip of paper. "I assume you know how to use the GPS on your phone."

"Couldn't get anywhere without it." Kyle grinned that grin of his, not so much stupid as silly. It made Gale remember childhood, and how his friend always thought he could grin his way out of trouble. He never could. Sean, on the other hand . . .

Pressing the twenty back into Regina's hand, Gale said, "I'm good."

"Take it."

"No, really. I—"

"I said, take it."

Gale should have taken his earlier advice and not argued. He stammered, "I work Monday, Thursday, Friday, Saturday, but if you need help on Sunday, Tuesday, or Wednesday, let me know."

"Why?"

Yeah. Why?

"Just thought I'd . . ." *Help out. You're doing something good. You shouldn't have to do it alone. I need service hours for my Eagle Scout project.*

"It's when I have time on my hands," he said at last. "That's not such a good thing for me."

Regina leveled a glare. Gale bore it without flinching. Much.

Scrubbing the tired from her face with both hands, she told him, "Leave me your number."

"We better get going." Kyle hefted the produce box full of soup containers and sandwiches in his arms. "I'm really sorry I can't help tonight, Chef."

Regina one-eyed him. "Don't call me chef."

Kyle colored. "Sorry. I thought it was safer than calling you Regina. I don't know your last name or anything."

"Regina is fine."

Nodding, Kyle headed for the back entrance. Habit, using the service door. Gale followed him. "See you, Regina."

She threw a tired wave over her shoulder. Gale was beat too, and now he had to go to Marco's and put in a full shift. With Frances.

She's not that bad.

No. She wasn't. Mostly annoying. Sometimes frustrating. Gale always thought it was how she ordered everyone around that set him off, but Regina was way worse, and he hadn't cringed or rolled his eyes even once.

DINNER SERVICE WAS OKAY. THE BOYS HAD SET REGINA UP WELL ENOUGH to be able to manage, and a few of her regulars pitched in to help serve. Too bad she couldn't call on them to fill Troy's shoes. Despite his rhythmic fall into a bottle, he was the only person she trusted in her kitchen. To know where everything was. To keep things the way she wanted them. Not to steal from her. She'd learned this the hard way; trust was a rare commodity in the always-on-the-edge world they all lived in. But this Gale kid . . .

She knew one when she saw one. A chef with potential. It was in the way he moved, how he smelled food, touched it before doing whatever needed doing to it, as if each piece of chicken or cut of carrot had some quality that made it right or wrong for the dish in question. She used to make chefs like him. And break them.

The other young man, Kyle. He'd do okay, but he didn't have it. Lucky for him, he didn't have the other part Regina recognized in Gale—the slightly pinched look of someone always hanging on by their fingernails. She saw it when Gale laughed, when he talked. But not when he cooked, even when he was in the weeds. An artist set free. She remembered the feeling. Queenie B did, anyway.

Cleaning up wasn't too bad. The two boys worked clean, well-trained. Despite her rule about not caring too much, she couldn't help worrying about Troy; this latest binge was lasting a long time. Was he eating? Getting to his nebulizer appointments at the clinic? The man wheezed like an old car chugging its last. He'd also disappeared for a while in 2012, but Troy had eventually come back to work; he just hadn't been the same since Petunia died. Neither of them had, really.

Exactly why caring too much was dangerous. The taut line she treaded made *selfish* and *survival* synonymous.

Stepping out into her yard, taking deep, deep breaths, she blinked free of those thoughts, the hurt. She spotted the Burger King crown over the cane fence that would buttress her peas in warmer months. The Burger Queen held her court of one, talking animatedly to the chain-link fence.

"Good evening, Gladys." Regina spoke gently. "What are you doing here? Didn't those boys deliver your food to you?"

The old woman sniffed. "I should fire that man."

Troy, of course. The Burger Queen labored under the delusion that Troy was her butler and driver, though, as far as Regina knew, Troy never owned a car.

"I'm sure he's doing his best. Can I give you a ride?"

"Thank you. Much obliged."

Regina offered her arm to the old woman, walked as slowly as her tiny steps required. The state-assisted building both Gladys and Troy lived in was as ramshackle as the rest of the area, but there was running water, heat, and shelter from the elements. It was more than many of Regina's elderly patrons had.

Helping Gladys climb into her Durango, Regina asked again if she'd gotten the food Kyle and Gale were supposed to deliver.

"Nice boys." Gladys sniffed in that imperious way. "The shaggy one even put it in the refrigerator for me."

"Then why are you here?" Regina asked. "How did you get here?"

"I . . . was . . ." Another sniff. "I am fully capable of going for a walk on my own, young lady."

"Of course you are. Forgive me."

Another consequence of Troy's benders; no one looked after Gladys. Rather, she allowed no one else to. Regina tucked that away. There was nothing she could really do, short of reporting the situation to whoever reported dotty old women roaming about dangerous neighborhoods. Then it would be a state nursing home, understaffed and overcrowded. Gladys was better off where she was.

She drove Gladys home, helped her to her apartment, and even warmed up soup for her before she left her in front of the grainy television tuned in to some game show. Hopefully, she'd stay put now. Regina had to get back to the kitchen, finish up. Thank goodness for Gale and Kyle's help today; she was in pretty good shape.

But then there was tomorrow.

In her Durango, heat blasting, she took her phone and the slip of paper Gale had written his number on from her pocket.

If you really meant it I can use your help tomorrow. Lunch or dinner lmk

Regina tossed the phone onto the passenger seat, headed back to the kitchen. In her head, planning. Breakfast was easy enough to see to on her own. A pile of scrambled eggs, toast. She could set up a slow cooker of oatmeal before she went to bed, like she'd done in the early days, and it'd be ready by the time the door opened. Could be she was hoping for too much from this kid, but she had a good feeling, and Regina didn't get those often enough to look a gift horse in the mouth.

Back at her kitchen, she set up the two massive slow cookers, grabbed the brown sugar and honey from the pantry, the frozen berries from the freezer, and set them on the counter. Eggs, she always had dozens on hand. Not from her own hens, but from the giant box store. Regina hated to use subpar ingredients, but sometimes cost and convenience had to win out. Money wasn't the issue. It only needed to seem so. Serving simple but tasty, nutritious food kept her off the wider radar. The locals kept Regina's Kitchen for themselves, for the most part. If she started cooking high end with organic, farm-raised and grain-fed products, word would spread. She'd be found out. And that was something she couldn't let happen.

Then she was upstairs. Home. Exhausted. Feeling pretty okay about things. Another day down. Another—with or without Troy—coming at her. She'd done it all by herself before. She'd acclimate to it again if she had to, and face it—she probably did. Or would, sometime soon, because Troy wasn't getting any younger or less of an alcoholic. She wasn't old, even if she felt it sometimes. Most of the time. This was what she'd signed up for when she'd chosen this balance, this form of atonement. If Regina could take pride in anything about her life, it was that she never quit.

Washed, dressed for bed, Regina slipped between the sheets—Frette, Italian-made—and turned out the light. Her phone on the nightstand lit up just as her heavy lids began their descent to slumber. A text from Gale bisected Julian's face on her lock screen—

I can do both. See you abt ten.

Regina texted him a thumbs-up, trying not to grin too smugly for being right. She cleared the screen, and there was Julian again, a picture she'd snatched off social media. A grown man. Standing with his father; she'd cropped Osvaldo out. Not because she hated him or resented him; because she loved him. She had when she was only barely someone—a chef with her own cooking show on public television. He'd been a guest, her producer's idea. Handsome and sophisticated. Foreign, with the name and accent to match, Osvaldo Balcazar had charmed everyone on the set, including her. Especially her. It had taken moments for them to fall in love, years for him to fall out of it. Regina never had. Never would. She owed him that much for all she'd done.

In the photo on her cell phone, her son wore a chef's coat, his smiling face driving home all she had done to him before he ever breathed his first breath. The thin upper lip, flat face, small eyes. The underdeveloped jaw she'd hoped beyond hope he would outgrow once he was a man. But he hadn't. He'd outgrown none of it. The behavioral issues. His limitations. Did Oz have him working in one of his restaurants? Or was it simply a photo op meant to prove the great Osvaldo Balcazar, sommelier and restaurateur, lived a shining, uncomplicated life since the vanishing of his wife, the infamous Queenie B?

She'd seen neither her son nor her ex-husband in years. Not since Bova, their little house in the cliffs. Italy. Rome had ruined everything. She had ruined everything.

Switching off the phone, Regina didn't worry someone might try to reach her in the night. Gale wouldn't, that was for sure. Anyone else who had her cell phone number—lawyers, accountants all overseeing her interests in an empire still bearing her name—wouldn't call during the night. No one knew how to find her. She, who had once been in every home in America, on billboards and radio and even—a cameo—on the silver screen. She, who couldn't hide if she wanted to, was now so incognito, no one in her present had a clue who she was. Had been. If she had anything to say about it, no one ever would.

8

All day: A phrase used to indicate the total number of orders needed; that is, if there are three orders of salmon on one ticket, and four on another, then there are seven orders of salmon all day.

2015

Gale's wrist still gave a little twinge now and then; he only noticed in passing. Too busy. Way too busy. Marco's, four shifts a week. Regina's Kitchen, sometimes every day, but mostly his three days off, lunch and dinner service. He'd fallen in beside her that first Sunday, and time just . . . flew.

Gale got to know the regulars, like the Burger Queen—Gladys, Gale learned. Otherwise, the faces changed a lot. Moved on. Got a job. Pulled themselves out of the hole they'd been in. Those were mostly families, down on their luck but striving for better. Many of the addicted—whatever it was they were addicted to—came and went and died. There were far too many elderly people frequenting the soup kitchen, too proud to do so on a regular basis. The guys Kyle worked with would come odd days, but hardly a week went by without seeing them at their regular table. Kyle had come a few times, but once he got his third job, he didn't have the time, nor the need.

Troy was still MIA; Gale was Regina's only regular help. And while she slipped cash to random people who offered to help serve now and again, Gale refused after that first, flustered time, politely but adamantly.

"I'm learning a lot from you," he said. "Call it an even trade."

It was the last time she offered. Regina taught him things he never learned in culinary school, like how to warm a basil leaf in your mouth to gauge how it was going to flavor the dish.

"No two basil plants are created equal," she told him. "Even the closest varieties are only related, not the same. The soil it grew in. How long ago it was picked, where it was stored, what time of year. Everything changes the potency. The flavor."

How had he ever thought otherwise?

Tonight was paid-job night, and Gale was in the zone. He had to admit, he and Frances were really working well together lately. Maybe working with Regina was teaching him more than cooking technique. At least he now knew he wasn't—consciously or not—one of those men who couldn't handle taking orders from a woman.

"Gale! I need to speak with you after shift," Marco called from the pass. "Stick around."

"Sure thing, Chef."

"What?" Frances shouted back.

"He was talking to me, Chef." Marco winked.

"Yes, Chef!"

Gale went back to the steaks he was firing, making sure they made it to the right doneness. One medium rare. One rare. One medium well. Frances claimed she never had, and never would, cook a piece of beef beyond medium. Period. No matter what the diner asked for.

"It's an insult to the animal that gave its life," she told him, but she didn't scold him for doing so. At least, not when Marco could hear. In a kitchen as small as theirs, the line cooks changed tasks by the specials. Gale was good at judging meat temp, so he got the grill, but what he liked best were the nights he got to be the saucier, who also helped Marco plate on the pass. Everyone knew any dish was all about the sauce that brought it all together.

Fast-paced as it was, service didn't fly in the same way it did in

Regina's Kitchen. Hot. Loud. Sometimes dangerous. Somehow, despite a whole—if abbreviated—brigade, it exhausted him way more. Though it was only eleven when Gale finally packed up his knives, the same ones he'd had since culinary school, it felt like two in the morning.

"Don't forget Chef wants to see you," Frances murmured as he passed. Then, "You've been doing exceptionally well since you came back."

"Thanks, Fran . . . Chef."

"You taking a course or something?"

"I did graduate from culinary school, you know."

Frances grimaced. "Of course I know. I wouldn't have hired you otherwise. You just seem more competent lately. Anyway . . ." She put her hand on his shoulder, squeezed it once. "Be safe going home. And congratulations."

"For?"

But Frances had already pushed through the swinging door, back into the kitchen. Knife kit over his shoulder, Gale met Marco out at the bar where he typically sat, chatting with whichever bartender was on duty. Marco's couldn't seem to keep its bartenders more than a few months. Gale had a feeling it had something to do with the boss lingering too late at their station after service, but he wasn't saying a word.

"You wanted to see me, Chef?"

Marco pulled a cigarette from the packet always in his pocket. He offered one to Gale.

"No thanks."

The bartender sidled off, nodding almost imperceptibly Gale's way.

Lighting up, blowing a thick stream of smoke, Marco pointed the lit end at Gale. "I'll get right to the point. You have any interest in being a sous here?"

Gale's kit slid off his shoulder. "Are you kidding?"

"I don't kid about that shit." Another long stream of smoke. "Santos is going home. Back to Costa Rica or some shit. He suggested you. Frances and I agreed. Monday and Thursday, lunch service. Sunday, Tuesday, Wednesday dinner. You interested?"

"Hell, yes!"

"You don't need to think about it?"

Gale would have laughed had he not feared it would get him in trouble. "No, Chef."

Marco chuckled, flicked ash from his cigarette. "You want to know the salary?"

A salary, man. A fucking salary!

"Yes, Chef," Gale said, adding, "please," for good measure.

"YOU ARE ONE LUCKY ASSHOLE." KYLE SAT, BALANCED ON THE BACK LEGS of the kitchen chair, as always in his boxers. "A fucking salary."

"No tipping out, though."

"Like you need it, with that kind of cash. Be happy. No more waiting to get tipped out, or getting your percentage cut. Or working a third job. Look at me."

"Do I have to?"

"Very funny."

It was. A little.

"Seriously, dude, congrats. I'm jealous as hell, but happy for you."

"Thanks, Kyle."

Letting the chair bang onto all four legs, Kyle groaned to his feet. "I'm too young to ache this much."

"You're working hard. Too hard."

"Gotta do what I gotta do." Kyle clapped his shoulder. "You working at Regina's tomorrow?"

Gale nodded. "It'll be my last Sunday dinner service with her. I'll be at Marco's from now on."

"You think she'll be pissed?"

"Nah. It'll mean some rearranging, but it'll work out. I think she likes me."

Another clap on his shoulder, a smile—kind of sad—and Kyle left him at the kitchen table. Gale considered just going to bed, but he hadn't checked his email in a few days, and the spam was probably taking over. Opening the laptop, waiting for it to wake up, he yawned big and contented.

You're on your way, man. Awesome.

"It's a step," Gale murmured.

Big one, though.

The screen blinked. And again. The laptop was really old, overloaded with all the stupid games Kyle played. Maybe he'd get himself a new one. All his own. Once he had a few paychecks put away. Which reminded him, he really needed to call his parents. But no; Gale wanted to see his dad's face in person. He texted his mother.

I have news. Want to meet up for breakfast?

The dots of an instant answer. Despite the hour. Gale tried not to let it bother him. Then again, he'd expected her to answer, hadn't he?

Sounds great buddy. Time?

What time? He didn't have to be at Regina's until lunch service. She'd never gotten anyone to help with Sunday mornings. The kitchen only served oatmeal and scrambled eggs. He could go in, surprise her, take his parents with him. They'd be proud to learn he was volunteering his time to a worthy, and educational, pursuit.

Can you pick me up at eight?

                                                            . . .

                                                            . . .

                                                            . . .

                                        So early on a sunday

A question? Or a statement. Gale let it go.

It'll be worth it. Promise

                                                            . . .

                                        Okay see you at eight. Love you!

Love u 2

Setting aside his cell, Gale noted the time. If he got to bed now, he'd get a solid seven hours before he had to be up. Even though the computer had finally chugged awake, he lowered the screen. Email could wait.

SHOWERED, KIT OVER HIS SHOULDER, HAIR STILL WET, GALE WAITED ON THE curb. There was no mistaking his dad's Baja, but his mom's car looked like every other silver-gray sedan on the road. Still, the streets were quiet, so when the nondescript car glided down his, he knew it was hers.

Lucy. Not his dad.

Don't jump to conclusions.

"Shut up, Sean." Gale opened the passenger door and slid inside. "Couldn't get Dad up?"

His mom tapped her cheek. Gale kissed it obediently. The musky scent of her perfume soothed. Like it did the bumps and bruises, the nightmares and thunderstorms of childhood. The hours she spent holding him while the drugs did their damage, making sure he kept breathing, didn't choke on his own vomit. Through withdrawals that lasted way longer than any thunderstorm or nightmare . . .

Rabbit hole, man. Don't.

"I wasn't aware you wanted him to join us." Lucy pulled away from the curb. "You didn't specify."

"Oh, sorry. Is he upset or anything?"

"Nah. I just told him you invited me out on a mother/son date."

"We could go get him," Gale said.

Lucy smiled. "How about we keep it just me and you. I miss this kind of thing. You're always so busy."

Ain't it the truth.

"So . . . what's the big news?"

"When we get there, okay?"

Gale directed his mother to Regina's Kitchen, ignoring the concerned tuts and tsks coming from her direction.

"Wow." She parked right out front. "One of these things is not like the other, huh?"

"That's what I thought, first time I saw it."

"A line going out the door?" Lucy got out of the car. "Must be great."

"It is, but . . ."

"But?"

Just tell her, man. She's your mom.

"It's a soup kitchen. Now before you go nuts, I volunteer here on my off days."

"Oh. Son, that's . . . it's really nice. I'm proud of you. But we can't actually *eat* here."

"Sure we can. I do all the time."

"If you needed money—"

"Can you just come inside?" Gale took her hand. "I promise, it's not what you're imagining. I want you to meet someone."

Gale waved to some of the regulars, bowed to the Burger Queen—"Your Highness"—but didn't stop to introduce them. His mother could only take so much at once. It wasn't that she was a snob, far from it. She knew what poverty looked like better than most, even if she'd not experienced it since marrying Danny Carmichael. Leading her around to the back entrance, he took some comfort from the now-pleasantly-surprised tuts and tsks coming from her direction.

"What are you doing here?" was the only greeting he got from Regina. Lucy's eyebrows rose.

"A lot of reasons," he said. "First, this is my mom, Lucy Carmichael. Mom, this is Regina."

Regina wiped her hand on her apron, held it out to Gale's mother. "Lucy Carmichael, huh? How's Ricky?"

Lucy took it. "Wrong show. But, yeah, I been getting that joke since I married Irish. Lucia, actually. I was born a Columbo."

"Paesana?"

"Born and partially raised. We moved to the States when I was a little kid."

"Well, Lucia, I got a breakfast service to get out, so whatever the reasons your boy has for this visit, it's got to wait. You here to help, Gale?"

"We both are," Lucy answered.

"Good. Pick as much as you want, but get food out to the dining room. Gale, open the doors."

9

Grind: To break something down into much smaller pieces; for example, coffee, peppercorns.

2001

Y ou can't. Saskia, come on." Queenie paces, her body vibrating almost as hot as her brain. "Not just before the awards. After, fine. Go. I'll give you a great reference. Please."

Saskia won't stay. Not this time. She can see it in the young woman's face. Something inside Queenie slumps even if it doesn't show on the outside. Pacing, pacing, pacing to keep from jumping out of her skin.

"I just can't do this anymore, Ms. Balcazar. I haven't been able to help you, and I can't just wait around for you to die."

"You're being dramatic. It's just too much caffeine."

"Only if there's caffeine in cocaine."

Queenie yanks at her hair. "I'm just trying to get through this week! The festival is my baby, Saskia! I've got to be on my game. Especially after . . . everything. This is the year everything changes. I feel it."

"Same story, different day. It's always something, Queenie." No Ms. Balcazar. Just Queenie, sadly spoken. This is it. Saskia's history.

Queenie tries to do that deep, cleansing breath thing. It used to work. It worked for a little while. She pretended it did.

"I'll stay with you through the festival awards," Saskia tells her, "on one condition."

"Anything. Name it."

"Mr. Balcazar comes to stay. Just for the week."

And Julian? Queenie hasn't seen him in months. Not since that leaked photo her PR people couldn't squash fast enough. The one Osvaldo did see. Fucking paparazzi. And it hadn't even been recent. "Give me my BlackBerry."

Saskia hands over the cell phone. Reluctantly. She'd taken it away when she caught Queenie calling her dealer. As much as she appreciates the girl's genuine love for her, Queenie has no patience for it, this week of all weeks. It's not like she's completely gone over the wall. She can catch herself. It's just a little cocaine, not booze. Everyone knows cocaine isn't addictive. All she needs is a little help to get through the food festival.

"Osvaldo, it's me."

"Hello, Regina. How can I help you?"

Always Regina. Never Queenie. "You going to pretend you and Saskia didn't cook up this little babysitting deal?"

He sighs. Queenie pictures him pinching the bridge of his long nose.

"She cares," he says. "I care."

"I know." She says it, but she doesn't intend to. It's nevertheless true. "I'm good. Really. Fine. Saskia is being overly cautious. I've had way too much coffee today, and—"

"Are you really trying to lie to me? Me?"

Now it is Queenie's turn to sigh. "I know you don't believe me, but this is the first little lapse since rehab. I fucked up, Oz. I'm sorry. But do you have any idea what my schedule looks like right now?"

"I know exactly what it looks like. You stretch yourself too thin. I used to think the alcohol and drugs were the result of that. Now I know better."

"What's that supposed to mean?"

The silence lingers too long. Long enough for Queenie to imagine, now, the sorrow in storm-blue eyes that once held her in awe.

"I don't know what it means," he says at last. "I just want it to end, Regina. I want you to be okay."

"I told you. I'm fine."

"Then why are you calling me?"

"So Saskia won't quit."

"And why is she threatening to quit?"

"Are we really doing this?" Queenie growls, less under her breath than she means to. "Will you come?"

Oz sighs. The kind that says he's done, but not done in. "I will."

"Will you bring Julian?"

Another silence, this one only long enough to half imagine his wild brows furrowed. "Not at first," he said. "In a few days, if you're . . . okay, I'll send for him. Maybe we can go to the award ceremony together. As a family."

The sommelier and the chef. Together again. Tears spill down Queenie's cheeks before she can even think about banishing them. She hands the phone to Saskia. "Make the arrangements. I'm going to get in the shower. Have a cup of tea ready for me when I come out." She hands her assistant the little vial only just delivered that morning. "And get rid of this."

OSVALDO IS AN ASSHOLE. SHE'S DONE AS HE ASKED, NOT A DRINK OR A snort or a pill all week. This week, of all weeks! Just so he and Julian would be at her side in her triumph. Didn't that count for anything? It was only three shots. Maybe four. If he can't cut her a small break, then fuck him. How the hell is she supposed to cope when every moment, from opening ceremony to the awards, rides on her shoulders. She has to be witty and sage and beautiful, all at the same time. Everyone wants a piece of her, and she has to give it to them or fade away like every other has-been in this business. This festival is everything. Everything! A new, more dignified stage of her career. The great Queenie B is back on her game. With the success of the festival, after last year's horror, she can slow down, maybe even let go of one of her shows. PBS has been trying to make changes she is unhappy with, anyway. Cohost? No way.

Osvaldo doesn't have to take Julian and go, her beautiful boy crying, arms outstretched, right there in front of everyone. But he does, just to spite her. To punish her. Their friends, colleagues, all those wannabes pretending to be thrilled at seeing the two of them together again are now snickering as she stands on the steps of the stage. Waiting for her cue. No Oz. No Julian. Just Queenie B.

She doesn't make a scene. Queenie blows a kiss, as if Osvaldo is only taking their overtired, special needs child out of a stressful situation. He'll go along with the story, once he hears it. He doesn't want the bad publicity any more than she does. But he won't let her see Julian again, damn him. As if he has the right to keep her from her child.

Which he does, according to the court orders.

"Queenie?"

She shakes herself out of it, shoulders back and chin up. Her heels are high, the steps are wobbly, and she's not exactly sober, but she nods to the kid wearing the headset and holding the clipboard. He points to the woman on the stage. Linda? No, Lydia. The woman PBS wants as her cohost. Lydia steps closer to the microphone.

"Few of us in the culinary world are recognized outside of it. We are big fish in small ponds, but!" She raises a finger. "Our pond is getting bigger." Laughter. A few whoops. Applause. Lydia waits. She knows how to work an audience, Queenie will give her that. "We all owe a huge debt to our keynote speaker. Not only a brilliant chef, but a charismatic woman who has been instrumental in elevating our art to celebrity status. The two thousands will usher in amazing things for the culinary world, for all of us. And we owe it in great part to our own, our magnificent, Queenie B!"

The applause. It is dizzying. Queenie climbs the steps, the headset kid giving her a hand. She looks amazing in her Zac Posen gown; her long hair drapes like an accessory. Her signature smile, the one made into a logo for both her shows, on cookbooks, menus, and personal stationery, sparkles in the spotlights more brilliantly than diamonds. It feeds her, this adulation. It proves them all wrong. Every relative and foster family who gave her back. Every smack and kick and curse aimed to break her. This moment validates everything. Almost everything.

Queenie takes her place center stage, waiting. Basking. A pair of attractive young men approach from the left. Unfolding the crisp black chef coat they carry between them, they wait on either side of her. To slip her arms into the sleeves. To cover the designer gown with the one item of clothing worn by every chef, from the prep cooks to Queenie B herself.

Arms raised over her head, she listens to the roar. Then she lowers her arms, lowers her head, and takes the bow they're all waiting for. The bow she has fucking earned.

10

Steep: The process of allowing dried ingredients to soak in a liquid until the liquid has taken on the flavor of the ingredient.

2015

Gale finally told his mother about the new position at Marco's, sitting in her car in front of his building. It would have been better if his dad was there, but Lucy's enthusiasm almost made up for it.

"That's huge, isn't it?" she asked. "Sous chef? And you're so young!"

"I'm thirty."

"But you only graduated a few years ago."

"Six, Mom."

"Can you just let me be happy for my successful son?"

"Brian's in Boston."

She smacked his arm.

"Ow!"

"Next time it'll be right across your face." And then she took both cheeks in her hands, smooshed them together so he looked like a fish. "I'm so proud of you, buddy. So happy."

Don't . . .

"Really? Are you?"

Her hands fell to her lap. "Son . . ."

"No, really." He tried to maintain eye contact. "It's okay. That whole . . . those years . . . they were bad."

"I don't blame you, Gale. Sean—"

"Don't blame him."

She can blame me. It was my fault.

"You never even drank in high school, like Kyle and the other boys. Sean is the one who introduced you to . . . all that."

It's true.

"It's not true." To Lucy. To Sean. "I made my choices, and I'm sorry. So, so sorry." Again. To Lucy. To Sean. "It just . . . it makes me really happy to hear you say you're proud of me."

"Sweetheart." Those hands on his cheeks again. Softer. Gentler. "I've never not been proud of you. You were always a good boy. A good son. Those bad years don't erase all the good ones."

"But they overshadow them."

"Only while we were in them." She let him go. "But that's all in the past. You're on to bigger and better things."

I'm not.

Tears stung.

Low blow, man. Sorry.

Gale didn't have it in him to stop their roll, but he did smile through them. "Bigger and better."

His mother pretended not to notice. "Thanks for today. I really enjoyed helping out and meeting Regina. Why does she look so familiar to me?"

"I dunno. She did to me, too, at first. But I'd never met her before." Gale surreptitiously wiped his eyes. "Actually, I should get going. This'll be my last Sunday dinner service with her."

"Why didn't you tell me? I'd have left you there."

"I didn't want you driving through that area by yourself. Anyway, this gives me time to relax a little. Check my email. I don't usually go in until around now, and I've already set her up for lunch."

"It's really amazing, what she does. And so clean. I wish my kitchen was that clean."

"She's obsessive about it." Gale chuckled. "I like being part of it. And she's really talented. I've learned a lot."

"From a soup kitchen cook?" Lucy waved him off. "Go. Get some rest. And don't work too hard!"

Gale waved to her from the curb, waiting until her car turned the corner before heading inside. The other guys would probably be up by now, but maybe only just. It'd be nice to get a shot at the computer before Kyle got on his games.

Up in the apartment, all was quiet but for the sound of the shower running. A quick peek showed Jimmy and Nando still asleep in the malodorous—garlic and onions, cigarette smoke and sweat—dark of their shared bedroom. He didn't hear them come in last night; it had to have been superlate. Maybe not even until dawn, which would be typical. The two of them spent more time at work after work than they did on shift, drinking and clowning around with their co-workers. Gale grabbed the computer while he had the chance.

So. Much. Spam. What good was a filter if it all got through? When had he ever bought anything from Pampered Chef? As if he could afford it. World Market. William Sonoma. Some political shit he vaguely remembered clicking on for the free sticker offered. *Click, click, click.* And gone.

Gale read the funny forward from his brother, who emailed him often but never anything personal. Brian's version of keeping in touch. Regularly. At a distance. Gale couldn't blame him, after all he put the family through. Lucy Carmichael forgave. Danny Carmichael did, too, but with a sharper edge. Brian? He probably never would. It was pawning Lucy's gold chain—the one that had been her nona's—that sunk Gale deeper than Brian was willing to go. His brother had bought it back, put it in their mother's jewelry box before she could go from wondering where it was to fearing it was stolen, and never said another word about it. But his brother remembered. Would always remember.

Brian's a dick, anyway.

"No, he's not. He's the good one."

You gotta stop that, man.

"Shut up, Sean."

More and more often, Sean's voice in Gale's head gave in. It took cheap shots now and then, encouraged and admonished, but when asked to kindly shut the fuck up, he did.

"Sorry."

Only you can prevent forest fires, man. Only you.

"What the hell does that even mean?"

Read your email so we can check out Insta. See if VagabondVictuals dropped any new pics this morning.

Gale clicked through what remained of his email. More spam. Newsletter from his old culinary school. Another forward from his brother. And . . .

"Holy shit."

"What?" Kyle stood in the doorway, towel wrapped around his waist. "Good holy shit? Or bad holy shit?"

"I don't know." Gale opened the email. Read it. And again. "They want me to send a video. An audition video."

Kyle came around to his side of the computer. "Who does?"

"*Cut!* The application you sent . . . to the . . . holy shit. Holy shit!" Gale pushed out of his chair, holy-shitting himself around the kitchen. "What do I do?"

Sitting behind the computer now, Kyle was all smiles. "We make a video. You have to do that vermouth chicken. It got you a job as sous, it'll get you onto the show. Dude. Dude!"

Gale's stomach roiled. Good, bad? He couldn't say. The email was old; he only had a week to respond. Kyle was already on the site, figuring out how to upload the video once it was done, saying things like, "You have to," and "You could go out first. Or you could win ten Gs!"

Not helping, Kyle. Sean's snicker echoed inside Gale's skull and, for a moment, the always-haggard phantom blinked brighter. *Was he always this . . . enthusiastic?*

Nothing ever got Kyle down. Not for long. The eternal Weeble. Gale wished he could be more like him in that way.

"I have to go," he said.

"What? Where? Not now. We have to do this!"

"Regina is expecting me. Gotta jet. We'll do this . . . later."

"I'm not letting you back out of it!" Kyle called after him. Gale slammed the door, trotted down the stairs, and blew out the front door. He had to tell Regina. If it was a stupid idea, she'd tell him straight. If it was a great opportunity . . . ?

She wouldn't. It was a stupid idea. One only an egomaniac would even think he had a shot at.

So, you're really going to back out of it.

"I'll bomb, Sean." Gale was already panting. "I'll embarrass myself, my parents, Marco, Regina. Frances will torture me."

Who the fuck cares, man? And, you know, you might win.

"I won't."

You don't know that.

"I do."

Okay, then, let's make a deal. If Regina's for it, you do it. If she's not, you don't.

"She'll tell me to stop being an ass and hand me a pot to wash."

Then you're off the hook. Deal?

"Fine. Deal."

If I had hands, I'd make you seal it with a handshake. But I don't, so I'll have to take you at your word. I have it, right?

Pant. Pant. Pant. Gale was mostly running now, but not fast enough to evade Sean's echo, chasing in his periphery. He'd get to Regina's Kitchen sweaty and disgusting. Slowing, he put a hand over his heart. Felt it pumping anxiety-fast. "Fine," he said. "You have my word. Now will you shut the fuck up?"

THE KID WAS LATE GETTING BACK, IF HE WAS COMING AT ALL. HE TOLD HER about the new position, but not when it started. Still, he'd set her up for lunch. All Regina had to do was serve. She hated serving, being out among the people too long. It gave them all time to look harder, place her face. It was why she never, ever smiled. If she did . . .

Setting sandwiches onto plates, plates onto a tray, Regina listened to those already in the dining room, gauging how many were out there by sound. Twentyish, she guessed. She filled bowls with vegetable soup.

"Hey, sorry, sorry, sorry." Gale was already putting an apron on.

"Take the sandwiches out," she said. "Get a head count for me."

Gale did as asked, without complaint. It's what she liked best about him. Nice kid. Without that ants-under-the-skin demeanor, she'd never have pegged him as an addict. Then again, the only kind she knew were those poor souls who came to her kitchen, and those wealthy enough to pretend regular spa visits rather than stints in rehab. Regular kids from good families? Unicorns, to her. Stories told and only loosely based in fact. People didn't fall into addiction accidentally. It was always a symptom of something else. What was Gale's something else?

They worked steadily until everyone was fed. Most of Regina's intermittent volunteers—and Troy, wherever the hell he was. Dammit—served food easily enough, but only Gale could be of significant help with the prep. The kid had skills. And instincts. She was able to do slightly more elaborate dinners when Gale was on hand. Tonight, lasagna, sauce made from scratch.

"Give that a turn, will you?" She jutted her chin sauce-pot-ward, her own hands deep in the ricotta and egg filling.

Gale nodded, stirring the sauce and turning down the heat. "It's simmering a little too heavy," he said. "Smells amazing. Better than at Marco's."

Regina grunted. "Marco never could make it as good as mine."

"You know Marco?"

Fuck. Fuck. Fuck. Fuck! She folded more eggs into the ricotta. "Long time ago," she said. "Don't mention me to him. Got it?"

"Sure. Okay."

That was all. No question. No prying. "You're a little distracted today," she said. "You have words with your mother or something?"

"Mom? No. Did you like her?"

"What's not to like?" Regina scraped lasagna filling from her fingers. "Turn the burner off and set the lid on." She washed her hands clean. There was still coffee left in the urn. She filled two mugs and brought them to the prep table, gesturing to one of the stools. "You nervous about your promotion?"

Gale sat, hands instantly curling around the mug. "Not really."

"Then what gives?"

His face scrunched, like he smelled something burning. "Do you watch any of those cooking competition shows?"

I invented them. "No. Can't say I do."

"I applied to be on *Cut!* Three rounds. Appetizer, dinner, dessert. No? Anyway, I didn't exactly apply. I filled it out, but Kyle sent my application in. Now they want an audition video."

"And?"

"And . . . I kind of don't want to do it."

"But you kind of do."

"Yeah."

"Nerves," she told him. "Don't let that get in your way. You applied for a reason, right?"

"Kyle—"

"No. You filled out the application for a reason."

"Temporary insanity?"

Regina smacked his hand. "Don't joke. So, what are you afraid of?"

"Bombing out. Making an ass of myself. Embarrassing you and Marco and my family."

Poor kid. He had talent. Definite talent. The innate kind no one can teach or learn. He just had no confidence. The world of culinary celebrity would likely beat the shit out of him. Then again, the culinary world that had nothing to do with celebrity could do that, too. It was hard, unforgiving work one had to truly love to keep at.

"Do you think I should do it?"

Regina shook it off. "Huh?"

"The competition," Gale said. "Should I do it?"

"I can't answer that for you."

Gale spun his mug one way, then the other. Wait. Wait. He'll come to it on his own. But she couldn't. "How about this? I'll make up a few mystery ingredient crates for you. See how you do."

"Yeah? Really?"

"Sure, why not. It could be fun."

His smile momentarily cleared that ants-under-the-skin look from his face. It was almost enough to make her smile in return. Regina looked away before he could see even the hint of it. "Clear these cups. I'll start layering the lasagna."

"Sure thing." Gale took their mostly untouched mugs to the sink. Rinsed, washed, dried. Putting them back in the wire rack, he said, "I thought you didn't watch the show."

"Huh? I don't."

"Then how do you know about the mystery crates?"

Regina lifted parcooked lasagna noodles from the water, layered them into the bottom of a massive hotel pan. She could find no cranky response, and so she made none at all.

11

Dying on the pass: A dish that has been sitting too long in the service window (the pass) and is at risk of being unservable.

2002

"Out! Get the fuck out of my kitchen before I throw you out with my own hands!"

Queenie glares at the young man who has ruined his last batch of scallops. How hard is it to sear scallops? He has no place in her brigade. Not in Cucuzza. Not while she's cooking because tonight, she's not just the face, the smile, the name. Queenie B is cooking because this is it. The tenth visit that will turn Cucuzza's two Michelin Stars into three, and nothing, *nothing* but perfection will go out.

The petrified kid hasn't moved from his station. Queenie might feel sorry for him if she had a couple glasses of wine in her. He might remind her that she has a son who gives her that same deer-in-the-headlights look when she's raging. But she hasn't had any wine. No whiskey, gin, or bourbon. No cocaine or Valium or any of her other go-to substances. She's going to make it this time.

"I. Said. Out." Between her teeth now. Scarier than the screaming. The kid hightails it out of the kitchen. Queenie dumps the ruined scallops, wipes the pan, and starts over. Four minutes. Two per side. Simple. "Is the risotto ready?"

"Ready, Chef!"

She slides the freshly cooked scallops onto the tray. "Scallops walking!"

"Risotto walking, Chef."

Immediate response. Her brigade runs tight. Except for the kid on fish. Who the hell hired him? She'll find out. After service. Now she plates the dish herself, suspecting if not knowing the diners at table twenty-eight are from the committee.

"Service, please," her expo, Lawrence, calls.

"I got it," she says.

"Yes, Chef."

Queenie is taking these herself. Nothing but the best, most personal service tonight. For everyone. From everyone. Even Osvaldo, who hasn't set foot in the restaurant in over a year, has had his sommelier tastevin shined for the occasion. Leave it to him to arrive for the accolades.

She delivers the plates to table twenty-eight. Casually. As if she delivers plates to tables any old night. She will tonight, that's certain. "Enjoy your meal," says she, that signature smile in place. She feels it. Almost. Maybe they won't notice the tightness of it.

"Thank you."

"Looks delicious."

And other such banalities leave their lips before her food goes past them. The scallops, the risotto, the crab cakes, the squash blossoms—all perfection. Queenie B doesn't have to see or hear their appreciation to know.

She returns to the kitchen, to the fish station. "What's up next?"

"Two halibut, Chef."

"Heard that."

The kid hasn't left, but is cowering in the service vestibule. Queenie crooks her finger, and he inches near.

"Who hired you?" She squirts olive oil into her hot pan.

"Chef Lawrence."

"Why?"

"Because I . . . I . . . I've done well until tonight, Chef. I swear."

She makes him wait. Flips the halibut. Seared to perfection. "Do I make you nervous?"

"No?"

"Don't lie. What's your name?"

"Michael, Chef."

Queenie lifts the edge of the halibut. It sticks. She leaves it, turns the heat down a little. Adding butter, she tips the pan and bastes the flesh so it glistens. "Hand me the bouquet, there."

Michael obeys. She has to give him credit; his hand doesn't shake.

"Why shouldn't I fire your ass?"

"Because I'm a good chef, Chef. I work hard. I fuc... messed up on the scallops, but I swear it'll never happen again."

Baste, baste, baste. A quick twist of the wrist. "Where do you see yourself in ten years, Michael?"

No hesitation. "Cooking."

"Not executive? Your own restaurant?"

"Only if I can still cook," he tells her. "It's all I want to do, Chef. It's the only time I feel... right."

Queenie tips the pan. The fish releases. Lifting it from the butter, she inhales the aroma. Beautiful. Flaky. Herbed and buttered. "Halibut walking!" She hands Michael the tray. "Go. And don't fuck up again."

"Heard, Chef. Thank you, Chef. Halibut walking!"

SHE CAN LEAVE, AT THIS POINT. THE DINERS AT TABLE TWENTY-EIGHT HAVE gone. What Michael said, though, lingers. He has spoken a truth she rarely acknowledges. Queenie B is not a natural mother, though she has come to love her son tremendously. She is not a good wife, though she has loved Osvaldo, too. She is not even, really, a good person. Selfish. Egotistical. Ruthless. The only time she feels good, *right,* is when she cooks, and so Queenie cooks the entire night, moving from station to station at will, because it's her damn restaurant and she can.

She—with Osvaldo—owns many restaurants, but she has no favorite, only the one most presently shiny. Food is all. It is everything. If she could just go back to being Chef Benuzzi, she could get her life together, be a good mother, a good wife, a good person. Queenie B has made her mark on the world and all the money she could ever possibly need. Maybe it's time for Queenie B to say adieu. Let her be the brand that endures, the personality remembered as the diva prone to tantrums in the kitchen and drunken, drug-induced mayhem. Regina can separate from her. Just step away, let the very competent people she hired run her empire while she, Osvaldo, and Julian live a quiet life, away from cameras and fans and her face on billboards from New York to Tokyo. Maybe Italy, in the tiny, centuries-old house she and Osvaldo bought when the money first started coming in. They never had more than that first summer of laziness and love at that house. Before Julian. Before fame. Before everything that came with it.

In the dining room, empty of diners but buzzing with her employees finishing up for the night, Queenie sits, still in her chef's coat. Black. Smiling logo on the sleeve pocket. Her name embroidered above her heart, just below *Cucuzza*. She pulls the elastic from her hair, shakes out her braid. It feels so good.

"Good night, wasn't it?" Osvaldo sits on the chair beside her, automatically tilting it back on two hind legs.

"You're going to fall and break your neck." Words spoken just as automatically.

He smiles, but lowers the legs back onto the ground. He is so handsome, in that mercurial way of Spanish nobility. Somewhere in his past, duchesses and counts and even a king splashed their blood into his veins. Blood now, too, in Julian's. The slight lilt left of Osvaldo's accent, meticulously maintained, still has a way of shivering through her.

"I think we're getting that star," she says.

"I do too."

Silence, but for the sound of cleaning. Clinks and clanks. A vacuum whirs in the vestibule. Laughter. Osvaldo reaches for her hand, and Queenie gives it. When he brings it to his lips and kisses it, she smiles. Not the signature smile, all teeth and red lips. A tired one. Slightly sad. Maybe a little hopeful.

She asks, "Remember Bova?"

Osvaldo squints, brow furrowed, then, "Our little house in Calabria? I remember it well."

"Let's go there. You, me, and Julian. What do you think?"

Osvaldo's eyes close. "Don't, my love. Please."

"I miss you."

"I miss you too."

"I've been sober for—"

"One year," he says. "When you can end that sentence with 'one year,' ask me again, and my answer will be yes. I'll go to Bova. I'll go anywhere with you. Forever, Regina."

Forever. Queenie cannot imagine forever. Only tomorrow. Next week. Months of engagements and appearances and performances. Forever? Does it even exist?

Leaning toward him, knowing he will lean in to meet her, she kisses him with those famous but tired, slightly sad and hopeful lips. No red gloss to smear, to come between them. No evidence of it at all besides the quickening of their breath and the hushed whispers of the staff still cleaning.

"I'll make it this time, Oz. I swear it."

Osvaldo. Master sommelier married to an alcoholic. Spanish noble hitched to an orphan. Her partner and husband and the father of her child damaged by her abuse before he was born. The irony of it all would be amusing were it not also tragic. He leans in again, fingers pushing through her hair and tugging her closer. He kisses her passionately now, and Queenie kisses him back. When they pull apart, they are alone completely.

"One year," he tells her, rising. And he leaves her alone in that darkened dining room. This place of their latest achievement.

Why he believes in her, Queenie B has no idea. He should never believe in her. Believe her. She will lie, if a year passes and she's fallen yet again. He has to know that by now.

She turns out the last lights in the dining room, makes her way to the kitchen by feel and the streetlights coming through the front windows. Silent. Empty. Spotless. Her people know their jobs, do them well. Even Michael. He'll be okay, given a little time and tutelage. Maybe she'll make him her protégé, give him a boost most would kill for.

Taking a clean pan from the stack, Queenie grabs a squeeze bottle of olive oil. She sets the pan on the stove to heat, grabs shrimp, garlic, scallions, olives, lemon wedges. She sautés and squeezes, sprinkles salt and just a tiny bit of oregano. Pasta would be better, but the water on the stove is set up for tomorrow, not boiling now. Bread will do. It is still today. It is still fresh. Enough.

Queenie B sits at the prep table, the first full meal of the day sending its aromas up into her nostrils, fork poised for that first bite. She gets up again, takes a glass from the rack, goes out to the bar and pours herself a white wine. Oz would have known the perfect one to pair, but she makes do with the house chardonnay. Bringing it back to the kitchen, she sets it by her plate, and leaves it there while she eats. A silent companion. Temptation to be denied. She smells it, once or twice, giving herself the illusion of tasting it on her tongue. She's always been able to do that—taste something by smell.

The shrimp is delicious. Of course. She made it. The bread, still crusty and light if slightly less so than it had been a few hours ago. The wine, untasted, if not untouched. Queenie takes plate and fork, wine and napkin to the sink. She turns on the water, waiting for it to get hot. Bringing the wine to her nose, she inhales deep, and more deeply. Steam rises, making the scent even stronger. Her mouth waters. Her brain screams.

One year.

Queenie dumps the wine down the drain, washes, dries, and puts everything away.

Standing in the doorway between the kitchen and dining room, she surveys her domain. Cucuzza isn't her first restaurant, or her shiny newest, but it is her finest. She can afford to hire the best. Chefs vie for positions in Queenie B's kitchens. For Cucuzza, she'd chosen young, exciting people, leaving only managerial positions for the more seasoned in their fields.

She wants fresh ideas. Molecular gastronomy intrigues, even if the end result doesn't quite mesh with what she considers a portion size. Maybe it's like fashion, all those models wearing garbage-bag dresses tied together with garden-hose belts and crowned by watering-can hats; it is only the artistic expression walking down the runway, not the garments a designer actually intends anyone to wear. Foggy dishes under glass domes appearing more like tadpoles in a terrarium is the runway show. And when Queenie B thinks about such things, she feels almost as right as she does while cooking.

Food is all.

It is everything.

Clicking off that last light, Queenie leaves through the service entrance. She locks up, pockets the keys, and gets in her car parked right there, at the exit.

Another Michelin Star. Her third for Cucuzza. It will happen, she is sure. In a year—less, because she's already been clean two months—she'll have it all again. This time, she is not going to throw it away.

12

Getting a push: When the order tickets are coming faster and the restaurant is getting busier, the kitchen is "getting a push."

2015

Sometimes, Gale wasn't even sure what day it was when he woke in the morning. Was it Tuesday? Yes, because he cooked lunch service at Marco's yesterday, dinner at Regina's. Right? Had to be right, because if it was Thursday, his other lunch service as sous, he'd wouldn't have been at Regina's the night prior; and he was never going to be able to forget the crate she set up for him, no matter how busy, how work-crazed.

Peanut butter, sweetbreads, brussels sprouts, and day-old glazed donuts.

Abysmal failure.

"I like the East Asian take on the dish," she told him. "Your sauce is perfect. The scallions you added from the pantry really kick it up. But the brussels sprouts are underutilized, and if you don't remove the membrane from the sweetbreads, they're pretty inedible. Someone else would have to really fuck up for you to be safe."

"I never made sweetbreads before."

"Not even in culinary school?"

If he had, Gale didn't remember. Regina showed him how to properly remove the membrane, poach the glands in milk, before dusting them in flour—in this case, the pulverized insides of the glazed donuts—and giving them a quick but careful fry.

"There's really no better way to cook them," she said. "I've . . . uh . . . watched a few shows, just to get an idea of how it goes. I'm telling you, in a crate like this one? They're not going to be looking for how creative you are with the protein, but how creatively you incorporate it with the other components."

A slaw of shaved brussels sprouts, fennel bulb, and daikon dressed in a light mirin vinaigrette. His peanut butter, soy, sesame dipping sauce with scallion garnish, plated impeccably; Gale had never seen, or tasted, anything so beautiful.

"The milk poach is kind of crucial," she'd told him, "to make sure they cook through when you fry them. Soaking them in milk for a few hours would be even better. Soften that offal taste a bit, but it's obviously not doable during the competition. As long as you poach and fry them to perfection, you're good."

That Regina turned humble fare into nutritious, tasty meals on a daily basis was established; that she was a true sorceress with food on a higher level was news that, after all, came as no real surprise to Gale. She exuded culinary confidence.

Stopping off at the apartment between Regina's and Marco's, Gale froze at the sight of his dad's yellow Baja parked out front. He trotted the rest of the way down the street, a smile on his face that faded when he saw his dad through the windshield.

"What's wrong? Is it Mom?"

Danny Carmichael was already out of the car, pulling Gale into a bear hug.

"Please. Just tell me."

"She's okay," he said. "But we had a scare. I didn't want to leave you a message, and you're not answering your phone."

Which most assuredly frightened Danny almost as much as whatever scare Lucy had recently given him.

"I've been doing back-to-back shifts," Gale told him. "You want to come up? Tell me what's going on?"

"Why don't you just come with me, if you can. If you have time."

"I'll make time. Just, Dad, come on. Don't leave me hanging."

"It seems she might have had a mild heart attack."

Oh, shit, man.

"It seems?" His voice cracked an octave too high.

"Okay, she did. She's in the hospital for observation, but they don't think she's going to need any of them stunts."

"I think they're called stents."

"Yeah, them things. Medication. Better eating habits. Exercise. You know she eats like shit."

Don't we all.

Gale was already calling the restaurant. Marco would cover for him; he was a good guy. There were still a couple of hours before Gale really had to be there. He could go upstairs, get changed, go see his mother, and be in the kitchen before the real dinner hours kicked up.

Cold, man. Real cold.

"Shut up, Sean."

"What was that, son?" Danny asked over his shoulder.

"Nothing. Wait here. I'm just going to change."

"I'M FINE, BUDDY." LUCY HUGGED GALE A LITTLE TOO HARD. "REALLY. There's no need for all this fuss. It was a wake-up call, nothing more than that."

"No work, three months." His dad wagged a finger. "You heard the doc."

"Yeah, well, the doc doesn't have bills to pay."

"Mom, don't be insane."

"Can you even imagine me sitting around doing nothing for three months?" She waved them both off. "I'd for sure have a real heart attack."

"Dad, don't let her—"

"Since when does your father *let* me do anything? Now hush and tell me about you. I haven't seen you since our breakfast date."

An entire month. Just about. Time didn't exist for Gale. He loved both the paid and volunteer jobs. What he learned from Regina—and her crazy crates—on a daily basis was invaluable.

"Well, I guess I do have some news."

"Tell, tell." His mother looked so drawn, dark rings around her eyes. At least, this time, it wasn't his fault.

"Remember that cooking competition show I used to watch with Sean and Kyle?"

"You watched a million of them."

"*Cut!* The one with the crazy crates of ingredients you have to turn into something edible?"

"Oh, right. I remember. Go on."

"I applied . . . well, I filled out the application and chickened out, then Kyle . . ." He laughed. "Never mind. Long story short, I got in. I'm going to be on television. Ten grand if I win."

"Ten thousand?" Danny grasped his arm. "For one day?"

"Yup. If I win. But—"

"Oh, Gale!" Lucy's cheeks pinked a little. "That's wonderful! When?"

"The taping is in a few weeks. I don't know when it'll air."

"So," his father said, "do they make you wait for the show to air? Or give you the money right off?"

Classic Mr. Carmichael.

Gale spent an hour with his parents, telling them about work, about Regina's, how much he learned from her, and that it was being able to tackle her insane crates that gave him the courage to go through with the competition. His mother still hadn't mentioned the soup kitchen to his dad; Danny took it in stride, even if he looked—momentarily—ready to pop when Gale confessed how he'd first found the place.

Lucy seemed fine, really. It was kind of a relief to know she'd be on medication, have to start taking care of herself. A doctor would monitor everything, make sure she was doing what she was supposed to. Scary, yes, but better to know than not to know.

"Don't you have to work?" Lucy asked, looking at the time on her husband's phone. "It's Tuesday."

"I got someone to cover—"

"Don't be an idiot!" Lucy slapped him upside the head. Gently. "Go. I'm fine. Create! When I'm out of here, we're coming in to the restaurant for a meal cooked by our chef son."

"I'll get you the best table in the house." He kissed her cheek.

Lucy held him close. "And tell Regina I'll have some time to spare in the next few months, if she wants an extra pair of hands."

"I will," Gale said. Against his better judgment. Not only did his mom need to rest, but Regina's was his domain, and he was a little surprised to realize how closely he guarded it. Only slightly less so than he guarded his mother.

MARCO MADE A FUSS ABOUT HIM COMING IN. "IT'S THE BEST PART OF BEING salaried," he said, expressive hands in the air. "Time off with pay!"

Gale didn't want time off. He wanted to cook and cook and plate and serve and cook some more. Sean rarely talked to him while he was busy, saving their conversations for quieter, more vulnerable moments. Fewer quieter moments meant fewer conversations that reminded Gale he was alive and Sean was not.

"I know, but she's the one who made me come in, so . . ."

"You sure?" Marco was already heading for the pass. "My sister had one of those mild incarcerations a few years back. She says she's still too weak to do shit she doesn't want to do."

"I think you mean mild *infarction*," Gale told him.

"Yeah, yeah. I know." Marco waved him off. "I was trying to be funny. Lighten the mood."

He wasn't trying to be funny.

"Really. It's all good. I got this."

Tuesdays were pretty slow, as a rule; this Tuesday, their last diners left at eight forty-five. The kitchen was cleaned and prepped for the next day before ten o'clock rolled around. Gale wasn't ready to go home. And he was hungry.

Marco had put, of all things, a fried sweetbread appetizer on the special menu. Probably not a coincidence, but a crap ton of lamb pancreas at the meat supplier. The sweetbreads had already been prepped and soaked in milk when he got in. There were still some of today's left. Alone in the kitchen—Marco, as always, at the bar—Gale poached and fried some up in a light rice flour and cornstarch coating. Instead of the tomato-based sauce Marco served them with, Gale dipped into his boss's secret stash of peanut butter and made the dipping sauce he'd put together at Regina's.

Plating the sweetbreads up on a bed of mesclun greens, he added the finely chopped scallion garnish and a squeeze of lime.

Looks pretty damn good, man.

It did. And the meal tasted amazing, too. Better, if he did say so himself, than what Regina made earlier. Probably because of that long soak in milk.

"What you got there, Gale?"

He didn't jump, even if he startled. Marco rarely entered the kitchen once it was clean and closed for the night. Gale finished chewing, swallowed. "I did up a couple of the leftover sweetbreads."

"Yeah? Doesn't look like mine."

"I . . . uh . . . thought I'd try something, you know, different."

Smooth, man. Real smooth.

"What's this?" Marco lifted the dipping sauce to his nose, stuck a pinkie in and tasted. "Not bad. Sesame sauce?"

"Kind of. Peanut butter, soy, and sesame."

"Mind if I . . . ?"

"Oh, sure." Gale shrugged. "I mean, it's your stuff."

Marco dipped a fried sweetbread in the sauce, took a bite. Gale was gratified to hear the crunch.

"That's damn good. Could use a little heat."

"I thought so too," Gale told him. "We only had jarred cherry peppers. I didn't think that would go as well. The vinegar, you know?"

"Yeah. But maybe some Thai chilies or something." Marco took another bite. "You come up with this yourself?"

"Pretty much. I . . . uh . . ." Gale's stomach lurched. "I guess I should tell you, I'm going to be on one of those cooking competition shows. Do you watch *Cut!*?"

"A postman doesn't go for a walk on Sunday, son. But I'm familiar."

"Well, a friend has been putting weirdo crates together for me, for practice, because that's how the show works. I prepared the sweetbreads all wrong, but the dipping sauce is mine."

"Why didn't you ask me to do it?"

"I didn't exactly ask her," Gale told him. "She just . . . took it upon herself."

"Chef friend?"

"Kind of. Regina runs a soup kitchen. I've been volunteering some of my off time. I've learned a lot from her."

"Yeah, huh?" Marco's eyebrow quirked. "Like how to clean sweetbreads."

"Yup."

"From a soup kitchen cook."

Gale laughed. "I know. Sounds strange."

Marco shook his head. If he had more to say about it, he decided against it, instead clapping Gale's shoulder. "A cooking show, huh? That'll be good advertising for the restaurant."

"If I win, I guess."

"Even if you lose. No publicity is bad publicity." He stepped into the walk-in, checked the container of sweetbreads soaking in milk for tomorrow's service. "What do you think? Switch it up for tomorrow? Do yours, see how it goes."

Dude!

"It's not . . . Italian."

Marco waved him off. "We do sesame tuna tartare. No one bats an eye. It's okay. It's good. This'll pair well with the swordfish special. Tweak it to make it work. Yeah?"

"Uh, sure. No problem."

"Write me a list. I'll get what you need at the market tomorrow morning."

More peanut butter. The Thai chilies. Limes. Scallions. The rest was all there, stocked in the pantry and fridge. Gale gave Marco the list, left the amounts up to him, thinking how funny it was that Marco's ego survived changing his own menu's recipes while Frances would have screamed bloody murder. Which she would do on Thursday, if Marco kept Gale's sweetbreads on the menu rather than hers, which weren't hers at all but Marco's.

Fucked-up, huh?

Gale didn't answer. He'd tried it before. Ignoring him. He sometimes thought Sean's voice in his head was his own guilty conscience. Like when he was happy and had no right to be. Not while Sean was dead and he was not. Or when he was sad, because Sean died and he hadn't. Or when he was playing video games with Kyle, because Sean couldn't, even though Sean was sitting right there with them, a haggard afterimage and a voice.

The only time he never showed up was while Gale was elbows deep in a service, whether at Regina's or Marco's. Even Sean respected the uninterruptableness of a chef immersed.

"Totally," Gale said at last. "Don't let my ego ever get that big, okay?"

Don't worry. Sean chuckled. *I won't.*

13

Knead: To work dough into a soft, uniform, and malleable texture by pressing, folding, and stretching it with the heel of your hand.

2015

Going to the fresh markets was risky, but Regina couldn't put together tough enough crates for Gale with stuff from the box stores. She needed out-of-the-ordinary. Proteins. Veg. Weirdo grains that weren't in fashion when she was a young chef. Stuff she was first to introduce to the "classic" world she'd come up in. The world she changed. That changed her.

Though that wasn't necessarily true. The culinary world was a tough one; it demanded stamina of all kinds. Life as a never-wanted foster kid gave Regina an abundance of it. But there'd always been something there, that same something she sensed in people like Gale only needing a shove in the wrong direction to start the chain reaction she and so many others succumbed to. The stumble that became a fall, that became a crash often fatal. Regina had survived it; she'd need a spreadsheet to calculate those who hadn't.

Eleven o'clock was usually a safe time to shop the markets. The chefs and shoppers who meant business had already come and gone. Regina browsed the produce vendors, found bitter melon and forbidden black rice. Farther along, she picked up a bottle of orange blossom syrup. None of which were particularly strange. Gale had proven he could put together just about anything she threw at him, but protein, if unfamiliar, messed him up more often than not. Those sweetbreads were a fail, but not as bad as the trotters and the geoduck, not to mention the expensive escamol he'd completely destroyed; there were very few ways one could prepare ant eggs and still keep their integrity.

In an unfamiliar corner of the market, where only those who spoke an East Asian language could shop without an interpreter, Regina found what looked like caramels left too long at the bottom of some granny's purse.

乾貝

She took the package from the rack, sniffed. She held it up to the woman eyeing her from behind a table.

"Gānbèi," the woman said, then, slower, "Conpoy. XO sauce?"

Ah. It definitely wasn't dried shrimp, so, "Scallops?"

The woman nodded, held up five fingers. Not even a quarter of an ounce, if Regina guessed correctly. She dug into her wallet for a five. Already, her own brain was concocting what she would do with the ingredients screaming East Asian. She'd go another route, make a chowder, New England creamy, not the Rhode Island kind. She would use the orange blossom syrup to pickle the bitter melon, grind the black rice into flour, coat the pickled melon and fry it nice and crispy to use as garnish floating atop the savory chowder. That punch of sour with the sweetness of the scallops already floated phantom-like in her mouth.

She bought another bag of the dried, fermented scallops, went back to the produce market to purchase another bitter melon, her brain buzzing. It was Wednesday; Gale would be working the dinner shift at Marco's. Regina's culinary vision would become real tonight, after the kitchen was closed. Tomorrow, she'd set the same crate for Gale, who would fall into her creativity trap by going Asian, she was certain. Then she would take out her chowder and show him how the game was—

"Pardon me, could I grab some of those scallions?"

Regina startled. The man standing slightly behind her smiled. Pow! Right in the kisser. She knew that crooked smile. Those lips. The ever-present stubble of facial hair. His curls were whiter, less abundant, but she knew them too. Turning quickly away, she moved aside. "Sure. Sorry."

In her periphery—because she certainly couldn't scurry away without drawing attention to herself—she watched Marco pick through the scallions, meticulous as she remembered him, rather than grabbing bunches for his prep cooks to sort through.

"Nice and fresh," he said, holding up a beautiful bulb. "Pete's got the best produce, am I right?"

"Yeah, right." Regina paid for her bitter melon, beating a less hasty retreat.

"Nice talking to you," Marco called after her. Regina waved over her shoulder but didn't turn back. Damn, damn, damn. Maybe that was sarcasm she heard in his voice, not recognition. He didn't call her back, or by her name. Either of her names. She hadn't seen the man in years. She was older, fatter, and crankier. Maybe he hadn't recognized her.

And maybe she wasn't Queenie B.

"IT'S GOOD." REGINA POKED HER FORK THROUGH THE FRIED RICE DISH. HE'D shredded the scallops—a detail she was surprised he thought of—and soaked them, reserving the liquid that he reduced before using as part of his XO sauce, another surprise. Though he worked in an Italian kitchen, Gale had a definite flair and affinity for East Asian cuisine, and where Regina had known he would go. Another fail, in her book.

"It's good, but?" he asked.

"Don't get me wrong," she answered. "It's a delicious plate of food."

"But?"

"It's safe."

"Safe."

"Yes. The crate ingredients said Asian, so you went Asian. Like all the other chefs would do too. You need to be more creative if you want to win the rounds."

"Creative is kind of dangerous in this competition. They say they want creative, but if you get too crazy with it, they say you're not being true to the ingredients. Remember the ant eggs?"

"No way I'm forgetting the ant eggs." She nudged him. "You have to know when to be creative with what. Some things can only be done certain ways."

"Like the escamol and the sweetbreads."

"Exactly. But you can be creative while still staying true to the ingredients." Regina lifted the lid from her chowder, warming on the stove—never the microwave—while he cooked. She ladled a bowl, set a bit of the fried, bitter melon—that wasn't crispy anymore, but he'd get the gist—on top. Watching him spoon it into his mouth, Regina couldn't keep the smile from her lips.

"Oh, wow." Gale ate more. "Wow. This is amazing. How did your brain go in this direction?"

"It's a process." She winked. "The point is, though, you need to stop grabbing the first idea in your head, and reach for the second, or the third."

"There's not much time to think."

"I know. But you're more creative than you give yourself credit for. This crate was meant to trip you up by being so Asian-forward. You came up with a delicious plate of food, but what if the other three contestants all went in that same direction? What's going to make yours stand out?"

Gale was scraping the last of the chowder into his mouth. "Going New England comfort food instead."

"Exactly."

"I'll try harder with the next crate."

How many more crates would there be, with filming due to start and market shopping now off the table?

"By the way," Gale said, rinsing the bowl and spoon, "my mom wants to come help out again."

"Isn't she supposed to be resting?"

"Resting is going to give her another heart attack." He turned off the water, set the bowl and spoon onto the drying rack. "She gave it a good month. I honestly don't see her taking the three her doctor told her she needed. If she doesn't do something soon, she'll end up back at the store. Then she'll be taking shifts for co-workers. At least, here, we can keep an eye on her."

We. Regina suppressed the smile this time. "You're a good son."

"I wasn't always."

"That's in the past," she told him. "Sure, I can use an extra pair of hands. Whenever she has time, I'll find simple tasks for her to do."

"Awesome. I'll let her know."

Regina finished wiping down counters, storing the various bits and pieces left to dry. Gale cleaned his mess, scraped together what was left of the fried rice that, while expected, was truly delicious. Regina grimaced at her reflection in the window over the sink; she should have given him a little more praise. Always what he did wrong. Rarely what he did right. Old habits died harder than old love.

"Leave some out for me," she told him. "I haven't eaten yet."

Gale wore his pride openly. Innocently. He filled a clean bowl for her. "It's an honor," he said. "Except when you're judging my stuff, I never see you eat."

"I eat." Regina patted her hips. "Believe me."

"Psssh. You're perfect."

Regina howled, too surprised to tone it down from Queenie B exuberant to Regina reticent.

"You have a killer smile," Gale told her. "Anyone ever tell you that?"

Millions. In fan mail. In endorsement requests. In the power of dollars spent on Queenie B–embossed merchandise. How had this kid, who'd been watching cooking shows since he was a teen, not recognized her yet? Maybe because his love of cooking coincided with her vanishing from the culinary world. No scandal. No big farewell. Just a vanishing everyone who was anyone had seemed happy to see happen.

Regina took the bowl of food from him. Still warm, if not hot. "There's more chowder if you want some," she said. "Help yourself."

GALE SUCKED IN A DEEP, UNINTENTIONAL BUT AUTOMATIC, BREATH THE moment he stepped out the back door. Regina's herb garden bloomed as fragrant as it was wild. Mint and rosemary, three kinds of basil, thyme, sage, oregano. Regina also grew tomatoes, peppers of all kinds, cucumbers, summer squash, zucchini, and green beans. Considering there were box-store-size cans of tomatoes and containers of dried herbs in the pantry, and frozen veg in the walk-in, he wasn't sure what she did with all of it. There was way too much for her to use herself; the fresh

produce they used in the kitchen was delivered in crates, straight from
the market.

Walking home, Gale's brain swished over and through all the other
things he could have created from the crate ingredients Regina had set for
him. Of course he'd gone for the first, the most obvious. He had to break
this habit or doom himself to going out of the *Cut!* competition for lacking
in creativity. That would be the worst. Bad plating? Okay, it was always a
rush to that finish. Undercooked this, overcooked that, all overlookable
if the creativity was there. And killer. It had to be superkiller.

You can do it, man. I know you can.

"I do too," Gale responded without thinking, and he knew it was true.
Not only had his skills improved with Regina's coaching, but his confidence had, too.

Thursday. Gale was off from his paid job until dinner service Sunday.
Of course, he'd go to Regina's, but she didn't need him full days anymore.
Between the two of them, they did most of the prep work necessary for
several services more efficiently than she'd been able to do with her un-
skilled volunteers. Troy was still missing. Some days, Gale even forgot to
wonder about him. Until Gladys the Burger Queen showed up. Alone. She
barely spoke to Gale, but he'd overheard her complaining about Troy's
continued absence to Regina, as if he were hired help, not some guy helping her out when he could. He wanted to ask Regina about it, but they
were getting along really well. She hardly ever crabbed at him anymore.
He didn't want to jinx it.

Trotting up the steps of his building, Gale called his mother.

"Gale? Is something wrong?"

He let himself into the apartment. "Wrong? No, why?"

"Because you're calling, not texting." She chuckled. It shook a little.

You got to let it slide.

"I'm fine. Everything is fine. I just figured it was easier to call and tell
you Regina would love to have your help if you still want to do it."

"Really?"

"Yeah, really. Did you think she'd say no?"

"You did too. Don't lie. It's the only reason you agreed to ask her."

"Okay, yeah, I did. I think she likes you."

"Does that mean she doesn't like many people?"

"Oh, Regina loves everyone," he said. "It's why she does what she does, I guess. She'd have to, right? She just doesn't, you know, warm up to most people. She even holds me at arm's length, and I know she likes me. I've only seen her smile a few times, but today, she actually laughed. I couldn't believe it. It was like she was someone else completely."

"There's a story there, buddy."

"Yeah, I suppose so."

"Did she say when?"

"Not really. Come with me when I go next time and see."

Lucy would pick him up tomorrow at eleven. Breakfast was easy, and mostly prepped. Dropping his backpack, kicking off his shoes, Gale was grateful for his mostly clean apartment of friends. He hadn't seen Kyle in a few days, their shifts at odds. Jimmy and Nando came and went. Good guys. They respected his space, his things, his quiet. That they were in the country illegally was a given. Always a low profile. No trouble. No unwanted attention. Gale was pretty sure they'd still be good, respectful, low-profile guys anyway. They weren't permanent fixtures in his life, though. Not like Kyle. And . . .

We should watch a few episodes. Keep sharp.

"The only ones left are the superold ones," Gale said. "Everything's changed since then. They're dated."

Everything comes back on trend. It goes from dated to vintage to new. You know that, man. Jeez.

"I guess." Gale poured the leftovers of Regina's chowder into a bowl, set it in the kind of slimy microwave, then took it out again and poured it into a pan.

Good call, man.

He heated slowly—on the stove the super had finally fixed—so the creamy broth wouldn't separate. Stirring, stirring. The aroma wafted on steam rising. He poured it back into the bowl and tipped it to his mouth. Rather than getting funky with every heat-up, the chowder took on depths of flavor Gale hadn't noticed before. The woman was a genius.

Grabbing the laptop, Gale took it and his chowder to his room. He clicked his way to earlier episodes Sean insisted would be relevant again.

They were not. Still dated. *Cut!*, in its infancy, hadn't hit its groove. The judges weren't the same, though the host was. And he'd eerily not aged at all. Still, it was good to see how the contest evolved, yet stayed exactly the same.

The crates are way tougher now.

"Yeah. These seem kind of tame."

You should look up some of these judges. Bet they were big-time, in their day.

"Big-time then isn't the same as big-time now. No Gordons or Giadas."

You still have a crush on her, you big nerd!

"Giada De Laurentiis is a goddess."

Well, I think you're wrong. Chefs before the Food Network were just as influential. It's the culinary world that expanded into mainstream, not the quality of chefs coming out of it.

"I never said anything about quality. I just said they weren't as big, as in famous. Name four celebrity chefs before two thousand who aren't Wolfgang Puck."

Easy. Julia Child, Emeril Lagasse, Jacques Pépin, Jeff Smith—

"Who the hell is Jeff Smith?"

You disappoint me, man! The afterimage burned brighter. *The Frugal Gourmet? We watched it on PBS, after school. You had your mom tape it.*

"Oh, right. Damn. I guess I didn't remember his real name. But he wasn't a celebrity chef like Gordon Ramsay is."

Even Wolfgang has competition with Ramsay. The ones who came first are the greatest greats even he looks up to, man! Get to know who they are, not just the ones on the current top ten list. It'll make you a better chef.

"It won't help me win *Cut!*," Gale told him. "But you have a point. I'll do it, after the—"

A knock, and the door cracked open. Kyle's voice, "You alone?"

Gale pulled the door open with his foot. "What's up?"

Kyle stepped inside, flopped onto Gale's bed. "Who were you talking to?"

"No one." *Thanks, man. That's real cold.* "I was watching old videos on the computer. You need it?"

"Nah. I'm wiped. I haven't seen you in days. I heard you talking, thought I'd say hi." Kyle turned the laptop so he could see. "Research for your big break into culinary stardom?"

"Funny." Gale turned it back. "Kind of. Regina's crates are great, but watching other contestants at it is really helpful too. One thing I've learned—never make bread pudding in the dessert round. Everyone makes bread pudding."

"Heard." Kyle snickered, fingers pushing through his hair. "I'm so envious."

"Fill out an application. You'll get—"

"I did." He shrugged. "Nothing. Now the site says they're not taking applications at this time. Bad timing."

"So try again when it opens up."

"Whatever." Kyle pushed off the bed, stretched so big his hairy belly peeked out from between shirt and pants. "I'm taking a shower, and getting to bed. See you tomorrow, or something."

"Yeah, okay. See you tomorrow."

Kyle left without closing the door. Gale pushed it shut with his foot. On the screen, the paused video waited. If Kyle was just getting home, it had to be after midnight. Lucy was picking him up at eleven. If Gale went to bed now, he could get a good eight hours and still have time to do laundry, maybe even clean out the fridge, before his mother got there.

Gale took his bowl to the sink, washed it, washed the pan, set them into the drying rack. Opening the fridge, the familiar tune of beer bottles *clinking* sang. The glands in the back of his jaw, under his tongue, watered. A beer would taste so, so good. Just one. He could do that, couldn't he? It wasn't like alcohol had ever been a problem. He could count on one hand the number of times he'd gotten fall-down drunk. High school stupidity. A college kegger or two.

Slippery slope, man. Don't do it.

"I wasn't going to."

Yeah. Okay.

Closing the door, he ignored the beer-bottle song. The specter was shaking his shaggy head. Gale shut down the laptop. Slipping it under his bed, he listened to the sounds of running water, Kyle singing, and Sean humming along, until he fell asleep.

14

Marinate: To impart the flavor of a marinade into food, typically requiring a few hours to allow the flavors to develop. It can also be used to tenderize a cut of meat.

2004

Bova. It is everything Queenie B remembers. Rustic charm. Spotty electricity. Gorgeous views of the blue Ionian Sea and the green Aspromonte mountains. The Greko spoken by the locals will take some getting used to, but she and Osvaldo get by with the little Greek they both know, and the Italian they speak fluently. Julian speaks only English, of course. If they stay long enough, he might pick up a few words and phrases. He's still young, even if his learning disabilities will make it harder. The child is too happy to have both his parents to himself to worry about being able to communicate with his peers.

The first week is bliss. Matrimonial. Maternal. They swim in the sea, walk in the hills, play and cook and eat. Julian's mood swings are difficult, often violent, but Osvaldo knows how to handle them. Queenie will learn. They're her fault, after all. When he hits her, fists clenched so tight his knuckles are white, she tamps down the urge to hit back. She remembers what it was like. The humiliation. The pain. The betrayal. Big hands hurt way worse than small ones. Big hands have to know better.

The second week is less blissful. Julian, used to having his parents to himself now, is bored. Osvaldo is always on the phone. Queenie can only do so much shopping, sunbathing, and cooking. Instead of ignoring her phone when it rings, she answers it.

It's just a local—if Rome can be considered local—appearance, judging an up-and-coming chef contest. Massimo will be there. She hasn't seen him in ages. How can she refuse?

Queenie tells herself it's just one night away from her boys. Two, tops. Because Osvaldo is angry and won't go with her. She knows he's only angry because he hasn't been asked to judge as well. Their love affair began in competition they both thrive on—he never had a chance of winning—and he remains entrenched in it. Sometimes, she thinks, he is so good with Julian because she is not. Queenie quells that thought before it can travel too far. Osvaldo is the good parent.

She travels to Rome the day prior to the event. It's been a while since her last visit, and then she'd been too drunk most of the time to enjoy more than being drunk. The city, its antiquity, imbues every molecule in her body. This is the way to see Rome—clear-eyed, clearheaded. Queenie wishes Osvaldo had come. Maybe not Julian, though. Meandering through the sites, the streets, on her husband's arm takes on a pall when she includes their son in the wishing and she chastises herself; a good mother would never have such thoughts.

The festivities start early the next day, with a brunch for the organizers, judges, and contestants. Queenie sits with Massimo, and they catch up. The man's frenetic energy puts her own frenzy to shame. By the time brunch is through, she's had to have a mimosa, just to take the edge off. Just the one. It'll be fine. She's been sober almost a year and a half and it's only champagne. A tiny bit at that; it's mostly orange juice.

The afternoon brings a series of interviews with the contestants, with television crews from all over Italy, with the local newspapers covering this small but prestigious event bringing the likes of Queenie B to judge. She feels bad that the focus is mostly on her. Falling into the attention, though, is what she does best. The smile flashes. The cameras zoom in on her. She is flirting with camera crews and contestants and the other judges without even meaning to. It's just the way things go, with Queenie B.

And she has to admit, she's missed it. Even though it has only been a few weeks since handing the final episodes of both her shows to guest hosts, claiming her mental health and her family have to take priority. Since turning down or canceling the endorsements, appearances, and engagements with television executives and committees always wooing. It had felt so good. Cathartic. Ditching every and all responsibility. Landing in Bova with her husband and son. In the house that needs more attention than they've given it in the years since its purchase. Queenie had, then, fully intended to spend at least a year getting the place in good order. Efficient. Classy. Nothing over the top. Fully intended.

"Buona sera, Oz," she purrs into the phone. "How are my boys this evening?"

"Missing you," Osvaldo tells her. "How is it?"

"Insane. But fun, I guess. I haven't missed this," she lies. "The final judging is in an hour. I have to get back down."

"I'll see you tomorrow, then?"

"Or the next day," Queenie tells him. "I'll know better after tonight. Any chance you'll join me?"

"Just me?"

"Julian too, of course." Another lie. "That's a given."

"Just come home tomorrow, and we'll be together here. I have a surprise for you."

"A surprise? For me? What is it?"

Osvaldo laughs. Oh, that sound. "It won't be a surprise if I tell you."

"Fine, be that way." Queenie kisses the phone. "I love you, Oz."

"Love you too, Regina. Julian? You want to say hello to Mama?"

Excited shrieking rises in the background. A muffling of words and a phone being grabbed, and—"Mama?"

"Hello, darling. How's my boy?"

"When do you come back?"

"Tomorrow, love."

"I want you now."

"I can't come now, sweetheart. I have to work. But I'll be back to—"

"You always say that! Always! I hate you!"

A loud clunk. Queenie imagines he's thrown the phone. A moment later, Osvaldo's tired voice says, "Bad idea to talk to him. My fault. I should have known better. He was fine, I promise. And he will be by the time you get here."

"All right. I'm sorry, Oz."

"It'll be fine. I love you."

"Love you, too."

Queenie taps out of the call, tucks the phone into her tiny beaded handbag. Julian has unsettled her. He is nothing if not brutally honest. Osvaldo tells her it's not her he hates, but her actions. Her being away from him. Julian doesn't handle transition well or process his emotions easily. It's part of his condition, along with his facial deformities and the learning disabilities. The child needs more than she can give him. He always has, even before birth. She is selfish. Putting her own needs first and foremost. Of course Julian hates her. Sometimes, she's not overly fond of him either.

It's only a minibar bottle of vodka. Two shots, at the most. Just to soothe her nerves. She downs it in two gulps, then reapplies her lipstick, adjusts her tight-fitting black dress over her famous curves, smooths her hair. She looks beautiful. In control. Queenie B is ready for whatever the evening brings. Good food, she hopes. And some fun.

WHERE HAS A WEEK GONE?

Queenie puts her suitcase down in the foyer of the Bova home. They're not here. She knows it already. Osvaldo left her a short but clear voicemail. He and Julian are back in New York. They do not want to see her. Ever again. Divorce papers were already being drawn by the time she sobered up enough to listen to the message.

She doesn't know what happened. All Queenie remembers is the final contest, the judging, the champagne fizzing and flying all over the place. She might remember kissing the winner—a lovely young man from Milan or Berlin whose bed she woke up in late yesterday afternoon. Three days. Four. No, five days unaccounted for aside from flashes of what she could have passed off as a fantasy if not for the pictorial evidence in rags like *Pettegolezzi*, feeding on her like she is actual news.

She's seen the video footage of her with that lovely young man from Milan or Berlin, the two of them still in their formalwear, drinking champagne in a hotel pool. Photos snapped of them together on a poolside

lounge chair, her bare breasts pixilated. And she hadn't even been looking. There were others. And reports. Of a hotel room trashed. A pair of
bouncers escorting a disheveled, shoeless Queenie B from a bar someplace in Monza. Oz saw them all, heard every detail. He has staff on retainer for the sole purpose of discovering her scandal before it explodes
on him. On Julian. Queenie has kept them busy for the last several days.

Walking through the empty house, Queenie picks up a toy here, a
stray jacket there. Left behind. Like her. They had to have left in a hurry.
What did Osvaldo tell their son? This time, she was close to certain, he
will not temper it with promises that Mama will be with them soon.
Better he told Julian she is dead, let it all be done with. Because she will
never change, never stay the good wife and mother. She will only have
flashes of Regina Benuzzi/Balcazar that shine brightly, but burn out in
the enormous solar flare that is Queenie B.

In the bedroom, she slips out of her clothes and into the silk kimono-
style robe Osvaldo gave her for Valentine's Day. Red, the color of passion
in most every culture on the globe. It had been a beautiful day, just the
two of them ice skating in Central Park, bundled against the cold. Dinner
in their own restaurant, the three Michelin Star Cucuzza, tucked away in
a corner that did not succeed in sparing them surreptitious pics snapped
and shared on social media. Then a night of making love without Julian—
spending quality time with his extremely competent nanny—in the next
room. A celebration of her sobriety, of their reunion. Neither of which
would ever last long enough.

Passing from room to room, she finds more evidence of their hurried
departure. A juice box left on the side table. The remote on the floor. Dishes
in the sink, rinsed, but not washed. Osvaldo, fastidious as he is, never leaves
a mess. Well, no mess but her. He has no intention of ever returning to Bova,
and the memory of bliss so quickly turned to despair. To betrayal. To yet
another failure to be a family.

Queenie looks up the number for a local realty office, leaning on the
new marble counter they'd only recently installed.

"Hello, English? Italian? Good, thanks. I have a house I want to put
on the market. I know it's not the best time of year but . . . no, I don't . . .
look, can you just come look at it? Fine. Tomorrow. I'll—"

Queenie catches sight of the La Cornue oven, a work of art in and of itself, that had not been in her kitchen when she left for Rome.

"I'll call you back." She taps out of the call, runs her hand over the smooth surface as red as the lipstick she wears.

I have a surprise for you . . .

Queenie bites down on her lip; the tears come nonetheless. The stove costs several times more than the house is worth. Osvaldo bought it and had it installed for her. For them. For this home that was to be their new beginning.

Instead of calling the realtor back, Queenie calls the housecleaning service they've been using since arriving in Bova. She arranges a deep cleaning. She can't sell the house. She won't. But maybe she'll be back one day. Until then, she'll hire a caretaker.

Packing what's left of her things, she weeps. Openly and intensely. She weeps for her failed marriage, for her son, for what she did to both. Julian and Osvaldo are truly better off without her. There's not a soul in existence who will disagree.

Her restaurants, her personal franchise, her celebrity all hinge upon her volatile, chaotic reputation. Without it, she's just another chef, because the old saying is true—there's no such thing as bad press. Every personal disaster causes an uptick in her finances, even as it hammers another nail in her personal coffin. Because people love a bad girl, especially a bad girl who hurts no one as much as she hurts herself.

Zipping her case closed—they really hadn't brought much with them to Bova—she catches sight of herself in the bureau mirror. Breath catches in her throat. She is forty-five, and beautiful. She is famous and rich and the envy of her peers. She is the idol of every young chef with dreams of her kind of success, of every woman who longs to behave badly and get away with it. She is the desire of men who wish to bask in her brand of wild.

She is Queenie B.

But the woman in the mirror is not Queenie B. Not really. She is Regina Benuzzi. Older. No wiser than she'd been when she walked with the rolled-in shoulders of a young woman afraid of the world. Strange, no matter where life takes her, Queenie B cannot shake Regina Benuzzi, no matter how hard she tries. She is always there. Waiting to remind her how unwanted she'd been. Waiting to be seen.

Unpacking her bag, Queenie doesn't think. Or she thinks so much there's no way to catch a single thought. Her mind unravels and winds itself back up again, almost without her noticing. But it's there. All of it.

In the bathroom so recently renovated it still smells like new paint and grout, Queenie scrubs her face clean. She braids her hair—two, not her signature one—and winds the plaits around her crown as the old women in town do. Putting on a pair of jeans and a plain white T-shirt, she talks to herself in Greko until she can ask for the items she needs like a local. She won't stay in Bova long; too many know who owns this humble little house decked out in the sort of luxury Queenie B and Osvaldo Balcazar are accustomed to. She'll stay only long enough to gain whatever equilibrium she can.

She's not even sure what that means, in fact. Maybe Regina Benuzzi won't die, but neither will—apparently—Queenie B. One of them has to give. Or both of them do. Outside of the spotlight that made it all possible. Somehow. Now, in this moment, she's heading down the hill to the market. Tonight, she's cooking. Elaborately. Simply. Deliciously. Tomorrow doesn't exist. Only the next meals needing to be created. Food is all. It is everything. On this Queenie and Regina can agree. Wherever they end up, they will get there. One meal at a time.

15

Heard/Heard that: When a chef calls out tickets, the cooking staff will shout "Heard!" or "Heard that!" to indicate they got the orders.

2015

Y ou're as ready as you're going to be." Regina chopped onions so fast, Gale's eyes didn't have time to water. "How do you feel?"

Taping was tomorrow. He felt like crap. "As good as I'm going to. I'm nervous. What if I make a fool of myself?"

"It's a chance you take. But you won't."

She scraped the onions from the cutting board into a mixing bowl. This afternoon, they were making spaghetti and meatballs for dinner service, a weekly favorite since long before Gale started volunteering.

"What are you even doing here? You should be at home, resting."

"No way," Gale said. "I'd go insane. As it is, my boss gave me the night off."

"Fine. Help prep dinner and then you're leaving. I have servers for tonight."

As if on cue, his mother shouldered in through the back door, bags of groceries looped over her arms. It was only Lucy's second time volunteering in Regina's Kitchen; she'd had a minor setback, but the doctors approved, as long as she took it easy. They knew, as well as her family did, she needed more to do than watch television. "I couldn't get all the pork you asked for. The ground chicken was on sale, so I supplemented with that. Good?"

"Ground chicken?" Gale asked. "In meatballs?"

"It'll be fine," Regina said. "I've done it before. You have to be able to improvise with what's available. That's the hallmark of a great chef. Now take those bags from your mother. Lucy, pour the milk over the bread."

"But Gale's the chef. I'll just—"

Regina leveled that glance even Lucy Carmichael didn't dare argue with.

"How much milk?"

"Until it's all wet but not pooling."

Gale watched Lucy, suppressing the urge to take the container of milk from her hand. She poured just enough, this mother of his who'd never actually cooked anything from scratch in her life.

"Gale, the meat?"

"Oh, right." He unpacked the ground beef, pork, and chicken. In a pinch, he'd have gotten veal, not chicken, but he supposed a soup kitchen couldn't afford that. He took the bowl of milky bread from his mother and tipped the meat from their Styrofoam trays into it. While he mixed by hand—gently, and not too much—Regina added the egg/onion/herb mixture.

"Good, good." She slid the massive bowl closer for inspection. "Just enough. Lucy, you going to roll with us?"

"Me?" His mother's cheeks pinked. Nice to see. "I don't want to mess it up."

"They're meatballs. How bad can you mess up? I'll show you."

Gale watched his mother carefully, looking for signs of fatigue as they rolled, but she showed none. Her meatballs were often too big, or too small. The first ones were rolled too hard. "Be gentle," Regina corrected. "You want your meatballs soft, not dense and hard."

When they were finished, the meatballs were lined up in the industrial tray, an army of fatty, pink warriors standing at perfect attention.

"Gale, sear them off while we get the tomatoes going."

"I never knew so much went into spaghetti and meatballs," Lucy said. "I never knew my son worked so hard."

"It's a chef's life."

Searing the meatballs on the stovetop, Gale listened to Regina teach his mother the intricacies of tomato sauce magic with half an ear. The only two women in his life who mattered were around the same age, both Italian, both blue-collar as blue-collar got. It was strange to think, after all the weeks, so much time spent toiling in the kitchen, that Gale knew almost nothing about Regina, personally. Like if she'd ever been married, had kids, worked in a restaurant. Like where she got the money to fund the soup kitchen, what organization she worked for, and if she got paid outside of use of the apartment above.

She doesn't know anything about you either.

Sean had a point. But Regina knew all she needed to, really. He hadn't fooled her. Not from day one. An addict knew an addict; she hadn't fooled him either. It was always safer not to ask.

Gale turned the meatballs again, searing those fatty pink warriors brown. Focused on that, he tried to let go of the anxiety building, even though he knew he couldn't. Wouldn't. Not until he was in the *Cut!* studio. Cooking.

GALE ATTEMPTED TO PROTEST ONCE AGAIN, BUT HE LEFT TO GO HOME AND rest up. Lucy stayed, even though Regina had a kind-of regular—who could use the twenty bucks—coming in to serve. But for boiling the pasta, dinner was done. Still, when the volunteer arrived, her little boy in tow, Lucy lingered on.

"It's going to get a little hectic." Regina dumped the first round of spaghetti into the boiling water. "They line up before I open for service. I've never run out of food yet, so I don't know why."

"Old habits," Lucy said. "Or fears. Tell me what I can do."

Regina didn't have the heart to tell her to go home. Lucy seemed happy, helping out. The woman needed a purpose, that much was plain.

"If you get overtired, your son is going to kill me."

"My son isn't the boss of me." Lucy winked. "I swear, I'll take it easy."

Lucy Carmichael couldn't take it easy any more than Regina could, which was why she caved. "Fine. I'll plate, you and Janie can deliver. Her little boy can pass out bread."

It did get hectic, as always, from six to seven. After that, stragglers came and went, but by eight o'clock, as always, Regina's Kitchen closed, having fed the local, hungry destitute. Janie and her boy went home with full bellies, leftovers, and a twenty in each of their pockets, wherever home was. Regina hoped it wasn't one of the nearby abandoned buildings where so many seemed to squat.

"That was fun." Lucy dried the industrial pan that had been left soaking in the sink. "It's really nice, you doing all this."

"I do what I can." She could do more; not without giving herself away though. The balance Regina struck had been working since opening the doors. "The faces here come and go. Sometimes because people make their way out of this sort of poverty. Sometimes because they die."

Lucy slid the pan onto the wire rack with the others. Her shoulders sagged, just a little. "I could go for a cup of tea. How about it, before I go?"

Tea. Like the old days, with Gladys. Troy's continued absence had put a stop to their after-service cuppas. Regina put the kettle on, firmly cutting off that train of thought. "I hope good old Lipton is okay."

"It's all I drink."

"You're good with caffeine?"

Lucy grimaced. "I'm not supposed to drink it, but I do. Not often. Don't tell Gale."

"I won't." Far be it from her to scold a woman about her vices.

Regina got mugs from the rack. Lucy poured hot water over the tea bags. Tea was never as good as it was in her Bernardaud teacups, but it would still feel nice going down.

"So." Lucy blew across the rim of her mug. "What do you think Gale's chances are? For real."

Regina set the tea bag on a folded paper towel. She stirred in a bit of sugar, a little milk. Sipped. There was nothing quite so comforting as that first sip of tea. Unless it was the first sip of something stronger promising the numbness to come.

Maybe Gale wasn't the only one anxious.

"He has plenty of talent," she said. "Good instincts when it comes to combining flavors. Good palate. Great technique."

"But?"

"He lacks confidence," Regina told her plainly. "And he lets his nerves get in his way. Once he's in the zone? There's no rattling him. It's getting there he has trouble with."

Lucy's shoulders sagged again. She sipped her tea, no sugar, no milk, the tea bag still steeping in the cup. "He's always been that way. Breaks my heart."

"It's who he is. Nothing to be heartbroken about." Unlike Regina's own son; she wasn't entitled to heartbreak she caused.

"I think it's why he did what he did," Lucy told her. "I mean, I can relate. Sometimes, I wish I could turn off all the noise in my head."

Regina could also relate. She kept her mouth shut.

"He nearly died a couple years back. Did he ever tell you?"

He didn't have to. Regina blew over the top of her cup. "Never mentioned it."

"It was awful. As if that even comes close. My boy. I nearly lost him, but he made it. His friend, Sean, he didn't. Gale blames himself." Lucy thumbed a tear from her cheek. "It wasn't his fault."

Of course he does. Survivors' guilt. Still . . . "We all make our choices."

"Yeah." She sat, mug in hands, staring at nothing. A sigh, and Lucy shook it off, smiling tightly. "Sorry. Don't know why I brought all that up."

Because your son is anxious and it brought back too many bad memories. "It's fine. No worries."

Lucy got to her feet, dumped what remained of her tea in the sink, washed and dried the mug. "I guess I should get going. You must be beat."

"It's a permanent state of being for me."

"I hear you." A chuckle? Or an attempt at one. The tightness around Lucy's smile showed in her eyes. "Can I come back next week?"

"Whenever you want to come," Regina told her. Truth was, she didn't mind Lucy's company as much as she thought she would. "I can always use an extra pair of hands. I give my volunteers twenty bucks at the end of a shift, if you're—"

"No. Thanks." Lucy held up both hands. "Put it back into the kitchen."

Regina couldn't admit she didn't need that twenty, though she was pretty certain Lucy could use it. She'd slip it to Gale, next time he was in. Tell him she forgot to give it to his mother in all the excitement over the competition.

She walked Lucy Carmichael to the service entrance, ready to lock the door behind her when movement in the garden raised her hackles. Reaching for the long flashlight kept near the door, as much a weapon as a light source, she told herself it was just a straggler looking for something to eat. Whoever it was, the odds of her knowing them were pretty high.

Unwilling to frighten Lucy, she said nothing until the woman got In her car and pulled out of the driveway behind the kitchen. Regina switched on the flashlight, shined it at the garden; light caught a faded sheen of papery gold.

"What are you doing here at this hour?" Regina took the box partially full of poorly picked vegetables from the Burger Queen's hands. "Why didn't you come inside for dinner?"

"I don't like spaghetti and meatballs." She sniffed. "It gives me heartburn. You said I could take vegetables whenever I wanted. Well, I wanted. Anything wrong with that, missy?"

Regina suppressed the exhausted sigh. Only last week the old woman had devoured two helpings of the spaghetti and meatballs she professed to dislike. "How did you think you were getting home with this?"

"That nice man said he would help me." Burger Queen pointed.

Regina shined her flashlight on the shadow stepping out from behind the compost bin. A man. Well-dressed. Shielding his eyes against the glare. Regina's breath caught in her throat. She lowered the flashlight.

"For fuck's sake."

"Hello, Queenie." Marco stepped nearer. "Long time, no see."

16

Bain Marie: A container of hot water into which a pan is placed for slow cooking.

2008

New Haven, Connecticut. Of all the places in the world Queenie B could land, this is last on the list. It has been a decade and a half since she left this city to film the pilot for the PBS show that would jettison her from obscurity to superstardom. She'd left it behind. All of it. Friends, jobs—she had two at the time—acquaintances whose names she can't recall. They had to all be gone, at this point. On to better jobs. Better cities. Better.

Except Marco.

Of course, Marco.

He said he'd never leave, and he hasn't.

She pulls up to the curb outside the dilapidated building she's come to see. It might have been lovely, once upon a time. Quaint. A good number of the original cedar shakes are still there. Big windows—currently glassless and boarded up—on the first floor. Those on the second—just as glassless and less carefully boarded—show signs of having had hurricane shutters, that meaning there are still a few mostly intact, creaking on their hinges. The shutter dogs remaining are not doing their jobs, but at least they're still there, and probably original. Regina is surprised they survived scavengers, though who in this neighborhood would even know what they are, let alone their worth?

From what she's learned from the realtor, the edifice was a fresh fish market from the time it was built in 1894 until the 1960s, when it became a pharmacy, and finally, in 1982, a head shop. The upper floor has been used as a residence, a storeroom, and a hookah bar—being ten years too late or fifteen years too early for trends—in that order. Abandoned sometime in the nineties, the place has been just another building in the once-bustling Rock Landing left to die a slow and withering death.

The perfect place for Queenie B to die, once and for all.

She walks around the perimeter of the building, keys laced through her fingers as she's read a woman alone in a sketchy area should do, imagining the garden she could plant in the yard apparently being used as a toilet by the local indigent. There is only one window cracked but not boarded, and she peeks inside. Empty, but for more detritus. The place will take at least a year, maybe two, to restore and get running. Queenie B doesn't have two years left. Regina Benuzzi, however and hopefully, does.

Getting back to her car—a white 2001 Durango she paid cash for not two hours ago—Queenie stands aside for an elderly woman wearing a fast-food crown. She is pushing a shopping cart full of empties and nods imperiously as she passes by. This is who she's doing this for, not herself. She wants to make a difference, a positive impact, in overlooked, apparently disposable lives. The impoverished. The addicts. The runaways. The mentally ill. The elderly with no one to care for them.

Queenie needs redemption.

So maybe it's a little for herself.

A lot for herself.

But doing good is doing good. She rose to fame and fortune by sheer will; she'll use that same will now. One day at a time. Alone. It's how she's lived the last several years. So far, so good. Tomorrow, she will go to the realty office and start the necessary paperwork. Tonight, though, she is heading to Wooster Street.

Not exactly Wooster, but a side street nearby.

To the last friend Queenie B and Regina Benuzzi have on earth.

New Haven has changed since last she drove these streets, but she manages to get where she needs to go. It's dark and it's cold and it rained earlier, leaving shiny puddles in all the potholes and dips. November in Connecticut is beautiful. November in New Haven, not so much; but like any other city, it has its charms.

The names on the bars and restaurants and shops have changed, but the basic feel of the place remains. The wealthy areas are still wealthy. The poor, still poor. Wooster Street is still Wooster Street.

And there is Marco's, exactly as it was all those years ago, from striped awning to the curl of letters on the window. Marco hadn't believed her when she said she'd be back. After a time, Queenie took his word for it.

She leaves the Durango parked down the block and walks the rest of the way. No heels clicking on the sidewalk, just the squeak of wet sneakers. Queenie doesn't wear makeup, especially not the signature red lipstick. The long ponytail pulled through the back of her ball cap— Huskies, picked up in the airport—is the last bit of her famous persona to remain. She's even gained just enough weight to take her goddess curves to matronly plump. Not on purpose; it's just the way it went.

Queenie goes around to the service entrance, even though, late as it is, no patrons remain inside. Marco will be at the bar, having a drink with whatever staff lingers to drink for free and smoke inside rather than in the alley.

The kitchen is clean. Empty. Garlic, onions, and olive oil still mist the air or are so permeated into every crack and crevice it's part of the decor. Sacred aromas. Queenie breathes them deep into her lungs. Hopeful. Listening. Voices on the other side of the swinging door tell her all is as she suspects. Marco's deep rumble tumbles around in her belly. He was never a drunk, but always a drinker. Every night. After hours. They'd gotten drunk together on more occasions than Queenie can calculate, back when it wasn't a problem for her. She wants to see him, and yet doesn't. Not at all. It's too much to hope she can slip into his office and get her property without him seeing her. Pushing through the door, letting it *flap-flap-flap* behind her, she hopes she's been vanished long enough not to be recognized by anyone but her old pal.

His eyes are the first to fall on her. They open wide. His lips pull back over his teeth. Sneer? Smile? Feral. Queenie puts a finger to her lips, slips back through the door still flapping before the bartender and hostess can turn.

"I'm heading out," she hears him say.

"Early night, Chef?" A male voice. The bartender.

"This old man's got to get his shut-eye."

The hostess laughs, low and throaty. "You're far from old."

"I feel it, these days." He sighs, and it doesn't sound put-on. "Once in a while, someone shows up and reminds you of your ill-spent youth, and you can't help remembering just how many years are behind you."

"I haven't had enough to drink to dissect that one." Still low and throaty, but muffled now. The clink of ice cubes. Queenie envies her so hard, she salivates.

She waits, arms crossed over her chest, for Marco to push through the door. Not long, because there he is. Far from old. They both are. But he's a little on the plush side too; he'd been so skinny, back in their day. All sinew, sweat, and passion.

"Regina." He says her name on an exhaled breath. Regina, not Queenie, even if it had been his idea to use the pseudonym. A good sign. "I thought you were dead."

"A lot of people do."

He opens his arms, and Queenie steps into them. No hesitation. It is, currently, the only place she wants to be. "How'd it all get so fucked-up, Marco?"

"It wasn't always."

"It feels that way." She pulls away. "You know why I'm here, right?"

He smiles. "I guess not for me."

"I think your wife might have something to say, if that were the case."

"How'd you know I'm married? We haven't spoken since the old days."

"I keep tabs." She punched his arm. "It's good to see you."

"Good to see you too. You look good."

"I look like shit." But she smiles this time.

"You want a drink?" he asks. Queenie puts up a hand and he doesn't press. "Hungry?"

"I wouldn't say no to a plate of your Bolognese."

"You got it."

Marco fills a small pot, salts the water, sets it on to boil. "Penne? Spaghet'?"

"Got any rigatoni?"

He chuckles, pulling a container of sauce from the fridge. "Still your favorite, huh?"

"Always."

Sauce heats, pasta cooks, Marco plates without finesse, just like when they were twentysomethings trying to impress each other with their inexperienced, culinary prowess. Grating cheese over top, he asks. "Enough?"

"A little more." Queenie digs in, suddenly hungrier than she should be. Rich. Homey. Garlicky. It needs salt. She would finely chop anchovies and dollop them on top. Marco wouldn't. Doesn't. There is little of fine dining to the plate of food she devours. Old-school Italian. Just like Marco himself.

"You want a soda? Water?"

"Soda, thanks. Diet whatever you have."

Marco pushes through that swinging door; he's gone longer than he should be. Thoughts of him calling his wife—*You'll never guess who just showed up in the restaurant!*—some newspaper or television station, or worse, Oz, are fleeting. Most would. He won't. Not Marco.

He returns with a glass of soda, and a book. Not a book. He slides both to her across the prep table. For a moment, all Queenie can do is stare. Then she swallows. Her hand is on the cover. Fingers trace the remaining gold flecks of the embossed words: *Holy Bible.*

Queenie opens to the frontispiece. The edge of the paper disintegrates, powdering her fingertips. Names in faded ink, almost illegible for as long as she can remember. She flips the fragile, onion-paper pages, the ink getting more legible with each careful turn.

And there they are.

Names of people she has no faces for, a family she knows is hers only because she's listed there with them, alongside her birth date, baptism, and bout with the chicken pox at the age of two. A mother, father, two brothers, and a sister all lost in a house fire she survived because as the story goes—she doesn't remember, even if the scent of woodsmoke never fails to chill her—baby Regina fell asleep under her sister's bed, playing hide-and-seek, tucked into a nest of blankets and stuffed animals. The firefighters found her sister dead in her bed, Regina alive and asleep underneath it.

Fanning gently through the pages still scented by the fire, the bible falls open to the *Ladies' Home Journal* recipe tucked inside, near the middle. Cheesy tuna-noodle casserole. Queenie can't be sure her mother put it there, but it was from the 1960s, so she probably had. It was the first thing Regina Benuzzi ever cooked. It was horrible, so she cooked it again, tweaking and amending until it was something slightly less than horrible. Considering the basic concept, there had never been much hope. Queenie tucks the recipe back in its place and closes the book.

"Thanks."

"No problem."

Moments pass, drenched in silence. Queenie finishes the rigatoni on her plate, gulps down the soda, which tickles her nose.

"So, what now?" Marco asks.

"What do you mean?"

"Are you back?"

"Hell, no. I just came for this."

"Where have you been?" Softly. "Where will you go?" Less so. "No one has seen or heard from you since . . . since . . ."

"Rome. That was on purpose, Marco."

"I've been worried about you."

Queenie snorts. "Liar. You haven't even thought about me in years."

"That's not true."

Maybe it isn't. Queenie can't let it matter. "I've been around," she says. "Italy, Spain, Croatia. I might try Russia next. I have an accountant I trust to keep my assets straight and me invisible. But no one's looking for me anymore. I'm like Orville Redenbacher or Chef Boyardee. All my brand needs is my face, and my old shows on Netflix."

"What about Oz? And Julian?"

Of course, he asks. "Remarried. Remothered. Assets and parental rights severed. They're both better off, I assure you."

"What about you?" Softly, again. So fucking softly.

"What about me?" Queenie bristles. Rising, she takes her dish, cutlery, and glass to the sink and leaves them there. "I'm fine. I have loads of money. I'm mostly clean four years now. It's a balance I can maintain as long as Queenie B stays vanished."

"But if you've been four years clean—"

"Mostly clean," she snaps. "The times I wasn't, it was because Queenie B came out to fuck with me. I don't fucking want her. I don't fucking need her!" Deep breath in, fingers pressed to temples. "Look. I'm sorry. This is hard, you know?"

"I know."

"Thanks for keeping this for me." She swipes the bible from the prep table. "And thanks for the rigatoni. I got to go."

"All right," Marco says. Nothing more. It's what she's always liked about him. That he has been a little in love with her, a little in awe of her, even when she was no one. Even now. Queenie leans over the table to kiss his cheek. He smells just the same as he always did—garlic, onions, and cigarettes. It makes her heart stutter. To go back to the days they were two young chefs sharing an apartment, eventually a bed, before she rose and fell and rose and fell would be . . . pointless. It would all happen again. She is Queenie B more than she was ever Regina Benuzzi, even before Queenie B existed.

"Take care of yourself, Reg."

"Don't you know by now?" She wiped her olive oil lip-print from his cheek. "It's what I do best. Don't tell anyone you saw me."

"That goes without saying."

Queenie takes her coat from the hook next to the door, slides the bible into the open mouth of her backpack. "I guess that's it."

"I'll walk you out."

"No need. I'm good." Another kiss on his cheek. This time, she lingers. Wife or not, he loves her still. Queenie suspects he always will. She loves him too, in her selfish, always-prideful way. It would be easy to fall into the past, if only for a night. Familiar. Easy. Comforting. But down that path, there be dragons slain and slain again. Queenie is too tired to take up that sword.

She's in the alley. She is walking along the sidewalk. She is in her

Durango, turning over the engine. Tonight, the hotel. Tomorrow, Regina Benuzzi is signing all the necessary paperwork to make the decrepit, rat-infested, trash-mound building in Rock Landing home. No one will ever find her there, not even Marco. He won't even look.

It is 2008. Barack Obama has won the White House. The global economy continues its spiral down a giant toilet. The governor of Illinois has been arrested on federal corruption charges, Fidel Castro has stepped down after fifty years in power, and an earthquake in China has left ninety thousand dead—of which Queenie B might have potentially been one, had she not left Chengdu when she did. That fact changed everything.

No more running, hiding, pretending. She is Regina Benuzzi, dammit, and it's time for Queenie B to go. Finally and at last.

Regina is going home.

The last place anyone will think to look for her.

The last place on earth she ever wanted to be.

She navigates the quiet streets. Unlike New York, New Haven sleeps. Queenie thinks she remembers this apartment building, or that little house tucked incongruously between a shoe repair and a bookstore. She lived in so many such places between the ages of three and eighteen, there's no telling if she's remembering or simply filling in blanks. This relative. That family friend. A foster home or two, in between suckering one of the former to take her in. Some were kind but uncaring. Others were uncaring and unkind. All a string of smiles and fists blurring into one another, just like the residences she never called home.

Pulling into the hotel lot, she reaches for her backpack.

A backpack.

Queenie B would never carry one. Regina Benuzzi used to. All the time. The change was already happening, and she hadn't even done it consciously. Maybe because she bought it in a thrift store, where Regina shopped because she had no choice. Where Queenie B would never step foot unless it was ironically. And she knows she's made the right decision, coming to New Haven, where it all began. She can't go back, but she has the money and the will to take a stab at a sort of do-over. It's a privilege most will never have; the least she can do is some good for those who won't.

17

Soigne: Pronounced swan-yay, it is French for "elegant." It is/was used to describe an exceptionally sexy, well-presented dish, but quickly devolved from trendy to dated and pretentious.

2015

Don't call me Queenie."

Marco bowed his head. "Good. I never liked that name."

"You're the one who gave it to me, you idiot."

"It seemed clever at the time."

Marco opened his arms, just like he had all those years ago when Queenie B landed in New Haven to die. Regina didn't melt into him this time. She was made of sterner stuff than chaotic, flighty Queenie had ever been. "I'm not a hugger these days."

Marco's arms fell. "Even with me?"

"Even with you. Listen, go inside, will you? Let me take Her Highness home. I'll be back in ten minutes."

"I'll go with—"

"Just stay here." She took the Burger Queen's arm. "And don't touch anything."

Regina drove the old woman home, brought her box of produce into her apartment, turned on her television, and left with a muttered, "Stay put. I'll see you tomorrow." On her way past, she rapped a little too fiercely on Troy's door. No answer. There was a notice taped to the peeling wood panel. She took out her cell phone, read by its light—a fifteen-day notice to quit.

"Shit." Resisting the urge to rip the notice from the door, she left. She had her own issues, dammit, and the most pressing was waiting for her back in her kitchen. But when she got back, Marco was still in the garden, in among the tomatoes she grew for her own use and to give away to those who wanted them.

Regina flicked on her flashlight, shining it in his direction. "Why are you here?"

"Good to see you too."

"You had to know I wouldn't be happy."

"It occurred to me." Marco turned in a circle, arms spreading wide. "Is this where you've been since that night?"

"Pretty much. It took over a year to get it restored and running."

"A soup kitchen?"

Regina nodded.

"How has no one recognized you?"

"Would you, if you didn't know me?"

"Yes."

"You're a liar. I'm old, fat, and I dress like a longshoreman." Her lip twitched; she suppressed the urge to smile. "Did you know me, that day in the market?"

"Can we take this inside? The bugs . . ."

Regina clicked off her flashlight, which had been attracting every moth in the vicinity. Marco devolved into shadow, highlighted by moonlight. "No chance you'll just go home and forget you saw me, huh?" Half joking, but only half. When he said nothing, Regina's shoulders sagged. "Fine. Come on in."

She walked ahead of him, more to gather whatever fortitude she needed than anger, but a little of that too. Seven years! Seven years in New Haven without being known by anyone but her well-paid accountant, who feared the lawyers she kept on retainer to fear betrayal. Marco wouldn't give her away. She was pretty sure. Still, the safe anonymity had been breached, and already her nerves were fraying.

Regina flicked on the light, gestured to the little table she often sat at with Gale or Lucy. Once, a million years ago it seemed, all by herself. "Sit. You want tea? Coffee?"

"I'm good." Marco whistled softly. "Nice kitchen. Big."

"Thanks."

"No one ever wondered how a soup kitchen cook came to have state-of-the-art kitchen equipment?"

"My clientele wouldn't know the difference between a Wolf and GE."

"GE's got some good stuff."

"Please, spare me."

They sat opposite each other. Marco slipped his coat off, hung it on the back of his chair. "Gale never noticed?"

"He noticed. Did he—?"

"Don't worry. I don't think he has any idea who you are," Marco said. "He mentioned your name once. Just Regina. You're the only woman by that name I've ever known, but then I saw you in the market that day."

"So you did know it was me."

"I doubted my own eyes, but not because I didn't recognize you. I thought you were dead."

"That's what you said last time."

"That's what I thought then, too."

"Wrong. Twice." She groaned. "Why are you here? Why couldn't you just leave me be?"

Marco slumped back in his chair. "You were my best friend, Reg. For a little while, I thought you'd be my wife."

"Well, you already have one of those, and it's been a long time since we were pals."

"I had a wife," he corrected. "Teenie died. About five years ago."

Regina had been right there, in New Haven. All the years she kept tabs on her only friend, she hadn't even once in all the time since coming back. "Shit. I'm so sorry."

He shrugged, eyes downcast. The part of her that wanted to embrace him fought the part that couldn't. Shouldn't. Wouldn't.

"I could say I don't know what made me come here," he said. "Pretend I was curious as everyone else. Why you'd let it all go, the fame and the money—"

"I have plenty of money, and I don't want the fame."

"Bullshit," he barked. "You don't want the fucking mess you were back then is all."

Regina's eyes narrowed in a way that should have warned him to shut the hell up. She'd used it effectively throughout her life, and only that moment realized it had never worked on him. "Okay, if not out of curiosity, why?"

"Because."

"Because? Wow, Marco."

"I don't need a reason," he said. "I saw an old friend's ghost buying produce, and I was happy. I wanted to see you. Tell me you wouldn't have done the same, if the roles were reversed."

"I wouldn't have."

"Still such a liar." He chuckled, then, "You do realize it's just a matter of time, don't you?"

"What is?" Yes, she was a liar; she knew exactly what he meant.

"I doubt I'm the first," he called her on it, "only the first to take it a step further. One of these days, it won't be an old friend glad to see you're still alive. Then what?"

Inside, the frenzy built. Regina inhaled through her nose, out through her mouth. The truth Marco spoke had shadowed her through the years. Someday, someone, the wrong someone, would recognize her, and it would all be over. She pushed away from the table, filled the kettle for tea neither of them wanted. "I won't be Queenie B again."

He leaned back in his chair, on two legs. Like Oz used to do. Or was it always Marco? He said, "You are her and she is you. You telling yourself they're two people doesn't do shit but give you reason to hide."

"It's how I cope. How I stay clean."

"It was how you coped, how you got clean. Now? It's just a good hiding spot that's going to bite you in the ass one of these days."

Regina dropped back onto her chair. She pulled the elastic from her braid, shook it out. White streaked the black, enhancing rather than aging. Looking in the mirror, sometimes, she'd smile and Queenie would smile back. Hopeful. Promising. *Let me out. We'll be good.* Regina did not trust her. No one ever should.

"What makes you think you can waltz in here and lecture me, anyway?"

"Is that what I'm doing?" He grinned, cocky and lopsided and not fooling her in the slightest. "I thought I was checking in on an old friend I thought was dead."

The teakettle whistled. Regina turned off the burner, wishing for a cup of tea she could hurl, even if it was in the Bernardaud. Or a shot she could belt back. "You checked. I'm fine. How about you beat it?"

Marco chuckled. So much like old times. Hauntingly so. He pushed out of his chair. "I've always been good at pissing you off."

"Some things don't change."

"Isn't that what you liked best about me, back in the old days? Isn't it why you ditched me? Because you didn't want anyone smacking you in the head with the truth?"

"Fuck you. I had Oz for that."

"Oz never told you anything you didn't want to hear," Marco said. "He helped you create the monster that was Queenie B, then discovered he couldn't handle it."

"You could have?"

"I've asked myself the same thing a million times over the years." Marco pushed fingers through his hair, thinner than it had been but still curly. His face was lined by kitchen heat and sunshine without sunblock. "Never did come up with an answer. Look, I just wanted to see you. I'll go now."

Ire rose, crackled in the roots of her hair. In her mind's eye, she hurled and she belted. Teacups. Booze. The frenzy that had been mostly quiet for the past seven years buzzed through her veins. From the bottom of that barrel she scraped daily for fortitude, Queenie B hailed, *You know he's right. That's why you're so mad.*

"Marco, wait."

He obeyed, of course.

"You . . . this is a lot. You took me by surprise. I . . ." Regina managed to smile and, for the split moment she held it, Marco's entire face lit up. Something inside her warmed. "I really am glad to see you."

"No, you're not."

"Ask me if I wish you'd never shown up, and I'll say yes," she told him. "But you did, and . . . really. I am glad."

"Thanks, I guess." There it was, that crooked smile she recognized in the market trying so hard not to happen.

"It's about as good as you can expect at the moment. Listen." She moved closer. Just enough. "Don't say anything. To anyone. Especially not Gale. Will you do that for me?"

"You don't even have to ask," he said. "I'm kind of hurt you think you do."

"I don't know you anymore, Marco. You don't know me either."

She stood upon a precipice, one she'd been standing upon for all the years since Bova, one she'd only just looked down and seen for what it was. Regina had felt the wind of it whip up at her now and then—most recently, when Marco spotted her in the market—but had never once cast a glance downward to acknowledge what it was. Her eyes stung so bad, she feared—hoped—he noticed them welling up, if not spilling over. Marco was, after all these years, still her friend. That was something.

"Come by next Wednesday," she said. "I'll cook. We can talk when my brain doesn't feel like it's going to explode out my ears. I owe you a dinner anyway."

His eyebrow arched.

"For the rigatoni Bolognese."

Marco's face relaxed into a smile, sad but genuine. "Can we make it Thursday? I'd rather leave Frances alone for service than Gale. He's good, but he's still new at this. He can't cook and expedite at the same time."

"She can?"

"Frances is fierce. She can do anything. Reminds me of someone I used to know."

"Don't wish that on anyone." She waved him off before he could counter. "Thursday, then. After service here. Around eight thirty."

"I'll bring the wi—the diet soda."

"And whatever dessert you have on the menu." Regina patted her plumpness.

"You got it."

They stood in the quiet kitchen made quieter for their unease. Two old friends who, in another life, wouldn't have an uncomfortable moment between them, brought down by a past they'd each only seen from afar.

He didn't open his arms. Regina wished he would; she was grateful he didn't. It spared her pressing her body to his, asking him to stay. Not just for another moment but for the night. It had been so long. Since anyone. Longer still since him. Safe, familiar Marco who loved her despite it all. There was no denying the pull toward him was no less real for that.

Her throat tightened around the words wishing. Her body tensed against the compulsion to latch onto their past, pull into the present. Giving herself over to compulsion had been the key to her success, and her downfall. Queenie B was all wild impulse, creative passion. Regina had been, too, once upon a time. When this man knew her. Loved her. So she remained silent while Queenie hailed from the bottom of that barrel of fortitude, promising promises she couldn't be trusted to keep.

18

Kill it: To intentionally overcook something is to "kill it."

2015

All the anxiety of the lead-up. The frenzy of the taping. The words *Gale Carmichael, you're cut.* Over and done. He hadn't won the ten grand, but at least he'd made it to the dessert round. Disappointing, but not embarrassing. And now he rode home in a fancy car with a minibar and plush seats. Probably because the producers hadn't had to put him up in a hotel like the contestants from farther afield.

It'd been a long, long day. The car picked him up at six in the morning. He wouldn't get home until around ten. Gale closed his eyes, but even the car's smooth purr didn't help him sleep; his brain played his performance over and over. What he could have done differently. Had his plating been equal to his creativity. Why he'd put overcooked octopus on the plate when it wasn't even a crate ingredient.

You're going to make yourself nuts, man.

The driver behind a thick, plexiglass wall bobbed her head in time to whatever music she listened to but Gale couldn't hear.

"I really thought I had it, Sean."

You did great. It was the dessert. Got both of you.

"But if I hadn't overcooked the octopus in the main course round . . ."

Yeah, but you did, and it's what went down. You did really well.

"I did, didn't I?" Gale felt his face smile, even if his stomach still twisted itself in knots. "I totally took the appetizer round."

You know Marco's going to want you to put that on the menu.

"Totally." Gale laughed softly. All in all, he didn't feel as bad as he thought he would. He not only didn't go out first but also won that round solidly with a perfectly executed risotto—ballsy, as one of the judges said, to attempt in such a short time—topped by barely warmed uni and a dollop of smoked caviar. One competitor edged him out in the main course because of that stupid octopus, but the other completely hammered the chard—which was a crate ingredient—and Gale had skated through.

"I really thought I had her in the dessert round," he told Sean. "She made bread pudding, for fuck's sake. What was she thinking?"

But she did it well, while your napoleon really sucked, man.

"It was more creative."

Inedible. Isn't that what Harold said?

"Shut up."

Just saying . . .

"Well, don't." Gale let go a deep breath. "Sure would have been cool to get that ten grand."

You're making good money now.

"Not good enough to get my own apartment."

That's not exactly true. It would just be more expensive, and for the first time in your adult life, you're not constantly strapped.

"Yeah, but I'm too old to be living with roommates."

Who says?

"Adulthood says."

Don't be an asshole. You're doing great. Way better than me, am I right?

Sean's sniggering sounded sinister inside Gale's head. Echoing. The afterimage always in his periphery blinked out. Sean knew, he *knew* exactly how to hit Gale hardest when he was most vulnerable. Always had, and wasn't that the truth? His gut welled up to his throat, glands in his jaw watering. Bile pooled in his mouth. His already-knotted stomach clenched. Heaved. Lunging for the divider, he banged on it even as it lowered. "Pull over. Quick."

Gale was puking out the open door before the car came to a complete stop. His driver came around to his side of the car, rubbed his back in that motherly way some people just knew how to do, without making him feel gross or weak.

"It's okay. Long day. I know. I can't tell you how many pukers I've had in my car."

Gale dry-heaved, his stomach convulsing long after it was empty.

Way better than me.

Way better than me.

Way better . . . way better . . . way better . . .

A sob welled in his still-convulsing gut. Let it go. Hold it in. Gale inhaled the eruption, making him gag all over again. Why you and not me? Goddammit, Sean.

Gale dropped onto his butt, right there at the side of the road, barely missing the pool of his own vomit. He reached for a cigarette that wasn't there. His driver pulled a pack from her shirt pocket, shook one out. Gale lit his first cigarette in months.

"Thanks."

"No worries."

She lit one too. "I'm trying to quit. I only smoke where my kid can't see me."

"I quit over a year ago," Gale told her. "You're right. It really has been a long, exhausting day."

Exhaling a long stream, he rested his arms on his knees. He tried to hold on to some semblance of dignity and failed even more horribly than he already had. Tears rolled warm down the sides of his face.

"Hey, come on, now." An arm around his shoulder. "It can't be that bad."

Nothing from Sean. No words of comfort. Or accusation. No afterimage burned into his retinas. Just that bomb dropped, leaving him alone to weather the aftermath.

She ducked into the car, came back with a bottle of water in one hand, a minibar-size bottle of scotch in the other. Gale took the water. He rinsed his mouth, spat over his shoulder. "Thanks."

"You're welcome." She took his elbow, coaxed him to his feet. "GPS says we have another half hour until we get to your place. You going to be okay?"

"I'll be fine. Thanks."

She held out her hand. "You're Gale, right?"

Cigarette stuck in the corner of his mouth, he took it. "Gale Carmichael."

"Jenara Bizzarro." She rolled her eyes. "Yeah, I know. Sounds like a DC supervillain."

"More Jedi Master."

She cocked her head.

"Chancellor Genarra? Sith Wars? No?"

"No, sorry," she said. "It's Italian. Jenara means January. Odd January, that's me."

"Were you born in January?"

Jenara laughed. "No! That makes it even funnier. My mom's kind of a kook, and my dad loved her for it. It makes for a good icebreaker, at least." She let go of his hand. "You feeling better?"

His stomach gurgled. Gale took another drag, tossed the rest. "Yeah, I think so."

"All right. Back in then. I got to get home to my daughter at some point tonight too." Jenara waved him into the back seat. "I'll keep the divider down, if that's okay. Then, if you need to stop again, just shout."

"Okay, good. Thanks." Gale got in, sprawled across the back seat. He could only see the top of her curly head from there, and a bit of her face reflected in the rearview mirror. Pretty eyes. Dark on dark. He imagined her eyelashes lush, if her brows were any indication, but he couldn't tell for sure.

You should ask her out, man. When's the last time you went out with a woman, anyway?

Gale put his arm across his eyes.

You not talking to me now?

Answering inside his own head never worked, even if that's where Sean's voice came from. Answering outside of it wasn't possible, not with his driver right there. Gale rolled onto his side, his back to her. He whispered, "Not now."

"You okay?" she asked over her shoulder.

"Yeah, fine. Thanks."

She turned the radio on. Turned the volume way down. All Gale could hear was the backbeat. And Sean.

When're you going to get over it, man? It happened. It's done. You didn't make me do anything. I could have said no when you brought it over. I fucking should have, right? I should have taken it from you and flushed it. But I didn't. Now you're alive and I'm not. Could've been the other way around. Or both of us could've bit the shit. But that's not what went down. It's not your—

"Mind if I stop for a pee break?" Jenara glanced at him in the rearview. "I thought I could make it home. There's a twenty-four-hour diner just up ahead."

"Go for it," Gale told her. He'd grab a coffee. Maybe a donut or something, to absorb the pukey taste in his mouth.

She pulled into the parking lot. "I'll be right out."

"I'm coming in," Gale said. "You want a coffee or something?"

Jenara smiled. Perfect, white teeth—definitely had braces at some point—and dimples. Deep ones appearing like magic. "I'd love it, thanks. Why don't you grab a table? I'll be right out."

Uh-oh. You asked her out and didn't even mean to.

"Shut up, Sean," he grumbled under his breath. Gale took a table in the window. The waitress, entirely too chipper for that time of night, set down two menus and two glasses of water. "Coffee," he croaked. "Please."

"Sure thing." Pink-lipped, toothy smile. She came back with two mugs and a pot of coffee. "Rough night?"

Gale managed to smile his thanks. "Long day." He sipped the coffee she poured. Dishwater. Trying not to grimace, he took two creamers from the bowl on the table, sugar packets from the sticky holder. They felt as if they'd gotten wet at some point and partially solidified. He dumped them into his coffee anyway. Passable, at best.

Jenara slid into the booth opposite before the waitress had a chance to move along. "I'll take one of those croissants." She pointed.

"Good choice. They just came out of the oven. And you?"

Gale glanced at the bakery window. "Two glazed donuts."

"They're from this morning," the woman said. "But the crullers are from about an hour ago."

"Okay, two crullers."

"You bake all night?" Jenara dumped cream into her coffee.

"Twenty-four hours a day. We get a lot of truckers on this stretch of ninety-five. You wouldn't believe how finicky they are about their baked goods."

The waitress returned with their food, left them with a smile. Jenara pulled her pastry apart. "I don't have to get home to my daughter," she said. "I mean, she's home, and I do have to get there at some point, but my mom is with her. She lives with us. I just wanted you to know I have a kid."

"I . . . uh . . . okay."

She pursed her lips, dimples deepening. "I know. TMI. I just like to get it out of the way when I meet someone. That way, if we have a good time, or whatever, he knows from the get-go. Too many guys hear the word 'kid' and suddenly have to be up early in the morning or whatever."

Gale bit into his cruller, brain whizzing. "It's . . . we're just having coffee."

"Duh." She winked. "But I'm about to ask you out and I wanted to be clear before I did. And, just so you know, I don't do this. Ever. I mean, I drive lots of guys to lots of places, and I've never once wanted to ask any of them out."

"Yeah?" Something warm pooled in his belly, and it wasn't the lukewarm coffee. "Why me?"

"Because you barfed and didn't get all weird and manly man about it." She ate a piece of the croissant she'd broken off, smiled as she chewed. Her dimples had dimples. Her curls kind of flopped around her face, soft and shiny and so, so black. "And you're cute."

"I am?"

"I dig redheads."

"It's chestnut."

"But it was red when you were a kid, am I right?"

Gale stuffed the rest of the cruller in his mouth. Heat Miser. Carrottop. Yukon Cornelius. Ron Weasley. He'd heard them all. "Yeah. I got my dad's red hair, but my mom's brown eyes. Irish Italian."

"Puerto Rican Italian." She winked. "Hot tempers."

"Every nationality claims that."

"Not the English."

"True. Or the French."

"I don't know about that. Swedish? Norwegian?"

"What are we even talking about?"

They laughed together. Jenara said, "So? Want to go out with me?"

Gale picked up his other cruller, broke it in half, and dipped it in his coffee. He hadn't dated anyone in years. Too fucked-up. Too much stress. Until recently, he'd always felt like he was still on that knife's edge. Until Regina and her kitchen and his promotion at work. The edge had dulled a bit, but it remained, and it was only fair to warn her.

"I'm an addict," he said. "I mean, not, like, currently. It's been almost two years."

Jenara covered his hand with hers. "That's a great accomplishment, Gale. Wow. So, do you want to go out with me?"

"You still want to?"

"Why wouldn't I?"

Because people don't trust addicts. Ever. No matter how long since the last fall. Because they believed it was never an if, but a when. Because it was mostly, exactly that.

Gale ate the rest of his cruller. Jenara ate her croissant. The waitress refilled their coffee cups without being asked, and they both seemed obliged to drink it.

"I did that DNA thing," she said. "I'm not really Puerto Rican Italian. I mean, I am, culturally. Mom was born in Puerto Rico, and Dad . . . well, that DNA thing shows just how mixed"—air quotes—"all those Europeans are. I've got a little bit of everything in me. I bet you do, too, even if you look Irish."

"What does it mean to look Irish?"

"Fair skin. Freckles. Red . . . sorry, chestnut hair. And that's an Irish chin if I ever saw one."

Gale rubbed his chin. "Irish chin?"

"Yeah." She reached out, stuck a finger in the deep cleft. "Irish chin."

"If you say so." He motioned to the waitress. "My brother's superfair. He can't go out in the sun without fifty-block on. I tan in the summer."

"Do you really, though?" Jenara cocked her head. "Or do your freckles just spread out?"

Laughing with her got easier each time he did so. Gale paid the bill, waving away her offer to cover her three dollars on the way back to the car. "Call it part of your tip."

"I'm not allowed to accept tips."

"I won't tell if you don't." He shoved his wallet back into his pocket. "Yes, by the way."

"Yes?"

"I'd like to go out with you, if you still want to."

Jenara pulled out her phone, scrolled. "How about this Thursday. You busy?"

Regina would be able to do without him. Maybe he'd get his mom to cover service for him. "Thursday is good. I don't have a car. Do you? I mean, obviously that one, but one of your own?"

"I do. And I already know where to pick you up. Do we do the requisite dinner thing? You being a chef, it might not be your jam."

"No, dinner'd be great." Thank goodness he hadn't maxed out his credit card's measly five-hundred-dollar limit. "You have a place in mind?"

"I might." She grinned at him over the open car door. "Why don't you sit up front? Less chance of you barfing up your donuts."

Gale grabbed his knife kit from the back seat, tossed it onto the front.

"GPS says we have another twenty minutes to your place. Seat belt."

"Oh, right." Gale clicked himself in. Jenara started the car, pulled smoothly from the lot.

This sure as hell ended different than either of us thought it would.

Dammit.

"Mind if I turn on some music?" Jenara asked.

"Please do."

Gale wished she'd talk, but she took her job seriously, and they drove the rest of the way listening to music in companionable silence. Head back. Eyes closed. Gale willed Sean to stay quiet. Except for a, *She's cute,* he obliged.

19

On the fly: An order needed in a hurry; that is, a server realizes they've forgotten to put up a ticket and the table has been waiting twenty minutes for their food. The order is put in "on the fly" to indicate it's needed ASAP.

2015

So it was dessert that tripped you up." Regina thumbed her lower lip. Gale tried not to fidget like he was in sixth grade and hadn't done his homework. "*Inedible,* I think was the word used. I don't think it was because it tasted bad. It just kind of squished all over the place when cut into."

"You overbaked the pastry."

"Maybe?" He did. Gale knew he did. "Dessert just isn't my thing. I did well before that."

"A good chef does it all. We'll work on your dessert skills."

"We will? Why?"

"Because it's a good skill to have. It'll do you well in the future. First up, we'll do an edible napoleon. How about Thursday afternoon?"

"This Thursday?" Gale's stomach twinged. "I . . . uh . . . I can't."

"You pick up a shift at Marco's?"

"No. I have a date."

Regina's eyebrows rose. "One of the contestants?"

"No. The driver who took me home. Jenara Bizzarro. How's that for a great name?"

More eyebrow raising. The corner of her mouth quirked. Gale wished she'd just smile. This way, he couldn't tell if amusement or derision hid behind the expression.

She resumed chopping carrots. "So, you here to work, big shot? Or just to tell me how it went?"

"Both."

"Great. Start on the potatoes. I'm doing cottage pie tonight. Oh, and your mother will be here in about an hour. Did you call her yet? About yesterday?"

He hadn't, but . . . "Why's she coming in?"

"I don't know. She called and asked if I could use her help. We have a lot of mise en place to prep. Should I have said no?"

"No, no." Gale tied an apron on. "I just don't . . . never mind. I'm not supposed to tell anyone the results, so don't tell her I told you."

"You told me, but won't tell your mother?"

"You're . . . you're Regina. You're my mentor."

She stopped chopping, back still to him. "I'm your mentor?"

"Aren't you?" Gale brought the box of potatoes to the sink. "I've learned more from you in the last few months than I ever learned in culinary school."

"That's bullshit." Regina's knife *snick-snick-snick*ed through the carrots. "You were already good when you first came here. Nothing I taught you got you your job as sous."

Don't argue, man. Can't you see you're making her uncomfortable?

The "Shut up, Sean" in his head stayed there. "You're amazing, Regina. I mean it."

A pause in the *snick*ing, momentary and maybe imagined, was her only response. Gale swallowed the sigh, ignored Sean still chastising him for making Regina uncomfortable, and started scrubbing the potatoes. He was halfway through peeling when his mother arrived, out of breath and typically frantic.

"Hi, buddy." She kissed his cheek. "I know, I know! You can't tell me if you won or lost. I won't even ask even though it's *killing* me. Hey, Regina. What can I do?"

"I saved you the celery." She pointed with her knife. "Wash it, then dice it. You know how to dice?"

"That's the little chunks, right?"

"Yeah, the little chunks. Gale, show her."

Gale grabbed a stalk and made quick work of it. "Like that."

"I won't be as fast," Lucy Carmichael said, "but I'll get it done."

Listening to his mother slowly slog through the pile of celery it would have taken him ten minutes to do, start to finish, made Gale's skin itch. Regina didn't seem to notice. She chopped onions with the precision and speed of one who'd been doing so for so long, it was like walking. More like running. Sprinting. By the time Gale had to leave for work, all the mise en place was done and ready to go into the pots. He untied his apron and hung it on the hook.

"It's just beef stew, when you come down to it," Regina was saying to his mother. "Ground beef instead of stew beef, and instead of the potatoes in the stew, they're mashed on top. Your husband is Irish, fercrissake. How've you never had cottage pie?"

"For one thing, this is called shepherd's pie in the freezer case. Second, I'm sure my son has told you all about my cooking skills."

"If it doesn't come out of a can or box," Gale teased.

Lucy swatted him with a dish towel, but only half-heartedly. "It's true. I was intimidated, I guess. Remember what a good cook Nona was?"

"Your mother was not a good cook," Gale told her. "She was just better than you."

"Well, I thought she was a good cook." She sighed, slumping a little. "I wish you didn't have to leave. I like spending time with my boy."

She smiled, her lips turning down instead of up. Gale put an arm around her shoulders. "What's wrong?"

"Nothing. Why?"

Regina moved to the sink, turned on the water, and pretended to wash what was in there.

"You look kind of sad."

"Do I?" Lucy touched his cheek. "Maybe I'm sad because my boy won't tell me if he's ten thousand dollars richer or not."

Gale jiggled her playfully. "I signed an NDA. The show airs pretty soon. You won't have long to wait."

"I guess." She checked the clock. "You're going to be late for work. Scoot!"

Kissing her cheek, he gave her an extra squeeze. The time he got to spend with her these days was good for both of them. He needed to see his mother was okay as much as she needed to see he was. "I'll call you later."

"Just let me know you got home safe."

"Will do." Gale headed for the door. "See you, Regina."

She waved over her head, barely glanced his way. Gale felt just a little bad about telling her but not his mother.

Regina is Regina.

"Yeah. But I don't like keeping Mom in suspense." He half walked, half ran from Regina's to Marco's, worrying about his mother. She seemed older, and more tired, neither having anything to do with curiosity about how he'd done in the competition. A heart attack, and she wasn't even sixty. The thought of losing her made his chest ache.

Maybe you should move back home. Keep an eye on her.

"That's the last thing she needs," Gale said. "Me, under the same roof."

You could help with the bills. It'll still be less than paying rent on your own place.

"But it kind of defeats the whole idea of having my own place, doesn't it? No, Sean. It's a terrible idea. What if I relapse?"

You won't.

"You don't know that. And I won't do it to them again."

Kyle found us, man, not your parents.

"Just drop it, okay?"

Fine. Be a tool.

"You're a tool."

Mature, man. Real mature.

Gale took the mature road and didn't respond. It was easy for Sean to say he wouldn't relapse. Again. Sure, it had been almost two years since the big one. He'd never gone that long without even a hiccup before, not in the dark decade of his drug abuse. That didn't mean he wouldn't. He feared it. Every minute of every day. Almost every minute of every day. The fear didn't follow him into the kitchen. Maybe that's all he needed to do, spend every waking minute in a kitchen, cooking. If not Marco's, Regina's. If not those places, another. Work until he only had enough energy in reserve to slough off his clothes and fall into bed.

It'll kill you, man. You're okay. Seriously. Have faith in yourself.

But Gale didn't. Not enough. Until the fear of falling wasn't always waiting in the back of his brain, he couldn't have much faith at all.

LUCY CARMICHAEL'S KNOT OF WORRY TANGLED AROUND HER SO TIGHT, Regina couldn't pretend it was just her normal air of dejectedness. The woman worried about Gale. Constantly. Regina got it. She'd been the focus of a lot of the same worry. She wanted to tell Lucy that Gale was going to be okay. Truth was, Regina worried too. There was just no telling which adversity would get weathered, and which one would send him into a tailspin. The longer weathering won out, the better equipped he'd be to avoid the tailspin. But less than two years clean? She'd gone as long as four without slipping. At least there'd been no major fuckups in more than ten. Most would consider Regina Benuzzi's sobriety a success.

She never would. That was the first step off a cliff she'd fallen—and leapt—from too many times before.

Drying her hands on her apron, she turned off the faucet. "So, what's really wrong?"

Lucy didn't even pretend. "I lost my job."

"Lost it? How? Aren't you union?"

"That doesn't mean I can't get fired." She heaved a drawn-out sigh. "I wasn't fired, exactly. The owners and manager at the grocery store love me, but I'm a liability now because of my ticker. They won't let me do full shifts anymore. They said I'll make more collecting my pension than I would doing what partial shifts they'd agree to. I guess it's for the best."

Regina leaned on the table next to Lucy. "But the pension isn't as much as you were making before."

"Nope."

"Shit."

"Yeah, shit. I can't sit around doing nothing, Regina. That and the hit to our budget causes me way more stress than anything else."

"What does your doctor say?"

"I've been told yoga would be great for me."

They both laughed. Regina had tried yoga. Several times. All those rehabs swore by yoga and meditation. She saw it work wonders for some; she was not one of them. Lucy, she could guarantee, wasn't either.

"We'll be all right. We always are." Lucy picked up a huge wooden spoon, gave the aromatic, simmering mirepoix a stir. "Is it insulting if I say this doesn't look very appetizing?"

"It's cottage pie. It looks like it's supposed to look. Keep stirring."

Regina added the rosemary and bay leaf and salt. Nutmeg, mustard powder, a little Worcestershire, wine. Nothing fancy or lovely to look at. Nothing saying, *Here is the creation of one of the greatest chefs in modern culinary history!* Something in her missed that. More than she used to. Lately, her fingers itched, the glands in her jaw winced, and she had to pull back. Even so, this cottage pie wasn't the usual nutritious and simple yet tasty fare served in her kitchen. She might have served it in one of her more casual restaurants, once upon a time.

It was Marco showing up, Queenie coaxing and promising. But it was mostly Gale. His help in her kitchen made it possible for her to be more creative. He made her *want* to be more creative. He called her his mentor—Regina's heart swelled exactly as it had when he said it—but Gale wasn't just learning, or taking some of the burden from her shoulders; he inspired without meaning to. And now, she had Lucy, whom she was beginning to like when Regina made it a habit of liking no one. A year ago, she counted Troy as her only friend, and that was always problematic. How had it happened? Again, the answer was Gale.

"You know," she said, "I could use more help around here."

"I'll come in whenever you need me. You know that."

"I meant, regular. Paid work, not volunteer, or those twenties I make Gale give you."

Lucy stopped stirring. "Come on. This place can't afford a paid staff. I know the shoestring soup kitchens run on. I watch TV."

Oh, if only she knew. "There's money in the budget. Look, the one person I've been able to mostly rely upon is an elderly man with a drinking problem and I haven't seen him in months."

"You can count on Gale."

"Gale has a job, and he won't take money from me. I've tried." *He called me his mentor.* "He's destined for better things, anyway. We both want that for him."

Lucy's face pinked, her smile almost teary. "That's good for a mother to hear."

"He's a good man, I don't know how I got along before him."

"But you did. You can. You're making up this job because you feel bad for me."

"Maybe. But the truth is, I need help. You need a job. And you're already doing most of what I'd need from you. I'd rather not have to scrounge for help when Gale's not around. And, like I said, there's money in the budget."

"How much money?"

Regina reined in the impulse to go exorbitant. "How's ten an hour?"

Ten dollars an hour. What a joke. But Lucy only needed to supplement her pension, and Regina needed to stay under the radar. "Off the books," she added.

Lucy thumbed her lip, eyes unfocused, her face that oft-mentioned open book running the gamut from happiness to worry. Finally, her expression settled on something that looked like resolve. "Before I say yes, I need to ask you something. Well, maybe confess."

"Okay?"

Lucy blinked, breaking eye contact. She leaned into the steam coming out of the pot. "It doesn't look great, but it smells amazing. You think I could take some home to my husband?"

"If I say yes, will you get to your point?"

Lucy stepped away from the pot. "I'm no good at . . . at . . . subtle, Regina, so I'm just going to ask." She breathed in deep, let it out slow. "Didn't you use to be Queenie B?"

The floor vanished under Regina's feet. She stumbled, canting headfirst into the hole, through the barrel Queenie hailed her from, waving her arms, jumping up and down.

"I'm sorry," Lucy said. "I figure you're incognito, because . . . all that happened . . . we all fall on hard times . . . thought you looked familiar when we met . . . when Gale got on *Cut!* . . . bingeing cooking shows and there you were on my TV screen!"

Lucy Carmichael's words jumbled and skipped, echoing from a great distance. Booming. Mingling with Marco's.

It's just a good hiding spot that's going to bite you in the ass one of these days.

This couldn't get her. Not now. A few years ago, it might have sent her scurrying. It would have. She couldn't let it. Not this time. The force of will she pulled from to survive—foster homes, poverty, drugs, ambition—reared up. Put Lucy's words in the right order. Made sense of them.

"I'm sorry, Regina," Lucy continued, as breathless as Regina felt but comprehensible. "I don't mean to pry and I won't. I mean, I got a little obsessed, but I won't do that anymore. I totally respect your privacy. It's been so hard, keeping my mouth shut. You have no idea. I have an idiot mouth sometimes, and I say things before I stop to think about it. It was hard enough as a volunteer, only here now and then. If I take the job, if you still want me, I mean, and don't worry, that's not, like, blackmail or anything. I swear. I'd never. But I'll be here all the time and . . ."

Regina put up her hands still flailing for a handhold. Queenie hovered, not triumphant, but wary, holding out a steadying hand for her to grab. Trusting her scared the hell out of Regina, even as she reached, but the reality was, her slow slide from obscurity hadn't begun with Marco. It wouldn't end with Lucy. It began as far back as Bova, the trail she'd left no matter how clever she thought she'd been, and Queenie knew how to navigate it.

"You've known since we first met, haven't you?"

Lucy's fingers entwined and untangled. She shook them out. "You looked familiar, that's all. I mean, you were everywhere when I was younger, and we both know I was no foodie. It didn't click. Then I saw your name on the health certificate over there." She pointed. "Regina Benuzzi. Regina is Queen in Italian. *Click!* Queenie B."

"Did you start bingeing my shows before or after you looked me up?"

Lucy bit her lip. "Okay, it was after. If it's any consolation, I'm sure Gale doesn't know. I honestly don't know how he'd react if he did."

The bigger reason for her silence. There was that worry, underlying everything else. But Gale would find out. Inevitably. "Just don't go telling anyone who I am. It's no one's business, is that clear?"

"Who am I going to tell?" Lucy tried to make light.

Regina glared.

"Cross my heart, hope to die, stick a needle in my eye. I won't tell anyone."

Another glare. Measured, not ferocious. Still capable of instilling fear—Regina had perfected it in a way Queenie never had—just to be safe.

Pulling hotel pans down from the rack, Regina tried to keep her heart where it belonged instead of pounding away at her throat. "Help me get these filled."

"Sure thing." Lucy took the pans from her, set them up on the prep table. She took the giant spoon from Regina's hand. "I'll load up the pans. You do the mashed potatoes on top. I'm sure there's a trick to it that I'll totally screw up."

She couldn't cook for shit, but Lucy wasn't stupid; she'd seen Regina's shaking hands. She was kind. Good. Fierce. A good ally. And, Queenie warned, a worse enemy.

"So, when can you start?" Her voice snapped a little too harshly. She leaned over the pot, inhaling deeply, as if to smell her stew and not calm her fraying nerves.

"When do you need me?"

"Mostly when Gale's not here. I'll work out a schedule for you. I'll pay you for today, and going forward."

"That's not—"

"Ask your son how effective arguing with me is."

"All right." Lucy chuckled. "You know, I could say the same."

Regina got to work on the potatoes to keep a retort she'd regret from spilling. Mashing felt good. By the time she was layering them—with a piping bag on top of the cottage pie, her hands no longer shook. Something like . . . could it be pride? Maybe not quite, but close. Lucy's confession hadn't leveled her, even if it did send her reeling. She'd gotten her feet under her. The urge to run subsided, leaving behind the strangest light-ness in Regina's body. Like when she set up mystery crates for Gale, showed him where he'd gone right, and wrong. When he called her his mentor. And Marco. Not finding him in her garden; that had been as aw-ful as Lucy's confession. But afterward, thinking about him coming back for a long-overdue dinner, planning what she'd make for him.

There was that sensation again, closer, now, to pride. Maybe a little like joy, fingering, clawing, glowing out of a barrel long ago and repeat-edly cracked, but never splintered entirely.

20

Clarify: Most often refers to butter, where the milk solids are rendered from the butterfat by gently melting the butter and allowing separation, then skimming off the solids.

2015

Gale went straight home after lunch service at Marco's to get ready for his date. The first date he'd made since that woman he used to score from, back when Sean was still alive. He didn't even remember her name, only that she was kind of hot, if constantly fucked-up. It made their relationship easier, because she rarely remembered him from one date to the next. *Fifty First Dates*, opiate style.

Nando and Jimmy were sleeping, but Kyle was up and about when Gale let himself into the apartment. The place stunk to high heaven; he grimaced before the look on Kyle's face could stop him.

"Sorry, dude. I'll spray some room freshener."

"Uh, thanks."

Kyle went through the apartment with the room freshener, spraying. "This is why I never make egg salad."

Gale chuckled. "Yeah, sure. Egg salad."

"Dude, if I stunk up the place this bad, I'd be proud. Then I'd head to the hospital because there'd be something seriously wrong with my digestive tract. You want some?" He held up a bowl of fluffy-looking egg salad. "My own special touches."

Gale grabbed a spoon from the drying rack, tasted. "Nice. That Dijon I taste?"

"It is. And I made my own mayo."

"Eggs dressed with eggs. What a concept, huh?"

"It's good though, right? I got some day-old pumpernickel from the restaurant, and microgreens. I'm thinking of slicing some avocado, too."

"Might be a little too rich."

"Yeah, you're right. I should try using the avocado instead of the mayo."

"That could be interesting. Squeeze of lemon, to brighten it up?"

"Awesome, dude. I'll try that."

"You testing something for one of the restaurants?" Gale asked.

"Yes and no." Kyle nudged him in the gut with his elbow. "Not the restaurant where I'm currently working. A food cart. *My* food cart."

"You have . . . you bought . . . ?"

"Not yet, but I'm hoping for this time next year. Maybe get a spot out on Long Wharf, you know, where all those trucks are down by the water near the IKEA? Or try to get a spot somewhere around Yale. It'd be a hit with the students, shoppers, businesspeople. Don't you think?"

You and every other food truck person.

"It's a fantastic idea," Gale answered. "Have you done any research yet? What's already out there? Where they are?"

"Some. I kind of wanted to see if I could come up with anything, you know, really good. Special. A concept."

"And?"

Kyle held up the bowl. "You're looking at it."

"Egg salad?"

"Not only egg salad. Just Eggs. That's what I want to call my truck. I'll do eggs in a bunch of different ways. Egg sandwiches with everything from serrano ham to my own cured bacon. Savory soufflés, sweet ones. All different kinds of egg salads. Great, right?"

It kind of is.

"I wish I'd thought of it."

"I always have room for you on my gravy train." Another nudge to the gut. "Say the word."

"I may just take you up on it." If it ever happened. If this newest idea made it to the end of the week. "I got to get in the shower before the boys wake up."

"Right, your date with the Uber driver."

"It wasn't Uber."

"You're really not going to tell me how you did?"

"Can't. I signed a nondisclosure thing."

"What if I sign one of those too?"

Gale shook his head. "Doesn't work that way. Sorry."

"Fine." Kyle put a lid on his bowl of egg salad, stuck it in the fridge. "Feel free to partake, if you get hungry. There's going to be a lot of egg stuff in there for a while."

Great. The apartment's going to stink for weeks.

"You can't smell it," Gale murmured on his way to the bathroom.

How do you know?

"Well, can you?"

No.

Letting the water get hot, Gale got undressed, set the timer on his phone. They had all agreed to no more than seven minutes in the shower, to keep the bills down. Mold in the grout between the tiles needed to be sprayed down with bleach. It was Jimmy's turn to clean the bathroom. Gale was pretty sure his roommate hadn't done so more than three times in the two years they'd lived together. Kyle always did it for him without saying anything. He was good that way. Jimmy was generous with his beer—which Gale never took him up on—and Nando took the recycling back for the deposits once a month without fail. For his part, Gale made sure all the bills were paid on time, reminding someone who would inevitably forget that the internet bill came due on the first and the electricity on the tenth. Aside from the occasional lapse in internet-bill contribution, they were good roommates; he loved them all. Gale just didn't want roommates anymore. He'd never, in his thirty years of life, lived alone.

Maybe it's time, man.

Tilting his head back, Gale rinsed the shampoo from his hair. The echo always there, always haunting, seemed more solid in the steam. Not quite as skinny, haggard, greasy-haired. Resisting the urge to throw back the curtain, catch the specter unaware, Gale closed his eyes instead. "How come you can hear what's in my head, but I can't talk back to you in there?"

How the fuck do I know?

"I think you're lying." Gale blew water from his lips. "It's probably boring, living inside my head."

It's crowded, is what it is.

"Then go."

The water ran hot down his body. The timer chimed. Gale got out of the shower, toweled off, and wrapped it around his waist. Still nothing from Sean. Not while he combed his hair, got dressed, put on shoes that weren't meant for the kitchen. Not until he started down the stairs of his apartment building to await Jenara.

You really think I want to hang around? You know how nuts that is, man?

"I've asked you to go. I've told you to."

But you keep bringing me back. I'm fucking dead.

"And it's my fault."

I didn't say that. I never did.

"You imply it. You're the reason I can't live alone. You yammering on constantly? I'd be using again in a week."

If that's what you want to tell yourself. I'm your excuse for everything. I was back then. I am now. Grow the fuck up, Gale, and take responsibility for yourself.

"When I do that, you tell me it wasn't my fault, that I shouldn't—"

You're not hearing what I'm saying, man. Sean sighed. Or the wind blew just a little brisker. Thankfully, a Mercedes pulled up. The window rolled down and Jenara's face appeared, banishing Sean, or, at least, keeping him quiet.

"You clean up nice." She grinned, then, "You coming?"

"Oh, yeah. Sorry." Gale trotted around to the passenger side, got in. Black leather interior. Plush seats. No juice boxes or granola bar wrappers on the floor, like his mom's car when he and his brother were kids. No fingerprints on the window. "Nice car. Did you borrow it from the livery?"

"Borrow it from . . . ? Dude. This is my car. They're all my cars. I own the service."

Heat crept up his neck. "Oh. I . . . um . . . didn't think . . . I mean, you have a kid. It's so clean."

"This isn't the car I cart my daughter around in." She snickered. "That one should be condemned. Kids, right?"

"I guess." Gale tried really hard to pretend his face wasn't burning off. "So, where're we going?"

"Buckle up," Jenara said as if he hadn't just marginalized her. "You'll see in about ten minutes."

THE POP-UP RESTAURANT, ARRANGED FAMILY STYLE ON THE COVERED patio of a spa/yoga studio, featured farm to table, wood-fired food. Everything from amuse-bouche to dessert was cooked over different woods, in gigantic grills made out of old oil tanks. The thing was on wheels and had a hitch. The proprietors, a husband and husband team, did private parties, pop-ups, and otherwise traveled around the country to cook at fairs and do competitions. Gale had to admit, it seemed like a pretty sweet gig. Kyle would love it.

You have to remember to tell him about this.

Fuck. Sean had been quiet all night. Of course, the moment Jenara left him to use the restroom, he showed up. He was full of shit with all that *you keep me here* crap. Gale hadn't been thinking about him, thinking about anything other than how cool this pop-up life was. The minute he was actually happy, almost care-free—

"Hey, did I miss anything?" Jenara slipped onto the chair beside him.

"Not yet. I think dessert's almost ready though. Did you want coffee?"

"I'd love it."

Gale poured coffee from the communal carafe into her cup, passed her the sugar and cream.

"Oh, good stuff."

"They roast it themselves."

"Of course, they do." Jenara took another sip. "Tastes woodsmoky."

"How'd you get tickets for this, anyway?" Gale asked. "I heard someone say it was sold out over a month ago."

Jenara sipped again, looked up at him over the rim, through thick lashes. Pretty eyes. "I have a confession to make."

"Uh-oh."

She set her cup down, chuckling softly. "I bought two tickets months ago, when I saw they'd be in town. I hoped I'd meet someone I wanted to take before the event. And look! I did."

"So you're saying I was your last resort."

"No, my mother would have been my last resort. But don't tell her that."

"Not much chance, considering I don't even know her."

"Well, I'm hoping that's not the case for long." She winked. No false modesty. No hedging. Just flirting that felt more like the good kind of teasing. "What was your favorite?"

"The sweet potatoes with curried yogurt."

"That was quick."

"Because it's by far one of the best things I ever put in my mouth. What about you?"

"I'm a carnivore," she said. "The wood-fired chicken."

"Everything's wood-fired."

"True. It's brined in pineapple juice."

"I saw that on the menu." Pouring them each another cup of coffee, Gale drained the pot. He held it up for one of the waitstaff to refill. "I love where I work, don't get me wrong, and I love Italian food, but it'd be great to be able to be more creative with the menu."

"People go to an Italian restaurant for Italian food."

"Yeah, that's what Frances says."

"Your boss?"

"She thinks so." Gale grinned. "She's the main sous chef. Marco owns the restaurant."

"But she runs it."

"Like a dictator."

They laughed together.

"She's not so bad." He took the full coffeepot from the waitress, held it up in offer to their tablemates. Pouring for several of them, he told Jenara, "I kind of get her now. She's as hard on herself as she is on everyone else.

Straying outside the lines? It's just not going to happen. It's who she is. We're way different chefs, that's for sure."

"Sounds like that's a good thing," Jenara said. "For you."

"Oh, definitely." Gale poured his coffee. "Thing is, she's been free with compliments lately. I think she appreciates how much I've improved in the last few months. Don't get me wrong, the food at my place is amazing no matter who cooks. It's just always the same. Even the specials feel done to death."

"Kind of like those artists who put out those seascapes that all look pretty much the same because that's what the people on the boardwalk want to buy. Pretty, but . . . yeah."

"Exactly. Is it conceited to consider myself a kind of artist?"

"Not at all. I wish I had a creative side." She tapped her still-empty coffee cup for another refill.

"Oh, sorry. I got distracted."

"It happens." Cream. Sugar. Stir. "I guess that's why I started my business," she said. "It takes no creativity whatsoever. It's all logistics. Practical."

"I'm sure it isn't easy, though."

"I sort of fell into it. Dad drove on the weekends. When he got sick, I did the driving. Then he died, I got a good buy on a nicer car and a low-interest loan. Most of what I did back then was airport runs."

"You obviously did well, considering you now have a fleet."

"Well enough to support my kid and my mom without pinching pennies."

"I'm really sorry about assuming—"

"Don't stress about it. I'm young. I'm pretty. I'm Hispanic. No one expects me to be a successful businesswoman."

The waitstaff serving the grilled peaches, and Tahitian vanilla and ginger ice cream—the only thing not made on the grill—saved Gale from more embarrassed fumbling. Jenara's confidence despite how others might view her seemed genuine. She dug into her dessert as if she hadn't already consumed five rounds of the six-course meal. Another reason to like her; she didn't pretend not to eat.

"I think that was the best thing I ever ate." Jenara licked her spoon. "Wow."

"It's good," Gale told her, "but I'd still take the sweet potatoes first."

"I'm a carnivore *and* a sweets gal."

"I'm more of a savory guy."

"Next time, we can trade."

Next time. Gale smiled. Jenara's dimples appeared. She placed her hand, palm up, on the table. He took it; their fingers entwined.

"I'm really glad the driver who was supposed to take you home bagged on me," she said. "This was fun."

"You weren't supposed to be driving that night?"

"Nah. I don't drive as much as I used to. Once in a while, just to break up the monotony of office crap. Doing the nine-to-five thing gives me more time with my kid. Being the boss lets me take time off when she's got school stuff."

"What's her name? How old is she?"

"Alicia. It was my grandmother's name. She's ten."

"Ten, wow. I kind of figured she was still a toddler."

"I had her young."

Gale hesitated. "Is her dad still around?"

"That's a story for another day." Jenara pulled her hand gently from his, smiling a little sadly. "Looks like they're herding us out."

Most of the diners were exiting the covered patio. Gale rose, held the back of Jenara's chair as his mother taught him to do a million years ago. He wasn't sure how much this all cost, but whatever it was, it had been worth it. "Do you know where I pay the bill?"

"It's all paid," Jenara said. "Remember? I bought the tickets months ago."

There came the heat again, up his neck, across his cheeks. "I . . . but . . . you shouldn't . . ."

"Please don't do that guy thing." Jenara kissed his cheek. "Okay?"

Gale could only nod. It was sort of old-fashioned to get weird about who paid the check, but he got weird anyway. Inside his head. Outside of it, he thanked her and said, "Next time it's on me," or something equally predictable, then, "How about tomorrow?," which neither of them predicted at all, even if her dimples deepened all over again.

21

Acrate: Passing ingredients through a sifter, changing the composition of the ingredient (i.e., flour).

2015

"Careful, it's hot." Regina set a bowl of soup on Gladys's TV tray. The Burger Queen only had three bowls in her cupboard, but they were vintage, leftover, Regina imagined, from the elderly woman's very first set of dishes.

"This is very nice. Thank you."

It was one of her bad days, Regina could tell. Gladys had no idea who Regina was, only that she was a nice lady who'd brought her soup. And still, she had to ask again, "And you're sure you haven't seen Troy around?"

"I had to dismiss him." Of course. "Unreliable." She sipped her soup, daintily. "I do believe he might have a drinking problem. My daddy had a drinking problem. It's why we lost all our money."

More insight? More delusion? It hardly mattered. The old woman's situation was becoming untenable. The notice was still up on Troy's apartment door. Regina circled the block every time she delivered food to Gladys, as if that might turn over whatever stone he hid beneath. She had to face the fact that Troy was gone, like happened to so many in Rock Landing. In her life.

"He was a nice man, though," Gladys said.

"Troy?"

"Who? My daddy's name wasn't Troy. It was Roger."

"Sorry. I'm sure he was lovely."

"It pained me to let him go." She lowered her voice. "I do believe he might have a drinking problem." Miming a tipple, Gladys let go a heavy sigh.

Regina switched on the tableside lamp. It was getting late. With Gale on his date, she'd had to keep Lucy to cover the kitchen while she delivered Gladys's dinner. Lucy had offered to do it for her, but Regina couldn't let her see how Gladys lived. She'd feel obligated to report it to someone, somewhere, just like Regina did on most days. Having been neglected and abused within the welfare system all her young life, she couldn't let it happen to the old woman. Gladys would be dead in a month.

"I'll leave you to your dinner."

Gladys waved imperiously, still gently slurping. The television on, her belly full, hopefully, she'd fall asleep.

Out in the Durango, Regina leaned her head on the steering wheel. She breathed in deeply, let it out slowly. Marco would be at the kitchen by eight thirty. The cioppino would be made with the last of her tomatoes, and seafood so fresh it had been swimming that morning. Simple. Elegant. He couldn't accuse her of showing off, even if she most certainly would be.

Pulling around the back of the kitchen, Regina remembered the basil she needed from the garden mostly gone to seed. Troy usually helped her put the beds up for the winter. She'd get Gale to help. Maybe that friend of his, Keith or Kyle. Pinching off handfuls that hadn't gone to seed, Regina stuffed them in her jacket pockets and headed for the back entrance.

Voices.

She paused, hand on the doorknob.

A woman. Lucy.

And a man.

She checked the time on her phone. Not even a quarter after eight. Dammit. She pushed open the door. "You're early."

Marco held up a cake box. "I brought cookies from Libby's."

"That doesn't make you any less early." Mental. Deep. Breath. "I assume you two know each other."

"Only through Gale," Lucy answered for them both. "We've been to the restaurant a few times. Can I see you a sec, Regina?"

Lucy Carmichael didn't wait for an answer; she grasped Regina by the arm and hauled her to the pantry, closing the door behind them. "Why didn't you tell me you had a date?"

"It's not a date. And it's none of your damn business."

"Don't get pissy with me. He walked into the dining room while I was wiping down the tables. He said you were expecting him. What was I supposed to do? Kick him out? That's my son's boss. A chef, Regina. Is that wise? He might recognize you."

Fierce mama-bird, Lucy Carmichael managed to pull a grin out of Regina's ire.

"I've known Marco for a very long time," she said. "He knows who I am. Was. But thanks."

"Oh. Whew!" Lucy dragged a dramatic hand across her brow. "I'll assume he knows you don't want Gale to know who you are."

"Lucy, go home." Regina guided her to the pantry door. "And thanks for covering for me."

"Fine. Be that way." Lucy pulled her into a quick but tight hug. "I'll see you tomorrow. You can tell me about your date."

Regina stiffened. "Not a date."

But Lucy was already out the door, telling Marco it was good to see him, and to have a good night. Regina gathered her thoughts, the emotions she usually kept as tight and brief as Lucy's hug. She joined Marco in the kitchen, kissed both his cheeks, Italian style, before she realized she was doing so. Floodgates breached were floodgates opened. She took the box of cookies.

"You remembered my kryptonite."

"I did. Haven't you been there, in all this time?"

"I haven't stepped foot on Wooster Street since the night I got my bible from you." She gestured him upstairs before the words he'd taken a breath to utter could get out of his mouth. "This way. I'm making cioppino."

"ANY CHANCE YOU'LL SHARE THE RECIPE?"

Marco slurped up the broth in that same old way Regina remembered. This same old guy with even less affectation than he had when they were young and ambitious. He'd never been overly so, just ambitious enough, successful enough.

"I could share the recipe, but Queenie B magic isn't shareable."

Marco's spoon froze partway to his mouth. "Did you just refer to yourself as Queenie B?"

She had. Dammit, she had. It was a couple of hours reminiscing, of skating shallow over the intervening years. That was all. Resting her chin on the heel of her hand, Regina ignored Osvaldo's voice scolding her about elbows on the table. He'd been infiltrating her thoughts a lot lately. Sometimes in a good way; most often not. "You were right, Marco. It's all starting to crumble."

"Something happen?"

"Besides you showing up here?" She removed her elbows from the table. "Lucy knows."

"She recognized you?"

"She said I looked familiar when we met, but then she . . ." Regina blew a breath through her lips. "She started watching cooking shows when Gale signed up for *Cut!*"

Marco reached across the table and took her hand.

Regina let him keep it. "I could move again. Start someplace else."

"But you don't want to."

"I don't know." She groaned.

"You can't spend your life running from who you are."

"Were."

"Are." He squeezed her hand. "Maybe you're not on billboards anymore, but you underestimate your influence still out there in the world."

There was no underestimating it. The money her name still pulled in said it all. Notoriety lived on; invisible as she was, Regina—correction, Queenie B—was a mystery that had yet to be solved. More than five years in one place had been an anomaly; in the earliest days, she'd rarely made it through a few months before a glance too long, a picture snapped moved her on.

"You going to tell Gale?"

She snatched her hand away. "No way."

An eyebrow arched. Marco wagged his spoon at her. "What if Lucy slips?"

"She won't."

"And you know her well enough to be sure about that?"

"What are you getting at? Huh?" She threw up her hands; threw up her hands! Like she used to, back when she was just Regina and Marco pissed her off. She reined it in. "Are you trying to freak me out? Or just being an asshole."

"Neither." Marco shrugged, tilting his bowl to scoop out the remaining broth. "Oh, the tangled webs we weave . . . just sayin'."

"I've never lied."

"You're not being truthful, either."

"I'm entitled to my anonymity."

"True." Marco gave up trying to scoop and slurped broth straight from the bowl. "Amazing." He smacked his lips. "He's going to find out, Reg. A week, a month. Tomorrow."

"I'll deal with it then."

"He's going to feel stupid because he should have recognized you because, well, you're *you*, and didn't, and then he'll be embarrassed. You know how he is."

Marco's calm unsettled her. He'd been as big a hothead as she. No more. Maybe she wasn't, either. Rising from the table, she took dishes with her, leaned heavily against the edge of the sink. "He called me his mentor, Marco. That means something to me. More than . . ."

Anything. But the word wouldn't come.

"And you think that'll change if he knows?"

"Everything changes once Queenie B hits the scene," she said. "You know that."

"You're not her."

"You just said I was!" She curled her hands into fists to keep them at her sides. "Which is it, Marco?"

He smiled sadly from his chair, shoulders going up, and falling down. "You make choices, Regina. Make the right ones, and you'll be fine."

He was right. And wrong. It was so much more than he could grasp, because Marco hadn't been there. He knew her before the drugs took over, when she was just a bit wild and slightly nutty, prone to dramatics and night terrors that started in fire and ended in fists. He'd held her through some of those nights when they were both too young and too inexperienced to know the turns it could take. Would take.

Regina washed the dishes by hand, as much to avoid the conversation as to spare her hand-thrown, hand-painted pottery plates the dishwasher. She could still conjure the street fair in that tiny Peruvian village, the bent-over woman who looked a hundred and ten but turned out to be only sixty-seven. The scents of food over flame and spices rich and pungent, mountain air she'd experienced nowhere else in the world. Osvaldo had haggled the artist down from her already ridiculously low price—the equivalent of twenty bucks—for four dinner and four dessert plates, all beautifully, disparately, and intricately painted. Regina paid her two hundred after he turned away, victorious. The woman had cried and given her four bowls that didn't match but were equally as beautiful. It cost almost twice that to have it all properly packaged and shipped back to New York, but worth every dime, as far as Regina was concerned. She didn't even ask Oz if he wanted them when they divorced. He wouldn't have remembered them, let alone wanted them. And she wouldn't have given them, anyway.

"Want me to dry?" Marco stood at her elbow. She hadn't even noticed.

"No, thanks. I'll let them air-dry."

"They're really pretty."

"They are." Regina smiled over her shoulder; it shined all over Marco's face. She averted her gaze from the infatuation she should have known would resurface. The infatuation she did know would resurface but pretended she didn't, even to herself.

She put the cookies on a plate, made them espresso, not even asking if he wanted cappuccino instead. Italians knew cappuccino was for breakfast, espresso for after dinner. So did chefs, even if their restaurants offered both after dinner.

"You want to watch a movie or something?"

"Sure. Sexy comedy?"

Light. Silly. Unrealistic. Exactly the kind of movies they'd watched, way back, because anything else was too exhausting. Marco remembered. Of course he did.

On the couch, the plate of cookies between them, they ate them and drank espresso while *The Proposal* flickered on her massive flat-screen. She leaned her head onto his shoulder. Marco put his arm around her, kissed the top of her head.

"Why'd you leave me behind, Reg?"

And there it was. The real reason he'd lifted the rock she'd been hiding beneath. Regina should have known this too. Had, all along. "I asked you to come to New York. You didn't want to."

"Because I'd just bought my restaurant. I thought you'd be coming back when you finished taping."

Regina had known, even as she kissed him goodbye, she wouldn't be. Marco was the house and home guy. The nice restaurant in a nice neighborhood guy. She had already been half out the door when the PBS producers called about the cheesy cooking show she put out on the local community access station. Regina broke his heart knowingly, if not maliciously. Not the way she'd broken Osvaldo, whom she loved so much. "Are you looking for an apology?"

"An apology? Nah." He took another cookie. "You weren't meant for the life I was offering you. I knew you, way back when, remember?" He pointed at her with the bit end of his cookie. "Straight out of foster care. You didn't talk about it much, but some things were obvious."

"Such as?"

"Such as"—he swallowed the last of his espresso—"you were busting to get out of New Haven. Out of Connecticut. I pretended it wasn't true. I wanted it not to be true. But, yeah. You were meant for bigger things, Reg. Bigger than me. Bigger than a nice, normal life spent cooking in a hometown you hated as much as you thought it hated you. I guess I just didn't realize how big big was going to be."

Regina tilted her head back. "I didn't either."

She looked at him. He looked at her. Words spoken and unspoken. Unnecessary between them, in this moment. He was right then; Marco was still right. Regina wriggled into a more comfortable position. "Watch the movie. And don't eat that last anginetti. It's mine."

She felt his laughter in the way his chest lifted and shifted. Regina allowed herself another Queenie B smile; Marco couldn't see it, the way they were sitting. She wouldn't have to ignore the effect it had on him.

22

Flake: Refers to the process of gently breaking off small pieces of food, often for combining with other foods. For example, you would flake cooked fish to combine with mashed potatoes to make fish cakes.

2010

Regina's Kitchen Hours

Breakfast: 7:30 A.M.–9:30 A.M.

Lunch: 12:00 P.M.–2:00 P.M.

Dinner: 5:00 P.M.–7:30 P.M.

B old lettering, but otherwise understated. The contractor hammers in the last nail, all smiles. Inspections passed, permits acquired, it's finally finished. At last. It has taken fourteen months, just as Mr. Koda promised. Right on time, and right on the dime. Honest as the day is long, Koda has never once taken advantage of the fact that Queenie always comes up with the money for all her add-ons and his unexpecteds. He had no clue of her identity at the start, and still has no idea at the finish, proving not everyone in the world knows who Queenie B is. Or cares.

Dining room set up, pantry stocked, she'll be able to open the soup kitchen in the morning, as planned. She isn't expecting a crowd or anything; she hasn't advertised in any big way. A few flyers distributed by a local priest to his mostly down-and-out congregation, and the flyer she's tacked up near the dumpster of the only restaurant in walking distance will suffice. Word of mouth will kick in after that. Low-key and local is what she's after. Maybe, for once, she'll be able to pull that off.

"Been a pleasure working with you." Mr. Koda shakes her hand. "I might even miss this place."

"You've done an amazing job. Everything I hoped for and then some."

"Still don't know why you'd open a place this nice down here." He scratches his head. "But you're a woman who knows what she wants and how to get it, that's for sure."

A slight chill slithers up her spine, but he doesn't know. If Mr. Koda is suspicious of anything, it's that she's in with some kind of cartel or in witness protection. She has paid everything in cash. No check. No proof.

Queenie reaches into her pocket for the wad of hundreds she's had—for the last time—her accountant withdraw. From here on, it will be credit cards paid by her newly-formed-for-the-purpose corporation. She isn't exactly sure how it works, but she's been assured it will.

"This is for you." She palms Koda a banded ten thousand. "And this"—she hands him another ten thousand—"is for the crew. Divvy it up as you see fit." She doesn't add any admonishment to see it goes to them; keeping it for himself won't even occur to him.

"I . . ." Koda stares at the money, then her. "I . . ."

"You're welcome." She almost smiles; she's learned not to do so overtly. "I hope I can call on you again if I need to."

"Of course, of course." He pockets the cash. Thankfully, his truck is right there, at the curb. It isn't that the locals are criminals, only desperately poor. Okay, there are criminals too—she hasn't had a high-tech security system put in for nothing—but Queenie prefers not to think about that.

She waves to him as he pulls away, keys to her new home, her great project, in hand. Letting herself in, locking the door behind her, she breathes in the aroma of fresh wood and paint. The black-and-white linoleum tiles aren't her style, but this part of the place isn't about style.

It's about function, economy, and invisibility. The exorbitant elegance of the place upstairs would cause speculation, but no one will ever see it. Her home is to be her sanctuary, as well as a reminder of who she'd been and how small her world has become.

Folding banquet tables and chairs for the soup kitchen dining room are easily stacked, and replaced if necessary. Two swinging doors—one going into the kitchen, and one coming out—are the only break in an otherwise pristine coat of deep red paint. White or beige, Koda had suggested, but Queenie knows it'll only be a matter of weeks before it's smudged beyond her ability to overlook it. She spent—a lot—extra on the easily washable paint the salesperson swore by. Used in all the day-care centers in New Haven, he said. Guaranteed to hold up, he said. Even with a daily cleaning service, Queenie will be happy if she gets a couple of years out of it.

Pushing through the swinging door into the kitchen, she's glad she hasn't skimped. Working with subpar appliances just won't cut it, even if her fine dining days are over. Cheaper, less ostentatious will never hold up anyway. Queenie runs her hand over the industrial-size Wolf. It's not the La Cornue still sitting, unused and unloved, in the Bova home—that she got in the divorce because Osvaldo wanted nothing to do with the place—but it's a stunning piece of equipment. Everything from that stove to the dishwashers to the gadgets, pots, and pans is, and not a single person who walks through the door is ever going to question it. This, she knows without a doubt, because she'll never let a chef into her kitchen. Only locals willing to volunteer, locals she'll slip a twenty to after a shift. Just enough to make it worth their while, not enough to raise suspicion.

Queenie preps for the morning, simple enough. Two huge Crock-Pots of oatmeal, jars of jam, honey, and brown sugar. She cuts up fruit. In the morning, she'll scramble several dozen eggs and toast several loaves of bread. Baking it from scratch crosses her mind—she's always loved the meditation of kneading dough—but only momentarily. She has no way of knowing how many will show. Simple is best until she gets the hang of things.

Lunch prep is even simpler. Sandwiches, PB&J, turkey, ham and cheese. She goes light on the mayo. It's hard to use jarred mayo, and even harder not to doctor it up with pesto or cranberry preserves. No arugula. No brie or caramelized onions. Simple, simple, simple.

Between breakfast and lunch, she plans to put up a pot of vegetable soup, so she gets to work on the mise en place for that. Store-bought stock, at least for now. Again, until she gets the hang of things. Dinner is lasagna, easy enough to put together and prebake; lasagna is always better for being allowed to sit overnight in the fridge. She hopes she's made enough of everything; sending people home hungry doesn't just go against her mission statement, it goes against every chef nerve in her body.

Not a chef. In this kitchen, never. She's a cook now. A soup kitchen cook making nutritious food for people in need. Her mission statement. Her balance.

Prep done, slow cooker timers set, Queenie goes upstairs for the first time since the final inspection. The whole apartment has been finished and furnished for almost a week. It's been difficult, not peeking, but the good kind of difficult. Like waiting-for-Christmas difficult.

She sets the alarm from the pad in her apartment and closes the world outside. Inside, it is perfect. Elegant. Beautiful. Richly textured from window curtains to the flowers on her Carrara marble counters, from the buttery-yellow walls to the burnished Brazilian teak flooring to the russet leather couch and armchair. Her television hides behind a mirror that isn't quite a mirror, but a very expensive trick of the eye. Her bedroom is a tranquility of sea-foam walls and comforting dark-walnut furniture. The bed is a luxurious pile of white. The bathroom is a spa complete with its own sound system. Koda is right about building so nice a place in an area that will never be prosperous again, but Queenie doesn't care. This is where she will live and someday die. Julian will do with it what he pleases when the time comes. Or Osvaldo will do it for him.

Julian.

Osvaldo.

She has done her best not to think about them and has mostly succeeded. The bible she retrieved from Marco sits there, on her bedside table. Atop it, an envelope she received months ago and has still not opened; she knows what it is. What's inside. The end of everything.

Queenie sleeps like the dead.

MORNINGS HAVE NEVER BEEN HER THING, BUT SHE RESOLVES TO BE UP BY six, every morning, to have a good breakfast before her long days. In her own home, she can be a chef. It is her joy, her art. Denying herself that piece of her soul is never going to end well. So Queenie makes herself a spinach and herb omelet—she will get chickens and put in an herb bed come spring—brews freshly ground coffee for cappuccino, and cuts a thick wedge of the fresh bread she bought yesterday before meeting Koda for the official sign placement.

Fed, dressed. Ready. Queenie gathers herself as she used to before stepping out onstage at an awards show or in front of a camera. It's a different sort of fortitude she needs now, and she draws as much as she can from a past that nearly killed her. Several times. Downstairs, the oatmeal gives off its nutty scent. She plugs in the coffeepots, the pot for hot water, and soon the aroma of coffee joins the nutty oatmeal. The buffet-style table is already set up with biodegradable cups, plates, bowls, and eating utensils—no sense saving the homeless if it destroys the planet; unlike most, she can afford to be environmentally conscientious. Tables and chairs line up neatly. She's as ready as she can be. This is going to be a great day.

Seven thirty, on the nose, Queenie unlocks the front door and barely gets out of the way before the onslaught knocks her over. The buffet table is stormed like the beach on D-day. Too much food ends up on the floor. She can only stare, dumbstruck. Queenie—no, Regina—remembers being poor, being hungry. She remembers savoring every bite of food, because there was no guarantee there'd be more. The only time she ate regularly was during her stint in a group home, run by the state, when she was seventeen and had no more relatives to tap. Edible was all it was required to be, and it was barely that, but it was there, and that was the important thing.

Dumbstruck turns to horror when, buffet tables empty, someone heads for the kitchen. Queenie bolts for the door, gets there just ahead of the man and his . . . girlfriend? The woman can be twelve, twenty, or fifty but the man is solidly somewhere in his forties. Queenie stands in the doorway, arms stretched from jamb to jamb.

"Sorry. No one goes in the kitchen. Health codes."

"Is there anything more? My daughter and I got here too late to get anything."

Queenie glances around him. People are filing out. Most are carrying food in those biodegradable vessels with them. It's only a quarter after eight.

"Sure," she tells him. "Just go sit. I'll bring something out to you."

Her hands shake, but Queenie manages two plates of scrambled eggs and toast. She cores two apples, fills them with a nob of butter, raisins, and brown sugar, then nukes them a couple minutes. When she brings the food out, there isn't a scrap of food except what's on the floor, and no one left but the man, his daughter, and the elderly woman Queenie recognizes because of the Burger King crown on her head.

"You too?"

"I couldn't get through the ravening barbarians." The woman sniffs. "No one has any manners anymore."

Queenie sets the plates down for the man and his daughter who, now that she gets a better look, is probably in her twenties and very, very high. The man pushes his plate to the Burger Queen.

"Go ahead, Gladys. I can wait."

She nods that imperial nod. "Thank you, Troy. You are a gentleman."

The daughter is already shoveling eggs into her mouth, almost as ravenous as the barbarians.

"Slow down," her father says. "You'll choke."

She does as she's bid. The man looks up at Queenie, his eyes sad but somehow smiling. He doesn't look much better than his kid, but he doesn't seem to be under the influence, at least at the moment. He has that look. Hunted. Haunted. Trying really hard and mostly failing.

"I'll be right back." Queenie goes to the kitchen, scrambles, toasts, nukes. It doesn't take long, but the daughter is finished with her food and trying to get the last dribbles of coffee from the urn by the time Queenie returns to the dining room.

"I'll put up another pot," she says, placing the food down for Troy.

"Sorry about all this." Troy waves his fork like a magic wand, maybe to vanish the sad evidence of her first step into philanthropy. "Someone should have told you a free buffet is never a good idea with really hungry people. Most of 'em's good sorts. But, still, you best have them line up and hand them what you offering."

"Good to know. I'll make sure to do that at lunch." Which is going to be difficult, with only her own hands doing the doling. "I'm Regina."

He rises halfway from his chair, tipping a nonexistent hat. "Troy. That's my daughter, Petunia. And this is Miss Gladys." He gestures to the elderly woman. "We live in the same building."

"Hello, Miss Gladys," Queenie says, and in response gets that imperial nod.

"Petunia, get away from there. She say she putting another pot on."

Petunia shakes the coffee urn. Troy shrugs, tucks into his food. "This is nice. Been a long time since I had fresh scramble. And a baked apple, just like my mama used to make."

"There was a fruit salad." Queenie pulls out a chair. Sits down. "This was an abysmal failure."

"Nah," Troy said around a mouthful of toast. "People just not used to anything lasting around here. They get it while they can. But you here to stay, I can tell."

"You can?"

"You wouldn't've made it this nice if you was going to up and leave. You just need some fine-tuning."

"Like a soup line instead of a buffet."

"Just like. Petunia, leave off that thing!"

"I'll get that coffee going." Queenie pushes to her feet, exhausted when she shouldn't be. It's not even nine o'clock. She makes a small pot of coffee in the automatic drip machine she keeps in the kitchen. No sense brewing a whole pot now. When there's enough coffee, she pours it into a disposable cup for Petunia and carries it out to her. At least there are still sugar packets and creamer near the empty urns.

"Thanks, miss." Petunia smiles, sips it black. She's not a pretty girl, looks too much like her father, who is not a handsome man. Maybe she could have been, he could have been, but the ravages of substance abuse and poverty are too deeply engraved. A perk of being a wealthy addict is the money to alleviate some of the damage she's done to herself.

"You okay?" Queenie asks.

"I fine." Petunia waves her off. "My daddy think I wasted all the time but I just wasted when he not. We look out for each other that way."

How healthy. Queenie tamps down the urge to lecture, to give the *I've been there myself* speech. She knows, as any addict does, that no one can coax, cajole, or coerce someone into getting clean. Staying clean. In the end, no matter the why behind it, the end is a decision made and kept despite the why that'll never go away.

Queenie takes coffee to Gladys and Troy. Petunia puts two sugars and half-and-half into her dad's. Her Highness dumps four packets into her coffee, but otherwise drinks it black. Torn between getting to the cleaning up or sitting with these three, Queenie gets to the former even if she'd rather succumb to the latter. Moments later, Troy wheels out the trash barrel, goes up and down between tables, cleaning up. Petunia asks for paper towel and spray cleaner and gets to work wiping down tables. The Burger Queen watches. Imperiously.

"So, what's with the paper crown?" she asks Troy. Quietly.

Troy chuckles, just as quietly. "Don't know. She been wearing it since I met her. Not in her house though. Every once in a while, she replaces it with a new one. Don't ask me how she gets to the Burger King. None in this area, that's for sure. Closest one is over on Whalley."

"And the attitude?"

Another soft chuckle. "All I know is she used to teach at some girls' finishing school. Least, that's what I got from stuff she's said. But who knows, really? Like the crown, she been like this all along."

"Well, thanks for helping. And for the advice. I really appreciate it."

"You need help handing out lunch?"

"Really?"

"Least I can do. I'll get Miss Gladys to keep Petunia till she come down. What time you need me?"

"Just be here by noon, when I open up again." Queenie doesn't add *only if you're not wasted*. Despite what Petunia said, maybe he's a few days clean. A few months. She remembers how precarious that teeter is, how the wrong comment can topple someone off it. Any excuse to justify using, even if it's cutting off their own nose to spite their face.

Queenie locks the door behind the three of them, even though it's only nine forty-five. No one else is coming, now. The same people who trashed her breakfast will be back to get lunch. Two meals in one day is a luxury. Three is nirvana itself. They'll be back. Maybe they'll bring others. Maybe they'll keep this boon for themselves. Whatever the case, she has to be ready.

23

Involtini: Meat, seafood, or veg wrapped around a filling like cheese, cured meats, or nuts.

New Year's Eve 2015

"Four! Three! Two! One! Happy New Year!"

Poppers popped. Confetti flew. People kissed and kids ran amuck.

Sitting a little apart, watching 2015 become 2016, Gale choked up a little. Celebrating a very dry New Year's Eve in Regina's Soup Kitchen with the familiar homeless, the destitute, his parents, Regina, Marco, and a sort-of girlfriend he still couldn't believe was his, hadn't been in his cards, not until way back in March, when Gale got robbed and life took a turn—strangely enough—for the better. The weeks had become months without him realizing. Without drama. Like a normal person. Even Sean had been cool. Quiet, for the most part, even as the anniversary of his death came and went without drama, only a few tears.

Gale wished Kyle was there, wished they saw each other more, but Jenara took up a lot of Gale's free time, and Kyle had taken a new third job, still working to save up for Just Eggs and getting no closer. Just eggs. Just dreams. While Gale was living his.

"You're far away." Jenara's voice in his ear, her chin on his shoulder.

Gale reached back and threaded fingers through her curls. "I'm happy."

"That's a good thing, right?"

"A really good thing." He pulled her into his lap. "Happy Bizarre January."

"Funny." She kissed him. "Happy New Year, Gale."

They were still kissing when his mother swooped in, nearly knocking them both off the chair. Jenara clung to his neck but also Lucy's. They'd taken to each other quickly and well, just like he'd taken to Jenara's mother, and her daughter. Everything was good, good, good. Even he and Frances were getting along better. She didn't immediately rankle at his changes and suggestions. Gale was pretty sure that had a lot to do with Marco, and that Marco's interventions had a lot to do with Regina, but with everything balanced so precisely, he wasn't asking any questions. Not even how Regina and Marco knew each other. Especially not that.

Lucy righted herself. "Dad and I are going to take Gladys home."

"Gladys?" Gale asked.

"Burger Queen."

"I know. I wasn't aware you knew."

She pursed her lips. "You sticking around a little? Or should Dad and I just go home from there?"

Gale looked to Jenara. "We'll be here," she said. "But I think Regina wants everyone out by one. She still has to open the kitchen in the morning."

"Three meals a day, seven days a week. Believe me, I know. Okay, we'll be back." She kissed Gale's cheek, then Jenara's. "Behave."

Pulling him to his feet, Jenara slipped from Gale's lap. She tugged him into the chaos of people dancing. Music bumped. Some sang/shouted the words to Prince's "1999," the ultimate New Year's song.

Loud, and momentary, garbling back into the rest of the lyrics few did know. Gale hopped and waved his arms in the air like everyone else. Sweat rolled from temples to chin. Jenara laughed and twirled. Marco was trying to lure Regina into the heaving bodies. Gale couldn't remember the last time he'd had so much—

But life is just a party, and parties weren't meant to last . . .

Clear. As if no one, nothing else existed. No phantom. Just Sean's voice. Gale's dancing feet stumbled. He bent over, hands on his knees as if to catch his breath. "Please. Don't. Please."

"Don't what?" Jenara leaned protectively over him.

Music bumped and boomed back into his ears. Gale pushed himself upright. "My back," he lied. "Gave me a twinge. I'm not old enough for this."

"Too many long hours on your feet." She tugged him from the dance floor. The music switched. Bowie's "Under Pressure." Regina's playlist was firmly entrenched in the eighties and had been all night. Jenara led Gale to the row of folding chairs lined up along the far wall.

"I'll be right back." He pointed to the bathroom.

"I'll be waiting." She kissed him quickly, flopped onto a chair. Curls stuck to her sweaty, adorably dimpled face.

At the bathroom sink, Gale wetted a paper towel, and pressed it to his face. The harsh lighting displayed his bright and blooming Irish cheeks in all their splotched glory. Jenara loved his white-boy flush in the way he loved her dimples punctuating beautiful brown skin. They were a contrast. Opposites attracting. Physically fitting. He was the luckiest guy on—

Did you know that song's about the apocalypse?

Gale closed his eyes, pressed the wet towel to them.

I never listened, really. Just the chorus, man. Partying like it's 1999 sounded like, you know, a fun song.

"I know the lyrics."

Yeah? I never did. Bombs and dying and the whole world going to hell. Pretty grim.

"Yup."

Something wrong?

"Nothing's wrong." Gale sighed. "Everything's great."

The door banged open. Two youngish guys stumbled over each other into the bathroom.

"Oh, sorry, dude," said one, then burst out laughing. The other pulled something from his pocket. A little something. A brown something. A vial Gale knew for what it was. His heart thudded; palms sweated.

"You can't do that here."

"Shit, dude. Don't be like that."

"Seriously, out. If Regina sees you, you'll be banned from ever coming back."

"How'll she see us in here?" The one with the vial held it up between forefinger and thumb, wiggled it. "You gonna tell?"

Sweat trickled from his brow. The other two hunched together, tipping white powder onto the base of their thumbs. The first guy snorted. The second leaned in, then up again. He held out his hand. An offering. A bribe. Gale reached. His hand shook.

He knocked the offering away. "Out! Both of you. If I see either of you again tonight, I'm telling Regina. And you definitely don't want to see her mad. Go." Neither moved. "Now!"

Again they scrambled over each other. This time, out of the bathroom. Gale stood in the doorway watching them beat a quick exit out as his parents were coming back in.

Across the cleared dining room, Gale caught Regina's eye. One expressive eyebrow raised. He only shook his head, stepping backward into the bathroom and letting the door close on the faces, the dancing, the noise, and Regina's quizzical expression.

Bent over the sink, Gale let his head sag. He hadn't knowingly been so close to drugs of any kind in what seemed like forever a little while ago, but instantly like just last week. How did it happen, that instant craving? What sort of chance did he have if it was always going to be that way? If every time was as close to a fall as any other?

You did—

"Shut up, Sean."

I'm just trying to—

"Shut the fuck up!" Gale roared at the mirror, at the wide and frightened eyes there. His. Sean's. "I don't want to hear you anymore!"

You know what to do then.

Tune out. Turn off. Gale knew. Too well. He closed his eyes to the men in the mirror, too afraid of what he'd see there.

Hey.

Gale opened his eyes. On his hand, just a sprinkle of white powder. A tremor rumbled through his body. He brought the hand, the powder stuck on sweat, to his lips. To the tip of his tongue. Just the tip.

Time never stood still. Outside the bathroom, his parents, his girlfriend, his mentor, his boss. His future. Danced. Gale's stomach clenched.

His hands shook. The water rinsing the powder and sweat from his hand was too hot, but he didn't pull away.

Happy New Year, buddy.

Gale barely heard Sean's sad, sardonic laughter over his own sobbing.

JANUARY 1, 2016, DAWNED AS ANY OTHER WOULD HAVE IN THE PAST, EX-cept Gale's hangover was emotional, not physical. Because he was cooking New Year's Day dinner at her house, for her family, he'd gone home with Jenara. It was only fair; they'd spent the prior evening with his parents, after all. Gale would have liked to see his brother. Maybe, if Brian stuck around long enough, he could talk Jenara into a quick pop in once dinner was done. Small chance. They'd met at Christmas, and it hadn't gone all that well.

"Well, he's a bit of a prat, isn't he?" Jenara had said it with a smile, and a fake British accent.

"A prat?"

"It's a British term."

"You're not British."

"So? I can't use it? Don't make fun of me."

"I'm not."

"I happen to like the word, and it fits your brother perfectly. Is there some rule about Latinas not appropriating British terminology? Is that only for supercool white people?"

"Hey, I never said any of—"

Jenara snorted. "Ha! Gotcha. He is though, but I liked him okay. His pratishness is kind of cute."

"Cute, huh?"

She'd made a face at him, as she often did. "His constant need of approval. He's like a puppy. I absolutely don't like how he's always one-upping you, but that's your dynamic and I shouldn't say anything about it."

To be fair, she hadn't mentioned it since. Gale had always been the deserving recipient of his younger brother's superiority. It was weird to know Jenara saw it so easily. Caught between defending himself and his brother, Gale hadn't mentioned it since either.

"Good morning." Jenara rolled into him, nuzzled his neck. "Happy twenty sixteen."

"Yeah, you too."

Her eyes opened all the way. Those eyes. He should feel better just looking into them. If only that worked.

"What's wrong?"

"Nothing."

"Don't bullshit me." Jenara came up on her elbow. "Spill it or I'm kicking you out of my bed. Not my house, though. I want whatever dinner you're making."

Warmth rose from his belly, spread out to his limbs, his face, made him smile. "You're something, you know that?"

"I do." She snuggled back into him. "Now tell me."

Gale traced circles on her shoulder, words tumbling through his brain still garbled with how quickly it had fallen into the demanding need for the white powder—didn't matter what it was—offered to him.

Just talk to her, man. Tell her.

A kinder Sean than last night. Gale didn't trust him, but he was right. He started slow. "I had to kick two guys out of the party last night."

"Bathroom?"

His circles ceased. "How'd you know?"

"I figured. They bolted out of there real fast. Freaked you out, huh?"

"A little." He shifted so they were face-to-face on the pillow. "A lot. They offered. I wanted it so bad."

"But you didn't do it."

"No."

Liar.

"It hit so hard."

"Because you were unprepared," she told him. "But you resisted, and that's the most important part."

"I guess." Gale avoided her gaze.

Dude. Come on.

"There was a little on my hand from when I knocked it away, but I"— actually touched my tongue to it—"caught myself and washed it off."

Way to go. Awesome. Chicken.

Gale couldn't look at her. He couldn't tell her either. He couldn't watch the affection fade from her eyes.

Jenara lifted his chin with the tip of one small finger "Hey. You wanted it. I get it. So it's not a total victory, but it's still a big one. Don't be so hard on yourself."

"I have to be. You don't understand."

Silence lingered too long. Gale couldn't look away; neither did she. Her eyes filled. His stomach roiled. A *whoosh* of sheets, and Jenara was out of bed, throwing on a bathrobe so ratty it had to mean something to her. "I can't do this without coffee."

Gale was already pulling on a pair of sleep shorts. "Do what?"

She didn't answer. Gale grabbed his T-shirt, hands shaking, from the foot of the bed. This was it. She was breaking up with him. He fucked up and she wasn't going to let it slide. He followed her to the kitchen where her mother and daughter were already having breakfast.

"Happy New Year!" Alicia bounced on her chair, milk and cereal slurring her words. She wore the 2016 crown Gale had brought her home from the party.

Jenara kissed her daughter's forehead, her mother's cheek. "Happy New Year."

"Morning, Mrs. Bizzarro. Morning, Alicia."

"Feliz Año Nuevo, hijo."

"Happy New Year, Gale!"

Jenara poured two cups of coffee, handed him one. "We'll be out on the sunporch," she told her mother. "We won't be long."

"Mija, Gale will freeze like that."

"He'll be fine." She grabbed his hand. "Come on."

Gale let her lead him out of the warm kitchen and into the sunporch. Morning light made it bright, and kind of warm, but he was still in a T-shirt and shorts holding a cup of coffee and hoping Jenara wasn't giving up on him, on New Year's Day of all days.

"It's time." Jenara sipped her coffee, her eyes still fixed on him.

"Jenara, please, don't—"

She held up a hand. Gale fell silent. Another sip, a deep breath, and she told him, "Remember when you asked me if Alicia's father is involved in her life and I put you off?"

His brain wouldn't keep up. Alicia's father? She wasn't breaking up with him? Scrambling for the memory, he found it floating around in the night of their first date. "I remember."

"Sit." She pointed to one of the deck chairs, thankfully cushioned but still cold on his bare legs. Jenara sat in the chair beside his, set her coffee down. "He's dead. Driving under the influence."

"Oh, wow. I'm so sorry."

"Thanks." She rubbed her eyes. "We were never married, but I loved him. So much. He loved me. Stan was a great guy. He loved Alicia. But he had drug problems long before I ever met him. I didn't know. At first. But I spent five years learning just what it is to love someone with addiction issues."

"And you still . . ." Gale couldn't say the words. He could only point to himself.

"And I still," she said. "I couldn't not love him because of his issues, and I can't not love you either."

"You love me?"

"Duh." Jenara smacked his arm. Coffee splashed out of the cup his fingers wrapped around. "I'm not saying it was love at first sight, but there was something there, Gale. What kind of person would I be if I passed up on something good, on someone as wonderful as you, because of your past?"

"A smart person."

"Stop." She picked up her own coffee again, blew across the top. "Everyone has issues. Everyone is entitled to love, to people who believe in them even if they falter. I just wanted you to know, I understand. I know the drill. I'm not saying I'll stick around if you fall hard down that rabbit hole and don't come back up. There's a line, and I'll know it if we ever cross it. But shit like last night? That's not going to send me running. I'm proud of you. I want you to be proud of you. Self-loathing is the quickest road to using again. I know this from experience."

The twittering inside his skull and the fluttering in the area of his chest was something out of old cartoons and comic strips. Catching his breath wasn't an easy feat, but Gale managed it enough to say, "Wow."

"Wow?" Jenara blew into her coffee cup. "That's it? Wow?"

"I don't know what else to say." Breathing came easier. "I don't deserve you."

"What did I just say about self-loathing?"

"Sorry."

"No, Gale. Don't apologize. I get it. I do. But you have to relearn how you see yourself. If you keep believing you're the user, the addict, the fuckup destined to go over the edge, you always will be." Jenara put her coffee aside, moved his out of the way. She took both his hands in hers, leaning in. "I can't believe in you more than you do. Okay?"

The "I guess" stayed inside his head. "Okay," he told her. "Okay."

"Good." She kissed him. "I'm waiting."

"Waiting for . . . ?"

"You to respond to the 'I love you' elephant in the room."

"Oh . . . oh!" Laughter, of all things, rose up from his gut, rolled out of his mouth. Relief. Joy. Fear. There was no pulling one emotion from the other. Gale pushed out of his chair, went to his bare knees on the cold, wooden floor. He'd never said it before. Not to anyone in that way of promises and forevers. It was harder than he imagined, even though she'd said it first. Even though she was waiting. "I almost said it a million times."

"I know." She draped her arms over his shoulders. "Maybe it makes me conceited, or whatever, but I've known you were mad about me almost from the start. I'm kind of something special. I know it. You know it. Love was inevitable."

"You're not conceited." He rested his head in her lap, eyes closed and heart beating the crap out of him. "It was from the start. I'm . . . scared."

"Yeah, I think we covered some of the reasons behind that. It's okay. Words are hard for some people. I get that."

"No!" The back of his head would have slammed her right in the nose if her reflexes hadn't pulled her back in time. "Sorry. Sorry."

"It's okay. You didn't get me."

Gale took both her hands in his, gathered them to his chest. "I do love—"

She put her finger against his lips. "Established," she said. "The words are nice, but I only wanted you to acknowledge what I said, not respond in kind. Don't get me wrong. I do! Want the words. But not now. Only when you're feeling it hard and can't help but tell me. That's what I want when you say it the first time, not a command performance. Not to be cliché but, straight from the heart." She pressed her forehead to his, their breath mingling and fogging just a little. "Just never lie to me, Gale. Ever. That's an unpardonable offense." She kissed his nose, scooting out of her chair. "Now come on. Let's go get some breakfast. Didn't you tell Regina you'd come in and help with lunch before you start cooking for me and mine?"

The storm door snapped closed behind her, cutting Alicia's blare of her party horn to something less earsplitting. Gale couldn't follow her inside, even if he was cold and his knees hurt. He needed a moment. To process. To accept. To ground himself. To give Sean the chance to put his two cents in.

Nothing.

"Now you're quiet?"

Still nothing.

"I didn't lie."

Groaning to his feet, Gale pressed hands to the small of his back. He really was too young for so many aches and pains. Jenara was right, too much time on his feet.

Maybe he needed better shoes.

24

Sweat: This refers to the gentle cooking of vegetables in butter or oil under a lid, so that their natural liquid is released to aid the cooking process. Often, vegetables cooked this way will end up looking translucent.

2016

January wasn't as much a letdown after the holiday season. Life was pretty good. Love life. Work life. Soup kitchen life. Routine, but rewarding. Even Sean had dulled back into the quiet he'd fallen into before New Year's.

And *Cut!* aired.

Everyone congratulated him on making it to the final round, consoled him for being second. All in all, Gale was proud of his performance, not that he'd do it again. Just watching it was enough to make his heart race and his head light. He didn't remember feeling those things during the actual cooking, only during the in-betweens when producers did their thing, the judges judged, and he and the other contestants were in what passed as a green room, waiting.

He watched the first airing at his parents' house with them, his brother, Jenara, Mrs. Bizzarro, and Alicia. Watched the DVR of it again with Kyle, Nando, and Jimmy at the apartment. The one he most wanted to watch it with was Regina, but, though she'd been invited to the family viewing, she hadn't come. Neither did Marco. He'd worked alone that

Tuesday night so Gale could have the shift off. Frances hadn't been pissy about it, but she refused the shift, citing personal reasons. Gale was pretty sure those reasons were of the envious variety, but they'd been otherwise getting along, so he didn't call her on it.

Dropping his keys in the bowl on the table, Gale flopped onto a kitchen chair and put his head in his arms. Lunch service at Marco's had been pretty exhausting. Ever since the episode aired, people came to the restaurant specifically when he was cooking. Marco loved it. Frances hated it, though she pretended not to. Gale was ready for it to die down.

"Dude." Kyle shuffled in, pulled out the chair opposite.

"Hey, Kyle. Not working?"

"Not tonight. I'm too beat, and Samantha needed the hours. You in? Or you going to Regina's?"

"Regina has Mom helping out."

"Yeah? She's okay?"

"She is," Gale said. And she was. His mother thrived in Regina's kitchen, maybe as much as he did himself.

"No Jenara?"

"Not tonight, no."

"Cool-cool." Kyle grinned. "That you're here, I mean. We don't see much of each other these days."

Gale had been looking forward to some quiet time on his own; it was one of the reasons he wasn't seeing Jenara. Much as he enjoyed her company, it was sometimes a lot. Her mother was noisy. Her daughter was noisy. Jenara was noisy even when quiet, strangely enough. She had an energy he loved, but sometimes it wore him down. Added to that, their conversation New Year's Day played out in his head—*Never lie to me*—whenever he saw her. Even if he never had, depending upon whether or not omission of fact constituted a lie.

"Want to play video games?" Kyle asked.

"Absolutely."

They played on the sixty-five-inch television—Nando brought it home one day and no one questioned it—in the tiny living room for a couple of hours. They cobbled dinner together from whatever was in the kitchen and ate it while watching *Chef* for the thousandth time. Food trucks, cooking, beating the odds—Kyle got a little melancholy, even if he'd been the one to suggest it.

Just Eggs languished, not for lack of passion, but lack of funding not even sixty-hour weeks could provide. Maybe Kyle wasn't the greatest chef, but his idea was a good one and he deserved better.

At least the place doesn't stink of eggs anymore.

When Sean did show up, Gale remembered why he shouldn't miss him.

"I guess I better get some shut-eye." Kyle stretched, yawning. "It was good spending some time with you, bud. I've missed this."

"Yeah, me too." And he did. Truly. Gale made a mental note to be better about making time for his friend in the future. Kyle was the only one who had stuck with him through the drug years, all the ups and downs, after Sean died. The rest of their friends—and Gale didn't really blame them—ditched him. Hard. And permanently, apparently, because none of them had even come out of the woodwork after the show aired.

Only nine o'clock. Gale wasn't really tired. It was a rare thing for him to have so many hours to himself, even if he'd spent many of them with Kyle. He'd be at Regina's all day tomorrow, breakfast through dinner. Setting a mental reminder to be in bed by eleven, Gale opened up the laptop to go through long-overdue emails.

Because he hated doing email on his phone and rarely touched the laptop these days, there were a lot. Several hundred. Mostly spam. He found a few from the Food Network, all old stuff pertaining to the show. The producers had typically called, only sending follow-up emails to cover their bases. Gale saved them all in a file he labeled, "second best," so he could always look back and remember.

He had a few emails from his fellow contestants, with whom he'd promised to stay in touch. Some were a couple of months old, but he answered them anyway. He really did want to stay in touch; having chef friends was a good thing, any way he looked at it. After deleting the exhaustive list of spam, Gale found an email from his mother, dated before the competition but after agreeing to do it.

Hey, buddy!

Here's a few more cooking shows you should check out. They're old! But these are the people who came before all the celebrity chefs we hear about nowadays.

Love you,
Mom

Too late to go down that rabbit hole of links and videos, Gale put the email in the "second best" folder. Maybe he'd check them out at some point. One thing he learned in the weeks leading up to the taping was there were way more cooking shows, competitions, and celebrity chefs than he'd ever dreamed possible, even before the Food Network came along.

Mouse hovering over the shutdown, Gale heard the ping of another email coming in. From the producers. He moved the mouse to it, clicked it just as his cell phone chimed.

"Hello?"

"Hey, Gale Carmichael?"

"That's me." On the screen, he read half-sentences. "Who's this?"

"It's Bernadette, from the Food Network. Remember me?"

In charge, but not in charge. Bernadette had done all the coordinating, start to finish.

"Crazy. I just got an email from you."

"I only just sent them out," she said. "Did you get a chance to read it?"

"Not really."

"Then I'll just tell you. Ask you, I suppose is more like it. I won't go into the spiel in my email. Bottom line, we're doing a show pitting runner-up contestants against one another. The ones we really thought got a bum deal. We're calling it a Grand Redemption Championship. Fifty grand to the winner. And we want you to be one of those contestants . . ."

FOUR QUALIFIER ROUNDS. THE WINNER FROM EACH QUALIFIER WOULD COMPETE in the Grand Championship worth . . . Fifty. Thousand. Dollars. Bernadette hadn't asked for an answer, only for him to think about it. She had other calls to make before it got too late.

"We start taping on this soon," she'd finished, "so don't take too long. We'd really like to give you a second chance, but if you don't want the spot, we have a long list to pull from."

He'd been one of sixteen runners-up, chosen out of . . . how many? Gale couldn't even fathom. Reading and rereading the email, he couldn't seem to process all the information. Bottom line—could he do it? Three rounds had been nerve-racking enough. Three to qualify, then, in the improbable event he won, three more to get through for fifty. Thousand. Dollars.

He needed to speak with Regina. It was too late. Mom? Jenara? Maybe Kyle wasn't asleep already. Afraid waiting until morning meant waiting too long, knowing that was stupid but fearing it anyway, Gale tapped into his contacts. His finger hovered.

What are you even doing, man?

"Not now, Sean."

That sigh that could have been wind in the drainpipe, water in the pipes. *You know what they'll all say. And even if someone advised against it, it's not what you want.*

"I don't know what I want."

Sure you do. You always do. You just look for someone to validate it.

Gale didn't argue. Sean was right. He rarely made a decision without consulting someone else first. Because he didn't trust his own wants, his own judgment. Though there was huge precedent for that.

You gotta stop thinking that way, man.

"It's hard not . . . hey."

Hey, what?

"I knew you could hear me the way I hear you!"

Ooops.

"Fucker." Gale laughed when he said it. Maybe it was the wind or the water, but he thought he heard Sean laugh, too. Opening up the email from the network, he keyed in his response.

"THIS COULD BE BIG FOR HIM." MARCO FILLED HER PLATE WITH SPAGHETTI, twisting it into a nest and topping it with a huge meatball. "Big for me, too."

"If he wins." Regina sprinkled cheese on her pasta. Freshly grated. Marco knew better than to put anything less on the table.

"Even if he doesn't. Nights he works are even busier than the weekends since the show aired."

"That's got to go over like a lead balloon with Frances."

"She's not happy. I'm afraid I'm going to lose her." Marco filled his own plate. They sat across from each other, after hours, at the prep table in Marco's. They'd been alternating kitchens every Thursday since that first dinner in her apartment. Regina had come to appreciate Marco's dishes, the same ones she used to consider lacking in sophistication. Homey. Comforting. Delicious. The gastronomic world of microgreens and foams had its place, but while such fads changed with the season, the relevance of tradition remained constant.

"You're more likely to lose him," Regina told him. "Forceful as she is, Frances is unfortunately timid."

"Are you fucking kidding me?" Marco's voice rose an octave. "You never met her."

"I know the type." She tapped her temple. "Talented, but her aggression comes from lack of confidence. The women-in-the-kitchen bullshit has gotten into her head. It's why she's so pissy about Gale being on the show. Why him and not her, you know? I can guarantee she never even applied. It feeds her anger, justified or not, and keeps her a big dictator-fish in her steamy little pond. She'll wait him out."

"Interesting." Marco twirled his spaghetti against a spoon, ate a mouthful. "I never thought about it that way, but you're probably right."

"You're a man. You never had to."

"Is that why you were such a nut?"

"Partially," Regina said. "I had to be a hundred times better than less-talented men. Good thing I was."

"Are." He twirled again.

"Yeah, yeah, yeah." Regina smacked his hand. "Stop that."

"Stop what?"

"Twirling with a spoon. It's barbaric."

Marco's laughter boomed. Were there anyone in the restaurant, they'd have come running. "Now that was all Queenie B! This is Marco's off Wooster Street, not your posh Cucuzza."

"Stop." But she laughed, too. "Cucuzza isn't mine anymore, anyway."

"It'll always be yours, no matter who owns it. It's still there, the jewel of Manhattan, still serving all your dishes."

Regina paused, midchew. "You've been?"

He tsked. "Talking with your mouth full? Now who's barbaric?"

"Fuck you. When did you go?"

Marco started a twirl, glanced her way, and purposefully set down his spoon. "Can I be honest without you punching me in the face?"

"My punching-people-in-the-face days are over. Spill it."

"After I saw you in the market," he confessed. "Don't get pissed at me!"

"I'm not."

"I know that pissy look."

"I always look this way. Ask Gale." Regina twirled and twirled and twirled her pasta. Not against a spoon. "How'd it look?"

"Exactly the way it did when you were there." He winked. "Whoever owns it now knew not to mess with anything. Your picture is still in the lobby."

Pride and satisfaction mingled with smugness, a little fear, and a smidge of reluctant excitement.

"Who sold it?" Marco asked. "You or Oz?"

"Hell if I know." She ate the overtwirled spaghetti, swallowed before speaking. "My lawyers were too good to sit back and let me give Oz everything, but I didn't get involved in who got what. I told them to do it. I let them deal with my husband, my child, my whole world." She sighed. "At least he got something out of our marriage. Whatever he got, he earned."

"Hmph." Marco poured diet soda into her glass from the lovely carafe he saved just for her. "So, you going to do more of those mystery crates for Gale?"

She wagged her fork at him. "What was that about?"

"What?"

"Don't fuck with me. You hmphed."

Marco set the carafe down. "It's none of my business."

"I'm sure it's not."

"Then forget it. I was thinking maybe I'd do a few crates for—"

"Don't make me beat you."

"I thought your punching-people-in-the-face days were over."

"You're really starting to piss me off, Marco."

His jaw worked back and forth, eyes focused on the food in his plate. Setting his fork down, he met her gaze across the prep table. "You want to know? Fine, I'll tell you. You were no innocent, Regina, but neither was Oz."

"Oz?" Regina shook her head. "What are you talking about? He wasn't the freak show."

"Give me a break. Osvaldo Balcazar has never been a victim a day in his life. You think he didn't bask in all that drama?"

"You're not being fair."

"To who? The man who profited, really profited! Off your reputation? The long-suffering husband role suited him just fine. Poor, charming, so-phisticated Osvaldo," he whined. "Fuck that shit, Reg. I wasn't there to witness it all firsthand, but I still knew *you*. And I knew what Oz was from the first time I met him."

"You hated him because I loved him."

"I admit that." Marco slammed a hand on the table, rattling dishes and cutlery. "You did a great job of cutting me out of your life entirely, but I watched through the years. The whole world couldn't help watching. Like a freakin' pileup on the freakin' highway." He leaned across the table, hands gripping the edge. "Did you ever see the interviews he did on TV after you vanished? Read his exclusive in *Gastronomica*? Or the big spread he did for *Food & Wine*? He paraded that little boy around like a tragic—"

Hackles raised. "Leave. Julian. Out of this."

Hands up, Marco's ire ebbed. "Okay, okay. Sorry. Line crossed. But you can't deny your ex-husband capitalized on your bad behavior. He didn't mind everybody thinking, 'Oh, poor Oz.' Hell, I can guarantee he encouraged it."

Marco's words echoed, hit her hard and low and dirty. Regina's whole body burned. Rage. Shame. Came at her from every angle.

Queenie would have launched herself at him, biting and scratching and shrieking. Regina held her temper. Barely. "You don't know Oz. You don't know what I put him through."

"The whole world knows what you put him through." Softly now. Almost defeatedly. Marco pushed fingers through his hair, and there they stayed as if his head would fall off if he didn't hold it on. "You two were a train wreck waiting to happen from day one. Yes, you were madly in love. Anyone could see that. But it wasn't the happily-ever-after kind. It was the toxic kind that eats away everything good and leaves only the really rotten."

A chord struck. Deep. Faint. Chilling. Regina closed her eyes. Cut Marco from her sight. She would not cry. "He tried to help me," she said. "Do you know how many times he forgave me? How many rehabs he sent me to?"

"He forgave you because it was in his best interests. Oz was a passive-aggressive asshole when I first met him and he only got worse. You did a lot of bad shit. I'm not downplaying that, but he . . ."

She opened her eyes when he fell silent. The look on his face. Raw. Trembling. Emotion he would not let fall any more than she would made his eyelashes thick. Sooty. "Look. I'm sorry. You showed up in my life after all these years and, happy as that's made me, it's brought up a lot of shit. Shit I wanted to say, back then, and couldn't."

"Because I cut you out of my life." Sharper than she intended. Apparently not sharp enough to cut. Marco smiled. Sadly. Gently.

"Because you wouldn't have heard me back then if I tried."

It was true. All of it. There was more he couldn't know, couldn't understand. Because he loved her. Marco always had, and he did again. But he saw clearly what she'd never seen at all. Maybe she hadn't wanted to. Maybe it was all part of her atonement. Take all the blame. Carry all the weight. She was doing it still.

It took Herculean effort; Regina lifted her shoulders, let slide some of that blame. Enough to see, truly feel, the truth in Marco's words. The truth beyond their past, together and apart. Beyond his broken heart then and his full one now.

Something like relief or joy or gratitude warmed her belly. Whispered truth, finally acknowledged, crackled like static along her scalp. Regina Benuzzi, Regina Balcazar, Queenie B reached across the table. Marco flinched. She rested her hand to his cheek rough with stubble and wrinkled by years, remembering so clearly when his skin was taut and his hair black as cured olives. His eyes still were.

She hadn't wanted him. Not then. Not even when they were living together, sharing a bed. He'd been a placeholder; more truth skated over once, and finally acknowledged. Marco had been everything she was running from without even truly knowing she was in motion. Oz had been the shine on her horizon. Blinding. Exciting. He was a whole world the unwanted little girl in her craved. And now?

Regina leaned. Marco leaned, took her chin tenderly in his fingertips. Caressing. Gentle. The kiss wasn't fireworks; it wouldn't have even set off a sparkler. It was an oven door left open to warm a whole room when the heat went out. It was soft sheets. It was a cool hand on a fevered brow. What it was not—thank every god in the history of humankind—was the crash and burn it had been with Oz. Those hovering and wrung-out days when it was all so exciting. Thrilling. Desperate. Love not happily-ever-after, Marco was right, but not toxic. Not in the beginning. But in the end when everything good had been burned away.

By both of them. Because Oz had been as addicted to the drama as she was to the drugs.

But mostly her. Because she had been addicted to both.

Rising from her chair, Regina took her plate and her kiss with her. "Your turn to wash."

She and Marco fell into the meditative process—wash, rinse, dry, rack—honed in their youth, in those dishwasher days before success. Across timelines and terrain. Common ground lived once together, then separately during those years she hardly ever thought about him at all. Then never. Regina couldn't remember what she *had* thought about. It was all such a blur. And a waste.

She had it all.

She lost it all.

"Hey, bull in a china shop, you want to be careful with that carafe? It was my nona's."

Regina hid her smile. Maybe not everything, after all.

Setting the carafe down, she took Marco by his soapy hands. She led. He followed. The puzzled furrow of his brow smoothed when she let go of one hand to untie her apron. Marco pulled it over her head, drying his hands on it and tossing it onto the prep table. He led her now. To his office. To the couch there. No windows. It smelled like cigarettes and garlic and onions. Like Marco. Like the past, before everything. Maybe like the future. Maybe. And for once, in her whole damn life, Regina let herself be led, with no kicking or screaming at all.

25

Grease: Refers to applying fat to a roasting tray or cake tin to ensure food doesn't stick.

2010

The days are a clichéd whirlwind passing in the kind of memory-erasing obscurity akin to Queenie B's most destructive days. Regina has barely enough time to bathe and sleep at the end of every long day, let alone fall from her precarious perch. But it's getting easier. She's learning, applying old lessons of organization and perspective. As long as she keeps things simple, she can get it all done.

Troy and Petunia help as a strange, unwholesome tag team; one or the other is always drunk, and thus annoying-yet-harmless fixtures in this corner or that. Gladys watches over them like a fussy hen, though the Burger Queen doesn't venture out after dark unless Troy accompanies her. Regina worries that Gladys doesn't eat during those dinner services Petunia's on duty. If there is a silver lining to their insobriety, it's that they serve as a reminder of all Queenie had been, all Regina fought. One day soon, she has to find more reliable help.

The holidays come and go in that same whirlwind. Regina is glad for that; she doesn't like to think about Julian opening gifts on Christmas morning, bought and wrapped by the woman he now calls Mom. Not that Queenie had ever bought the gifts he opened while she sprawled on the couch or floor, nursing a hangover. Regina remembers few Christmas mornings, but she holds on tight to those she does, hangover or not.

New Year's Day—that day of always-days—brings fewer homeless and destitute in for breakfast. She sets out only hot and cold cereals, puts up pots of coffee and hot water. For lunch, sandwiches. Dinner, more sandwiches and a big pot of—what else?—soup. She's been working so hard. Regina deserves a day that she doesn't have to spend with exhaustion.

The whole day is slow. Dinner service is over by six thirty, and though her doors stay open until eight o'clock, as always, she's able to prep for the next day. Tomorrow will be easier, especially if her tag team shows up. Tonight, Regina is cooking herself something special, something not one pot or leftovers. She's already bought the necessary ingredients.

Seared and basted filet mignon, butter-poached lobster tail, roasted fingerling potatoes with horseradish, and fresh spinach wilted in olive oil with garlic. Simple ingredients demand perfect execution, and Regina doesn't disappoint herself. It's been a long, long time since she's eaten fare so fine; she doesn't dare go to a restaurant. The preparation and consumption fill her soul with an almost-forgotten joy. She weeps. It's not just food. It's the all. The everything. It is art. Her art. Living without it has starved her core, and that will lead to nowhere good. Regina reaffirms her vow to ply her art as dedicatedly as she feeds the homeless and destitute. Privately, where no one will guess she's anything other than a soup kitchen cook.

Cleaning up, she takes care with every lovely glass and dish. She puts them away with a reverence she's not felt in her kitchen downstairs where everything is serviceable. Durable. Part of her feels slightly guilty about keeping such opulence to herself, but, like the meals she's vowed to create, Regina understands these fine things also feed her artist soul, the one she sacrificed on the altar of excess but will now honor and respect.

Nine thirty. Her kitchen is clean. Regina doesn't watch much television, in part because she fears what she'll come across. Accidentally. On purpose. It's better to avoid the pitfalls of vanity and—worse—truth. Maybe, one day, when some of the shame has mellowed into wisdom, she'll be able to watch herself, watch Queenie B, in all her former infamy.

She bought herself an electronic reader for Christmas, but hasn't opened it yet. No time. Now she fetches it from under the Christmas tree. Setting it up is simple. She downloads a few books, chooses one, and shoulders into her comfy armchair. A flick of a switch, and the gas—never woodburning—fireplace glows.

REGINA WAKES TO THE SOUND OF A CAR ALARM SOMEWHERE OUTSIDE. NOT hers. The Durango is parked in the garage, behind a chain-link fence. It's after two. By the percentage of the book read, she's been asleep almost since settling into the chair. It's okay; there will be other nights like this one. She's promised herself.

Taking the e-reader to her bedroom, she opens the drawer of her bedside table but stops short of putting it inside. The bible she'd gone to Marco for all those months ago stares back at her. Under it, the un-opened envelope of the-end-of-everything papers likewise shoved away and forgotten—not forgotten; never.

Fortified by the food, the fire, her resolve to do better, be better, Regina sits on the edge of her bed, takes out the bible, the envelope. She opens the bible, takes from it the recipe clipping, then sets it back between the pages. Thumbing to the frontispiece, she finds the names. Her family of strangers. The habit of love fills her. The wanting and wishing. Things that had never been or could be.

There is her name. Birth date. Baptism. Chicken pox. The entirety of her identity, scratched and fading in her mother's long-dead handwriting. She takes the pen from her crossword puzzle book atop her nightstand. Under her name, she writes—

Regina Benuzzi marries Osvaldo Balcazar October 14, 1989. Divorced December 13, 2004.

And under that—

Julian Osvaldo Balcazar . . .

His birth date. The surgeries she can remember, which aren't many, not because they hadn't been, but because so much of that time was a blank. Under what she can remember, she writes what she can never forget—

Parental rights relinquished to Osvaldo Balcazar April 27, 2006.

Adopted by Fernanda Balcazar née Colón May 28, 2007.

Regina puts the unopened envelope of papers she signed making all that so, back into the drawer. On top, the bible. She closes the drawer on that part of her past, will probably never open it again. There's no point. There never will be. She gave him away. Her son. To a woman she doesn't know. A woman Oz met while visiting Queenie B, during a stint in a rehab she can't pry from all the others. A woman whose husband ended up dead, DUI, while Queenie and Oz were in Bova making a go of it.

There's no scotch or bourbon or vodka in her home, but there is wine kept for cooking. A boogeyman, a tightrope. "If you wouldn't drink it, don't cook with it." An old mantra she's spoken to countless television cameras and devotees. The wine she keeps is very good.

Head hanging, she balls the edges of her comforter into fists. Almost five years since the bottle of vodka she took to bed after signing those papers giving up her son. Not even Julian's adoption had sent her toppling again. This couldn't. This remembering. If she caved now, she was lost forever.

Do better.

Be better.

Growling low, a dog cornered, Regina bolted from the edge of her bed. Into the kitchen. To the pantry. She takes the open bottle of wine from the shelf, uncorks it. The scent. Oh, the aroma! Pouring it in the hot pan, basting her filet with it, she hadn't hungered. Not like she does now. Intoxicating. Irresistible. Regina puts the uncorked bottle to her nose. She breathes like drinking. Her eyes water.

Winging it across the kitchen, Regina roars. The bottle of excellent wine smashes on her Carrera counter, splashes on the Brazilian teak floor. She punches the pots and pans hanging from their rack, flings lovely dishes and cups. Regina smashes and rages as she used to when wasted and out of control. It frightened her then, even if only shadows— and pictorial evidence—of such tirades haunted her. It frightens her now.

Surveying the destruction, hair in tangles around her face, body quivering with rage spent, Regina takes deep breaths until she can do so without shuddering. She turns her back on the carnage of her kitchen. Tomorrow, the stains will be set, but she doesn't, in this moment, trust herself to clean up without putting her lips to the floor and slurping up what she can.

Regina shuffles to her bedroom, strips to nothing, and climbs in between the expensive sheets of her expensive bed. "If money can fix it, it's not a problem." Another of her mantras. She has plenty of money. Whatever she's ruined, she can fix. All she knows is, if she doesn't find her own oblivion now, it'll find her in ways she'll never recover from.

26

Coddle: To cook something in water just below the boiling point.

2016

Gale tapped out of the email from the network. Filming for the elimination rounds was set for February. Four groups, of which Gale was in the second, would compete for a spot in the final, airing sometime in March. Grateful as he was for the tight timeline—less opportunity for him to freak out—Gale wished he was in the first group. He was certain he'd be less anxious if he could get it all over with sooner rather than later. Second was okay, though. Only four days after group one.

Who would be the judges? Anyone from his last appearance? Maybe that wouldn't be such a good thing. The crates were sure to be superhard, although he couldn't imagine a harder one than Regina's crate of limoncello cake, pickles, champagne, and crickets; where the hell did she even get crickets? Crazy ingredients he could manage. Ingredients that didn't go together in any way, he struggled with. He'd used the champagne to repickle the pickles. Limoncello cake became a sort of tart shell he filled with those repickled pickles mixed with raspberries. He used the too-sweet whipped cream icing that became the perfect balancing vehicle to top it off. Coating the crickets in white chocolate had been a bit lazy, but they were a nice complement to the inherent acid and tartness. Regina was impressed, even if it hadn't been the most delicious bite.

"Hey, there." Jenara slid into the booth, opposite him. "Sorry I'm late."

"Don't worry about it." He tucked the phone into his pocket. "Hungry?"

"Starving. I want a huge cheeseburger and fries. And a chocolate malted."

"That sounds awesome." He handed the diner menus to the approaching waiter already writing down their order. Gale didn't love diner food, but Jenara did. More than anything. It was, in his opinion, always too salty, and too abundant, but it did satisfy in a way other food didn't.

"Sorry about tonight." Jenara slipped her arms from her coat. "I swear if Boomer bags on me again, he's history."

"You've said that a million times."

"I mean it this time."

The waiter set glasses of water onto the table.

"Alicia's really disappointed. She was looking forward to movie night."

"You could have brought her with you."

"Nah." She leaned on the table. "If I only get an hour, I want you to myself even if it's just a burger at the diner. But you're coming Sunday, right?"

Sunday. Sunday. Sunday. Father/daughter bowling party with Alicia's Girl Scout troop. He'd had to let the soup kitchen down, but Alicia asked him, so shyly and sincerely. He'd melted completely. Besides, Lucy filled in for him more and more lately; it was as if Regina didn't even need him anymore. "You picking me up?"

"You really need to renew your license, Gale."

"What for? I don't have a car."

"Hmm." Jenara pursed her lips, gave him that look.

"I can take the bus."

"Don't be an ass. I'll pick you up. But I'm not staying. This is a daddy/daughter day."

You're not her daddy, man.

"Don't forget I have to be at work by four."

"I didn't forget."

The waiter brought their food. Jenara wolfed hers down in half the time it took Gale. She picked at his french fries while he finished. They talked about nothing, debated over the worthiness of the latest Marvel movie. Before he knew it, the hour he had with Jenara was gone, and she was sliding her arms back into her coat sleeves as she scooted out of the booth.

"I hate to leave." She kissed him quickly. "What will you do tonight?"

Friday night. His first alone in a long time. "Probably just go home and watch something."

"You practicing?"

"With Regina, almost every day."

"Good. Right, then." Jenara patted her pockets, found her keys. "I'll see you Sunday."

For daddy/daughter bowling day.

"Shut up, Sean," he muttered the moment Jenara was out of earshot. Sean had gone back to ignoring his thoughts, despite Gale catching him listening to them. "What do you have against Alicia?"

Nothing. She's a cute kid. You're just not her daddy.

"So?"

It's a big responsibility. You're not ready for it.

"Why the fuck not?"

You tell me.

"Can I get you anything else?" The waiter stood just over Gale's shoulder, probably listening to him argue with himself.

"No, thanks. I'll take the check."

"The lady already paid it. She said you can leave the tip."

She got you again, man.

Gale swallowed the "Shut up, Sean." He slapped a ten on the table and left the diner. Cold as it was, his apartment was only a few short blocks' walk. Hands jammed in his pockets, he walked at a good pace in the hopes of avoiding the burger-bomb that would inevitably form in his gut.

"I'm not a moron, you know."

You talking to me?

"Who else would I be talking to when I'm by myself on a mostly empty sidewalk?"

I never said you're a moron.

"I know what you are. You're my conscience, my anxieties."

If that's what helps you sleep.

"Fuck you, Sean. Alicia is a great kid and I'd be lucky to be her dad."

Yeah? You ready to make that commitment to her mother? Because, ever since she dropped the L-word, you're easily annoyed by the things you used to find cute. Playing daddy and being daddy are two seriously different things.

Gale refused to engage further. Sean always did know how to get into his head, feed his every want, his every fear. It'd been Sean's oxy—prescribed when he got his wisdom teeth pulled—they first dabbled with. His insistence heroin was a cheaper option when buying oxy broke their bank accounts. His research into the most efficient ways to get it into their systems. Kyle warned him Sean was a bad influence. Over and over. Gale was too far gone before Kyle even figured out what they were doing. Sean, even further. Gale only found out it hadn't been Sean's first time abusing opiates when they tried to get clean. Not even his second. Gale caught up with him quickly, and then he lost count of who'd done what, when.

His pulse raced. Sweat beaded his upper lip. There were few memories from those oblivion days, only sensations that left him wanting and nauseated. Unzipping his coat, he let the cold air smack some sense into him. He should have known better than to let his mind wander down dark paths. Taking the front steps two at a time, Gale reached his apartment door before his keys were out of his pocket. He stood there fumbling with the lock, fingers shaking, wishing he had to work, or Jenara didn't, or Regina needed him.

"Dude! We meet again."

Gale jumped a mile, dropped his keys.

Kyle picked them up, unlocked the door for the both of them. He squinted in the dim lighting, looking intently into Gale's eyes for, he knew, the telltale pinprick pupils. "You okay?"

"Yeah, fine." Gale took his keys back a little too roughly. "You startled me."

"Sorry."

The apartment was strangely warm, considering they kept the thermostat at sixty-eight. A quick check showed it was set correctly, yet read seventy-five on the thermometer.

"Dammit." Kyle pulled his phone from his pocket. "I told the super about this. He was supposed to fix it this morning. We're not paying for all this extra heat."

"How long has it been broken?"

"On and off for about a week." Kyle nudged him in the ribs. "Something you'd know if you weren't shacking up with Jenara most of the time."

Gale decided not to take offense.

"Pretty serious, huh?" Kyle asked.

She thinks so.

Gale let go a deep breath. "You home tonight?"

"Yup! Slow night. Chef asked who wanted to go home."

Kyle wasn't lazy, just disenchanted. Gale had seen it before, that flame of enthusiasm burning bright and burning out. He still wasn't sure if Kyle was unlucky or had no real follow-through. Maybe a little of both. The death of Just Eggs weighed him down; it was hard to see.

"What're you up to tonight?" Kyle asked.

"Nothing. One of Jenara's drivers bagged on her, so she has to drive. We just had burgers down at the diner. Regina's pretty much done for the day, and besides, my mom is with her."

"She's there a lot, huh?"

"It makes her happy." Gale shucked off his coat. "She loved the grocery store, but I think she might love the soup kitchen even more. She's actually starting to be a better cook."

Kyle pretended to stagger backward, clutching his heart, then— "Oh, sorry, dude. That wasn't cool."

"It's okay." Gale hadn't even thought of his mother's heart attack until Kyle felt bad about feigning one. "Hey, that reminds me. She sent me links to some really old cooking shows she thought would help me with the competition first go-around. Want to watch some with me?"

"Sounds like an exciting Friday night." Kyle chuckled. "Actually, that sounds great. I'm supertired. And hungry." He held up the take-out container. "I'll heat this up, you connect the computer to the TV."

Gale grabbed the laptop. He could have synced it with his phone, but he knew how to do it via laptop already. Pulling up his mother's email, he clicked on a random video, and couldn't get it to play. He tried another. Same. Maybe he didn't know how to sync the devices after all.

Gale signed in to Netflix, searched for the name of one of the shows in his mother's links. Score! Season after season, right there. No syncing necessary. He chose season four; plenty of time for a show to find its groove. Kyle flopped onto the couch beside him, blowing on his food.

"How about this one?"

"Awesome. Hit it, dude."

The picture wasn't great, but not bad for a twenty-some-odd-year-old show. The opening music was dated. And the logo, a red-lipped smile zooming around, chased by a bumblebee. The two kissed, center screen, the words *The Queenie B* curling out of a flower. Then a woman. Long, black hair. Amazing smile. Arms raised to the applause of the audience clapping her in.

"Dude."

Gale's mouth went dry.

"Dude! Are you seeing this?"

"I'm seeing it."

Queenie B. The name was suddenly, gut-wrenchingly familiar. The woman addressing the audience was too. But she wasn't Regina. Not the Regina he'd known nearly a year. His mentor. The unsmiling, cranky woman making lasagna and oatmeal and pots of vegetable soup for the homeless and destitute of Rock Landing. He'd never have put two and two together.

"What the fuck, dude?" Kyle was already tapping around on his phone. "Did you know?"

"Obviously not."

"What the fuck!" Kyle whooped. "I remember her now. I mean, who she used to be. Queenie B's got a massive Wiki page! Look."

"I don't want to see it."

"Why the hell not? This is huge, dude. She vanished from the cooking scene before we got obsessed, back in—"

"I said I don't want to know." Gale paused the on-screen woman he knew so well and didn't at all. "If she's running a soup kitchen in fucking New Haven, Connecticut, she obviously doesn't want people to know who she is. Was. She's Regina."

"Oh. Yeah, I guess." Kyle slumped into the couch. "Dude, can you imagine what one of the big foodie magazines would give for information of her whereabouts?"

Gale's blood curdled. "You wouldn't do that, Kyle. I know you wouldn't."

"I don't know." He chomped down, talked through his mouth full of burrito. "That's a shit ton of money."

"Kyle, you can't—"

"Chill, dude." Kyle guffawed, chewed-up burrito flying. "Even if she didn't scare the crap out of me, I wouldn't. I'm not an asshole. But DAY-um!" He slapped his thigh. "She's a bona fide celebrity."

"Was."

"Yeah." Kyle swallowed hard. "Well, come on. Hit play already."

Gale's finger hovered over the play button. It was there, after all, for anyone to view; why not him? He pressed rewind, started at the beginning with the flying red lips. Regina was Queenie B. Animated in a way he'd never seen her. Young. Probably around his own age. How had she gone from the vibrant woman on-screen to the woman he knew?

Gale squashed the impulse to do exactly what Kyle had. Take out his phone and look her up. Dive into a past she obviously wanted left behind her. Wanted to, but didn't. Because there she was, and here he was, diving even if he didn't open his phone.

27

Dead plate: A dish of food that is deemed unservable, either because it was sent back or prepared incorrectly. Dead plates are typically fair game for servers or cooks to eat, dependent upon the restaurant's policy.

2012

Petunia is dead. Wasn't it inevitable? Neither she nor her father has ever even suggested they get clean; they simply take turns being drunk. Petunia had been taking more than her fair share of turns the last several months, leaving Troy more often sober. A parent's love? Regina supposes it is, in its way. The Burger Queen does not think so. She thinks, if Troy loves his daughter, he won't enable her.

Regina hates that word in all its forms—*enable, enabling, enabler*. It's a bullshit word, the psychobabble catchphrase of the moment, and destructive to all parties concerned because it's just another label to slap blame on.

The dining room is buzzing, breakfast, lunch, and dinner. First with Petunia's death, then with Troy's disappearance. On his knees, wailing a siren sound as the ambulance took his daughter's body away, is the last anyone has seen of him. Not even Gladys has, and she is angry. Regina wishes she could be angry. All she can be is worried. For the time being, she sends Gladys home from lunch with boxed dinners so she's not walking to the kitchen after dark, even picks up a new Burger Queen crown for her when hers gets shabby. And she keeps eyes and ears out for any sign of Troy climbing out of his bottle.

In the meanwhile, she's running meal services with the haphazard assistance of those in need of that twenty-dollar bill she offers for their trouble. Sometimes, she can't find anyone interested in more than the sandwich and cup of soup. It's not that they're lazy—another word she despises—just too old or too young, too exhausted or too lost inside their own heads. Then there are those who come in drunk, or high; Regina doesn't send them away unfed, but neither does she ask for their help.

Busy day turns into busy day, and Regina hasn't enough energy left at the end of one to even think straight. The learning curve is indeed curvaceous, and she's still figuring out how to navigate the course. Meals become simpler. No one complains about soup and sandwiches, day after day. Or the cereals. Though a few mumble about missing Troy's eggs. Bottom line is, she can't do it on her own, but she's afraid to hire someone. Hiring means a paycheck, means health insurance and Social Security deductions and a million other things that leave a paper trail she is absolutely not willing to leave.

But something's got to give.

Regina has made baked ziti and sausages, figuring it's at least as easy to serve as soup and sandwiches. It is certainly less time-consuming to make. Word has gotten out; even Gladys could not stay away. The line is longer than usual, and Regina is only one person.

"Help serve, there's a twenty in it for you." Over and over she asks. Grunts, heads shaking. No takers. Regina plugs on, her feet sore and her back aching. She might have to cave and hire someone, under the table to avoid that paper trail. She'll have to be careful when the various inspectors come. If they come. This part of the city is largely ignored. Once acknowledged, someone would have to do something about it and, in Regina's experience, past and present, no one wants to. It's one of the reasons she chose Rock Landing to begin with.

By six forty-five, most of the hungry are served. Regina is ready to drop right there, but she can't leave the dining room unattended even to clean the kitchen. It is going to be a long night, too long to indulge in the meal she'd planned for herself. Her back, that old injury, screams *I told you so*s from her past. She scoops herself a plate of ziti, skewers a sausage, and eats standing there in the doorway. If she sits, she won't get up again.

The entrance door opens and closes with a bang. Great. Another hungry person to serve. Regina lowers her plate to the table, but the woman, leggy and curvy and not at all dressed for the weather, doesn't get in line. She clacks on high heels to the far corner of the dining room, finger to her red lips. Hiding behind a group of elderly folk, she can't get low enough for the poof of her hugely teased Afro. It sticks up over the head of one old man, making him look like a fuzzy brown mushroom.

The door opens again with a bang. A man stands in the doorway, scanning the dining room, door held open by one meaty hand. He is big, his puffer coat making him even bigger, and he is angry, if the red blotches of his face are to be believed.

"Close the door," the Burger Queen calls out. "You're letting the cold in."

He takes another step inside, lets the door go. "Have you seen a tall Black woman, really pretty, wearing one of those flowy shirts and a leather miniskirt? Hair out to here?" He holds his hands wide around his head.

Heads shake. Mumblers mumble. Gladys is already on her feet, head high and shoulders back, that imperious air as grand as any Victorian lady's. She moves closer and the man steps back, eyes on her paper crown and eyebrows expressing derision, but Gladys says, "As you can see, there's no one fitting that description here. Now, if you'd like something to eat, young man, take a seat like a gentleman," and he takes another step back.

"Eat?" He scans the room, grimacing. "Here?"

"Don't be rude." The old woman claps, just once. "If you require no sustenance, then I'll thank you to leave."

The man scans the room again, squinting and shrugging in turn. His face is no longer blotchy red. Regina watches, puzzled but amused. Silence follows his departure, everyone focuses on the old man/mushroom. Eyes, followed by a nose, and a red-lipped smile appear above his head. Several laugh. The woman kisses the crown of the old man's pate. "My people!" She dances about the room, kissing this head and that cheek. Regina is certain whoever she is, she doesn't know everyone, but she seems to know many. The rest have simply gotten caught in her whir.

"What have you to say for yourself, young lady?" Gladys stands before her, as imperious and authoritative as she'd been with the blotchy man.

"Excuse me?"

A sniff, nose just a fraction higher than it had been. "Racing in here, being chased by that man, dressed like"—and higher—"that."

"Maybe you should be minding your own business." She adds, "Ma'am," though it comes off more like a sneer. Regina can't exactly place her accent, but it isn't American. And she can't place her age. When she ran into the dining room, she'd have said twentysomething. Looking at her closer, she thinks she has to be in her late thirties.

"If I had minded my own business, you would have been dragged out of this establishment by your hair. Caveman that he is. Now button those top buttons and sit. Regina," she calls, waving. "If you please."

The tired has been shooed from her legs. Gladys the Burger Queen resumes her seat off to the side, almost in the corner, where she always sat with Petunia or Troy, and now alone. Regina scoops baked ziti onto a plate for the newcomer, delivers it to the table where she sits, old-school chastised and properly submissive, buttoning her top buttons.

"Thank you," she says when Regina places the plate in front of her. Then, "She always like that?"

"Always." It's a lie. Gladys is Gladys, but rarely so cogent.

"You run this place?"

"I do."

"I heard about it before, from . . ." She points to the diners. "Anyway, thanks for not giving me away. He'll calm down soon enough."

"Maybe you shouldn't date men like that."

"Date? I don't think you can call what we do dating." She waves a hand from head to toe. "Some think they pay for all this, not just use of certain parts. They're wrong."

The impulse to smile siphons away. Regina doesn't want to be judgmental; she has no right to be. She's done way worse than accept money for sex. She hands the woman a can of soda. "Just be safe."

"I always am." She grimaces, holds up the can. "Got anything diet?"

THE DINING ROOM IS MOSTLY EMPTY BY A QUARTER AFTER SEVEN. A FEW latecomers still sit in a corner, eating what is left of the baked ziti. Regina planned well. No leftovers. That is where she wants to be, going forward. Just enough. No waste. And no one going hungry.

The chased woman is still there, sitting on the edge of the latecomers' table, chatting. Three boys and a girl, all late teens. Regina thinks they're runaways, but she can't be sure. When they get up to leave, the woman waves them off but makes no move to leave herself. Instead, she approaches Gladys at her solitary table, head bowed.

Regina joins them, slightly afraid but not knowing exactly which woman she fears for.

"I want to thank you, for what you did."

Gladys glances up. The imperious expression lingers only around the edges of her features. There is a question there. Confusion. This is the Gladys, the Burger Queen, that Regina knows best. She goes to their rescue.

"There's a twenty in it for you if you help me clean up," she tells the younger woman. To Gladys, she says, "I'll be done soon. I'll take you home."

Gladys sniffs, nods almost imperceptibly.

THE DINING ROOM IS CLEAN IN HALF AN HOUR. PREP TABLES ARE ALREADY wiped down. All that is left to do in the kitchen is clean the hotel pans now soaking in the sink and set up the Crock-Pots for the morning.

"Thanks for your help." Regina hands the woman a twenty.

"Thanks for the food, and . . ." She holds up the bill before stuffing it into her bra. "I guess I should be going."

"Will you be safe?"

"Safe is as safe does." She tries to smile when she says it; Regina can tell by the way the corners of her eyes crinkle. Too much hardship, hard living. This close, she looks more like fifty.

The kettle Regina's put on to boil sings. She locks the front door after the woman leaving before attending to it. Gladys is still in her little corner. Waiting. Her memory might be broken, but some things are too ingrained to fall through those cracks.

Pouring tea into the Bernardaud cups, Regina inhales. Peppermint is never her go-to, especially late in the day. Too rejuvenating. Tonight, she needs it just to get up the stairs.

"Thank you." Both Gladys's hands wrap around her cup. Knuckles are boles keeping two rings, both on middle fingers, both neither expensive nor cheap, from falling off. One is set with a rather large red cabochon that should look incongruous but somehow doesn't. Regina can't get away with big rings; her fingers are too stubby. Earth hands, a palmist once told her, though she remembers being the exact opposite of what that was supposed to make her. Gladys's fingers are long and must have once been graceful. They dance on the hot mug, a symphony of clacks from her rings.

"She'll be dead within the year." Gladys blows across the top of her teacup. "Mark my words."

"You're probably right." Regina does the same. "You all right?"

"I'm fine, dear. Thank you."

Is she playing at senility? Regina believes it's mostly real, and sometimes convenient. She's never known anyone like Gladys the Burger Queen. Not in any life.

They finish their tea in silence. Regina takes the cups to the kitchen. She'll wash them when she gets back. The two-block drive to Gladys's apartment building also happens in silence. Regina walks her up the stairs, to her first-floor apartment directly across from Troy's. She's tempted to knock on the door.

"Here." Regina hands Gladys the to-go containers she'd packed. "In case Troy isn't himself tomorrow."

"Thank you, dear."

No mercurial sniff. Her expression is concerned, her watery eyes on Troy's door. "Petunia was a good girl."

"She was."

"I'm so very sad she's gone."

"Yeah, me too."

More silence, less comfortable than before. Regina still has a few things to do, and she is exhausted. "Well, good night, Gladys."

The old woman dips her head. "Good night, Queenie. Pleasant dreams."

The door closes, and Regina can only stare.

28

Al dente: To the tooth; the texture of cooked pasta when it's tender but firm and chewy when bitten into.

2016

The kitchen door opened, letting in cold air and Gale already shucking his coat. "Sorry I'm a little late."

"You can get started on the dinner rolls." Regina jutted her chin toward the bagged, partially baked dinner rolls on the largest of the prep tables, her hands too busy slicing carrots to point. "I want a milk wash on them so they get nice and brown. There's nothing more disgusting than pale dinner rolls."

"I can think of a lot more disgusting things." Gale set down his bag, put on his apron. No chef coats in Regina's kitchen. "It smells amazing in here."

"Yankee pot roast," she said. "There was a special on chuck at the C-Town. I bought out all they had yesterday. It's been braising since lunch."

"Only you can make chuck roast into something delicious."

Regina grunted. "Anyone can make chuck taste good with some salt and a Dutch oven."

"But you've got more than that going." Gale gave a long sniff. "I smell garlic, onions, rosemary. And thyme. And—"

"Great, you know the recipe. Can you get a move on with those rolls now?"

Despite his light, teasing manner—too light, too teasing—Gale hadn't yet met her eyes. His presence thrummed like the wire on an egg slicer ready to snap. Maybe it hadn't been a great idea, encouraging him to do the competition again. She'd been trying to decide whether that had been for his benefit, or Queenie's. Regina felt her more often, lately. Not insisting, but no longer pleading. Just sort of . . . there.

As always, once Gale got into his groove, the jittery thrum of him eased. The rolls were basted and he was putting them into the oven before Regina finished slicing carrots. "We're roasting these, too." She drizzled oil over the hotel pan of carrots, gave them a good shake before sliding them across to him. "No one likes a boiled carrot."

A little butter, salt, and dill after they were nice and caramelized, and they'd be delicious. It was nice, being able to be more thoughtful about the food she served. Missing Troy—the usuals still missed his eggs—didn't diminish the benefit of Gale's competence in the kitchen that allowed her to think more about the food, get slightly more creative. Like the apple crumble waiting to be assembled, according to her dinner service checklist. Everything else was done, or in the process of cooking.

"Now just the dessert," Regina said. "Apples are prepped and in the walk-in."

Gale fetched the apples, two buckets at a time. "That's a lot of apples," he said.

"I think we have enough for four trays."

"When did you peel all these?"

"Your mom did them earlier. You should have seen her with the apple peeler. I never saw anyone have so much fun. She made winding a whole apple without the skin breaking into a game."

"That's my mom." Gale smiled, kind of winced. He turned his back on Regina to dump the apples into the colander.

Regina mixed the oats, brown sugar, butter, and dried cranberries by hand. Gale had already portioned the sliced apples into four hotel pans and was coating them with her mixture of cornstarch, cinnamon, cloves, salt, and nutmeg. She went behind him, sprinkling a thick layer of crumble on top. They spoke little, and only when necessary while they finished making dessert and got it into the last oven. In the short time he'd been in the kitchen, Gale had gone from overly cheery to uncomfortable to silent. That could mean only one thing.

"You're nervous." She set a mug of coffee in front of him, breaking his stare into space. "Having second thoughts?"

"Huh? What?"

"The competition."

He rolled his eyes dramatically. She nearly smiled.

"You don't have to do it, you know."

"I signed the contract."

"Those things are breakable." She stirred sugar in her tea, a little milk. "If you're going to back out, do so sooner rather than later."

"I'm not backing out. I'm not really nervous. Well, I am, but I'm excited too. I know what to expect. I've . . . uh . . ." He thumbed the handle of his coffee mug, studying it like he was trying to find a chip. ". . . been doing some research."

"Research, huh? I thought you exhausted that the first time around."

"Ha! Not quite." Wild-eyed. Almost scary. Almost sad.

She sipped her coffee, giving him a moment. "Is Marco making up crates for you? Is that it? I'm not going to be insulted, even if he has the creativity of a—"

"I saw all your shows."

Thwunk. Right between the eyes. Coffee splashed over the top of her mug, onto her hands, the table. "You . . . what?"

"Saw all your shows." Gale wiped up the coffee with his sleeve, gaze everywhere but on hers. "Well, a lot of them. Enough to . . . anyway, I didn't know they were yours. I mean, I knew as soon as I saw you, but I didn't start watching them because it was you. Mom sent me links way before the last competition, and I never got around to watching them, then I couldn't get them to play, but Kyle and I had nothing to do so I tried Netflix and . . ." He finally looked at her, eyes so strained around the edges it made her heart thump. ". . . there you were."

Regina slumped back in her chair. A dull drone buzzed up from her belly, into her ears. It wasn't anger. Not even fear.

It's just a good hiding spot that's going to bite you in the ass one of these days.

It felt more like . . .

"I didn't Wiki you or anything," Gale blurted. "Well, Kyle did, but I made him stop. I knew you wouldn't want . . . I mean . . . I figured you didn't . . . point is, I didn't dig into your past. I just watched the shows. I swear. I couldn't help myself. You were . . . you are . . . I mean, big doesn't even come close to it. I can't believe it took me this long to . . . Regina?"

. . . relief.

"Regina, I'm so sorry."

Her vision blurred, but only around the edges. Hadn't she been expecting this? Since Marco? Since Lucy? Since the beginning?

She tapped his hand across the table, attempting a smile she feared, hoped, came across as her usual grimace. "You have nothing to be sorry for."

"I swear I'm not going to tell anyone."

But Kyle would. Maybe not yet, but eventually. He was a nice guy, but the whereabouts of Queenie B was too big for him to sit on forever. He'd tell someone, who'd tell someone, who'd tell, who'd tell, who'd tell. Reporters would show up at the soup kitchen. Paparazzi with their cameras. Old photos would be dredged up. Speculation would be made.

"I know you won't." She pushed away from the table, took his full mug and hers to the sink, saying over her shoulder, "Finish the crumbles and get them into the oven."

"Okay." He pushed away from the table, chair legs scraping. "Yeah, sure. No problem."

Gale got to work, looking over his shoulder so often he looked like a bobblehead. Regina stirred this, checked that. Outwardly, calm. Inside, she was already running. Searching for that next place to hide in. Mentally saying goodbye to her soup kitchen, its regulars. Gladys and Lucy and Marco and . . .

Gale.

Her chest squeezed, knocking the breath from her body.

"I'll be back in a sec," she said, darting for the door leading up to her apartment. In the dark of that stairwell, she pressed fingers to her eyes, fought that old monster hiding under her bed since the fire. Quiet for a time, it now clawed the lifesaving blankets away. Regina couldn't catch her breath. How many times did she have to lose everything?

She hid from the monster's gnashing teeth. Run, it said. Run fast. Run now. Regina longed for the unlongable, for the oblivion that had been the only thing to ever hush the rushing, pulsing, screaming inside her. Back then. Now. Hitting her as it hadn't in so long, she'd almost felt safe. A lesson in some things never changing. Because it all balanced on the edge of a chef's knife.

She dropped to the bottom step so she wouldn't go upstairs. To the bottle of wine she kept for cooking but never opened after the rage that resulted in replacing all the marble in her apartment kitchen. The cell phone in her back pocket jabbed. Pulling it free, she was tapping Marco's number before her brain could stop her flying fingers.

"Hey, what's—"

"I need you," she whispered. "Now."

"I'll be right there."

That was all. Her summons. His compliance.

No.

Her plea. His empathy.

How long she sat in the dark, Regina couldn't say. Moments. Hours. It felt like hours battling the churning in brain and gut and heart. Nothing had changed. She told herself that, over and over. It was only that Gale knew.

Gale knew.

Gale knew.

A tidal wave crashing.

The door opened a crack, then all the way and quickly closed. An arm slipped around her shoulders. Any other arm, and she'd have flailed and kicked herself free of it. Resting her head on his shoulder, she matched her breathing to his. In. Out. In. Out. Focused on the warmth of him. His arm, his presence.

"Gale knows who I am," she said into the dark. "First you, then Lucy, now Gale. And Kyle, too. You were right. All this hiding is coming to bite me in the ass." She groaned, heels of her palms pressed to her eyes so she wouldn't cry. "I can't do it again. I can't run. I can't hide. I can't lose all of you."

"Shh," he said, rocking her now, as if she were a little girl. "Shh."

She hadn't flailed and kicked herself free of him; Regina didn't rage against his soft command either. Leaning more heavily into him, she let herself be rocked and shushed, the motion and sound lulling the monster near enough to sleep for the muscles in her shoulders to unknot. But it never slept. Not completely. Even through these years of atonement and redemption, the monster born in fire who became all the worst of Queenie B kept one eye open, waiting.

"You're not her," he said, so softly she couldn't be sure he'd spoken at all. "She's you."

The truth in his words trickled through her, starting in her ear, worming into her brain. Down her throat. Into her belly. Tingling to fingers and toes.

Not Marco's words.

Not Marco's voice.

Not Marco.

Gale.

"Regina?" Marco called. From the kitchen. The door flew open, letting light into that dark stairwell. Gale smiled awkwardly back at her. His arm fell away and up he got, without a word or backward glance.

"Hey, Marco." He nodded in passing.

"Hey." Marco glanced from Gale to Regina, eyebrows raised.

Regina watched him go, her eyes adjusting to the sudden light, her heart not so much pounding as it was swelling. A lump rose in her throat, thwarting any words that might have tried to form. Memorizing the contours and taste of it, Regina swallowed the lump gently down.

"You okay?" Marco helped her to her feet. "What happened?"

In the kitchen, Gale checked the braising pot roasts as if he'd not just proved his bravest, kindest love. Without declaration. Without show. A rush of panic and love and gratitude swept over her, bracing as wind blowing in off the Sound.

She closed the door behind Marco, closed them into darkness. Thick silence muffled the simple chaos of emotion trying to come clean.

"Reg?"

"Shh." She nestled into him. "Shh."

Marco's arms came around her. Her plea. His empathy. It melded with the remnants of Gale's devotion lingering like the scent of freshly baked cookies, good and sweet, in the stairwell. Sparked by kindred chaos, cemented in food. The all. The everything. Grown into love that braved the dragon in her den.

Gale.

Marco.

And Lucy too.

What had she done in her ill-spent life to deserve any of them? Regina couldn't guess. She didn't even try.

29

Reducc: The procċss of simmering or boiling a liquid, usually stock or sauce, to intensify the flavor and thicken the consistency.

2016

"You sure about this?"

Regina struggled with the huge pot of boiled potatoes. "Will you stop asking me that? You're the one who was pushing for it months ago."

"I just want to make sure . . . here, let me help you with that."

"I can do it."

Marco knew better than to take the pot from her, instead adding his muscle to hers. Together, they dumped water and potatoes into the industrial-size colander.

"It's come out of hiding, or run again. I can't run. I won't. Before someone outs me, I have to out myself." Regina wiped her hands on her apron. "You said it yourself"—and a little internet searching proved him right—"I still have influence in the culinary world. I can use that, get in touch with some of the old greats. Emeril. Lydia. Ina. Eric. Tony would understand better than anyone. He always had a thing for me."

"I know *of* those people," he reminded her. "And you don't know them anymore."

Regina shook the colander of potatoes, steam rising up in her face. "Someone has to remember me fondly, right?"

"A lot of people do," Marco said. "But can you really know who's safe? Who's not going to turn it into a circus? You think it's going to be, 'Hey, how the hell are you? Where've you been the last decade or so?' You burned a lot of bridges."

"Nothing's going to be safe." She checked the time. Four thirty. Lucy should have been back from the box store by now. She'd been counting on her to go pick up Gladys. It had taken the old woman a while, but she tolerated Lucy when Regina couldn't be there. At least she'd stopped waiting for Troy. "There has to be someone. Think, Marco."

"How about an interview?" Marco asked. "There are lots of talk shows that would kill to have you on."

"That would absolutely turn into a circus." She scooped potatoes into the massive ricer she had ordered from an online kitchen supply warehouse, squeezed with all her might. "I need more control."

"No, really? I'd never have guessed. For fuck's sake, Regina, let me." Marco took the ricer from her. "Glare all you want. My hands are bigger."

The bastard. But she laughed.

He riced. She mixed. Butter, salt, a little cream. A handful of parsley. There would be no infusion of truffle or garlic, no horseradish kick, but they'd be the smoothest, silkiest potatoes to pass the lips of anyone in the dining room tonight. Layering the mashed potatoes into hotel pans, sliding them to Marco to set into the oven so they'd be golden brown and slightly crispy on top, Regina moved on to the veg. If Lucy didn't get there soon, she'd have to go get Gladys herself.

"This is too high. You'll dry them out." Marco adjusted the temp on the oven. She smacked his hands away.

"You're the sous in this kitchen. Don't touch anything I don't tell you to."

He backed off, hands raised. Regina put the temperature back up to where she wanted it. Marco leaned on the edge of the prep table, hairy arms crossed, smiling.

"What?" Regina chopped without pause.

"I think I got it."

"Don't just stand there grinning, out with it?"

"You do a magazine interview," he said. "Like Oz did, after you vanished. It's not in your face, like a television spot."

Regina's scalp prickled. "That's not a bad idea."

"I think it's genius."

"Let's not get carried away." Her brain was already sifting through possibilities. Any magazine would jump at the chance to stage her comeback. But which one? *Gastronomica*? *Food and Wine*? Queenie B knew every editor, most of the journalists, and many of the interns on every food magazine staff—a decade ago. Slept with a lot of them too. Regina did not. But if she could pull it off, it would be . . .

"Kind of like a soft open."

Marco nodded. "Exactly."

"I like this idea. A lot."

"You're welcome." He winked.

She would make it an offer no one in their right minds would refuse— an exclusive she'd, of course, get final approval of, that would ensure no one leaked the news and risked someone else getting a jump on the story of a lifetime. She could dictate when Queenie rose from the ashes. Her way. In her time. And once it was done . . .

Regina untied her apron and threw it at him, that scalp-prickling sensation coursing through her whole body. "Baste the chicken in about ten minutes," she said. "I have to go get Gladys. If Lucy doesn't get here by five, turn the ovens down to one seventy. Don't touch them a minute before that. Understood?"

"I didn't leave Gale in charge at my place to come take orders from you, woman!" he called after her, but Regina was already flying out the door.

A magazine exclusive. It could work. It wasn't hubris to know all she had to do was make the call to get what she wanted; it was straight-up fact. She'd stop at the newsagent on the corner of Gladys's block, grab whatever foodie magazines she could find. Publishing was even more changeable than the culinary world, but maybe she'd get lucky and recognize a name or two. Someone she could trust; or at least trust their ambition enough to risk contact.

PULLING UP IN FRONT OF GLADYS'S BUILDING, HAND ON THE PLASTIC BAG of glossy magazines to keep them from sliding off the seat, Regina took in its dilapidated glory. The building had been beautiful, once. Prewar elegant. Current-day graffiti everywhere. Garbage in huge piles, bagged, and picked apart by crows. It was as if the city of New Haven had forgotten it existed at all.

She hated that Gladys lived there. Hated that she lived alone, vulnerable to the vagaries of the neighborhood, the city, and her failing mind. The alternative was worse—a state-run nursing home, understaffed and overcrowded because the system had never been devised for so many to get so old. Heartbreaking, backbreaking, soul-breaking work few had the stomach for.

Regina let herself in the main entrance—Troy had given her a key long ago—navigated the shopping carts and bicycles cluttering the narrow path to Gladys's apartment. Across the way, where Troy once lived, the notice to quit was gone from the door; the loud and messy sounds of a family came muffled from the other side. She took a breath in, and let it whisper out.

Not now. Too much. Regina had to accept that she might never know what happened to him.

She knocked on Gladys's door, and waited. Regina had a key to this lock, too, but had sworn she'd use it only in an emergency. Gladys's mind might be a sieve that only caught thought or memory on occasion, but she deserved all the respect and dignity Regina could give her. Just as she was about to knock again, the door creaked open.

"Oh. It's you."

"It's me." Regina smiled.

Gladys seemed momentarily taken aback. "Let me get my purse."

"Take your time." But don't. Regina had to get back to open the soup kitchen. Hopefully, Lucy would be there even if Marco would be gone. He'd left Gale in charge of Marco's for prep; he wouldn't for service. And Marco called *her* a control freak. He was, at least, starting to teach Gale the less glamorous side of the restaurant business, something Regina herself had never been good at. She'd had Osvaldo for that. And all the experts she could afford to hire.

Gladys stepped into the hall, closed her door, and locked it, jiggling it for good measure. She lifted her chin in that mercurial way, going first down the hall, navigating the carts and bikes with tottering yet elegant steps. Resisting the urge to put out a steadying hand, Regina was nonetheless ready should she falter. She reached around the old woman to open the front door for her. A gust from outside whisked the paper crown away.

"I got it."

For all her tottering slowness, the old woman had made it down the steps in the time it took Regina to chase down her paper crown. Placing it back on the Burger Queen's stiff and thinning hair, she resisted the urge to curtsy.

"Thank you, dear."

"You're welcome."

Gladys needed help getting into the Durango. Regina moved her magazines to the back seat, buckled the old woman in rather than argue with her to do it herself. At least she didn't complain.

"What's for dinner tonight?"

"Chicken, mashed potatoes, and peas."

"Canned or frozen?"

"Frozen."

"Good." She sniffed. "I never could abide canned peas. Only Mother's. Well, she didn't do the actual canning. Susie did. But Mother did take credit for it when she gave the jars out to neighbors."

Gladys talked the whole way back to Regina's Kitchen, barely pausing for breath. Mother and Susie. Her dog, Lassie, so named long before the television program, and wasn't that utterly too-too? She talked about the peas Susie shucked with her long thumbs, and how mesmerized little she had been by it. How she pretended they were tiny babies cocooned in the pods and cried when Mother made her eat every last one on her plate. She talked and talked, even once inside the kitchen where Lucy was waiting, apron at the ready. She escorted Her Majesty to the dining room, to her table for one, without the old woman missing a word, as if she had to set the memories free before they got locked inside her brain again.

"Is she still talking?" Regina asked as Lucy came back through the swinging door.

"I told her to hold her thought, and I'd be right back with her tea."

"She'll forget by the time you get back."

"I know." Lucy poured hot water into a mug from the urn always warming on the counter, set a tea bag into it. "I put the ovens down to one seventy and basted the chicken. What else do you need me to do?"

"Marco was supposed to baste the chicken."

Lucy dunked her tea bag. "He had to rush off as soon as I got back. Gale was having some issue with the grill."

It was always something, in a kitchen. "Sit with her," Regina said. "We're good until people start coming, then I'll need your help serving."

"You got it." Lucy poured a second mug, dunked another bag. Holding both mugs aloft, she said, "Wish me luck!," and pushed backward through the swinging door.

Regina stood alone in her kitchen, hands on her hips, surveying her queendom. Pride swelling, she didn't deny the prickling behind her eyes. Before long, it wouldn't be hers anymore. Like Cucuzza. Like all the other jewels in her former crown, long gone. Lost. Given away. They didn't matter anymore, but this kitchen always would. On everything she hoped to be, Regina swore it.

"It's going to be different, this time."

Spotting her bag of magazines there on the counter where she'd dropped them, Regina whisked them into the stairwell where Lucy wouldn't see them. She'd never guess. Not in a million years. She wasn't even sure the woman knew she'd unintentionally outed her to Gale. Probably not. Lucy would have apologized, clearing the air before it could get foggy. Regina would tell her what was going on, once she knew, herself.

GASTRONOMICA. FOOD & WINE. COOK'S ILLUSTRATED. BON APPÉTIT. THEY were all several months behind, but at least the newsagent still carried them. She was way behind, too; Regina hadn't so much as flipped open any of their covers in years.

Lingering long over *Food & Wine*, she conjured the Classic in Aspen, where she'd debuted, then reigned as literal queen for so long. She'd added a few new and trendy magazines to her pile—she hoped they would make it, even if they probably wouldn't—also a couple of months out of date and catering mostly to chefs who not only saw the beauty in a plate of food, whether artistic expression or mom's meatloaf, but lived for it. She had too, once upon a time. Until the food took a back seat to her fame, then to her addictions that were part of that fame. Regina's Kitchen had healed, but it hadn't nurtured the all, the everything.

The magazines were kindling; she devoured the pictures, gorged on the recipes and the spotlights on old greats—her heart did little flips; did she get as old as they did?—as well as those up-and-coming chefs she couldn't know, but who most certainly knew her. Breathless. Unsatiated. Insatiable. Midnight neared before she knuckled down to searching through editors and journalists in the credits and bylines.

It was after midnight when she, gritty-eyed and a little deflated, gave in to bed. Of course, it wasn't going to be that easy. She knew no one. Not a single editor or journalist from back in her day. Oh, it was entirely possible she did, in fact, know some of them but simply didn't remember. Their names. Faces. What she'd done to them. Probably just as well. Uncurling from the club chair by the gas fireplace, she grabbed the last two magazines from the pile. One appeared to be more of the supermarket endcap category. The other seemed a little too *Ladies' Home Journal* or *Good Housekeeping* for her purposes. Tomorrow, she'd go to another newsagent, or the big bookstore over by Yale. They'd have larger selections than a kiosk on a street corner in Rock Landing that only carried months-old magazines.

Under the covers, propped up on piles of downy pillows, Regina tossed the supermarket endcap magazine to the floor. An exclusive in such a mag said too many things about who she'd been and where she'd landed than she could stomach. Flipping through the last one—*A Chef's Life*, fifth anniversary edition—she had to admit it wasn't the house and home variety she'd judged it to be, only old and worn, even the inserts torn free.

The once-glossy cover now dulled, though the artwork showed merit, had luxurious heft. From last autumn. A carafe of wine, dewy grapes, a hunk of Roquefort putting Regina's salivary glands into overdrive, and a crusty hunk of break. Simple. Elegant. Maybe done to death, but classic for a reason.

She scanned bylines. Went back to the table of contents. Typical autumnal fare, from food to article to spotlight. On the second page, she found the letter from the editor—"Five Years After the Dream Came True." Maybe a bit uninspired, but concise. She scanned but didn't read. Phrases popped—gastronomic daring; trends already passé; classic reinvented—enough to get the gist. At the bottom, beside a barely legible signature, the tiny photo in the bottom corner made Regina sit up higher.

"Holy shit."

Bringing the magazine closer to her face, she couldn't quite tell, but . . . was it? She grabbed her phone, tapped *editor a chef's life* into the search engine. And there she was. Older, of course. No longer the young woman Queenie B handpicked, the young woman Queenie B had nearly broken. The young woman who'd left her when she could no longer watch her employer destroy herself.

Saskia Specter.

Of all those she'd hurt and lost, Saskia was up there, just below Oz and Julian. Until seeing her picture, searching for her name, Regina didn't even realize it. Now the splinters embedded all those years ago pricked fresh, bleeding her from the inside.

Wide awake now, Regina read the letter from the editor in its entirety. Saskia wasn't just executive editor, she founded the magazine itself. It's mission: to speak to the hearts of chefs and food critics while still being accessible to food lovers of all kinds.

When had she gone from personal assistant to journalist? Regina wished she could remember anything personal about the young woman Saskia had been. Still, it couldn't be more perfect. Redemption, times two. Regina didn't even have it in her to feel devious about it. If Saskia would do it. Of course she'd do it. Saskia hadn't gotten to where she was by being stupid.

She couldn't call the magazine offices. No way she was getting through without name-dropping. But Saskia would—for ambition or love—take a call from an old friend of Queenie B's.

Tapping into her phone, Regina scrolled through the few numbers stored there to the one that would pick up any time of day or night.

"This better be a booty call."

"For fuck's sake, Marco, shut up and listen. I have a plan . . ."

30

Core: Removing the central section of fruits that contain seeds or tougher material that can't be eaten.

2016

I t's really simple. Forget about me. If either of you blab, it's bad for Gale."

"How is it bad for Gale?"

"Think about it, Lucy. If the producers find out, he could lose his spot on the show."

"But what if he wins and they disqualify him after the interview comes out?" Kyle asked.

"They can't disqualify him for who he knows," Regina said. "Sometimes the competitors have been mentored by the judges. What I'm saying is, if anything about me gets out before the competition ever happens, it could get Gale booted just to avoid any hassle."

"It's not about me." Gale's gut churned. "This is Regina's business. If she doesn't want people to know who she is, that's the end of it."

His mother stood, arms crossed, while his best friend sat, shoulders slumped. Marco perched on a counter nearby, elbows on his knees, head bowed, fingers entwined. Tense when he was never anything of the kind. He'd not said a word the whole time Regina spoke, which wasn't long. True to the woman Gale knew, her speech had been short and blunt.

"Well, I've known all this time and haven't said a word," Lucy said.

"Not even to my own husband. I'm a little insulted you thought I needed to be in on this meeting."

"It's not for you, Mrs. Carmichael." Kyle's head hung lower. "It's for me. But, honest, I'd never say a word. Not a single word. To anyone."

He's such a liar. You know he's already told everyone at work. Good thing no one'll believe him.

Gale gritted his teeth.

"Just be sure you keep it that way," Regina said, but she smiled a for-real smile. Gale couldn't help conjuring the lips, the bee, the logo. "For now, it's business as usual."

"What do you mean 'for now'?" his mother asked.

"Let's just get Gale through the competition, okay?" Regina glanced at the clock. "I have an appointment to get to. Lucy, go home. You look a wreck. Gale and Kyle can cover service prep."

"Me?"

"Aren't you staying?"

"Of course, Chef."

"Don't."

"Sorry. Regina?"

"Better."

He'll be here all the time, now that he knows.

"I could use an afternoon off my feet," Lucy said, and only then did Gale notice the rings under her eyes, and the way she rubbed her hands together, as if they hurt.

"You okay?" he asked.

"I'm fine, buddy. Never better."

She's not. She's worried about you, that all this is going to tip you over the edge. You got to be diligent, man. You have to prove—

"We have the kitchen covered," Gale said a little too loudly. He kissed his mother's cheek. "Go home."

Marco hopped down from the counter, heading to the door with Lucy and Regina. "See you tomorrow, Gale. We'll go over your grocery list."

"Heard, Chef." He tried to smile, didn't quite pull it off. The tension across his shoulders ached a bit. Too much chopping. Not enough sleep. That's all it was.

"I'll be back for service," Regina said. "Gale, plan on staying late. I have two practice crates set up for you."

"Can I stay and watch?" Kyle asked.

Told you so!

"Up to Gale. See you later."

"Do you care if I stay?" Kyle asked after they were gone. "I can jet after service. Seriously, I don't want—"

"Don't be an idiot. Stay."

"Sweet. Thanks."

He's going to be like a barnacle. Mark my words.

"I better call Jenara." Gale took out his phone. "Tell her I won't be over tonight."

"So you . . . did you tell her? About . . . you know."

"Of course not." Gale tapped her number, kind of wondering why he hadn't. That was boyfriend stuff, wasn't it? But it hadn't even occurred to him to tell her any more than it had to keep it from her. They were one in the same. Weren't they? Instead of calling he texted.

Hey, not gonna make it tonight practicing with reg

💩 I'm starting to get jealous. I never see you anymore.

Hadn't they just hung out? Work. Regina's. After-hours practice crates. He'd invited her to his parents' house for dinner—he cooked—but she'd been unable to make it. When had he seen Jenara last? Life was coming at him fast, these days.

Fifty thousand $$$

The only excuse he could grasp.

😂 Tomorrow night not taking no for an answer

It's a date

She's too possessive, man.

Gale tapped out. Lunch still needed to be finished before they could start on dinner. It'd go way faster with Kyle than with his mom. If Sean would knock it off, he might even have fun.

"You want to do sandwiches or cut up veg for salad?" he asked.

"What kind of sandwiches?"

"Does it matter?"

"Well." Kyle shuffled. "I thought I'd make one of my famous egg salads. Do you think she'd mind?"

"You stinking up the place?" Gale laughed. "Probably. There are deli meats in the walk-in, and a slicer on that rack over there."

"Oh." More shuffling. "I guess I'll do the veg. Meat slicers scare me."

Kyle got romaine, carrots, tomatoes, and bell peppers from the walk-in, set them onto the prep table. Gale wasn't overly fond of the meat slicer either, but he was probably the safer choice.

"Hey, Gale?"

"Yeah?" He carried the slicer to the prep table.

"It's kind of cool, don't you think?"

"What's cool?" The suction cups were superstrong. Once placed, moving the slicer was a process.

"You, being Queenie B's protégé and not even knowing it."

Gale dropped the edge of the slicer. "Don't call her that. And I'm not her protégé."

"Dude." Kyle shook his head. "You're nuts. You know how many chefs would kill for—?"

"I considered her my mentor way before I knew who she was. It doesn't matter to me. She's Regina. End of story."

"Mentor. Protégé. Same difference, dude. It's just cool, you know? Being here. Being part of a bigger story, even if my bit in it is really small."

He's jealous.

Gale wedged a butter knife under the suction cup, pried it up. Taking care to place the slicer correctly on the metal prep table, he didn't even tell Sean to shut up inside his head.

"I guess. Get chopping. We have a lot to do before she gets back."

Kyle chopped. Gale sliced. For a while, there was no other sound in the kitchen than the slicer's whir and the *thunk* of Kyle's knife. Even Sean kept quiet. Slice, slap, slice, slap. The repetition of motion lulled, though

Gale knew better than to lose focus. Losing a finger at this point in his life was probably not the best—

"I've been reading some stuff." Kyle's voice startled Gale, his finger too close to the blade. "Regina's . . . just wow. And all she's been through."

Slice, slap. Slice, slap. Gale couldn't regain the lull. "You shouldn't be prying."

"Why not? It's all out there. She's a celebrity. I'm curious, is all. I can't believe you're not."

"Well, I'm not."

Liar, liar, pants on fire, man.

"You don't have to worry. I'm not going to blab and I'm not going to, like, ask her shit. She kind of scared me before, but now?" He shrugged. "I don't know. Less scary, I guess."

"Less?"

Less?

"She was a train wreck, dude. I mean, like, a Charlie Sheen/Amy Winehouse train wreck. Maybe even worse."

"Don't you dare fucking pity her."

Kyle paused his chopping. "Calm down, dude. Why would you even think that?"

Gale unwrapped the deli meat. "Then what do you mean?"

"I'm in awe, I guess. She was just like us, once. Then she had it all, lost it all, and ended up here, a soup kitchen cook, making life better for people who need it. She made it out. Like you."

Unlike me.

"I'm not out. Not yet."

"But you're doing great." Kyle gave him that big doofy smile of his. "You know she's got to be bankrolling this whole thing, right?"

Gale turned off the slicer, watched the blade slow to a stop, exhaling a deep breath he hadn't felt go down. "I hadn't thought about it."

"So she must not have lost everything, even if that's what the internet said. Did you know she has a kid?"

Whoa.

"No."

"Yeah. He's about our age. Name's Julian. He has FAS or some shit, because she—"

"Enough." Gale knocked his knuckles on the metal table. "It's none of our business. She'd be pissed if she heard you talking about her life like it is. Now quit yapping and finish up the salad so we can start assembling sandwiches."

"You need to chill, dude. You're starting to sound just like her. Why are you so angry?"

"I'm not angry. I just don't think we should be talking about her. She's been—" Hiding? Incognito? Pretending? "—just Regina for a long time. Let it go."

He won't. He'll keep looking shit up, and if you won't listen to what he finds out, he'll tell someone, no matter what he promised.

"Whatever, dude." Kyle grabbed another large mixing bowl from the rack, plonked it on the table a little too hard. He started on the bell peppers, knife a blur even if his eyes were on Gale.

"You're going to cut off a finger."

"I could do this blindfolded."

Kyle's knife nevertheless slowed. Gale's heart fell to his stomach. Kyle was his best friend. Maybe his only friend. He wasn't angry with him, his curiosity, or even his prying, unless it came from the fact that Kyle did what Gale only wished he could. Rubbing a hand over his face, he leaned against the prep table. "I don't want anything to change."

"They've been changing since you first stepped foot in this place last year," Kyle told him.

This time last year, there was no Regina's Kitchen, no Regina, no Jenara, no sous position at Marco's, a job he earned long before Marco knew his old friend was also Gale's mentor.

"I guess."

Kyle set his knife down, leaned as Gale leaned. "Be happy, dude. It's all good stuff."

"Is it?" he said. "Because she's not going to stay, you know. Here in Rock Landing, or even New Haven."

"Probably not. I hadn't thought that far."

Gale crossed his arms over his abdomen, hunching a little when Kyle placed a hand between his shoulder blades. "Once people know she's here, this place stops being a soup kitchen for the local poor and homeless. People will come from everywhere. She'll leave before that happens."

"But we're not going to say anything to anyone, dude. No one's going to know."

I can't do it again.

Gale swallowed the bile rising.

I can't run.

Sour. Burning.

"Dude, you okay?"

I can't hide.

That left only one option that Gale could think of.

"It's only a matter of time."

"Then don't think too far ahead." Kyle rubbed rough circles on Gale's back. "Everything's going to turn out great. You'll see."

Gale met Kyle's big silly smile with the best he could manage, which seemed to satisfy his friend because he went back to chopping as if their conversation never interrupted it. Gale wished he could put things from his mind even half as easily. Maybe it made Kyle look a little clueless sometimes, but Gale was one hundred percent certain he didn't stare at the ceiling most nights, just trying to get his brain to stop.

Gale grabbed a loaf of whole wheat bread and brought it to the prep table. Sandwich assembly wasn't lulling like the slicer had been, but he could go on autopilot and not lose a finger for it. Bread, meat, cheese, mayo, bread. Over and over. The repetition should have soothed somewhat, but it didn't. It gave his brain room to chew on his own words. On Kyle's. Even Sean's. And it came down to the fact that the life he liked—Marco's, Jenara, Regina, the soup kitchen—was on a collision course with Queenie B and there was absolutely nothing Gale Carmichael could do to stop it.

31

Braise: Cooking method that first sears the food at a high temp, then finishes in a covered pot at a low temp while sitting in some form of liquid.

2016

Regina hadn't dressed up for the occasion. Better to be who she'd been since vanishing than risk showing up as Queenie B now. Not yet, at any rate. It was coming. Probably soon. She hoped soon. Because the buildup inside her wavered less toward scared and more toward enthusiastic this last week of waiting for the call. For this lunch. For this. Besides, it was only Marco's.

Marco approached her table, brow furrowed and eyes on his cell phone. "She's running a little late. You want a soda or something?"

"Sure. Thanks."

Traffic? Maybe. More than likely, she was a very busy woman taking time out of her day to speak with an old friend of her ex-boss, who happened to be Queenie B. Only the fact that Marco's former relationship to Queenie and her local-access television show from eons ago was easily verifiable made him worth Saskia's effort. This, alone, gave Regina confidence in her plan. If talking to an ancient acquaintance of Queenie B's could get the executive editor and founder of *A Chef's Life* magazine—cautiously well-regarded in the industry, as she'd discovered—out to New Haven,

Connecticut, from her offices in Manhattan, Regina was more than certain she'd be interested in an exclusive.

Close to certain.

Marginally.

If the bridge leading to Saskia Specter was only singed, rather than incinerated.

"Hello?"

There she was. Standing at the hostess stand, taking off her coat. Queenie had loved her more than most, even when Saskia left her. Maybe because she'd had the courage to leave her when staying might have been heartbreaking but better for her career.

I'm sorry. Saskia, I'm so, so sorry.

Words, as a young woman, Saskia had heard too often through those insane years. Used and abused years. Queenie had lied to and sometimes fooled her. Like everyone else in her life. Regina forgot most of them. They hadn't mattered, then or now, truth be told. But how did one truly apologize when the apology was too long in the offering? When words were insufficient?

You offered the chance of a lifetime, for the second time, and hoped.

Regina rose to her feet. "Over here."

Marco came out of the bar area that same moment, backed quietly away. Saskia stood frozen at the hostess stand, face betraying nothing.

And then her lip trembled. "Queenie?"

"I go by Regina these days."

Saskia crossed the dining room in a rush, as if she would take Regina in her arms and pull her in tight. Had she always been so tall? Regina didn't remember that, but she supposed, even as a younger woman, Saskia had been able to look Osvaldo in the eye.

Saskia stopped just short of the anticipated—Dreaded? Wished for?—hug. "I can't believe it's you."

"It's me. Sit."

Saskia sat. More like her legs gave way and a chair happened to be there. Regina sat in the chair adjacent. Silence fell. Saskia couldn't seem to stop staring.

And then there was Marco, setting a glass of soda in front of Regina, a white wine for Saskia. "You ladies ready for food?"

Saskia blinked, and she smiled even if it was a little stiff. "You must be Marco."

"That's my name, don't wear it out."

"Has she been here in New Haven with you? All this time?"

"We're not there yet," Regina cut in. "Marco, food."

"Sure thing."

Saskia sipped her wine. "I don't usually drink during the day," she said. "But I think the occasion warrants it." She looked pointedly at the glass of soda on the table. Regina chose to ignore it. The topic would come up again—her sobriety, her vanishing act, her rise from the ashes of the life she'd destroyed—just not now.

"I'm assuming this isn't a social call." Saskia set her wineglass down. "So I'll dispense with the niceties for the moment. Why did you have Marco arrange this?"

Right to the point. She'd always liked that about Saskia.

"It's time I come out of hiding," Regina said, "and I'm offering you the exclusive. Where I've been, what I've been doing, where I'm going. That kind of thing."

To her credit, Saskia took it in stride, wiping the lipstick from the rim of her glass with a slightly shaking thumb her only reaction. "That's fluff," she said. "And unbefitting the occasion. That's not what you want."

Regina sat up straighter. "No. It's not."

"What do you want, Queenie? Really?"

She'd never dared to think this would be easy; neither had she considered just how hard it would be to say the words she practiced—

My story isn't over. I want a happier ending. Marco's idea of a quotable response to the inevitable question.

The chance to make things right. Hers. She'd done her penance, atoned as she could. But it wasn't the truth, and it wouldn't come out of her mouth.

"I fucked up everything," she blurted, "but I worked damn hard for what I had. I miss it. All of it. I didn't, but now I do. Most of it, anyway."

"Fame? Fortune?"

"I still have both." Regina almost reached across the table to grab her hand. "It doesn't matter what I did or how long I've been gone. I miss the life, Saskia. I miss the people, the culture, even some of the chaos. But what I miss the most is the food. The joy of discovery and creation. Haute cuisine or low country, it's everything."

"And I'm your path of least resistance. My magazine."

"Exactly." Regina smiled, let Queenie shine.

Saskia rewarded her with laughter. "You haven't changed."

"I'll be honest, I'm scared shitless. I'm fully aware of what a mess I was, that there are some bridges I can never mend. Barely a day goes by that I don't crave the oblivion I used to live in, especially since making this decision. But I haven't felt this . . . this . . ." Happy? Alive? Hopeful? ". . . focused in a long time. My best shot is a sort of soft open, letting some of the dust settle before I have to be in the spotlight again. You get the story of your career; I get to come back on my terms. Win, win."

Saskia squinted one eye. "I'd say, 'Aren't you full of yourself?' but we both know you are." And half a smile. "With reason. So let me ask you something."

"All right."

"I've seen you with my own eyes. I know where you are, where you've been, who you've been with." She gestured to the door Marco most assuredly hid behind. "What if I say no?"

"You won't."

Her nose wrinkled. "Indulge me."

Marco backed out of the kitchen bearing a platter and a breadbasket, a culinary hero on his improvised white horse. "Here we go, ladies." Though he met only Regina's eyes. "House-roasted red peppers, fontina and provolone, house-prepared tapenade, sun-dried tomatoes and"—he set the breadbasket beside the antipasto—"fresh bread. Not house-made. Rocco's."

"It looks lovely," Saskia said. "Thank you."

"Yeah, thanks," Regina echoed, then, "Now beat it."

But she smiled and Marco backed his way to the kitchen with a wink. "He thinks he needs to save me from the tough questions."

"You've never needed saving."

"There's a whole lot of people who'd disagree with that."

"I'll spare you the whole 'you only needed to save yourself' speech, because obviously, you did, and it's all pretty trite at this point anyway. So?"

Regina placed a variety of victuals on a plate, handed it to Saskia before filling one for herself. Stalling. Trying to find the right words, settled for, "If you say no, then report to the world I'm staging a comeback, I'd handle it. Maybe not well, but I'm not the Queenie B I used to be. I'm the Regina I was when it all began. Better. Wiser. A hell of a lot fatter. I've made up my mind, Sas. You know better than most there's little anyone can do to change it. With you or without you, this is happening."

"And you knew before you had Marco call I wouldn't refuse." Saskia held her gaze, unblinking. Half smiling. Love and memory. Skepticism. Hope.

Regina grinned. "Of course I did."

"Why now?"

Gale, of course. On many levels. "You'll find out soon enough."

"All right, then." Saskia's gaze held a moment more before falling to the food on her plate. "Shall we? This tapenade looks especially delicious."

"That's because I made it." Regina grinned. "Marco did the rest."

"Then you're still cooking?"

"In a matter of speaking, but let's not get ahead of things." Regina popped a slice of fontina in her mouth. "I have a . . . let's say a request."

"That's actually a demand."

"Tomato, tomahto."

"Go for it."

"I stay vanished until the day the interview drops. My life is about to get blitzed, and there are things I need to make happen before the circus begins."

"That goes without saying. If I could put you in a closet until the interview drops, I'd be even happier. Anyone involved with production will be required to sign an NDA. I'm assuming you're sober." She gestured to the glass of soda.

"As a nun on Sunday. Almost since Rome."

"That's a long time." Saskia nodded, sipping her wine. "Like I said, this isn't going to be a fluff piece, Regina. I'm going to hit you hard. Will you be able to handle that?"

"I expected nothing less." It wasn't an answer, but Regina feared tempting the fates with some optimistic declaration she'd not had to put to the test in a long, long time. "That brings up another demand."

"No mincing words, huh? Okay. Let's hear it."

"I won't talk about Julian. Osvaldo, okay, but nothing about my son."

"I can live with that. But I have one condition."

Regina quirked an eyebrow.

"*A Chef's Life* gets a three-month exclusive. You give no other interviews."

"I'm coming out of hiding, not diving back into that pandemonium." Regina heaved a huge, silent sigh. "There won't be any other articles or interviews. Not that I'll take part in."

"There's going to be backlash. You're going to need an advocate big enough to counter it."

Regina grinned. "Angling for a follow-up?"

So did Saskia. "Naturally."

Of course, Saskia was right. The backlash would be swift and brutal. Journalists would come crawling out of the woodwork, finding stories wherever they could. Breaking off a hunk of bread, Regina waved it like a maestra's baton. "I'll give you a six-month exclusive. That includes two follow-ups in *A Chef's Life* during that time. Good?"

"Way more than I could have hoped for."

Way more than Regina had planned to offer, but this worked out well for both of them. "Then we have a deal."

Saskia took her offered hand. "We have a deal. I'll get my department started on a contract. If all goes well, we can begin the interview process in the next couple of weeks."

"ASAP," Regina told her. "I want this done last week."

"Just like old times." Saskia's voice broke. Pressing her napkin to trembling lips, she kept it there until she regained her composure. "Sorry, it's just . . . dammit, Queenie. It's so good to see you."

Regina still had Saskia's hand in hers, no longer a deal being made. A truce or a lifeline. A promise of a different kind. Hers or Saskia's or Queenie B's. Gently squeezing her former-assistant/future-editor's hand, Regina swallowed down the emotional, the trite, the pat—*It's good to see you too*—nevertheless sincere response. Instead, she said, "Let's hope you still feel that way in six months," and let go of Saskia's hand. "I hope you're still hungry. I'm pretty sure Marco made Bolognese. I'll deny it if you say it, but it's better than mine."

MARCO INDEED BROUGHT OUT PLATES OF RIGATONI BOLOGNESE. HEAVY, for lunch, but Regina appreciated the private sentiment. Her hero, indeed. She and Saskia ate. They chatted, mostly about Saskia and her magazine, her husband and children. Nothing about Regina or Queenie. Not yet. Only Gale and the importance of timing the release of the article to come after the *Cut!* competition. Saskia agreed to release it after the Grand Redemption Championship filmed, should Gale make it through the first round. Tight, but Saskia promised to bump articles and lash her entire staff if need be. She was editor in chief; if she said it would be done, it would be.

"I'll get that contract to you by the weekend." Saskia slipped into her coat at the hostess stand, wrapped her scarf around her neck. "Early next week at the latest. Should I send it to your lawyers? Do you have an agent?"

Deep, deep breath. "I'll text you the info."

"Perfect. Okay, then. I guess I'll speak with you next week." Hesitating, Saskia bravely threw her arms around Regina, hugged her until Regina hugged her back. "This is the start of something great. You know that, right?"

"Something, anyway."

Jostling her back and forth, Saskia kissed both her cheeks before hurrying out of Marco's and into the cold New Haven winter.

Regina stood in the vestibule until she couldn't see her anymore. The afternoon had passed quickly and gone better than she could have asked. Saskia Specter was older, wiser, more poised and wicked smart, but she was also kind and compassionate. Still—not to be smug, but hey, Regina was who she was—she knew that even after all these years, Saskia was more than a little captivated by the queen. By memories of the past or hope for their coming future, it didn't matter. It felt good, and Regina chose to bask in it.

Marco's arm slipped around her shoulders. "Everything you hoped for?"

"Don't pretend you weren't listening to every word." She elbowed him, sort of gently. "Thanks for closing down service."

He kissed her temple. "Queenie B still moves and shakes the world, huh?"

After all this time. After all she'd done.

"Yeah."

There was no way she was coming out of this unscathed; dropping out of the culinary scene at the height of her infamy, if not of her glory, had only forestalled the inevitable. The culinary world would react, some kindly, some curiously, some vindictively; at least Regina had chosen how it would begin. It was, indeed, something.

"Don't forget me when you're famous this time."

"Don't be an asshole."

It was everything.

32

SOS: Sauce on [the] side.

2016

True to her word, Saskia delivered the promised contract before the weekend, not to the lawyers Regina kept on retainer, but to Regina herself. Though she bullied Marco into going over it with her, it was straightforward, honest, and exactly what Regina wanted. That Saskia was also and most certainly ensuring the continued success and survival of her still-fledgling magazine was irrelevant, and personally satisfying. It was the only apology Regina could offer that was actually worth a damn. Step one of her rise from the ashes done, Regina could focus on step two. And three, four, fifteen . . .

The qualifier round of the Grand Redemption Championship loomed. No matter what crate she concocted, Gale smoked it. Pickled herring and eggplant lasagna became fried herring bites with a caponata dipping sauce. Oyster crackers, preserved lemon, and candied bacon became maybe not the best lemon meringue pie Regina had ever eaten, but pretty damn good.

"You're as ready as you're going to be," Regina told him the night before he left for his qualifier round in New York. "You feeling good?"

"I am."

"Just do your best. Don't get flustered. You're a star."

He'd hugged her then, quick and close and gone.

The day of taping, Regina was as useless as Lucy used to be in the kitchen. It was nothing like the first time Gale competed; then, she'd been cool, prepared for either outcome. Now, she wanted him to win. So bad. That was Queenie, had to be. Queenie wanted Gale to do her proud, to bring home the prize. Queenie loved that rush, the accolades. Queenie couldn't exist without them. Regina had to keep reminding herself that she could and had for all these years.

Kyle came in to help out, cheerful and optimistic, certain Gale was going to win. Without Kyle the meal service would have been disastrous. He wasn't great chef material, but he was competent and willing. A good follower with the ability, if not the ambition, to be a good leader.

Regina wasn't stupid; Kyle's sudden willingness to volunteer so much of his time had everything to do with who she was. She was okay with that. It was honest, and understandable.

After service was finished and the morning prepped for, Marco showed up with dinner—pollo scarpariello—even though it was her turn to cook. He didn't ask her if she'd heard from Gale. She didn't ask him. He'd call. One of them. Her, of course. Marco pretended not to be jealous of that.

Long hours after Marco went to bed, Regina sat in a club chair by the fire, wrapped in a blanket and legs tucked up, reading over the pages Saskia had sent her and trying not to worry about not hearing from Gale. Preliminary stuff, but it had been rough. Saskia hadn't been kidding about not pulling any punches, especially the bits revisiting a past she barely remembered. But she trusted Saskia to have the details right. Saskia had absorbed and processed all that had been Queenie B. To rise from the ashes meant first to burst into flame. Queenie B had done her part; it was Regina's turn to do the same.

A crash of empty crates in the yard. Chickens squawked madly in their coop. Marco was already at the overlooking window before Regina could untangle herself from her blanket.

"There's someone out there," he said.

"What was your first clue?"

Bam! Bam! Bam! A fist on the back door. A muffled shout. Whoever it was had hopped the chain-link fence. Had to be a young someone. Probably high. Probably hungry. Sense told her to call the police. Compassion forbid it.

"Dammit." She jammed on her Crocs, flew down the steps, Marco close on her heels.

The pounding continued. Less forcefully, then more. Regina struggled with the locks, yanked open the door, a mag flashlight raised to the body stumbling forward.

"Gale?"

He reeked of alcohol, fell into her arms. Marco caught them both before they tumbled. Righting herself, she grasped Gale by the arms and hauled him all the way inside before closing the door behind him.

Oh, Gale.

She wouldn't say it aloud. She couldn't. He'd be harder on himself tomorrow than she could ever be. Leading him to a chair, she peeled off his coat and handed it to Marco.

"What happened?"

Now Gale was sobbing. Racking sobs that pulled so hard at her heart, she felt the tendons and muscles stretch.

"Gale, come on. It can't be that bad. You've lost before."

His head came up. Eyes bloodshot and bleary. Face streaked by tears. A smile splitting his face like a horror-show clown. "I won," he said. "I fucking won."

GALE SAT WITH REGINA IN HER APARTMENT ABOVE THE KITCHEN, HANDS wrapped around a mug of coffee that couldn't hope to counter all the alcohol in his system. He wished he could remember how it happened. Exactly how it happened.

You totally remember.

Gale slurped his coffee.

Own it, man. Lie to yourself and it'll be worse.

Regina sat opposite him, her hand reaching for his. Gale could almost weep all over again. Her brutal kindness. Her harsh understanding. She was the only place he considered going to when all was said and done. Not Jenara. Not Marco or Kyle or even his mom. Regina.

"I'm going to hit the road." Marco slipped his coat on, kissed Regina's lips. Gale's heart swelled. He loved these two people to an absurd degree. Tears stung. He slurped again.

The door closed softly. Regina's hand squeezed his. "So, you won, huh?"

He nodded.

"Care to elaborate?"

"I smoked the other contestants." He sniffed. "Every round. I won them all. Even dessert."

"What'd you make?"

"Brie ice cream in a cone cup of crushed Pringles and chocolate shell made with olive oil."

"Wow."

"That's what the judges said." He went to rub his eyes, forgetting he had coffee in his hands. It spilled. "Sorry."

Regina mopped it up with a dish towel. "Don't worry."

"I couldn't believe it," he said. "I mean, I knew I took every round. But when Tom cut my competitor after the last round, I nearly fainted."

"You did not."

"No, I did. Everything went kind of fuzzy. I honestly don't remember much of what happened after that. My brain just . . . cut out. I sort of remember the postcompetition interview and all that, but we finished early and I ended up in a bar with some of the producers and the other contestants and I . . . I fucked up, Regina. I fucked up bad."

"Yeah, you did." She brushed the hair from his face. "But one slip doesn't make you a failure."

That's technically the definition of failing.

Gale closed his eyes. The specter grimaced. Head swimming, stomach roiling, he really had no recollection of taking that first drink, or how many he belted back after that. He almost remembered emptying the livery-car's minibar, maintaining the warmth, the comfort, the way alcohol made his thoughts slow and his mind drift away from the fact that he'd won. That he'd have to do it all again. That he had a real shot at fifty grand, and everyone would be counting on him and failure wasn't just his if he lost. It was Regina's. Queenie-Fucking-B's.

"Ohhh." Gale pushed away his coffee. "I think I'm going to puke."

"Not in here, you're not. Let's go, hero."

Her shoulder in his armpit, Regina helped him to the bathroom. Gale wanted to vomit, knew he'd feel better if he did, but couldn't. Dry heaving, brain sloshing, thoughts muddling, he couldn't tell if he was still drunk on alcohol or anxiety. He slumped against the toilet, trying not to cry again, and failing miserably.

"Just stay put. I'm going to draw you a bath." Regina pointed. "I'll be right in there. Okay?"

Gale nodded without picking his head up. In the adjoining room, water roared. It made him weep all the harder.

Jeez, man. Get it together.

"Fuck you."

This is what I died for? For you to have it all only to throw it away? Jenara's going to kick your ass to the curb. Marco's going to fire you. Regina's—

"I said shut up!"

No, you said "fuck you."

"Well, fuck you and shut up."

It should have been you who overdosed. Not me. You're the one who bought the drugs. You're the one who talked me into it. You're the one who found a vein when I couldn't.

"*You* bought them. *You* talked *me* into it."

Convenient memory to have, man. Lets you off the hook, doesn't it? I notice you don't deny finding the vein I couldn't.

Gale pressed hands over his ears, as if it would silence Sean. His lies. His truth. As if he could banish that ghost now like a horror-show zombie, shambling and coming apart, bit by rotten bit. Half dead. Never gone. Always there. Always waiting to strike.

"Hey, hey, hey." Regina was there, pulling his hands from his ears and him into her arms. "Gale, it's okay. Come on. You're all right."

She helped him to his feet, out of his clothes, into the bath. Coconut-scented warmth invaded his skin, his nose. Coconut cream pie. Coconut curry. Coconut carrot soup. Bubbles soothed bunched muscles, swallowed his tears. Regina petted his head, trickled water onto his cheeks. A little by a lot, Gale calmed down enough to understand just how drunk he actually was.

I'm sorry, man. I didn't mean all that.

But Sean meant every word. Head lolling, Gale gazed up at Regina still petting him like he'd had a nightmare.

"You must have been a good mom." He smiled despite tears now gently rolling.

"No. I wasn't." Still petting. Over and over. "I lost custody of my son a long time ago."

"Because of . . . you know."

"Yeah."

"I'm sorry."

"Me too."

"He's about my same age, isn't he? Julian."

Regina's petting faltered, only a moment. "A little younger than you."

"Oh." Gale closed his eyes, sunk lower in the tub. His buzz slipped closer to alcohol-induced slumber. Yes. Oblivion. Turn off. One more drink or ten, and he'd slip away.

Gale. Gale, come on. Come on—

"Gale." Regina was tapping his cheek. "Stay with me."

Tears trickled, joined the coconut-scented bubbles. "I killed my best friend," he said. "It was all my fault."

"We all make our choices." She didn't miss a beat. "Your friend made his."

Listen to her. It wasn't your fault.

"It's all so mixed-up in my head." Gale choked.

"I know." Regina stroked his cheek. "I know exactly."

Gale leaned into her hand. "Please don't tell my mom I fucked up. Or Jenara."

"I won't. But you will. Hiding isn't going to change what happened." She sighed. "Believe me, I know that too."

She knew. Regina knew everything. Gale sniffed back tears, closed his eyes. "I love you, Regina. I mean it. I really love you."

"Yeah, yeah, yeah." Flying red lips chased a bee. "I love you too."

Slumber oozed up from the warm water again. Gale slid lower. Lower. "No, you don't."

Water cascaded over his head. Gale shot up, wiping bubbles from his face. "Hey!"

"No sleep for you until some of that alcohol works its way out of your system." Regina hooked an arm under his shoulder, pulled him upright. "Come on. Let's get you dried off. I have a robe you can wear."

Out of the warm tub, Gale shivered. That he was completely naked and dripping skipped just out of self-conscious reach. The softness of the towel registered higher than that it was Regina toweling him off. Cloth at least as soft as the towel enveloped him, shoulders to knees.

"It'll do." Regina tied the sash. "Let's get some food into you. Marco left some of his scarpariello."

Food. The all. The everything.

Gale was suddenly ravenous. Aside from tasting the components for his own dishes during the competition, he was pretty sure he hadn't eaten all day.

Regina set a plate of food in front of him. He shoveled it in, pretending not to hear Regina on the phone with his mother, telling her Gale was with her, exhausted and a little worse for wear. He was spending the night, and would she let Jenara know? Thanks, it's better to not have her worry. He pretended, because if he didn't, he'd be a sobbing, quivering mess again.

You fucked up, man, but it doesn't mean you'll do it again.

Make up your mind, Sean.

No. You make up your mind, Gale.

He closed his eyes, breathed in deeply through his nose because his mouth was full of delicious food. He could taste it, even drunk as he was. Tomorrow, he would pay the price of his fuckup, but at least, unlike Sean, he'd live to fuck up another day.

33

À la carte: Separately priced items from a menu, not a meal set.

2016

"Nothing doing."

Regina took the apron Gale had been about to put on the next morning, in the hopes of pretending last night hadn't happened. Idiot.

"I'm all ready for breakfast. You, go. You have some people to see."

Jenara. Mom. Marco. Even Kyle. They all knew by now. He'd told them as much by not telling them anything at all. While they all covered for him, excited and happy for this mad opportunity, he'd let them all down.

They love you, man. You owe them.

He couldn't face his mother. Not yet. He called, not texted, Jenara first. That she was breaking up with him was a given; better to get it over with.

"Diner. Fifteen minutes."

That's all she'd said. Obedient as a chastised dog, he was there in ten, waiting.

"I got you coffee," he said when she slid into the booth. "I didn't know if you'd want anything else."

"Good call." She sipped hers black. "This coffee really does suck."

He couldn't laugh. Apparently, neither could she.

"I won't make excuses," Gale told her. "I messed up. Over two years sober, and I messed up on one of the best days of my life."

Now Jenara smiled. "You won?"

He managed one too. "Don't tell anyone. I could get disqualified."

"Gale, that's fabulous!"

"Shh." How could she be so cool? So amazing. His smile faded. "I'm sorry, Jenara. If you want to break up with me, I totally—"

Jenara took his hand across the table. "I'm not breaking up with you. I love you, but I have my own form of PTSD when it comes to this kind of thing. I need a few days to process."

"It's never going to happen again."

"I know you mean that. I hope it's true, but . . . just give me a few days. I'll call you."

"Okay."

"I needed to see you with my own eyes. Now I have." Sliding her hand from his, she got up from the table, coffee untouched but for that first, gross sip. "One slip can either be just that, or the excuse you use to slip again," she said. "Don't let it be the second one."

Yeah, what she said.

"I can't be your watchdog," she said, more gently than he deserved. "Been there. Done that. It never works. This is up to you, Gale. Okay?"

"Okay. Yeah."

Eloquent, man. That's sure to instill confidence.

Jenara traced the line of his jaw, smiling sadly, but smiling. She bent and touched a kiss to his cheek. "Congratulations," she said and left without a backward glance. Gale's heart kept time with the mass of curls bouncing down her back. Life had been too good to be true. All of it.

"That's the last I'll see of her."

Not if you don't fuck up again.

"I can't put her through it."

You won't if you don't fuck up again.

"And Alicia." Gale put his head in his hands. "I don't deserve either of them."

Come on, man. You know where this leads.

"Can I get you anything else?" A waitress Gale didn't recognize stood over him, pen in hand.

"No, just the check."

She tore it from her pad, slapped it onto the table. "Have a good day!"

Far too cheery for his mood. Gale nodded, put a five on the table, and left the warm diner for the cold street. Breath fogging, fingers freezing, he started texting his mother and stopped. He should go see her. She deserved that much. Anxiety rushed through his body, pooled in his cheeks. He couldn't face her. Couldn't see that look in her eyes. The terror. The disappointment. The sorrow. Gale called instead.

Chickenshit.

"Fuck y—"

"Hey, buddy!" A little shrill. Lucy Carmichael had seen it all, heard it all, and couldn't be, wouldn't be fooled ever again. "Big day yesterday! How are you this morning?"

"I know Regina called you, Mom."

"Oh."

His heart hammered way too fast. Gale could barely breathe. "I went to a bar," rushed out of his mouth. "I got shit-faced after the show. I'm sorry."

Dead silence, then, "Oh, thank god."

"Huh?"

"I was afraid it was worse. I knew Regina wasn't telling me every-thing, and I thought . . . I thought . . ."

"It wasn't that," he told her. "But it was bad enough. I have no excuse. It was stupid. I'm sorry I let you down."

Again.

"I'm sorry you let yourself down." She sighed. "But you know what they say. Get back on the horse. Or . . . off? I don't know. You know what I mean."

Too shrill again. False cheer. Panic he knew was doing terrible things to her wonky heart. Everything welled up again. Every thought, fear, im-pulse. Gale held his breath. Willed it all back down. He could promise her never again, but she wouldn't believe him any more than Jenara could. He'd promised so many times before.

It's different this time, man. Make it different.

How could it be any different? The cycle he only ever saw in hindsight was the same. Success after failure after failure after success. The rush of thoughts and sensations overwhelming him was never going away, and neither would that need for oblivion. Gale didn't know how to change it. *If* he could change it.

"Gale? Honey? You still there?"

He put one foot in front of the other, partly so he wouldn't freeze, partly, simply, to move. "I'm so sorry, Mom. I love you so much."

"I love you too, buddy. Always and forever. No matter what."

You got a good mom, you lucky dog.

"I'll be better. I swear."

She didn't answer, and Gale knew it was because she couldn't. He imagined her silent tears, the relief and the sorrow and the fear all mixing together in a confusion she could never parcel out.

Tell her, man. Give her something.

"There's something else I have to tell you," he said. "Don't worry. It's nothing bad."

She sniffed. "Okay."

"I won."

"You . . . you won?"

And now Gale imagined her smile, that instant proud-mama moment lifting at least a little of the burden. "Every round. I don't know when the next set of rounds is, exactly, but I get to compete for the fifty grand . . ."

GALE TALKED TO HIS MOTHER THE WHOLE WALK HOME. MAYBE IT DIDN'T DO all that much to allay her fears, but it made him feel a hell of a lot better. She promised not to tell anyone, not even his dad, about the win, and maybe that meant she wasn't telling him about the bar either.

Gale felt bad, but he hadn't asked her not to tell. Lucy Carmichael was good at keeping secrets; she'd been doing it for him a long time. And if his father, after all, knew too, he never let on, so he had to be good at keeping secrets, too.

At work that night, Marco didn't say a word. About anything. He didn't watch Gale more closely or pretend nothing happened; he just acted the way he always did with nothing more than a grim sort of nod when Gale entered the kitchen. Likewise, the next day, Regina had returned to her normal self, all signs of the motherly woman who gave him a bath, food, and a place to sleep it off gone. Four days later, life was kind of back to the way it had been before his greatest achievement collided with his most recent failure.

And Jenara hadn't called.

Sitting at his kitchen table, eating a bowl of cereal, Gale watched an old cartoon he, Sean, and Kyle had been obsessed with when they were teens. The picture quality on the communal laptop was awful to begin with, and the cartoon itself had to be fifteen years old. Was the animation always that bad? Gale laughed anyway. Funny was funny, even if his stomach still felt kind of hollow.

"Dude, where've you been?" Kyle pulled a kitchen chair up beside Gale's. "You don't answer your phone anymore?"

"Sorry. Work. Regina's. It's been a crazy few days since . . . you know."

"Yeah." Kyle leaned over to see the computer screen. "Shit. I don't think I've watched this show since we were in high school."

"It's still on."

"Seriously? I wonder if it's still funny."

"I don't think I want to know." Gale pointed his spoon at the screen. "Better to remember it fondly."

"True. Pass the milk and cereal, will you?"

Gale passed him both. Kyle got himself a bowl and spoon. They sat side by side, crunching their sugary breakfast and watching old cartoons, not speaking. Just like the old days.

Not like the old days, man. Come clean. You know he knows, anyway. Just like everyone else.

Pushing his bowl away, Gale heaved a huge, fortifying sigh that didn't really help much. "I fucked up. After the taping. Fucked up bad."

Kyle swallowed. Milk flecked the corners of his mouth. "I figured."

"How?"

"Your mom called in a panic that night."

"Before or after Regina called her?"

"After, apparently. She . . . uh . . . asked me to search your room."

"Did you?"

Stirring the colorful milk, Kyle nodded. "I had to, dude. She was, you know, freaking out. I was, too."

"It's okay."

"If it helps any," Kyle said, "it made us both feel better when I came up with nothing."

"It was alcohol, not drugs."

"Alcohol is drugs, dude. Just the legal kind."

"Yeah, I know." Another fortifying sigh that didn't do jack shit. "I don't know how it happened."

Fercrissake, this is Kyle, man. Kyle!

Gale hung his head. Four days pretending he could just go back to life as it had been. Pretending nothing had changed. But everything had, and it wasn't just his fuckup. It was winning. It was setting foot on a new path when he had absolutely no idea where it led. Deep breaths were just not going to cut it.

The truth shall set you free, my man.

"I'm lying." He exhaled the words. Oh, how they stung. "I went to that bar knowing it was a mistake. What was going to happen. I went anyway."

The bar. The other contestants. The producers and the camera crew and the interns. All buying rounds, celebrating his win.

"I never even pretended I wasn't going to drink every shot that got put in my hand."

"Sometimes the demons win." Kyle heaved a deep breath. "Put it behind you. It's all you can do, right?"

Gale tried hard not to cry. It hurt to cry. It hurt not to. "Two years, down the shitter."

"That's not true."

"No? I'm back to square one in the trust department. My mom, Jenara, Regina, Marco. You."

"Not square one." Kyle nudged him with his shoulder. "Maybe square five."

"What does that even mean?"

"It means you fucked up, but you kept it cool for two years. And, it wasn't, you know . . . the other stuff."

"You can say *heroin*."

Kyle shuddered theatrically. "It feels like saying *Voldemort*."

Gale snorted, laughter tumbling from his lips.

He got you, man.

"I'm sorry, Kyle. I swear, it's not going to get there again. Shit-faced as I was, I swear it wasn't even a consideration."

Kyle smiled sadly. Maybe it was hopefully. Gale didn't trust himself to decipher which, but it sure as hell wasn't confidently.

"Don't apologize to me, dude. I'm here for you. No matter what."

He always has been. If not for him, you'd probably be dead too.

Gale had thought talking to Mom would be the worst. Or Jenara. They weren't. Because he'd been avoiding Kyle for days without acknowledging—

"Why?"

"Huh?"

"Why, Kyle? After everything, why have you stuck it out when no one else but my mother has? Even my dad and brother checked out. Don't get me wrong, I don't blame them, but . . ." Gale pressed fingers to his eyes, smooshing away the tears. "I killed Sean. My best friend. *Our* best friend. I let you down a million times, a million ways. Why are you still here?"

Kyle put an arm around Gale's shoulders in that gruff and tender way of old friends not completely comfortable with displays of affection. "Where else am I going to be, dude? It's you and me. Been that way since we were kids. It's never going to change." Letting him go, Kyle shoved him in that same gruff and tender way. "And you didn't kill Sean. Sean killed Sean. That you didn't die too doesn't make you a murderer."

And here it came, that thing that would break them if anything could.

Don't do it, man.

"Finding a vein for him does though."

Kyle pulled away. A needle hitting a nerve would have hurt less. Spectral rage burned in his periphery.

You know why you're doing this. You know what you're planning. Go ahead. Use this. Fucking use me! You're an asshole.

"Is that what you remember?" Kyle asked. "For real? Because, that's bad shit, dude. I mean, really bad shit."

"I wish . . ." Gale sputtered, choked on the pain of his own words. He wailed, "I don't know if he bought the stuff and talked me into it or the other way around. I don't know if I helped him find a spot or he helped me. It's all fucked-up in my head, Kyle. I don't know what happened or how or in what order. I'm never going to. But he's dead. He's fucking dead. And I'm sure as hell not innocent."

Pushing his chair away from the table, Kyle got up, fingers tugging at his hair. A pit opened up underneath Gale, one promising the kind of oblivion drinking himself blind hadn't provided, could never provide. Then Kyle's arms were around him, hugging him close from behind. Gale grabbed those arms with both hands, holding so tight it had to hurt.

"Sean made his choice, same as you," Kyle said. "He died, you didn't. End of story."

Kyle held him until the choking eased; Gale had no idea how long. Sean stayed surprisingly quiet through it all, though Gale could feel him there. Waiting.

"I'm sorry, Kyle. I shouldn't lay all this on you."

He let go of Kyle, or Kyle let go of him. Either way, his friend was in his chair again, forcing him to meet his eyes. "I'm probably talking out of my ass, but maybe that's part of the problem, Gale. You don't talk about it. You never did. You're not the kind of guy who can bottle it all up and hope to survive the boom."

Gale ripped a paper towel from the roll they kept on the table. Mopped his face. Blew his nose. "It's a lot to expect someone else to carry."

"Not carry, dude. And there are professionals who get paid for that shit."

Another paper towel. No words.

"I've never seen you happier than you've been since . . . I was going to say Jenara, but really, it's since we went to the soup kitchen that first time. Things started happening for you then, dude. Regina, getting the sous job. The competition and Jenara. The Grand Redemption Championship and the chance to win fifty-fucking-grand! You got to let yourself be happy."

"But you just said I *was* happy."

Kyle broke eye contact. "You won, didn't you?"

Gale blew his nose. "Yeah."

A smile. The ghost of one. "I'll leave you to work that out for yourself." Rising, Kyle kissed the top of Gale's head. "I love you, dude."

I love you too, man.

"I love you," Gale told both of them.

Kyle gathered their bowls, set them into the sink. "You going to Regina's?" And there they were. Back to normal. As only with Kyle it could ever be.

"In a bit. You working?"

"Nope."

"Want to come help out?" Gale managed a smile, watery as it was. "I think she's starting to like you."

Kyle's big doofy grin flicked on a light inside Gale. If he could grab it with both hands and hold it tight, he would have. Instead, he settled for letting it warm him from the inside.

"I'll drive," Kyle said, already halfway down the hall. "I have time to hop in the shower, right?"

"Go for it."

The water turned on, that white-noise hush. Gale blew his nose again, tossed the wadded-up paper towel into the trash. He put away the milk, the cereal, wiped down the table, feeling better than he had since the day of his win. Less hollow. Slightly stronger. Maybe even a little wiser.

You know what he was getting at, right?

Afraid. To be happy. For it to all be taken away. That he didn't deserve it, to begin with. "I've always been this way."

What happened made it worse. I'm sorry about that.

"Me too."

Sean sighed. Or it was the shower's white noise turning off. *He's better than both of us.*

"Yeah," Gale said, even though Kyle, stepping into the hallway wrapped in a towel, could probably hear him. "He's the best friend we ever had." Even if he pretended he didn't.

34

Whisk: The process of using a whisk to incorporate air into food or to blend ingredients to a smooth consistency.

2016

Regina was pleased by Saskia's interview process. Difficult as it started, it got easier. Saskia was patient, kind, and tough. She pushed Regina to limits that had her hanging up on more than one occasion, but she always called back. Like pressing on a canker sore, it felt good.

The Grand Redemption Championship filming date was confirmed, so too was the article's release to hit the stands after filming was done. No cover photo; Regina had been adamant about that. There was still every chance the story would leak once the magazine had gone to print, but it was the best she could do to stick to her self-imposed timeline. She felt a little bad about not telling anyone her plans—aside from Marco— but she would before the interview came out. After Gale competed. He had enough on his shoulders, and she had other things to accomplish before life changed once again, for her and everyone she loved.

The last detail, maybe the most important one, was Gladys.

"I can't just leave her and hope for the best," she told Marco one night during their weekly dinner. "I can't get power of attorney and I'll never get guardianship. I'm no one to her. Even if all my money could move mountains, the process will take too long. She doesn't even have a social worker checking in on her. The state will take her as soon as I bring her situation to anyone's attention."

"Then it's out of your hands."

Regina pushed food around on her plate. Salmon in a Dijon pan sauce over sauteed spinach. She wouldn't admit to trying to shed a few pounds before whatever was coming came, but she had a good enough idea of what shape it would take to know she'd rather face it a little more camera-ready.

"I can take her with me, hire full-time care."

Marco met her gaze across the table. "With *you*?"

She did her best not to roll her eyes. "With us."

"Are you sure?"

"I'm not doing this hand-holding stuff, Marco. You helped me come up with this plan and made damn sure I included you in it. Now can we just move on to Gladys without you getting maudlin on me?"

"I'm not maudlin." Marco pushed away from the table, took their mostly empty dishes to the sink. Leaning against it, he scrubbed his face with both hands.

"Second thoughts?" she asked.

"And thirds and fourths."

Regina wasn't prepared for how that slammed her in the gut. She sat up straighter. "It's not too late for you to back out."

Marco's hands fell to his sides, his grin tired but a grin nonetheless. "And give you the satisfaction of ditching me twice? Nothing doing. I have my pride."

"Okay." Some of the breath slammed from her body wheezed back in. "Fine. Good."

"Your enthusiasm is staggering. My ego might just pop."

And there came the rest of it, filling her lungs so that her snarled "Fuck you" tripped out on laughter.

"I love you too." He pushed off the sink. "Listen, you, *we* can't cart a demented old lady around, caregiver in tow or not. It would technically be kidnapping for all the same reasons you can't get power of attorney or guardianship. Besides, she's too old to deal with all that, or to leave her in an unfamiliar place with unfamiliar people, because you're not going to be able to babysit her then any better than you can manage now. Why not just hire a caretaker now, leave her where she is?"

"In that dump?" Regina shook her head. "Any competent caretaker will report it to the state."

"Yeah, you're right." Coming to stand behind her, Marco kneaded her shoulders. "Have you spoken to Kyle yet? Lucy?"

"It's too soon," she told him. "I don't want to tip my hand. Gale's whole future is—"

"His own to decide."

"You think he won't do it?"

"I honestly don't know, Reg. Either way, he's on to bigger and better, whatever he chooses. That kid's got real potential."

"Duh." Regina let out a long breath.

"There has to be a solution that doesn't ultimately land her in the hands of the state," Marco said. "I mean, consider this. She's been flying under the radar all this time, right?"

"Well, technically, it hasn't been an issue until this past year. Had anyone called attention to her mental state, she'd have passed. They'd have left her alone. Especially with Troy across the hall, taking care of her."

"But no one's caught up to that, right?"

"Right? Where's this going?"

Marco tipped her chair back, smiled upside down at her.

"What the hell?"

"It's probably not, technically, legal, but I might have a plan."

IT HAD BEEN OVER A WEEK.

Seven days and fourteen hours, to be exact.

Gale went to work, helped at Regina's, played video games with Kyle—now that he had all the time he used to spend with Jenara—and stressed. Work. Sleep. Play. Stress. Eat, on occasion. Stress some more.

It's not helping, man.

She'll call. Give her time.

Don't use this as an excuse to relapse.

You lived without her before, you'll live without her again.

There was no point in responding to either Sean's encouragement or his taunts, even when alone. So Gale didn't. Sean was only echoing his own thoughts, anyway.

"Do you think you can stay a bit?" Regina asked him as they finished dinner service cleanup. Lucy had already gone home, and Kyle hadn't been in for a few days. Just him and Regina, like in simpler times.

"Sure, what do you need?"

"I promised Gladys apple crisp for tomorrow and haven't even started it yet."

Simpler times. "Sure. No problem."

"Great. Apples are in the walk-in. Get peeling."

Peeling, chopping, layering, baking. Gale had made so many apple crisps by that point, he could do it in his sleep.

"You hear from Jenara yet?"

Gale nicked a finger. "Shit."

"Quit chopping! You'll get blood in the apples. Come here."

Obedience was a given, but she took his hand and led him to the sink, ran it under cold water. From the first aid kit, she took antiseptic, a bandage, and a finger cot—which he, Kyle, and Sean always called finger condoms, because they were idiots that way—and fixed him up. Except for the usual scowl he'd come to recognize as concentration rather than anger, he caught a glimpse of the Regina who'd taken care of him the night he arrived on her doorstep, drunk off his ass and panicking.

"I know how you're feeling right now," she said without looking up. "Will you be forgiven? Will the ones you love ever trust you again? It sucks, but this is how it goes. Use that to avoid fucking up again rather than an excuse to do so."

"That's what Sean says," Gale muttered.

"You got marbles in your mouth?" And there was the regular, old Regina back. Gale kind of preferred her. "Speak clearly, will you?"

"I'm not going to do it again. I swear it."

"Take it slower, Sparky." She grinned. "Today. You're not going to do it again today. Tomorrow, you tell yourself the same thing. You keep doing that until you forget to even remind yourself."

"Have you forgotten?"

"I've had a few days here, a few weeks there," she said. "It's getting to be more often lately, but I'll be okay."

"Lately? Because of me?"

Regina laughed, flying lips chasing a bee. "Not the way you're thinking." And then it was gone, not replaced by the scowl he was more comfortable with, but a softer smile she rarely offered. She pushed the hair from his face. "You're making me remember what it was to be young and passionate and royally fucked-up, but happy. You make me want stuff I haven't in a long, long time."

"Is that a good thing?"

"I guess we'll see soon enough."

"Huh?"

"Back to work." She whisked the first aid paraphernalia from the counter. "These crisps aren't making themselves."

Two hours later, they had four hotel pans of apple crisp baking in the ovens, water for tea was already boiling on the stovetop, and the familiar, companionable silence they usually worked in left Gale far too much time inside his own head.

"Another twenty minutes or so should do it." She passed him his mug. "I should have asked you if you were staying before I forced you into a cup of tea."

"Where am I going to go?" he asked. "Home to play video games with Kyle?"

"Glad to know I'm a better option." Regina blew over the top of her mug. "He's a good kid."

"He's the same age as me."

"You're both kids."

Gale sipped his too-hot tea. The days, the confessions, the waiting and wanting and wishing balled into one another. Not only had Jenara not called, but Lucy seemed to be avoiding him too. When they did see each other in the kitchen, she seemed shaky, always close to tears.

"Out with it."

No sigh. No smile. Just, "Is it always going to be this hard?"

"Yup. But hard doesn't mean impossible. It doesn't mean you'll never fuck up again. It doesn't mean you will. What matters is getting back up, brushing yourself off, and trying again."

Gale's eyes unfocused.

Fess up, man. You know you have to.

If anyone was going to understand, it was Regina. He took another too-hot sip, kept his gaze off in the distance, unwilling to look her in the eye. "At the party on New Year's Eve? I chased two guys out of the bathroom. They were using . . . something. I wanted it so bad. They offered, and it took everything I had not to. But I did, kind of. I got some of whatever it was on my hand when I smacked it away. It . . . I . . . it was just the smallest bit on the tip of my tongue. But . . . yeah. I caved."

She was silent way too long. Gale's face burned.

"You do understand," she said, "that's when you decided to use, right?"

Gale blinked, focused. "I didn't *decide* anything."

"Of course you did. It was the tiniest taste, but it was a taste. You didn't just wash it off. Once you make the decision, conscious or not, it's only a matter of time. Believe me, I know. And if you don't acknowledge it, it'll happen again. Sooner than you think."

"You're losing me here," Gale told her. "I didn't take them up on their offer. I kicked them out. I should never have told you I tasted it."

"Maybe. But *you* still know you did. Did you tell anyone else?"

Sean, he imagined, didn't count. "Jenara."

"Everything?"

Gale looked away.

"There you go. The decision was made when you didn't tell her. You crossed a boundary and didn't step back. Get it?"

You know she's right.

"Shit."

Told you, didn't I?

"It took me years and more denial than I care to admit before I actually got my head wrapped around that. Learn from it, Gale. It's all you can do at this point."

"Yeah."

More dejected than he'd been since the morning after, Gale drank his tea in silence. Funny thing was, he had absolutely no desire to drink, or do anything else for that matter. Zilch. Nada. It was as if the fiery alcohol fall from grace had sapped every desire for oblivion from his brain.

It won't last, man. You got to know that. You got to keep diligent.

Gale wanted to cry.

Gale did cry.

Without sobbing and snot.

Only a few tears he pretended Regina didn't see.

35

Running the pass: The "pass" is the long, flat
surface where dishes are plated, then picked up by waitstaff.
The chef who "runs the pass" is in charge of calling out orders
as they come in, making sure the courses run smoothly
and tickets are filled in a timely manner. It's also their
responsibility to make sure dishes sent out to diners are
properly plated.

2016

I'm perfectly fine right where I am, young lady. And I would appreciate
it if you did not bring strange men into my home."

Regina leveled an I-told-you-so glare at Marco. "He's not a stranger,
Gladys. That's Marco. You remember him. From the kitchen?"

The Burger Queen, in full regalia, looked down her nose, sniffing.
"It's unseemly."

"I'm just here to help carry your bags, ma'am."

"Bags, what bags? Where am I going?"

"They have to fumigate your building and you're going to stay with
me for a few days. Remember?" Regina felt a little bad, lying, but Marco
was right; inviting her to stay with her wasn't illegal, as long as she went
with them willingly. The trickery made it a bit hazy, but she was willing
to take the chance.

Gladys's eyes darted back and forth, whispering, "Is it cockroaches?"

"Uh, yes. Roaches."

Shuddering, the old woman put hands over her ears. "I cannot abide cockroaches. They crawl into your ears at night and lay eggs in your brain."

"Then let's get you out of here and over to Regina's." Marco reached for the suitcase and overnight bag straight out of the 1950s that Regina had hastily packed, and in front of which the old woman immediately stepped. Every stitch of clothing Gladys owned, all the creams and over-the-counter medications from her medicine cabinet—some equally as old as the cases—fit into them. It was both sad and satisfying to know a life could be distilled down to so little, so quickly.

"Take her down to the car," Regina murmured to Marco. "I'll do one final sweep and be right behind you with her bags."

"I can—"

"Don't do the chivalry thing," she snapped. "You'll have your hands full with Her Highness. Besides, I'd rather be the one seen with her bags. Less suspicious."

"No one's going to notice, let alone bat an eye."

"Just do it, will you?"

"This way, ma'am," Marco said a little more loudly than necessary, and before Gladys could balk added, "Is that a roach on the carpet?"

She was pretty spry in that moment, hightailing it out of the apartment with her hands over her ears, leaving Marco following in her wake. He left the door open; Regina heard her scolding him the whole way down the hall. Doing another quick sweep, she told herself they were doing the right thing. It was for Gladys's well-being, now and continued. The timing was tight, but it would all work out. It had to.

On her way out the door, Regina remembered to check the fridge. Much as she hated to do it, she grabbed a plastic grocery bag from the caddy under the sink and tossed all the food, most of which was from Regina's own kitchen. There were also decade-old condiments, an ancient brown bottle of Geritol, and a tub of Country Crock. If all went well, the Burger Queen would never rule over this domain again. Anything now left behind had come with the apartment and would be someone else's problem in a month or two.

A flutter of paper stuck to the side of the refrigerator caught her eye as she swept past. Regina paused, almost left without looking. Freeing it from the Liberty Bank magnet, she swallowed down the lump rising to her throat.

Eleven digits, starting with a one, written in Gladys's careful, beautiful hand.

And a name.

Troy.

Shouts from across the hall, from Troy's old apartment, snatched her attention. A door opened, letting loose the noise before slamming it off again. Dammit. Marco was wrong; all the neighbors would be watching from windows.

Stuffing the slip of paper into her pocket, Regina hurried out of Gladys's apartment. With any luck, neither of them would ever see the place again.

BY THE TIME SHE ACTUALLY HAD A MOMENT TO CALL THE NUMBER ON THE slip of paper, Regina had stopped believing it was the way to Troy she hoped for.

"You've got all you need here," Regina told the old woman now ensconced in the guest room, most recently and only used by Gale, of her apartment. "If you want to come down to the kitchen, you just ask Abigay and she'll bring you down, okay?"

Gladys suspiciously eyed the smiling caregiver Marco had hired. "I'm perfectly capable of taking care of myself."

"I know." Regina resisted the urge to kiss the top of her head. "She's here to make me feel better. Just until you know your way around, how to work the remote, that kind of thing."

Tugging her down to her level, Gladys whispered, "Daddy hired a colored girl once. Mother preferred hiring Irish, so we had to let her go."

Regina glanced Abigay's way, but the woman was all smiles and silent reassurances. Abigay was set up in what had been Regina's office. Taking care of one mostly healthy old woman with a patchy memory in a luxurious apartment was a pretty sweet gig. Once the chaos of Queenie B's resurgence into the world settled down, Gladys would move into Regina's bedroom, Abigay into the spare. Anything to make the old woman's last years good ones, even if Regina wouldn't be there to witness them.

Life hadn't given her a grandmother when she was a child needing one so desperately, but it gave her Gladys. The grandmother who vexed her, but who needed her. Truly needed her. There was something to that Regina would never have understood had the Burger Queen not shown up in her soup kitchen. Gladys had forgotten Troy; she'd forget Regina, too. But Regina would never forget the Burger Queen.

"Apple crisp today," she told her on her way out the door. "Just like I promised."

Deep in a cozy chair, her feet not even touching the ground, the Burger Queen reached for the remote control she had no idea how to use. "I don't like apples," she said, and to Abigay, "Can I get game shows with this contraption?"

Regina left her apartment as quietly as she could. Downstairs, Marco and Lucy were laughing at something; she could hear them through the door. Poised between here and there, between lives, she took a few of those deep, cleansing breaths. It would all be fine. At least, okay. As long as she took it one day at a time, just as she'd preached to Gale.

Dropping onto the top step, she pulled the cell phone from her pocket. The slip of paper from Gladys's refrigerator was a little worse for wear, having spent several hours in Regina's pocket, but the old woman's pristine handwriting made that irrelevant.

Months of wondering where he was, what had become of him, and here the answer could be, right in her hand. Gladys had, at some point and for too short a time, known enough to write down his name and a phone number. If this was any such thing at all.

"Only one way to find out."

Tapping in ten of the eleven numbers, her finger poised over the last one. Worst-case scenario, it was nothing. And maybe, by some miracle, Troy himself would pick up the phone.

Last digit. Tap.

"Northern State Prison, how may I direct your call?"

Regina nearly dropped the phone. And yet, it made perfect sense. His past. His present. Apparently, his future. As the whole dreadful notion landed in her belly, relief mingled in there too. He wasn't dead. Troy might have drunk himself into trouble, but not death.

"Northern State Prison," repeated the voice on the other line. "How may I direct your call?"

Steadying her breath as best as she was able, she said, "I'm trying to reach an inmate I believe is incarcerated in your facility." Regina let go the words. "Can you help me with that?"

36

Infuse: To allow the flavor of an ingredient to soak into a liquid until the liquid takes on the flavor of the ingredient.

2016

Eleven days.

Jenara called.

She wanted to see him.

Gale paced in his apartment, waiting for five o'clock, the time she asked him to meet her out front. They'd go to the beach. March was proving unusually warm.

It sounded promising, so it couldn't be. If she was going to forgive him, she'd just out and say it, right? Jenara was trying to break it to him gently, in public, so he couldn't make a fuss. Not that he would. Gale wasn't a fusser. He'd shut down. Walk away. Never beg. It just wasn't him.

Maybe that's your issue, man.

"I'm not doing this, Sean."

Sounds to me like you are.

"The Grand Championship is next week. What am I supposed to do?"

Your best. One thing has nothing to do with the other.

"Says you."

"Says who?" Kyle shuffled into the kitchen, scratching his belly and stretching. "Damn, I slept in, huh?"

"You haven't been up yet today?" Gale checked the time. "It's four forty-five."

"I worked a double yesterday. Didn't get home until two."

"That's still sixteen hours, dude."

"Fifteen. And I didn't go right to bed when I got home. What's it to you, anyway?"

"Nothing," Gale mumbled. "Sorry. It's just . . . Jenara's picking me up out front in a few minutes."

"Dude." Kyle dropped onto a kitchen chair. "That's good though, right?"

"Fuck if I know."

"She could have ghosted you."

He has a point.

The tiniest spark of hope pricked Gale's anxiety.

"How long until you have to go down?"

"Ten, fifteen minutes."

"I'll distract you until then." Kyle play-punched his shoulder. "You ready for the big day? The competition, I mean. This is a big day too."

"I knew what you meant." Gale blew a breath through his lips. "Ready as I can be. The crates are going to be brutal."

"It's fifty K, man. They better be. You got it, though. None of your competitors is being mentored by the one and only Queenie B, that's for sure."

Another point for Kyle. Wow. Maybe he's smarter than we give him credit for.

The "Shut up, Sean" stayed in his head, but Gale was confident he got the point. "You're going to help her out the day I'm gone, right?"

"Yup."

Kyle's smile made Gale smile too. "You really like working there."

"I do, and not because . . ." He made a gesture in the air. "It feels kinda good, you know? Feeding hungry people who can't afford to eat regular. I don't have to be a great chef or anything, just a competent cook. It's cool."

"It is."

For you. The thought—his, not Sean's—came at him like a smack in the face; it was nevertheless true.

"I thought that was enough for me," he confessed. "I never thought about anything more than cooking, to keep my head straight and make enough money to get by."

But Kyle was unsuccessfully, and obviously, laughing behind his hand. "What?"

Kyle shoved Gale gently. "Dude, you had *aspirations*, back in the day. How do you not remember all the restaurants we planned to open? You even had a notebook dedicated to that one with the hipster name. Menus and floor plans. Crap, what was the name?"

The notebook. Cartoon burger, fries, and a striped cup on the cover. Buried so deep, it came to him fuzzy. "The Flight Fantastic."

"Right! The microbrewery."

"Craft burgers and sausages."

"That's still an awesome idea."

Maybe it was. Maybe its time had come. Or passed. Gale hadn't thought about it in a long, long time, but he bet his mom still had the notebook stashed away someplace. The laughter died like a balloon deflating inside him. "I lost a lot of years."

"Don't go there, dude. It's done. Now look at you." Kyle jiggled him by the shoulders. "You got this. Win or lose next week, you're a *Cut!* champion. You're besties with Queenie B."

"I'm sure she'd love that designation." But Gale managed to smile, glancing at the clock on the microwave. "I better go. Jenara's probably downstairs waiting. Thanks for distracting me."

"Any time, dude." Kyle hugged him. "Whatever happens, you're good."

Simple and trite, and, somehow, Kyle's sentiment made Gale feel better. "Thanks. See you later."

"Yeah. Later, dude."

Gale trotted down the steps, gathering whatever fortitude he could muster.

Whatever happens, you're good.

Though Gale's heart stuttered a little, Kyle's words repeated inside his head. Promising. Reassuring. Gale grabbed onto them with everything he had.

Jenara's black town car awaited him, slick and newly washed. Not her personal car. A livery car. Maybe even the same car they'd met in. Gale wasn't sure what to make of that, or if he should make anything of it at all.

"Sorry, I'm late." He ducked inside.

"You're fine." Her smile, slightly stiff, but not stilted, was the clichéd parting of clouds on a stormy day. "Savin Rock sound good to you?"

"Sure. I haven't been there in years."

"It's really pretty this time of day."

Jenara leaned over and turned on the radio. Gale took her hint. They'd talk at the beach. It wasn't a long drive; the silence between them was comfortable enough. Familiar. Filling the space between them with words had never been necessary. Jenara liked to read; Gale liked to watch her, the way her lips moved so slightly. He didn't watch her now. That would be weird. Only an occasional, surreptitious glance. Every time, her eyes on the road, attention focused, slightly stiff but not stilted smile in place.

Pulling into the lot, Jenara found a spot near a park bench overlooking the beach. Other cars were there. The walking paths made Savin Rock a popular spot for beach-walking, even in the colder months. Dogs. Kids. Lovers. Sandy beaches. Rocks for kids and dogs and childlike adults to climb. The Sound's abundance of oyster and slipper shells to pick. Seawashed rocks and glass. The view of sand and sea and grass, especially at the turn of day, couldn't be beat.

Gale got out of the car, followed Jenara to the park bench, sat when she sat. Hands jammed in his pockets to keep from putting his arm around her, he waited.

And he waited.

Be cool, man.

Gale somehow managed to obey.

"I thought I could do this." Jenara blew out a long breath.

Here it comes.

"I had it all rehearsed. I knew exactly what I was going to say and how I'd say it, but . . ."

"But?" Had the word come out of his mouth? Soft and calm and not at all trembling like his insides.

Jenara faced him. "Now I'm seeing you, like, face-to-face, and it's all jumbled. I don't want to say any of it anymore. I thought I could . . ."

"Take your time. Say what you need to say. It's okay."

She took a deep, deep breath. When she blew it out, a little cloud forming in front of her face told Gale he should be cold, even though he was burning up.

"At first," she said, looking out to sea, "I just thought I needed a few days. Time to process, you know? Instead of calming down about it, I got angry. So, so angry. How dare you do this to me, knowing what I've been through? Then I remembered when we first met, and you warned me, and I told you something that boiled down to it doesn't matter to me. That I wasn't going to *not* like you because of it. And then I got mad at myself, because I never wanted to be the kind of person who'd write someone off because he has issues."

She looked at him now, tears in her eyes. "It's why it took so long to call you, Gale. I needed to stop being angry. What finally calmed me down was coming to the realization that I just can't do it again."

Vision narrowed. Jenara. Her hair blowing in her face. A hand pushing it back.

"I can't put Alicia through it, either. She misses you so much, but she'll forget, you know? And maybe I'll get lucky and another super-amazing guy'll come along who I won't have to worry about every time he leaves the house."

"It's never going to happen again."

"I know you mean it with all your heart, but I heard that, I *believed* it, a thousand times. You have to see it from my perspective. Do you? Can you?"

Damn it all to hell. Gale nodded.

"That's what I came here to tell you." Tears rolled, her lip quivered, her face contorted in her efforts not to let either happen. "But now I don't know that I can even though I know I have to. Fuck, Gale. I don't know what to do."

This is exactly what she doesn't want, man. This is what loving you is.

No lingering shadow. Just Sean's voice, not mocking or mean. Sad. Resigned. The infinite wisdom of the dead. Then Jenara was leaning into his shoulder. Gale's arm encircled her, tears prickling. Tucked into each other, on the bench, at the beach, as the sun slowly set, Gale and Jenara sat, the months of their love story unraveling behind them. A ribbon caught in the sea breeze poised in that last moment before someone caught it, or let it fly free.

Courage, man.

"I have to tell you something," he said. "About New Year's Eve . . ."

AT SOME POINT IN THE TELLING, JENARA HAD SHIFTED AWAY FROM HIM. SHE stared out to sea, hunched over and hands in coat pockets. "You told Regina and not me?"

"Not then. Only recently. I should have told you everything on New Year's morning."

"That you didn't says things I don't want to know." She shook her head, slowly back and forth. "I don't know what to say."

Do it for her, man. Do it for you.

"There's only one thing left to say." Gale's lips ached with the effort to keep them from trembling. He tipped her chin up, needed to see her eyes when he told her, "I'm thirty years old, and you're the first person I've ever been in love with. I hate it, but this is—"

Jenara put a hand gently over his mouth, smiling though she wept. "That's the first time you've ever said it." The kiss she pressed to his lips before the warmth of her hand got snatched by the cold now coming in off the Sound was not passionate or sad but full. So full. Emotions Gale had no words for and would never try to find. They'd be irrelevant.

"Bye," she said.

Hair swinging.

Hands in her pockets.

Jenara got into her car, turned over the ignition.

Tires crunched. Then surf. And seagulls. And wind.

And gone.

Gale bowed his head. March wind ruffled his hair. He was cold in so many ways, the words for them would be irrelevant too. The sky burned bright orange and pink, the crimson on the horizon getting darker, richer, moodier. Gale shivered now, cold being the only appropriate word. He was too far from home to walk, even if it would do him good. Pulling his phone from his coat pocket, he stretched, his back popping from sitting hunched for so long. He texted:

Can you come get me? Savin Rock Beach. Near old museum.

The immediate dot-dot-dot that said Kyle had been waiting, then—

Be there in fifteen.

He was there in ten. Gale stayed on the bench, now too cold to step over his heart lying in bits at his feet.

"Hey." Kyle dropped onto the bench beside him. Shorts and a track jacket, his working Crocs with no socks. Probably no shirt underneath. Gale's eyes prickled all over again.

"Thanks for coming."

"No problem."

Winter, spring, summer, or fall, Sean sang, *all you had to do was . . . text.*

"You okay?"

Gale choked out a stunted sort of bark, like laughter, like a sob, startling gulls into flight.

Kyle put an arm around his shoulders. "Let's go home."

They drove the whole way in silence. The kind only longtime friends who'd been through a lot together could maintain.

I fucking love this guy.

"I do too."

"Huh?"

"Nothing. Just talking to myself."

"Alrighty then." Kyle grinned, eyes on the road. He drove a shit-bucket, but he was a good driver. "How about we order a pizza from Sally's. Text Nando or Jimmy. They're both working. We'll get it free."

Gale didn't need to get his pizza for free anymore, but he texted Jimmy. They'd bring a couple of pies home with them; Sally's Apizza was closing early. Slow night. They'd all hang, play video games. Eat pizza. Drink beer, all but Gale. Not tonight. Not ever.

Not tonight. Let forever speak for itself, man.

"Shut up, Sean," Gale mumbled, but he didn't mean it.

Kyle looked at him sidelong, shaking his head. "Tell him hi for me."

In the dusky-dark, Gale couldn't tell if Kyle was smiling.

37

Curdle: When egg or fat-based mixtures are cooked too quickly and the protein separates from the liquids, leaving a lumpy mixture behind.

2016

The Grand Redemption Championship filmed in a few days. The interview was done and already on its way to print. Everything Regina had been planning for, preparing for, was so close, the pins and needles she lived on never let up.

She worried for Gale. Not about the competition; he'd smoke that, she was certain. He was just strangely calm about his breakup with Jenara. Regina had handled his drunken tears easily enough. They were familiar in the most personal way. This calm, she had no idea what to do with.

"He'll be okay," Marco assured her over the prep table in his restaurant. "You, of all people, have to trust him. How's Her Highness doing?"

"Fine. Settling in. It won't be long before the landlord figures out she's gone. Hopefully, I've timed it all right so that Queenie B's lawyers can handle whatever comes of that."

"Whatever the backlash, we'll handle it."

Marco took her hand across the table. Sex was easy, comfortable, and surprisingly good. It was his gestures of love and support Regina found hard to deal with, but she was trying. She was going to need him when all the shit hit the fan. He steadied her in ways she'd forgotten about in those years after she ditched him for fame and fortune.

And Osvaldo Balcazar.

Oz.

No matter how long it had been, what she'd done or he'd done or they'd done, Queenie had loved him. Maybe it was the toxic kind Marco claimed, but there had been joy and passion and the sort of forever-after found mostly in movies and novels. She couldn't help the twinges in her body when she thought of him, even with Marco holding her hand across the table. Regina was no fool; Queenie or Regina was never going down that road again. But for the first time in a very, very long time, she could remember their days with some of the good, rather than all of the bad.

Oz would most certainly contact her when the interview dropped. Through his lawyers. He'd get ahead of all the surprise and joy for the beloved culinary star, back from the public-dead. The detractors. Those claiming it was all a publicity stunt. Those taking bets on when her first big disaster would hit the headlines. He'd be ahead of the old friends coming out of the woodwork, whether sincere or hoping to board her crazy train back to stardom. Yes, Oz would contact her first, because Marco was right; if there was another fifteen minutes of her fame he could latch onto, he would. He was also the only one who knew how to reach her, even if he didn't know her at all anymore.

Like a summons, the phone in her pocket vibrated. Regina pulled her hand from Marco's to answer it, almost expecting to see his number on the screen.

Newark, NJ.

The hair on the back of her neck prickled.

"Hello?" she said over the long beep in her ear. "Hello?"

"Regina? That you?"

She would not cry. "Holy shit, Troy." But she did. "Holy shit."

"It's me." Troy howled. "Damn! How'd you find me? Did Her Highness finally remember?"

"No, but she had your name and a phone number pinned to her refrigerator. Dammit, Troy! Why haven't you called me?"

"Now how was I supposed to do that? No phone in the kitchen and it's not like your number is listed or whatnot. I called Gladys, gave her the number, and hoped she'd remember to tell you."

Marco was making *Who is it? What's going on?* gestures. Regina put up a hand, turned her back. "Tell me what happened."

PRIORS AS FAR BACK AS THE EIGHTIES. BURGLARY. LIQUOR STORES. Convenience stores. Petty thefts. The house Troy robbed in 2009 was the one that would have put him away for a while, had he and Petunia not skipped bail.

"The law finally caught up with me," he finished. "Gladys made a fuss when they took me away. I felt so bad, leaving her all on her own like that. How is she?"

Thank goodness they hadn't caught up with her too. "She's fine." Regina sniffed. "With me."

"At the kitchen?"

"Yeah." She blew the word through her lips. "There's been a lot . . . since you . . ." Another breath. "It's complicated. What about you? Do you have a lawyer?"

"Had," he said. "You know they got to give me a lawyer. It's all said and done."

"How long?"

Troy laughed. Softly, not at all sadly. "Probably the rest of my days. I'm an old man, Regina. This place is minimum security. Bunch of men too old, too ugly, or too harmless to be interesting. I get three squares, a roof over my head, and ain't no way even I'd drink the liquor they got in here. I'm good."

"But you don't belong in prison, Troy," Regina said. "You're a good man."

"Nah, I ain't that. I tried, but . . . I never hurt no one. I swear that. But I did wrong to all them people I stole from, to my own daughter. It's time to pay up."

The counter bubbled up in Regina's throat. In a few months, she could hire lawyers, get his sentence reduced. Something! But there would be no arguing with him, like there was no arguing with her once her mind was set. They were, after all, birds of a feather. Except she'd never gone to prison outside of her own making. Because poverty exacted its own price. And if money could fix it, it hadn't been a problem for Queenie B.

A muffled voice on the other end gave Troy five more minutes.

"It's real good to hear your voice," he said. "I can almost smell the kitchen in it."

"Everyone misses your scrambled eggs."

"Lot of the same faces?"

"Some," she told him. "You know how often they change."

"Sure do. Except for our Burger Queen."

And you, until a few months ago.

Regina bit her lip until it stopped trembling. "I'd bring her to see you, but—"

"She don't remember me."

"I think she would, if she saw you."

"That bad, huh?"

"Pretty bad, yeah. It's gotten worse this past year."

Silence fell and lingered. Regina's heart sat heavy in her chest. All this time, and they had so little left to say to each other. Rather, she had so much to say and couldn't. Not now. But even he'd know, soon enough.

"Don't you come neither, Regina." She should have predicted his train of thought; it might have hurt a little less. "All around better that way, know what I'm saying? I been the best person I can be these last years with you. I mean that. It's why I here in prison, doing my time. You're why I ain't dead, like Petunia, when I should be. When it shoulda been me."

The countering argument got stuck in her throat. He was her friend, no matter what he'd done. No matter how many times he gave himself over to his demons. The fact was, visiting him wasn't happening anyway. The approval process would take time, and by then, she'd be long gone. Not even Regina anymore. At least, not only.

"Can I call you again?"

"I'd like that. You leave a message, I'll call you back. I can call you too, during hours."

"If you ever need anything..."

"Like I said," he told her, "I got all I need. I even got some buddies I play cards and such with."

"We'll talk soon, then."

"Yeah, real soon."

"Okay, well . . ."

"Yeah, well. G'bye, Regina. Tell Her Highness her driver say hello."

"Will do."

She tapped out, head hanging. Marco stood behind her but didn't touch her. Good call. How well he knew her. How lucky she was. To have this, now. With him. A man she'd abandoned, but not broken. He wasn't dazzling. Not in any way. Marco was Marco, content to be who he was. Not content. Proud. Happy. Whole. In Regina's eyes—though she'd never let on—he shined all the brighter for that. Not everyone was lucky enough to find a Marco. Troy never had.

"You okay?"

"Yes, thanks." Tucking her phone, and the conversation, into her back pocket, she turned to face him. Tomorrow, she'd tell Gale about their old friend. Right now, the slow simmer of her life was building to a full boil she'd never have guessed at a year ago, but one that had been building since she left Bova.

One thing at a time. Isn't that what she told Gale?

"Did you talk to Frances yet?"

It took a moment for Marco to catch up, but he nodded. "No. Tomorrow, before her shift."

After Gale's. "How sure are you she'll go for it?"

"Executive chef?" Marco snickered. "Even if it's only interim, she'll jump at it. The bonus pay'll sweeten any reservations she might have. Which she won't. Gale's not going to be happy, though, being under her again."

"In theory, and only until after the competition. He'll never actually have to be her sous."

"He's still going to be pissed."

"Better pissed than freaked the hell out before he competes." Regina put her arms around Marco's waist, looked up into his face more owl-like now than the lupine contours of youth. "I have to do this. All the parts are in motion, and there's no stopping it. But Gale can't be the cost. I won't jeopardize him. I won't be the reason he fails."

"You're being a bit dramatic, aren't you?"

"Fuck—"

Marco caught the rest of her curse in his mouth, holding her tight and close as if his kiss or his touch could soothe her temper. If only it had ever been that easy to accomplish.

"I know you're right," he said. "I know this is for Gale. All of it. I know, I know, I know."

"But?"

He pulled back just enough. His kiss hadn't soothed. Neither had his touch. As always, with Marco, he didn't take it personally. He got her, and that soothed way better—and less perilously—than passion.

"It's a lot to juggle and hope it comes off all right. This could all go tits up."

"How very British of you." She gave him a squeeze. "You have to admit, it's fun."

"Is that what we're calling it?"

She let him go to clear their plates from the prep table. He was right behind her with the rest. Side by side, he washed, she dried. Normal. Easy. Quiet. For a little while longer, anyway. Her roller-coaster car was *click-clack-clicket*ing near the first apex. In her mind's eye, her arms were going up and a whoop gathered in her throat. And Regina remembered what it felt like, all those years ago, to be on the precipice of something great.

38

Butterfly: To split food through the center, thinning it out, but not cutting through it entirely.

2016

You sure you want to do this?" The accompanying *click-click-click* conjured Saskia tapping a pen against her teeth. She'd done that a lot during the interview process. "It's pretty risky."

"Risk I'm willing to take," Regina said. "Can you arrange it?"

"Of course. I'll text you the details."

"Great. Thanks."

"So?" Saskia prodded before Regina could sign off. "Less than a month. You ready?"

Regina didn't need to ask for what any more than Saskia had needed an answer to begin with. They were both nervously excited. "Just a couple of details to cinch up, but yeah."

"Anything I can help with?"

Regina laughed Queenie's laugh. "You got all the information I'm giving you."

"For now." *Click-click-click.* "You owe me two more interviews."

"I haven't forgotten." A car door slammed outside the kitchen service doors. "Here comes one of those details. Got to go. Text me the details. And thanks, Sas."

Regina watched Kyle and Lucy enter from the darkened stairwell leading to her apartment. Upstairs, Gladys played rummy with Abigay, a game the caregiver didn't have to let her win. She might not know what day it was, or even what decade, but Her Highness was a crackerjack card player. Rather than Gladys's company making Regina feel claustrophobic, she was kind of enjoying it. Maybe knowing it wasn't going to last long had something to do with it.

A lump rose to her throat, almost beating out the thrill chasing itself across her skin. This was it. The last bits and pieces. There was no going back, as if halting the locomotive that was Queenie B had ever been possible to begin with. She stepped out of the stairwell and into the light.

"Regina." Lucy rushed her. "What's wrong? What's going on? Why did you ask us to come in without telling Gale? Is he okay?" She grabbed Regina by the arms. "Is this an intervention?"

Removing her hands, Regina pushed her gently into a chair. "Gale's fine."

"I tried to tell her."

"No offense, Kyle, but you never told me the truth of things, back when—"

"Enough." Gratified, it hadn't been cantankerous Regina, but decisive Queenie B who had silenced them so effectively. This was about Gale. It was all about Gale.

Mostly, anyway.

At least half.

"I'll get right to it," she said. "There's a lot going on I haven't told anyone about, including Gale, and—"

"Good stuff?" Kyle asked. "You're not dying or anything, right?"

She leveled a glare, this time, all Regina. It was kind of cool, being able to call upon either. It was getting easier. Soon, Regina and Queenie would be one person again. Maybe for the first time.

"Sorry," he murmured.

"Good stuff, but big stuff," she said. "And I don't want Gale to know anything until after his competition next week."

"Because you're afraid he'll freak out," Kyle said.

"Because there's no point in taking the chance beforehand. Now quit yammering and let me finish."

"Yes, Chef."

It didn't rankle. Not this time. Yes, Chef. Exactly what Regina *and* Queenie were. "I'm going to tell you everything," she began, "because I trust you, and because I need your help to pull it off . . ."

"SURPRISE!"

He knew, of course. Marco had given him the night off, he said, so he could rest up before the big day tomorrow. There was no way Gale was relaxing at home, or even sleeping until he was too exhausted to stay awake. But Regina wouldn't let him come in either. When Gale called his parents, Lucy said they had plans. And, as far as he knew, Kyle wasn't working, but he wasn't home either.

Then, "Can you come in after all?," Regina had said only half an hour ago. "I just need a little help getting breakfast prepped for tomorrow."

At eight o'clock. Regina never needed help prepping for breakfast. Kyle walked in not five minutes later, offering to drive him to the kitchen and lend a hand, considering he'd gotten off work early. Lies, but the good kind. The loving kind.

Don't be an asshole and spoil it for them.

As if he'd needed Sean's prompting.

"Surprise!" they—Kyle and Regina and Marco; Burger Queen, his parents, and even Brian—shouted. One glaring absence Gale registered and let go. Of course Jenara wasn't there. No surprises, good or sad, but Gale still cried. It didn't take much, lately.

"Thanks, everyone." He thumbed the tears away. "You're too much."

"It's not every day your son competes on television for fifty thousand dollars." Lucy kissed both his cheeks.

Danny Carmichael clapped him on the back. "Win or lose, son, we're proud of you."

"Not me." Brian mock-punched him. "I want the win."

"Shut up, nerdface."

Yeah, shut up, Brian.

The brothers hugged, a real hug. There went the waterworks again. Gale got passed from Brian to Marco to Kyle to Gladys—who allowed him to shake her hand—and finally to Regina, who held him like she had the night he'd come to her shit-faced and raving.

"I have one more surprise for you." She handed him her cell phone. Gale took it. "Hello?"

"Hey! Just wanted to say good luck tomorrow."

Holy shit; would he ever stop crying? "Troy?"

"Yessiree." He hooted that big laugh Gale remembered only now, hearing it again. "I'm that bad penny, always turning up."

The phone got passed, even though, aside from Regina, only Kyle and—technically, though not actually—Gladys knew who Troy was. It was a party, celebrating Gale. He tried his best to enjoy it, and he did, until the glaring absence that hurt more than it had since that day at Savin Rock poked him in the ribs.

Jenara had been everything new and wonderful, then became part of his everyday to the point of him taking her place in it for granted. And now, the truth had broken her in a way Gale could never fix. They'd done right, for themselves and for each other. At least there was that.

Because everyone at the party—including his father and Brian, who weren't supposed to know but Lucy had broken Regina down—knew who she was, Regina had prepared "light hors d'oeuvres" Queenie B style. Crispy prosciutto-wrapped figs, stuffed with goat cheese and drizzled with honey; smoked trout and garlic cream on rye toasts; spears of endive with lobster, avocado, and grapefruit; skewers of tomato, basil, and mozzarella with a light drizzle of olive oil, which Mom had prepared all on her own, having watched a video until she could do it exactly the same way. Kyle had been in the kitchen all afternoon, helping pull it all off. Everything was beautiful. Perfection. It excited Gale's palate and his imagination. So used to taking whatever Regina gave him and turning it into something else, he switched out the goat cheese with the garlic cream, the lobster and the smoked trout. Inside his own head, every amazing morsel he ate became something else. If he could think as fast tomorrow, maybe it wouldn't be the embarrassing disaster he feared.

"Ten o'clock!" Lucy clapped them all silent. "Everyone, go home. Gale needs a good night's sleep."

"There's no need to be rude." Gladys, hands over her ears, scowled. "Why are Italians always so loud?"

"Why are old ladies always so cranky?" Lucy straightened Burger Queen's crown. "You're up past your bedtime too."

"I'm not a child. Where is Abigay?"

Everyone fell silent, glancing at one another. Heavens to Murgatroyd, she remembered. Regina said, "I gave her the night off."

"And who are you to tell *my* maid what to do, when?"

"She's not your—" Marco began, but Regina put a hand on his arm. "She'll be home any minute."

The old woman hmphed, glaring off into space.

"You want to come spend the night at home, son?" Danny put an arm around his son's shoulders. "Having both you boys there would be fun."

"Yeah, Gale. I'll let you get all the sleep you need in our old twin beds. I promise not to fart too much."

"Don't be disgusting." Lucy swatted Brian.

"Wonderful as that sounds," Gale answered, "the car's picking me up in front of my place real early tomorrow. I don't want to try changing that now."

"Right, right." Danny squeezed him gently. "You'll do great, son."

"Yeah, you'll do great." Brian's sincerity, questionable as it was most of the time, warmed. "If you need to talk after, win or lose, just call me, okay? I'm always here for you, bud. We all are."

Silence. Awkward glances. Except for Regina, who scowled at the rest of them.

Ah. Clarity. The warmth ebbed, just a bit. Nothing he didn't deserve. Nothing they shouldn't expect even if they hoped it wouldn't happen.

Gale hugged his parents, his brother. He promised to call them, one way or another. And he would. There was no way he was fucking it up this time. No way.

No way, man. The afterimage burned bright; Sean's version of a smile. *No fucking way.*

"Hey?" Lucy smooshed Gale's cheeks, thumbing those damn tears springing a leak. "You okay?"

"I'm fine. Honest. Just, this is a lot, you know? I'm happy."

"You don't sound sure."

"Go home," he said. "I'll call tomorrow. It'll probably be late."

"Late never bothered me." She smoothed back his hair, pressed a finger into the dimple in his chin. "Love you, buddy."

"Love you too, Mom."

"I'm out of here too." Marco jostled him back and forth. "Got to cover for my lazy-ass sous chef tomorrow."

Gale chuckled. "I'll do you proud, Chef."

"I know." Marco let him go. "You got this, kid. Any way it goes, you're a star. Remember that."

A star.

Yeah, man. A star. Wear it well. You earned it.

"I'm not a star," he told them both, barely above a whisper.

"That's what she said." Marco jabbed a thumb over his shoulder. "Once upon a time."

"I never said any such thing."

"Do you always got to ruin my best lines?" Marco grabbed Gale's face, kissed each cheek, Italian style. Slinging an arm over Regina's shoulders, Marco only laughed when she shoved him off. Damn, Gale loved them. He loved all of them.

They love you too, man. Lucky dog.

"I got a long day tomorrow, too." Kyle was the only one left, besides the Burger Queen still staring moodily into space, though Gale would bet she no longer knew why. "You ready to roll?"

"You go home. I want to help Regina clean up in here."

Kyle looked one way, another. "It's just a few paper plates. We can have it done in—"

"Dude."

Understanding dawned with that goofy, beautiful smile. "Gotcha. You want a little one-on-one with the mentor."

"Something like that," Gale told him, though it wasn't the whole truth. What he wanted, even more than a few last moments with Regina, was time alone. All alone.

You're never alone, man.

Tears built behind his eyes. He wouldn't let them go. Not in front of

Kyle, who'd misread them. Like everyone did. Everyone but Regina, who'd understand it all.

"LOOK WHO I FOUND." REGINA PUSHED OPEN THE BACK DOOR, ABIGAY IN tow. "See, Gladys? I told you she'd be home any minute."

"Who's home?"

"Me, Miss Gladys." She bent just a bit lower. "Abigay. We play cards and watch game shows together."

The Burger Queen backed away, tugging Regina to her level. "I have a colored maid?"

"You have a caregiver who takes wonderful care of you."

"Daddy hired a colored girl once, but Mama only hires Irish. We had to let her go."

"Nah-nah, Miss Gladys." Abigay shook her head at Regina, smiling. "Let's go on upstairs now. It's way past bedtime."

Regina watched them go slowly up the stairs, Abigay always ready to catch the old woman if she fell. She would have gotten one of those chair-lift things, but the stairway was too narrow and Her Highness was far too spry and ornery to use one.

"I'll be up shortly," she called after them. "Shout if you need me."

She left the door open so she'd hear if anyone did shout. No one would, but she felt better doing so. Most likely, the old woman would be out like a light before Regina got upstairs, and Abigay would be settled into her makeshift room in the office for the night. Saskia had done as she asked and texted the information she needed; Regina had a long day ahead of herself tomorrow too. She needed to get to bed, even if sleep probably wasn't happening.

"You two don't need to stay and help."

Gale lowered his head, started collecting garbage. Kyle gesticulated behind his back, nothing Regina could actually decipher, but she got the idea. She shooed him out. He gave her a thumbs-up, that grin of his making her smile too. He would never be a great chef. His big break wasn't going to be culinary stardom. But he was a good cook, and he had a big heart. Regina had done well, choosing him.

Gale rolled the industrial garbage barrel about the kitchen, tossing empty plates—not a morsel of her hors d'oeuvres to be seen—and cups into it. She expected the too-tightly-wound aspect to be radiating off him.

"Put that down." Not too tightly wound. Unraveling. Gale did as she asked. Regina sat down at the little table in the corner. The one where she'd sat with Petunia. Gladys. Sometimes, but rarely, Troy. Until this past year, the only people she'd allowed into her life. Until Gale. And then Lucy and Marco and now Kyle. Her world opening up like the flower a bee being chased by a pair of smacking, crimson lips used to land upon.

"Talk to me."

Tears rolled. She'd noticed it happening a lot tonight, put it down to nerves or excitement or even Jenara not being there, and it was. But that wasn't all. Regina took his hand across the table.

"I honestly don't know what's wrong with me," he said. "Everything?"

"That doesn't tell me shit, Gale."

He laughed, softly, wiping his face with the back of his hand. "I've been feeling . . . fragile, I guess is the word. Like, I cry for no reason. If I'm happy. If I'm sad. Excited or nervous or tired. The only time I don't want to cry is when I'm cooking."

"That bodes well for tomorrow." She smiled, just as softly. "It's understandable. This whole thing with Jenara—"

"It's not that so much," he said. "Part of it, yeah, but I know it was the right thing for both of us."

She knew the feeling, especially since coming to her decision, since making all her plans. The need to contact Osvaldo, to pull him and Julian back into her world, this new and brilliant world she swore to every god and star in the heavens she'd make right this time, overwhelmed. Thank those gods and stars for Marco. But Jenara was not that grounding force for Gale.

"I liked her," she said. "But you're right. Too much of the same baggage makes a heavy load."

He snickered, watery and trembling. "You read that on a magnet or something?"

Regina Benuzzi of 2015 would have bitten his head off. Regina soon-to-be Queenie B did not. "I should copyright it."

"You'd make a fortune."

"Another one." Her smile faded with his. Patience. Something she'd never had before but found somewhere between her biggest fall and this moment. Her hand still covering his, she stroked it with her thumb.

"I didn't think I'd be this nervous," Gale told her. "It's not like I don't know what's coming. Maybe it's because I want to win so bad this time. Not for . . . well, for the money, but it's more. It feels like it's . . . like I'm . . ."

"On the verge of something great?"

His smile broke through the dam of tears, dazzling. "Food is all I think about. Not, you know, *food*. The art of it, I guess. All the things I want to do with it. It's like when I was younger. Before drugs and Sean and these couple of years doing just enough to survive myself. I had dreams, Regina. Dreams I forgot all about. This last year and some with you?" Dazzling, dazzling, dazzling. "It's like I finally woke up or something. That sounds stupid."

"No, it doesn't." Hadn't she felt the same? He'd been the light in her dark. She'd been the light in his. Accidental mentor and mentee. Guiding stars. Life preservers tossed overboard on a sea, if not turbulent, too dreadfully still. Pick a cliché. Regina hadn't the words to articulate any of it, nor the mouth that would even if she could. She'd never been made for anything so flowery or deep.

"It sounds right," she said. "Don't be afraid to shine, Gale."

"I'm not sure I know how. I think too much."

She had too, once upon a time. Until she stopped thinking completely, and everything went to hell. "You can't live with the past like the new monkey on your back. You did shit. I did shit. We picked ourselves up and we kept going. You want to look back? Look back on that and let it drive you instead of pull you down. Don't stop thinking, but try not to let those thoughts beat the piss out of you."

Gale hung his head, picked at his thumbnail. Regina resisted the urge to smack his hand, tell him to stop. She wasn't his mother. He had one. A good one. And Regina had been a poor one. Taking her own advice, she let that go. Julian had a good mother now too. And Gale needed a friend.

"You'll be nervous about tomorrow until you look into that first crate," she said. "It's not the competition, but the lead-up to it. The lead-up to every new crate. But you shine when you're in the groove, Gale. Hold on to that really, really hard. Trust that euphoric rush is going to come, because it always does."

"My new drug." He lifted his head, tears rolling. "Don't you see? I'm just changing where I get the rush from. I'm always going to need it to function."

"So what?"

"What do you mean, so what?"

"Everyone has their thing, Gale. For some, it's love, or money, or thrill of the chase, or a million other reasons they have for doing whatever it is they do. We traded ours for something bad, for something false. But we got it back. Don't you get that?"

Not dazzling now. A little sad. A little relieved. A whole lot skeptical. But he heard her, and Regina had to remind herself that all her hindsight, though sparked by him, was still new in Gale's past. And he'd lost a friend, for which he felt responsible. That was a whole level of hurt she'd escaped, even if all her levels had been so public and well-documented.

"Come on. I'll take you home."

"Nah." Gale pushed out of his chair as if he carried a precariously perched burden. "I need the walk."

"All right," Regina said, keeping to herself all the worry for him walking the streets in this area, so late. The trouble he could get in, considering his admitted fragility and his nerves and the thousands of pitfalls he could fall into along the way. Regina knew better than anyone there was no saving him from any of it, except maybe the mugging like the one that led him to her in the first place. Hugging him a little closer, a little longer than necessary, she didn't say anything at all. She'd see him tomorrow. In his groove. In his euphoria. Not so much battling his demons as rising above them.

39

86'd: When the kitchen runs out of a dish, it's "86'd." It means, "We're all out." Dishes can also be 86'd if the chef is unhappy with the preparation, and in that way takes on the other connotation of the term, "to get rid of."

2016

It didn't smell like a place where a whole lot of cooking got done. Gale remembered that from the last two times. Though the studio had no discernible odor upon entry, by the end of the day, it would be a smorgasbord of aromas, heady and extraordinary. He steered his focus to the anticipation of that rather than the anticipation of the competition itself. It wasn't easy; circumventing the familiar spirals in his brain took a lot of effort and probably some strange facial expressions, but Gale had thought hard on his long walk home the night prior. Regina was right about a lot of things, including the fact that it was the lead-up to anything that freaked him out, not the actual act itself.

I told you that a million times, man.

"You did not."

Did too. Jeez.

"You're not?" The man beside him bounced on the balls of his feet, shaking out his hands and jerking his head back and forth like a fighter warming up.

"Sorry, what?"

"I asked if you're ready for this." No calm energy there, not like the woman sitting off by herself, eyes closed and face unmoving.

"Ready as I'm going to be." Gale attempted an easy smile that felt way more like a grimace. He offered his hand. "Gale Carmichael."

His competitor took it. "Steven Adonucci. My friends call me Nucci."

Great. He even sounded like the kind of chef who went celebrity. "Which week did you win?"

"Third. You?"

"Second."

"So she's either first or fourth." Nucci jutted his chin in the serene being's direction. "I wonder where the last one is?"

"Traffic, maybe?"

"Yeah, maybe." Again the bouncing, shaking, jerking. Nucci was wound even tighter than Gale. Maybe he had something, there. Focusing on the end-of-day aromas took the concentration of Serene Being's approach. Gale didn't want to look like a copycat, in either case.

Want me to sing to you?

Gale kept the "Shut up, Sean" in his head, focusing again on those end-of-the-day aromas—garlic, onions, charred meat—while taking deep, even breaths, and flexing his fingers into tight fists, and letting go. Tight fists. Letting go.

"Last contestant is fifteen minutes out." Some guy with a headset around his neck called to the woman with a tablet. Then, to the three contestants present, "Might as well go ahead and have something to eat. Get coffee. Betty'll show you where."

They followed Betty and her tablet through the studio, to the break room Gale remembered waiting in—nutmeg, apples, cinnamon—between rounds. The set and studio were already busy with sound checks and lighting. Gale tried to get a look at who the judges would be, but no one so notable was present yet. Just the three of them and the production crew.

Despite his nerves, Gale was hungry, and the mistake of not eating all day was still too fresh to overlook. The food was good. Scrambled eggs, bacon, rye toast. Nothing fancy, but well done. He had a bowl of fruit, too, because Serene Being's bowl of yogurt, granola, and fresh berries made him feel like he didn't care about nutrition.

"Vegetarian." Nucci said around the bagel in his mouth. "Guaranteed. Easy pickings."

"She made it to the grand championship, same as us."

"Could be a fluke."

Never underestimate a vegetarian, man.

Gale was sure Sean had a point; he was just not inclined to parse it out at the moment.

Contestant number four was hurried in. Another man, this one much older than either Gale or Nucci. When he spoke—to Betty—Gale detected an accent, though he couldn't say from where.

"We go in twenty," Headset called—butter, citrus, alcohol burning off wine—and left the break room. Betty followed behind. Gale moved through conjured aromas until the newcomer, glancing only momentarily in Serene Being's direction, approached him and Nucci, hand extended. "I am Avraam," he said, "and I will be winning this championship."

"That's funny." Nucci took his hand first. "I'm Steven, and I'll be the one winning the fifty grand."

"Gale." He didn't bother with the posturing. Confidence was great; overconfidence led to mistakes only someone clueless about their own shortcomings made. At least, that's what Gale told himself.

"I'm Rhiannon, if anyone is interested." No longer Serene Being. Rhiannon.

"Gale." He shook her hand. She made the rounds. Unlike Nucci and Avraam, the smile on her face matched the amused glint in her eye.

Gale moved away from the posturing men, got himself another cup of coffee. It was exceptionally good. Cream and sugar. Light and sweet. The way he'd been drinking it since he and Jenara had coffee at that dive diner on the highway, the first time he'd competed on this show.

Focus, man.

Aromas. Olive oil, dill, scallions. Phantom. Focusing. It was right. They'd been right. Whatever they had was doomed before it began. *Too much of the same baggage makes a heavy load.* Cake. Sugar. Chocolate. Maybe someone would have the guts to bake something in the dessert round.

"It's going to come down to me and you."

Rhiannon stood just behind him, at his elbow.

"What makes you say that?"

"Those two? They'll blow it, first and second. Mark my words."

"You psychic or something?" He grinned and she laughed. Nice laugh. Easy.

"No, just a good judge of character. Look at them. They've already decided we're going to be easy to pick off and are circling each other like a couple of puffed-out pigeons. That's going to tank them, I'm telling you."

"Maybe they're just that good."

Rhiannon snorted. "No one is as good as those two think they are."

Told you not to underestimate the vegetarian.

"Can I ask you something?"

Rhiannon groaned. "No, I wasn't named for the song. It's an old family name."

"That's not what I was going to ask."

"Oh. Sorry. Everyone does. Or they assume. Okay, shoot."

"Are you a vegetarian?"

"Me?" Her laughter didn't wobble or pitch too shrilly. It was actually deeper than it should have been, given her voice. "No, I'm not a vegetarian. I'm sous in an artisanal steak house, and there's nothing I like better than a locally sourced, grass-fed, humanely butchered piece of beef."

Close enough.

Rhiannon held out her hand. "Good luck in there."

Gale took it. Warm. Calloused. Nice. The tip of what he assumed was a chef-knife tattoo peeked out from the cuff of her chef jacket. Kindred, of a kind. All of them. Even Avraam and Nucci still posturing. "Yeah, you too."

IT WAS KIND OF HARD TO SEE FROM HER VANTAGE POINT, BUT REGINA wasn't going to kick. They were in an observation room packed with old equipment and file boxes filled with obsolete forms now stored digitally that no one thought to recycle. Saskia had gotten her into the studio without any fanfare and very little stealth. It was the reputation of her magazine—and the promise of a focus piece in *A Chef's Life*—that got them into the taping of the Grand Championship, not Queenie B. She still had a little time before that inevitability. At the moment, she was still just Regina. And she was here for Gale.

"You want me to get you coffee or something?" Saskia asked.

"I'm good. You sure no one'll come up here?"

"I told you I have it all covered. No one will know you're here." Saskia leaned on the back of a chair. "But, you know, it'd be an amazing bit of publicity, if you'd just go down there, after the competition's over, of course, and—"

"Saskia. Stop."

But Saskia shook her head. "Did you see who's down there? I couldn't have scripted this better."

Tom, of course. He was a staple of the show. Regina had indeed spotted him, along with two judges she might or might not recognize, and Harold Javian. Culinary star turned culinary royalty, and an old friend. Harold had aged in that way of good-looking men who got frustratingly better-looking, somehow. Silver fox, she believed was the term, dressed like he didn't care in the obviously expensive—Loro Piana, if she guessed right—T-shirt showing off his tan, toned arms. Tom had, eerily, not aged at all. Queenie B had been brash and beautiful, completely wild and flamboyantly talented. What would Regina look like to them? She did not care to speculate. The old days were not only a blur, they were a long time ago. The one thing that had changed dramatically was, now, Regina didn't really give a shit.

"I'm here to see Gale compete." Regina kept her cool. "End of story. Got me?"

"Fine." Saskia deflated. "You can't blame me for trying."

No, she couldn't. Queenie had been pestering Regina for days. The publicity. A sneak peek leading up to the interview. Even the gratification of seeing the looks on all their faces—Harold's especially, the bastard. Damn, she missed him and hadn't even realized it until seeing him down there. Regina held firm. This was about Gale's moment, not Queenie B's rise from the ashes. Hubris made her confident she would, indeed, rise, but would it be fame or infamy lifting her up? None of that was going to touch Gale. None. She'd watch him. She'd go home. Only later would she tell him she'd been there the whole time.

He had spooked her, last night. His fragile unraveling, the dazzling smile laced with tears. Queenie had never been like that. Her chaos had been the aggressive kind; her unraveling took whole cities with her. Last night, she'd been afraid to let him go home alone, but did. Because, as Regina knew from the most intimate experience, either he would, or he wouldn't, and nothing she could do would change anything. And now there he was, filing into the studio with the other contestants. Smiling without the edge cutting through it. Joking with the lone woman in a room full of men. Regina would risk being there in that studio, full of people who'd know her in an instant, a million times over, just to see that.

"I'm going to have to go down and say hello during a break," Saskia was saying. "Otherwise it'll seem suspicious."

"Whatever you need to do. Just keep me out of it."

Cues were called. What are you competing for? Regina could have scripted the answers herself. The older man—whose name and accent were Greek—said he wanted to take his wife on a well-earned vacation around the world, but the truth that he did not speak was, he was really there to prove he still had it. She could relate.

The young guy who was not Gale claimed he would use the fifty grand prize money to buy the motorcycle of his dreams, but the truth he did not speak was that he was really there in the hopes of becoming one of the famous chefs sitting as judges. She could also relate.

The only woman in the competition said she'd pay off student loans accrued when she thought she wanted to be in finance, only to discover her heart was in food. Winning would prove to her parents she'd made the right choice. Regina believed her. Regina also instinctively knew the truth she did not speak; she was there to prove a woman was as good in the kitchen as a man. Regina could absolutely relate.

Then it was Gale's turn.

"I'm here because a friend sent in the application I chickened out of sending." Dazzling. Flirting with the camera despite the roil inside him. "And there's a woman I want to impress the hell out of."

"That's my boy," she muttered so low even Saskia didn't hear her, savoring the burn of knowing she was the woman he wanted to impress.

The contestants got the rules they already knew by heart. Took their marks. Opened their crates. And . . .

Frenzy.

First round. Gale moved with confidence. Kept his cool. No roiling now. Gale, in cooking mode. Controlled. The gears in his head clicking through flavors and aromas and textures. Motorcycle guy was cocky, putting on a show, calling out prompts to the judges as if they'd think he was clever. Harold absolutely would not. Know your audience, kid. Greek's experience showed, in good ways and bad. The woman moved with quiet confidence, as if she'd forgotten everyone else was in the room. She was Gale's biggest competition, without a doubt, if not in skill, in determination.

And, just like that, the round was over. The contestants brought their plates to the board for judging. After the initial sampling and comments, the contestants filed out again.

"The young lady won that round," Saskia leaned in to whisper. "But looks like your boy's going to be safe. Who do you think's going out?"

"The older guy, unfortunately. Not innovative enough."

"It's going to be a while before they send someone packing. You want that coffee now?"

"That'd be great, thanks."

Saskia left her alone in the dark, crowded observation room. Regina stayed well back from the window, even if no one would actually be able to see her if they looked. She watched Harold. She watched Tom. She itched to be in the break room with Gale, or at least a fly on the wall. Not just for him, but for her. For Queenie. The closer she got to this world, the harder she ached for it all.

"Sorry it took so long." Saskia backed in through the door, only one coffee in hand. "I said my hellos and got a few quotes on the first round while I was down there and ended up drinking your coffee. It'd have looked weird to stand there holding it. I wasn't sure how you take it these days. I brought creamers and sweeteners, just in case it's no longer black."

"Good call." Back then, Regina drank it mostly to sober her up. She added both cream and sugar now.

Saskia reached into her messenger bag, pulled out a bagel with cream cheese, and a paper coffee cup that held smoked salmon, capers, and red onion. "I thought you might be hungry."

"I am now." Regina spread out a napkin, assembled her feast. "Thanks."

"You're welcome. No trouble at all."

Saskia sat back in her chair, hands resting on her belly and an amused grin on her face, this woman who'd once taken care of her even when she didn't deserve the loyalty. Regina wished she could have loved Saskia then, the way she deserved. The way she loved Gale now. But Regina hadn't even been able to love her own son. Not then. Not during those oblivious, oblivion years when love was a stumbling block between her and the next high. Yet here was Saskia Specter—older, accomplished, a woman with a family and a career and clout in the world she'd flirted with from Queenie B's dressing room. Saskia was once again taking care of her with a smile on her face. As if no time had passed at all. It gave Regina hope that, maybe, she hadn't been as unlovable, as unloving as memory—and childhood—told her she'd been. If Gale loved her now and Saskia loved her still, maybe Julian could, someday, too.

AN HOUR AND A SURREPTITIOUS FORAY TO THE BATHROOM LATER, THE contestants filed back into the studio.

"You called it," Saskia said.

"I'm sure he's a good chef," Regina said. "Set in his ways, but good. Cuisine needs to evolve, just like everything else."

Saskia tapped into her computer. "Good line. Mind if I find a place to use that in the next article?"

"It's not original."

"It will be." Saskia winked. "Once it's a quote from Queenie B."

Tom called the second round. Again, the frenzy. With only three contestants, it would have been logical to assume it wouldn't be as nuts as the first. It was. Maybe more so. The woman stared a little too long at the honking-big pork shoulder thirty minutes would never cook. Gale and Motorcycle both went for the meat grinder at the same time. Motorcycle beat him to it.

"You have the knife skills," Regina muttered. "Use them. Come on, Gale."

As if he heard her, Gale got a second knife from his kit and sausaged the hell out of that pork shoulder. The woman sliced hers superthin, got it into a marinade. Regina felt bad for her; she should have gone for the pressure cooker. Stir-fry was a good idea, if a bit expected, but it wasn't a long-enough marinade to tenderize, too short a cook time to break down the collagen. She would lose this round. Regina would put money on it.

Then Motorcycle burned his meatballs.

As far as she could tell, Gale was whizzing through this round with bulgogi pork meatballs—Asian, yet again, though she might have gone that route herself—in lettuce wrappers, some sort of sauce concocted from the guacamole in the crate. Time ticked down. The contestants pushed through. Sweat glistened on skin, lined chef jackets, and darkened armpits. He was going to do it. Gale would win this round. Regina's heart raced way too fast.

"Time's up!"

Laser focused on Gale, Regina took heart that he laughed without that shaky wobble. He glanced left and right, at the dishes his fellow contestants put up. And she could see, even from high above, his confidence.

"Looking good."

"Very good," Regina agreed. "Who are you calling out this round?"

"Hard to say without tasting, but burned meatballs?"

"Her meat is going to be like shoe leather. Which is the greater culinary sin?"

Apparently, burned meatballs.

Regina would have rather seen Gale go up against Motorcycle. The woman had clearly taken the first round. Gale, clearly, the second. That meant it all came down to the final round, and dessert was still not his forte.

STANDING AT HIS STATION, HANDS ON THE HANDLES OF HIS MYSTERY crate, stomach in knots and his brain whirring, Gale maintained his focus. Not on phantom aromas, but on the round he'd just won. He wanted to win. He wanted the money. It wouldn't change the fact he was a recovering addict whose dead best friend lived inside his head, but it would make life a little easier. For him. His parents. He just had to get through the dessert round. Not just get through it. Win it.

You got this, Gale.

Not Sean's voice. Regina's.

"Open your crates."

Corn nuts. A piñata full of hard candy. Chocolate sausage. Saltine crackers.

Gale's brain flicked through the textures, the tastes of each ingredient. How they'd go together. How to make them go together. The easy route would be currant and chocolate sausage ice cream, some sort of brittle made with melted-down hard candies from the piñata. It was the first place his mind went, and so he discarded it. Rhiannon was already at the refrigerator, gathering the makings for an ice cream base.

He unwrapped a yellow hard candy. Lemon. Unwrapped several more and got them in a pan with a little water to melt. The brittle was still a good idea, and he was sticking with it. Grabbing a lemon from the pantry, he spotted marshmallows. It would be better to make his own, but time didn't allow. The dessert forming in his head coated his tongue. Sweet on sweet. He needed the saltines as a salty element . . .

And it hit him.

Years and years of his mother's brand of cooking. The only "cookie" she'd ever made successfully—mock toffee cookies. He'd elevate it, somehow.

Discarding the marshmallows, Gale grabbed saltines. His heart pounded. Mom would be thrilled if he won with her Christmas standby. She might swat him with a towel if it cost him the round. Either way, she'd be proud.

He tossed the lemon candies, replaced them with cherry. His brain palate told him there was too much sweet. Back to the pantry. Wonder of wonders, there was the tart cherry liqueur he hoped would be tart enough, because he wasn't tasting it. Not even a drop.

While the candies melted in the liqueur, he rough-chopped the corn nuts, to add once they were. Gale buttered a cookie sheet, layered saltines. Using the underside of a saucepan, he crushed them up just enough for the syrup to seep in. A taste of the chocolate sausage proved it more bitter than he'd like on its own, but a perfect counter.

Candies melted, butter incorporated, he poured the cherry caramel over the saltines. On top of that, chocolate sausage chopped up with some more of the corn nuts. Gale slid it into the oven. They'd only need a few minutes to melt together. Good thing, because a few minutes was all he had.

Salt, sweet, acid. His dessert lacked a creamy element. Rhiannon was getting her ice cream from the machine. It looked perfect.

Creamy, creamy, creamy that wasn't ice cream or the too-easy whipped cream.

Darting to the pantry one last time, Gale grabbed the mascarpone cream. And there he saw it. His coup de grâce. A container of coconut cream.

Was there enough time? The clock was winding down fast. The blender was his only hope. Tossing the coconut cream into it with a splash of the cherry liqueur, a pinch of salt, and a prayer, Gale went through all the ingredients in his head. He took his version of his mother's mock-toffee cookies from the oven. Perfect. Just melted enough. He drizzled caramel still in the pan onto the plate, set the slab of cookie on top. Went through his ingredients again. The coconut cream wasn't whipped enough. Dammit! But all crate ingredients were on the plate.

"Five, four . . ."

The coconut cream was nearly there.

". . . three, two . . ."

Gale grabbed a spoon, threw some of the cream from the blender on top of one of the cookies.

". . . one! Time's up! Step away from your station."

Looking down at the one dish he got the cream onto, Gale knew he had a winner. Hands down, more creative than Rhiannon's ice cream and saltine waffle bowl. But only on that one dish. Without the coconut cream, his dessert wasn't finished. Maybe he should have gone with the easier—and way more expected—whipped cream. Too late. It was what it was.

"Good job." He offered his hand to Rhiannon.

She smiled up at him. He hadn't realized how tiny she was. In the break room, she seemed much bigger. "Thanks. You too."

Their hands fell, heads turning to the judges' table, to those whose decision would change one of their lives. For the better. For the worse. Maybe a little of both. Or maybe not at all. Gale wasn't all that much older than he'd been when Kyle sent his application in, but he was way wiser. He told himself over and over, on his long walk home the night prior, that Regina was right. He had to let himself shine, to stop living with his past as a monkey on his back. And who knew better than Queenie B? Today, in this moment, coconut cream or no coconut cream, Gale believed it with every foodie fiber of his being.

40

Scald: To heat a liquid just below the boiling point (to 180 degrees); to blanch fruits and vegetables to facilitate removal of the skin.

2016

Regina paced the observation room. Side to side. Front to back. Corner to corner. She tried not to look down at those judges taking way too long to decide whether the woman's perfect ice cream trumped Gale's ingenuity. In all honesty, she didn't know which way she'd go herself. Gale's dessert—according to them—tasted like heaven. The right amounts of sweet and salt, acid and fat. On the one plate. They had to judge him on the other three that didn't get the coconut cream. It was the only thing sinking him. An incomplete dish was an incomplete dish, and the woman, while not necessarily innovative, had done simple to perfection. That went a long way.

"You're going to pace a hole in the floor." Saskia barely looked up from the laptop she tapped away on. "They only just started deliberating. Try to relax."

Leaning on the arm of Saskia's chair, Regina read over her shoulder. "Were you here for the other parts of the competition that haven't aired yet?"

"I was given access to the episodes."

She straightened. "You still have them? Gale's?"

Click, tap, tap—Saskia's screen changed from document to video. "I can send it to you, if you want."

"Can't I just watch it on your computer?"

"I'm working, if you hadn't noticed."

Regina pushed off the armrest, went to the observation window. The damn boom obstructed her view of the judges. She didn't have to see Harold to know what he said, how he said it. Exacting. Barely reined acerbic. Fair. He hadn't changed a bit. His vote would go to the simple perfection. Or maybe the innovative. Damn it all to—

A quick rap on the observation-room door already opening sent Regina scooting behind an insufficient tower of boxes.

"Saskia, are you—"

"I made it clear I wasn't to be disturbed." Saskia wasn't quick enough putting her weight against the door. Harold Javian was already in, one hand pressed to the door, the other to the jamb, smiling a puzzled smile.

"I missed you downstairs. I heard you were up here and wanted to say hello."

"Hello, Harold. Nice to see you. Now if you don't mind . . ."

"You're being weird." He smiled, perfect and pearly. He was older, most certainly, but even closer up, had truly aged well. The boxes Regina hid behind weren't enough; she tried becoming a shadow behind them causing them to sway. Harold's brow furrowed. Squinted eyes went wide, homing in. Another step into the room. This time, Saskia didn't try to stop him. There was no hiding. No going back.

"Queenie?"

Saskia wrung her hands, teeth biting into her lower lip, eyes welling. "I didn't do this. I swear."

Harold was coming closer, hands outstretched, face lit by wonder and maybe a little love. Fight or flight, Regina could do neither. This was it. The risk she'd been willing to take because after all, hindsight proved intention was a terrible liar. She wasn't there for Gale; if that were so, she'd be back at the soup kitchen, still anonymous, waiting along with everyone else. Waiting on the sidelines had never been her style. She'd come to the studio for her. To feel it all again, just a hint before the article that would bring it all swarming back, through Gale.

Stepping out of box-shaped shadows, not Regina or Queenie, both, and neither, newly born, not newly risen, she took Harold's hands still reaching for her.

"Hey, Harry."

His mouth worked. A fish on the butcher block having no idea it was about to be gutted. "I . . . have no words. You've rendered me speechless."

"Grab me a jacket, hell just froze over." Regina flashed Queenie's smile. It felt, if not appropriate in this moment, on this precipice, natural. She motioned to Saskia. "Shut the door, please."

"Oh, yes. Of course." Saskia pressed the door gently closed, as if she didn't want anyone to notice. As if the jig wasn't totally, completely, and most royally up. Because there was no way Harold Javian was keeping his mouth shut, even if Regina could still get out of the studio without being seen. He would keep it to himself until the decision was called; the man did have integrity. But Gale would know, so she couldn't skulk off and pretend she hadn't been there the whole time. He'd be hurt, if he won. Embarrassed, if he didn't. And the culinary world would be abuzz before morning with the news that Queenie B had shown up on the *Cut!* set, to watch her protégé compete for fifty thousand dollars.

Regina's carefully laid plans for the soup kitchen, for Gale, for this day of competition splattered like a mixer set too high. The way from infamy to obscurity had been all ducking and dodging. She should have known obscurity wasn't that patient or wily when seeking fame. She had to salvage this, turn it right, make it work. And if she couldn't do it Regina Benuzzi style, she'd do it Queenie B's.

"Did you already make your decision on the competition?" she asked.

Harold blinked, shook his head slightly. "Yes? Before coming up here. Meera and Karin are still debating. Why?"

"And you can't change it once it's been handed in, right?"

"Right. Jesus, Queenie, my head's about to explode. What the hell is going on?"

What the hell, indeed. Below, muffled calls for Harold Javian ruffled about the studio.

"Get back down there." She shoved him toward the door. "Don't say anything. We'll talk after taping's done."

"But—"

"Seriously, Harold. Don't say a word. I mean it. Let me handle this my way."

That cocky half grin. "I see some things haven't changed."

But he was right. Queenie would have threatened. Regina would have run. She reined them both in with a deep, deep breath. "Listen," she said. "Gale Carmichael is my friend. He doesn't know I'm here and my presence can't in any way change the outcome of this competition."

"It's insulting you'd think—"

"Please, Harold, for old friendship's sake, go back down there and keep your mouth shut until after the competition's called."

"Does that mean you'll be down after it is?"

Regina looked to Saskia. Wide eyes went wider. She nodded.

"I won't be vanishing again, that's for sure." She kissed his cheek. "It's good to see you, Harry." And shoved him out the door.

Saskia closed it firmly behind him. "Will he keep quiet?"

"We can only hope," Regina said.

"What are you planning?"

"Planning? I'm winging this, Sas. Do you have a lipstick?"

"Just the color I have on."

It would have to do. Regina took the tube of lipstick Saskia dug out of her purse—red, but not Queenie B red—muscle memory making a mirror unnecessary. She pulled the elastic from her hair, gave it a shake. Streaks of white in her otherwise black hair. Jeans and button-down. The new Queenie B allowing only traces of the old to identify her. It was kind of perfect, if she did say so herself.

"It's amazing, how such little effort brings her back."

The understatement of the century. In so many ways.

Saskia smoothed stray flyaways, smiling slightly dreamily. "Do you have any idea how much I loved you, back then? How hard it was for me to leave you when I did?"

"I wish I could say I did," Regina told her. "I didn't know much of anything, back then. How do I look?"

"Like you." Dreamy smile faded. She looked beyond Regina, to the set below. "Looks like they're about ready."

The judges sat at their table, contestants returning. Only a matter of moments now. Gale would win or lose. Either way, Regina would be there.

"Let's go."

Saskia only nodded, opening the door Regina had only just pushed Harold through. In her mind's eye, she saw it all unfold. Not watching from the wings and confessing it to Gale in an airplane—Regina hoped; Queenie knew—winging across the ocean. Nothing like the soft open of the interview she'd planned. It was now cameras and booms, startled expressions turned whoops or groans. It would be a circus, the kind she'd been hiding from for over a decade. She'd blown it, but Regina Benuzzi was a survivor, and Queenie B was nothing if not opportunistic.

41

On deck: A phrase that means, "This order is coming up!" Cooks might call out new tickets and let the line know what's on deck. They'll also give servers a heads-up if their orders are "on deck" or coming out soon.

2016

Gale and Rhiannon stood on their marks. Her hands clasped at the small of her back, military style; he didn't know what to do with his. Pockets seemed wrong. At his back brought that copycat feeling. Arms crossed, too combative. Flopping at his sides, too defeated. On his hips, too superhero. These thoughts pelted through his brain in the time it took to entwine his fingers, cat's-cradle style, at his abdomen.

The judges sat at their table, stone-faced. The cloche covering the losing dish sat at the edge of that table. Tom's hand on the knob. Stage directions were called. Tom's famous, "Whose dish is being cut?" would be dubbed in later.

Gale heard only garbles in the background of his brain chatter, eyes fixed on that cloche. Win or lose, he was ready. He'd had fun. Back home everyone waited. Mom and Dad. Kyle and Marco.

Regina.

His stomach did a little flip. He'd done her proud. No question about it.

I'm proud too, man.

Tom lifted the lid.

To her credit, Rhiannon didn't whoop or fist pump the air. She folded into a squat, her hands over her face, holding back the joy she should be whooping.

Gale put a hand on her back, between her shoulder blades. "Congratulations."

"Oh, my god! Gale. Oh, my god!" She jack-in-the-box leapt into him, arms flung around his neck. "I thought you had it. I really did. Oh, my god. Did this just happen?"

The director was calling for him to exit the set. Rhiannon unwound herself, let go of him. He would shake hands with all the judges first, just like Regina told him to do whether he won or lost. It showed character, and he had that in spades. At least, she said he did, and Gale would do her proud even if she'd never know.

"It came down to splitting hairs," Harold Javian told him. "Had you gotten that coconut cream on all the plates . . ."

"Rhiannon outcooked me," Gale said. "Plain and simple."

Harold held on to his hand a bit longer than necessary, smiling. "Something tells me you're headed for big things, Chef."

He shook the other judges' hands. Tom's. It was over. Behind him, Rhiannon basked in her glory. He was really happy for her. At least it hadn't been Avraam or Nucci. Gale would nevertheless wish them both well when he got to the break room, as long as neither of them said anything crass about being beaten by a girl.

You did great, man.

No echo. No Sean. Maybe not even his voice, after all.

Yes it was.

Gale followed Betty's ponytail off set. He had done well. His brain didn't crash over what he could have, should have, would have done. Gale's foodie heart knew he'd have won if that coconut cream got onto all four plates. It wasn't hubris, just the confidence that, if he had to do it all over again, he'd do nothing differently except time that last round thirty seconds faster.

"Excuse me, ma'am!" Betty waved her tablet in the air. "This is a closed set. You can't be . . ."

Gale nearly bowled into Betty's back.

"Holy shit. Holy shit! Holy shit! Holy shit!" And off she scurried, back the way they'd come, leaving Gale turning in a confused circle.

"Hey, Gale."

It took a moment for his eyes to catch up with his brain.

"Regina?" He took a step closer. "What are you doing here?"

A tall woman Gale had never seen before stood behind Regina, tucking dark hair behind her ear and smiling awkwardly. He looked from her to Regina and back again.

What the hell?

Gale echoed Sean's sentiments, all the confidence and excitement and disappointment bursting out of him. Regina. Here. In New York. In the *Cut!* studio. Where everyone—including Betty holy-shitting her way through her discovery—would recognize her. And Gale could come up with only one reason for Regina to be in the studio.

"You didn't trust me."

"Didn't . . . what?"

"You thought I was going to crash and burn again."

She reared back, the most irritated Regina expression he'd ever seen on her face. "Fuck that, Gale. I'm not your babysitter. I'd have sent your mother for that. You're not even remotely close."

"Then what are you doing here?" He put himself between her and the click and squeak of hurrying shoes coming up behind him. "Are you insane?"

Regina raised a finger over her head; clicks and squeaks silenced. Listening. Waiting. Gale had to imagine the judges and camera crew, the boom guys and scripters and directors and producers, all held in thrall by that finger raised, because he couldn't have turned around if he wanted to.

"I wanted to see you compete," she said. "Without you knowing. Without anyone knowing." Her gaze flicked to someone beyond him and back again. "That obviously didn't work out. But it was all in the works, Gale. I was going to tell you everything after the competition."

"Tell me? What?"

She pulled him closer, the raised finger only implied but still holding back the most immediate future. "I can only hide for so long, and it's been getting harder and harder, because I don't want to lose everything again. You and the kitchen and Marco and . . . my life, Gale. I can make a go of it this time. I know I can."

Regina was looking up at him, waiting for a response. No tears. Never tears. How had he never realized it was she who had to look up at him? From the moment he met her, Regina loomed large, and he hadn't even known who else she was. Queenie B. A culinary star who'd risen, burned bright, and went out before he ever stepped foot in a kitchen, but still had the power, in a single raised finger, to stop the world.

Cameras and mics were zoomed in on them. Gale was no longer second in the *Cut!* Grand Redemption Championship; he was a starring player in Queenie B's reemergence into the culinary world. Center stage. This scene, their words, would be everywhere. Pictures. Sound bites. Video clips. He was fully aware of, if slightly dislocated from, his surroundings; he saw only her. Not Queenie B, after all, despite the red lips and hair unbound. She was Regina. His unintentional mentor. His unasked-for friend. A woman who knew all his demons and still believed in him more than he believed in himself.

Gale scrubbed his face with both hands. He technically had a right to be angry that she'd hijacked the day, and hurt that she'd kept him in the dark. He'd deal with that later. Something bigger boiled up inside him now, the same something simmering during the competition when confidence overpowered his racing brain and let him have fun rather than simply survive the ordeal.

You got this, superstar.

Turning without actually looking at the gathered throng behind him, Gale offered his arm to Regina, who looked at it as gruffly impatient as only Regina could.

"Your Highness," he said. "Your people await."

She smacked his arm but she took it, smiling a smile he remembered from the grainy video of days gone by. Not for the camera, but for him. *Thank you*, it said. *I owe you*, it promised.

And then the world burst open.

42

Waxing the table: Giving a guest/s special VIP treatment.

2016

No matter what else the day had become, the *Cut!* Grand Redemption Championship had to finish taping. Gale and Rhiannon got herded off to do the interviews that would later be inserted in between all the rounds. Wherever Regina was—or should he start thinking of her as Queenie B? Nah—he was certain she was dazzling everyone in her path. He'd seen Queenie in her heyday; he knew the Regina of today. She'd find him later, she promised. The producers were sending them back to New Haven. In a much nicer car, of course. She and Gale had a lot to talk about.

"Wait in here while we make sure we have everything we need." Betty, no longer perfunctorily crisp, wiggled like an excited puppy. "Just some forms to sign. You remember."

"Sure." He could use a huge glass of water. Better, coffee. He wanted to call his mother, talk to Kyle, tell Marco what had happened on the set, but he wouldn't get his phone back until all those forms were signed.

You still got me, man.

But Avraam and Nucci were already descending.

"You're Queenie B's protégé?"

"What the fuck, kid?"

"I help out in her kitchen," Gale said. They were already talking over him, not really interested in fact, only conjecture coming from their own mouths. How had the vegetarian won when Queenie B's protégé competed against her? It was rigged. Had to look good. No way he wasn't robbed just so it didn't look like favoritism.

Gale stopped listening, edging closer to the coffee machine and the hit of caffeine he needed desperately.

"Psst! Gale." Rhiannon motioned to him around the side of the bank of refrigerators.

"Hey," Gale whispered, wiping off the coffee her *psst!* made him splash on his hand. Checking over his shoulder, making sure the puffed-up pigeons were still at it, he darted around the refrigerators to join her.

"They're a lot, huh?"

Gale grimaced. "I'm sorry about all this. It's supposed to be your big moment. In Reg—Queenie's defense, she had no intention of upstaging anything. She was watching from an observation room."

"Sorry? Are you kidding?" Rhiannon's eyes shined; her cheeks flushed. "You have no idea, Gale. A woman? That big in the culinary world, way back then? She's been my idol my whole life."

"She was a catastrophe back then. She'd be the first to admit it."

"That doesn't take away from her greatness, what she accomplished. It's because of her I can be here, right now, winning a competition no amount of talent would have gotten me into to begin with. And now she's back, today of all days. I feel like . . . like . . ." Tears welled. ". . . like it's an omen or something."

Yeah. Good outlook. I like this woman.

"Congratulations, again," he said. "You really did deserve the win."

"Thanks. I'm over the moon. I really did think you had it, though."

"It's all good." And it was. Mostly. He'd still have liked the win, so much so he was already thinking about where else he could send an application. Confidence was arrogant like that; the more he trusted it, the bigger and bolder it would get. New Haven and Marco's was too small for him now. Part of the same complicated life, but behind him.

Like me.

Emotion lumped in Gale's throat. *Like you.*

". . . not even going to cover half my loans," Rhiannon was saying, "after taxes and all. I was a finance major, remember."

Gale sipped his coffee, cleared the lump and the words inside his head that were heard nonetheless. "You really going to use all your prize money to pay student loans?"

"I have to," Rhiannon said. "The thought of them keeps me up at night."

Gale laughed, quietly, so Avraam and Nucci wouldn't hear. "All the more reason to use a little piece of it to do something fun. Go on some sort of foodie vacation. What's five thousand bucks in the grand scheme of things?"

Rhiannon put her hands on her hips, looked up at him through narrowed but smiling eyes. "You're a very bad influence."

"I'm just saying, you got to live a little. Quit worrying."

For fuck's sake, man. Look who's talking. But Gale heard the cocky, amused smile only a glow out of the corner of his eye. Ghostly. Real. He would never know for sure. Maybe it didn't actually matter.

"Gale?" Betty called from the doorway. "You're wanted on the set."

"I am? What for?"

"Just some after-show footage. Rhiannon, stay put a minute, okay?"

"What about us two?" Nucci crossed his arms over his puffed-up chest.

Betty's nose wrinkled. "I'll find out if you can come watch. Hold tight. Gale, this way."

"One sec." Gale turned back to Rhiannon. Blond, blue-eyed, the kind of girl he imagined living in a California beach movie, not Brooklyn, where she worked in that artisanal, cruelty-free steak house. A finance major turned chef, who didn't know how hard he'd once fallen, and how long it took for him to get back up. No baggage to make his load heavier. "Do you go out with chefs?"

She chuckled, that deeper-than-should-be sound. "Smooth, Gale. Real smooth. You'd come all the way into the city from New Haven?"

"It's just a train ride." Heat crept up Gale's neck; he smiled through it. "Don't get any grand ideas or anything. I'm just trying to swindle you out of some of that prize money."

"Hardy-har-har." She shoved him. "I'd like that."

He patted his pockets. "I don't have a pen."

She pulled one from her chef coat pocket, wrote his number on her hand. "I'll text you once they give me my phone back. Then we'll have each other's numbers."

"Okay, good."

"Great."

They stood awkwardly, face-to-face. Handshake? Hug? Rhiannon held out her hand.

"Just so you know," she said, "I'm only going out with you to get in good with Queenie B."

"I assumed."

"So, to be clear, you're after my money, I'm after your influence. Honesty is the best policy, after all."

"Agreed."

Pulling him down to her level, Rhiannon kissed his cheek. "Talk soon."

"Gale?"

He turned to Betty's impatient call to follow her swinging ponytail down the narrow hall, back to the studio where Regina would be waiting to do whatever publicity thing she'd agreed to do. And him by default. Because of course she did. She was Queenie-fucking-B, and he wasn't just a guy who helped out in her soup kitchen anymore.

HAROLD HAD SUGGESTED A SINGLE COURSE HEAD-TO-HEAD—HIM AND Rhiannon against Regina and Gale—insisting he was as unprepared as she when Saskia raised some concern.

"It's okay," Queenie, not Regina, said. "Gale and I got this."

Maybe Harold had the advantage of having judged hundreds of such contests, but he'd never cooked with Rhiannon before. Regina and Gale were a muscle-memory tag team of culinary greatness. Poor Harold wouldn't know what hit him.

The crate ingredients—low-sodium kielbasa, a tube of polenta, a package of preshredded cheddar, and a jar of mole—were even harder for the showrunners to put together than crazy but well-considered ones, considering the spontaneity, and the depletion of the pantry that had been set up for the Grand Redemption Championship. Regina's brain whirred. Her body thrummed. Years in the soup kitchen had taught her to be creative with less, to make do, to keep it simple. Queenie B, however, had never embraced simple.

"Are you thinking what I'm thinking?" Gale asked.

"Shrimp and grits?"

"What? No!" Gale snorted. "I thought kielbasa tacos, but shrimp and grits is way better."

"Time!" Betty called over the chatter on set. "Contestants, to your crates."

Gale showed her where to stand. The judges, now only Meera and Karin, didn't sit at their judging table; they were to be part of the show. Meera stood at the end of Regina's workstation, Karin at Harold's.

"Okay, Chefs." Tom stood between them. "Open your crates!"

Regina dumped the tube of gelatinous polenta into a pot, added cream. "Smash this up and stir it until it's smooth. Add the butter—"

"Got it, Chef. Get on the rest. Let's show them how brilliant we are."

Gale winked. He winked! Regina's heart did stupid things she'd have scolded it for that morning. "Just don't forget to add cheddar."

Grabbing shrimp from the freezer—thankfully, already cleaned—she tossed them into a bowl and filled it with water. Regina sliced the kielbasa and got it into a pan, cooking it down while the shrimp defrosted. The mole was rather disgusting, but nevertheless a crate ingredient. Her knife—Gale's actually, the kid had a good kit—diced scallions, a serrano, and bell peppers like it was part of her hand, fast, perfectly uniform as she'd once demanded of the entremetier in her kitchens. She threw them into the pan with some garlic and the kielbasa, tossed it one-handed while sprinkling a bit of salt.

"Chef, the shrimp," she called over her shoulder.

"Heard, Chef." Gale took his polenta off the burner, spun, grabbed the bowl of shrimp, and dried them off. "Tails on or off?"

"Leave them on."

"Heard, Chef."

Handing them off, Gale flipped the burner back on and continued stirring, now sprinkling in the packaged, grated cheddar, another knob of butter. Even in her periphery, she could see how smooth and creamy it was.

"Don't forget to season it."

"Heard, Chef." But he smiled when he said it. Regina allowed herself a smile back.

Spooning some of the rather-disgusting mole into the pan of veg and sausage, she tossed one-handed again. Her wrist twinged just a little, but she was in the zone. Taste. Still gross. She grabbed cherry tomatoes from a pint container left on her station by the previous contestant. Smashed them with the back of a wooden spoon. Stir, salt, butter. Better. A squeeze of lemon gave it the brightness she was after, but not quite enough. Racing to the fridge, she grabbed fresh dill.

"Two minutes!" Betty called. Later, Meera and Karin's comments would be dubbed in. Tom would call his usual, "Two minutes remaining, Chefs." Regina heard almost nothing of what any of them were saying now. The zone was the zone. That fluid place Gale cooked in. She was in his or he was in hers, but she remembered it now more intimately than when she watched Gale and knew that's where he was. Where he shined. Where she shined too and always had. From rinky-dink local access with barely a working stove, to PBS, to the biggest, brightest sets in the world.

Regina was a little out of breath now. She put the shrimp into the pan with the mole and vegetables, gave it another toss. Her wrist gave, only for a second.

"Gale, plate."

"Already on it, Chef."

He'd gotten his polenta into a bowl and was chopping the dill while Regina spooned the shrimp and kielbasa pooling like buttery, spicy magic on top of the grits. Gale sprinkled the dill over top while she did the same with a last pinch of salt.

"Time! Step away from your stations!"

"Whew! That was amazing!" Gale threw his arms around her, lifting her slightly off the ground. She didn't insist he put her down; Regina held on tight, head back, joy flying from her lips, lipsticked red, if not Queenie B red. No bee buzzing. No flower to land on. That had been the glorious, thrilling, tumultuous then; she wasn't that person anymore. Whatever she was, whoever she turned out to be, she was wiser now. Prepared for the ups and downs, the fame and the infamy. It was all still there, waiting as the world would soon be waiting, to see what she would do with them. Regina kind-of-sort-of-definitely couldn't wait to see herself.

AS IF THERE HAD BEEN ANY DOUBT SHE'D WIN. QUEENIE B, HAVING CLIMBED out of the black hole she'd slunk into all those years ago, winning against the great Harold Javian was television too good to pass up, after all. It was sure to hit headlines in the coming days.

Saskia was over the moon, already on the phone with her staff. The advance buzz was going to require more than their usual copies printed. And was there any way to change the cover of the magazine no longer heralding Queenie B's return, but showcasing the event like a queen's coronation?

Whether or not her win had been preordained by the *Cut!* producers, Regina had no doubt she earned it. For his part, Harold was a good sport. He was one of the great culinary rock stars, come up the same way she had. James Beard Awards, Michelin Stars, Iron Chef. Respected. A master of his craft. Regina was just better. She had been, way back when, and she still was. There was no point in being modest about it. The modesty would be false. Whatever else Queenie B had been, she'd never lacked in confidence. Regina would be no less now. And that included what might look like hubris on anyone else.

Taping finished; people hung around. Waiting for Queenie B to kick the party into gear. Regina could have held court all night. Contractually bound not to share anything that would be in the article—and unwilling to, anyway—there was still plenty of the past to talk about. She chatted, kept her cool, tried not to swear too much, though if that was all they were getting of the old Queenie B, she probably shouldn't have been stingy. When Harold approached, what was left of those still hanging on melted away in clumps like cornstarch in warm broth.

"You going back to Connecticut?" Harold was putting his coat on, keys in hand.

"Yeah. You still have the place in Chelsea?"

"We do. Charlotte is very grateful for your divorce."

Snide humor intact. Thank goodness. Regina couldn't have dealt with a schmoozy, gushy Harold Javian. "She still hate me?"

"Queenie, for goodness' sake. Charlotte loves you. You know that." Sarcasm didn't bite so hard when one was in on the joke. Charlotte had, in one of Queenie's less obliterated moments, made it abundantly clear that not only did she hold no love for her whatsoever, but she threatened to wipe the floor with her if she ever went near her husband again. That, Regina remembered, though she had no recollection of ever making a pass at Harold Javian. He had never been her type, though that wasn't saying much.

"You call her yet and tell her I've risen from the dead?"

"Texted." Harold pulled out his cell, showed her the wide-eyed emoji, followed by the head-exploding one that sufficed for his wife's response. "She never believed you were dead. Something about being a bad penny."

They chatted as they hadn't yet been able to, catching up as old friends would. As if there were no more to it than that. She asked after his daughters, and the grandkids born in the intervening years. Harold kept his own questions to the less intimate. He hadn't spoken with Osvaldo in years, though he'd seen this and heard that on occasion. It wasn't hard to find out what people were up to, aside from her. And then, "Gale's about the same age as Julian, if I remember correctly."

Regina had been braced to hear his name, but, still, it hurt. "He is."

"Anything to that?"

"Nothing at all." Quickly. Too quickly. Ice cracked through her veins. "What makes you think you have the right to ask that?"

Harold shrugged, his grin only a little snide. "Better me than some reporter, no?"

Regina sagged just a little. It was after eleven. She was beat to hell, and her day wasn't over yet. "I didn't think so, when he first came into my soup kitchen," she said. "But I'm not an idiot. I can see how it looks."

"A soup kitchen? Is that where you've—"

"Shh!" She covered his mouth with her hand. "I wasn't supposed to tell you that."

"I won't tell."

"You have a big mouth. Don't make me find you and punch it. I know where you live, Harry."

He chuckled. "No one calls me Harry but you and Charlotte."

"Because we knew you when you were still a peasant."

"We were all peasants, back then." Harold patted his pockets for the keys already in his hand, tossed them up and caught them, sighing a little dramatically but sincerely. "I miss the old salad days, sometimes. That rise to stardom. Now that you're not dead, I envy you, getting to do it all over again."

"Don't envy me. It's not worth the price I paid." *Julian. My Julian.*

"But you're a fool if you don't enjoy every moment of it," Harold told her. "If I don't show my face on the network and commercials and side appearances for a decade, even a couple of years, the public will forget me. You, on the other hand, are Queenie B. By this time tomorrow, you'll once again be the most famous culinary rock star in the land."

Maybe not by tomorrow, but soon.

"It was so good seeing you, Queenie." Harold pulled her into an embrace. "I'm very grateful I got to be part of it."

They'd been good friends, better adversaries. She hugged him back. "I'm glad you were here too."

"I want a rematch." He let her go, held her arms, smiled. "Soon."

"We'll see. Say hello to Charlotte for me."

"Will do."

Regina. Queenie B. Stood alone in the studio no longer full of people watching her every move. Only the blonde with the tablet, still herding those left into finishing whatever tasks they had so they could all go home. She reminded Regina of Saskia.

"You ready to go home?"

As if conjured by her thoughts, Saskia stood beside her looking as weary as Regina felt.

"I thought you left."

"I was going," she said, "after you and Harold battled it out but I . . . this whole night got me thinking . . ." Saskia moved to face her, laptop clutched to her chest, teeth biting her lower lip, just like when she was a young woman scared to death and completely in love with her disaster of an employer. "What do you think of me doing a biography? Yours, I mean. Not a tell-all from way back when, though I would have some keen insight to those years, now that I think about it. Still, I meant yours. I'd never do a tell-all, especially after all this—"

"Saskia, stop. Take a breath." How their roles had reversed. Regina's hopes for her future burned a little brighter.

Saskia took several deep breaths, morphed back into the accomplished woman who'd come to Marco's that day in New Haven to resurrect the dead. "I just thought . . . you know there will be more unauthorized books. Did you read any that came out after . . . you know?"

"Not one."

"Good. They were all trash. But it's going to happen again. You know it and I know it. It's not just ambition, Que—Reg . . ."

"Queenie is fine."

"It's not just that, though I won't deny it wouldn't be a dream come true to write. You deserve to have your story told. You deserve the respect you've earned for all you accomplished. There's more to you than the shit that kept the tabloids in business all that time." Saskia reached out, grasped Regina's arm. "Just think about it, okay? It would be an honor, and an act of love."

Slightly dramatic, but Saskia Specter was nothing if not kind, sincere, talented, and at least as opportunistic as Queenie B.

"I'll let you know."

"They canceled the inconspicuous car I got you here in." Saskia let go of her arm. "The one the network got you and Gale is out front."

"I heard. Thanks, for everything."

"Get home safe," she said. "I'll be in touch."

"You have my number."

Regina took herself—she couldn't deal with the blonde and her tablet—to the break room where Gale waited for her. He'd been chatting it up with the chef who beat him for the fifty grand. Another little bit of curls with an easygoing nature, but everyone had a type. Rhiannon was a chef. She understood his world. If Regina had her way, Gale wouldn't be around to date her; it would be a long-distance relationship at best. Maybe there was something of Julian to him, but it had been buried under everything else he became long ago. Gale had walked into her soup kitchen at the exact right moment to change both their lives. If that wasn't kismet, nothing was.

43

Mince: To finely cut up food into uniform pieces smaller than diced or chopped foods.

2016

Wow." Gale slid into the limo waiting in front of the studio for Regina—correction, Queenie B—and him. "Snazzy."

"The network knows how to take care of the talent."

"I'm just along for the ride." He dropped onto the long bench seat. "The gossip columns are going to call me your boy toy. You know that, right?"

"Not my first rodeo." She snickered. "It'll change tack after they snap a few photos of you and Rhiannon canoodling in New York. I can see the headlines now. *Queenie B loses boy toy to Grand Champion.*"

The car glided from the curb. Smooth jazz played on the sound system. New York City lights, in this city that never slept. "You're her idol, you know."

Regina shrugged. "You like her?"

"She's nice. I asked her out."

"I hear a but coming."

"I'm not looking for anything more than casual," he confessed. "I was kind of thinking, maybe I'd apply to do another competition. *Top Chef,* maybe. It's been a dream, you know. I mean, not one I ever took seriously." *Not before her. Not before now.* "I thought, maybe we could work on elevating my skills. I know I have a good palate and ideas, but I'm still all over the place. If you could—"

Regina reached across, grabbing his hand. "We need to talk."

Gale's insides gurgled. He knew what was coming. He'd avoided acknowledging it for weeks, but he had absolutely known since the moment he saw her in the studio, standing on the precipice between his Regina and the world's Queenie B, finger raised. Sitting up, he held tight to the hand holding his. "You can't go."

"I have to, Gale. The soup kitchen can't survive the return of Queenie B. Not if I'm there. It'll be nuts for a while after the article drops, but—"

"Article?"

She blew out a deep breath. "I told you, this has been in the works for a while. That woman I was with? The tall one with the dark hair? She was my assistant a long time ago, and now has her own food magazine. Marco contacted her for me—"

"Marco was in on this?"

"Will you just listen? I did an interview for *A Chef's Life*. It's coming out in a few weeks. I made sure it would be after your competition, because I didn't want it to impact it in any way."

"Why didn't you just tell me?"

"Because it's not just doing the interview. It's me coming out of hiding and all that brings with it. It's me going away and your mom and Kyle taking over the kitchen and—"

"Hold on, hold on." Gale's gurgling insides threatened to spill. "Mom and Kyle? Not me?"

"No. Not you." She let go of his hand, fingering hair from his face the way she'd done that night he'd come to her drunk and coming apart. "I asked your mother to run the everyday and keep an eye on Gladys. Kyle's taking over services. I'm hiring a proper kitchen crew to help them, but it has to stay the way it's been if it's going to serve the community it's meant to serve."

"Where do I fit in?"

"You don't. You're not for the soup kitchen, Gale, any more than I am. We were, but not anymore. I want you to come with me."

"Come with you? Where?"

"Bova, Italy," she said. "I have a house there being converted into a culinary school and adjoining restaurant. I haven't figured it all out yet but the plan is to have great chefs from around the world teaching master classes, all volunteer, of course. Who wouldn't jump at the chance to spend a week in Calabria as part of Queenie B's next great endeavor? The prestige alone will be worth it."

"Sounds expensive," Gale said. "What chef hopeful will be able to afford that?"

"Students will be on scholarship," Regina answered. "It's the restaurant that'll bring money in. Can you imagine eating in a place where Harold Javian could be your chef one night? Queenie B the next? We'll get chefs from the French Laundry, El Bulli, La Marine, Ginza Kojyu. You name it! They'll come, because Queenie B asked them to. Personally, and with charm, I promise. And the students get the best culinary education on the planet in exchange for creating and cooking and working harder than they've ever worked in their lives. Marco's going to help me run it. And you, if you will."

"Me?" Gale's voice cracked. "I'm no—"

"Don't," she snapped. "Don't say you're no one. You're a *Cut!* champion."

"And two-time loser. Seriously, Regina, how do I qualify to be part of this?"

"You don't. Not yet. But you will, Gale. Look." She flopped back in her seat. "I'm not going to force you. Marco's keeping his restaurant open. He's making Frances executive chef. You can go back to life as it was before if you want. I'll even tell Kyle you're—"

"No. You can't do that to him." Gale pushed fingers through his hair. "All he ever wanted was a food cart and he got chosen by Queenie B herself to run her beloved soup kitchen. It'd kill him."

"Just Eggs?"

"He told you?"

"He might have asked if I wanted to invest after he found out who I am."

"No way."

"He did." Regina stretched her neck, side to side. Gale had seen her after a fourteen-hour shift, splattered in food and oil and flour, and she'd never looked as tired as she did right now. Her neck finally cracked. "Got to give him credit for having the nerve. I was honest with him. It's a kitschy idea with a five-year shelf life he'd never break even on. He understood."

"I thought he'd just given up on it."

Like every other time? Even Kyle had to grow up, man.

Head back on the plush seat, Regina closed her eyes. Gale picked at his thumbnail, his cuticles, searching his gut for a reaction to all she'd told him. He understood why she'd kept it to herself, let everyone in on it but him. Mom and Kyle. Marco. It made perfect sense, even her wanting him to come with her, because, in all honesty, he couldn't imagine life without her at this point. Apparently, it went both ways.

"Okay," he said.

Regina picked up her head. "Okay?"

"Yeah." Relief, happiness, excitement, fear, flew out of his mouth like a thousand butterflies released from a net. "I'll go with you to Italy. One condition."

An eyebrow quirked.

"I get to sit in on those master classes."

And a smile. Tired, but all Queenie B. "How else did you think you were going to qualify to be part of my next great endeavor? Jeez, Gale. Get a grip."

Burn, man.

Gale would have laughed if he wasn't certain he'd start blubbering instead. He settled for a smile, flopping supine onto the long, luxurious bench seat, arms over his head. "When?"

"It was going to be a few days before the interview came out," she said. "But I think we have to move it up, after tonight. You have a passport."

"Mom has it." Gale closed his eyes. "She's going to have a cow."

"No, she won't. The last thing she wants is you hanging around New Haven the rest of your life."

True. She's been saying for years you needed to get out.

"Does she know? About Bova?"

Regina chuckled. "I had to tell her. She wanted to know why I was asking Kyle to run the kitchen instead of you."

Good old Lucy Carmichael.

Leaving his mom. New Haven. Kyle and their apartment and the soup kitchen and Marco's. This morning, when he left for the filming, he never could have imagined any of it. And now he was going to Italy with the one and only Queenie B, to be part of something truly great.

Gale tried to imagine how it would be, but he couldn't picture Italy. He'd never been. Never out of the country but the once, when his parents took his brother and him to Ireland. Danny Carmichael had family there. Lucy felt out of place. He and Brian had been so close, back in those days before Sean and drugs and the chaos of both. Gale felt bad for having lost that. Maybe he could somehow get it back. At least a close approximation. Or something better. Brian was an asshole, but Gale had, in part, created that.

Stars exploded in his brain. Confidence. Regina on the seat across from him. Italy. A brighter future than he'd ever have imagined, than he once thought he deserved.

Don't fuck it up, man.

"Shut up, Sean," he said and rolled over onto his side.

REGINA'S PHONE VIBRATED, WAKING HER JUST AS THE FIRST SNIPS OF A dream—a blue coast, the smell of fresh paint—flickered behind her eyes. Digging it out of her pocket, she squinted sleepily at the screen. She tapped into the call.

"Hey, Oz."

"Hello, Regina." Always Regina.

"Harold called you, huh?"

"Actually, it was Charlotte."

She'd have laughed louder were Gale not softly snoring from the luxurious bench seat across from her.

"I wanted to call before . . . everything that's coming. Whatever that everything entails."

"I'm glad you did." Thanks, Charlotte. Though it hadn't been done kindly, Regina was grateful. She'd never have called him. "How's Julian?"

"He is doing very well." Clipped, but not unkind. Regina couldn't blame him; it hurt, nevertheless.

"He with you?"

Gentler now. "Currently working at one of my restaurants in Jersey City. He's happy."

Jersey City. So close. Right now, she could divert the driver and be there in less than half an hour. Does he remember me? Ever ask about me? Hate me? She had no right to ask. Not yet. "That's good to hear. And your wife?"

"Fernanda is also doing well. She is a good mother to our son."

Our son. It could have meant all, or theirs. Regina left it alone. Silence hovered, threatened to smother. "I'm going to be in Bova for the foreseeable future. I'm starting a culinary school in our old house."

"I'm glad the La Cornue will finally be put to good use." He sniffed a very-Oz chuckle, turning what could have been a dig into a gentle jest. "I'm glad to know you're alive and well, Regina."

"You knew that all along. You were pretty much the only one."

"You know what I mean."

And she did. "I'm glad to be alive and well, too."

Laughing with him, softly and sadly, loosened something inside Regina, a conflicted feeling she'd only ever had for him. She closed her eyes and let it go on a breath exhaled, without even trying to dissect it.

"I hope only the best for you." The catch in his voice brought one to her own.

"Thanks. Same."

"Maybe, in time, we can even be friends again."

They wouldn't be. But it was a nice thought. A nice thing to say. And he meant it, no matter how much truth there was to Marco's opinion. They'd damaged each other so thoroughly, she and Osvaldo.

The sign-off hovered like the silence had. Across from her, Gale dreamed; she could tell by the batting of his eyes. Not Julian. Not even a substitute. Maybe just the chance to do right by someone who looked up to her. Loved her. Despite everything she'd ever done.

"Oz?"

"Yes, Regina?"

"I'll never just show up, but if Julian ever expresses any interest . . ."

"He has." So gently, it hurt. "He does."

"Really?"

"You're not easy to forget," Oz told her, the gentleness of his tone falling away. "We both know what's going to happen now. He's a grown man. He won't need my permission to contact you, but I swear on his life, if I feel you're a danger to him, I'll do everything I can to stop him."

"Fair enough."

That was all. It was sufficient.

"It is good, talking to you, Regina." Again clipped, yet not unkind. "I'm glad I called."

This time, it didn't hurt. "I'm sure it wasn't easy."

"It was not."

She would not promise. Anything. Regina had no right, and she had no heart for it. For him, yes, but for her, too. Time, that great, silent prognosticator, would tell. For now, she was too happy, too hopeful, to let the thoughts fly into their old chaos.

Staring at the lights flashing by the window, Regina didn't remember saying goodbye. Or hanging up. Across from her, on that long couch, hands tucked under his head and eyes batting dreams, Gale smiled in his sleep. The world was only just opening up for him. A grueling, backbreaking, spirit-crushing world that was brilliant and rewarding and thrilling at the same time. She'd be there for him, the way she'd never been for Julian. She couldn't make it up to her son, but Regina—Queenie B—could do better. She would do better.

Scooting across to his side of the car, Regina reclined as he reclined. Her hands tucked behind her head, eyes closed but not yet batting. The tops of their heads not quite touching, but close enough to imagine his dreams somehow mingling with hers beginning to form.

REGINA'S PHONE VIBRATED—*HEY, OZ*—BUT GALE WAS TOO TIRED TO LISTEN in. She'd tell him, if she wanted to. And if she didn't, that was okay.

The competition. Losing. Bova. Rhiannon. Bova. Regina. Queenie B. Thoughts swirled. Merged. Formed. Dreaming came like clouds rolling in over the Sound. Not a threatening roil and boom, a fog as soft as cornstarch between fingers.

"Hey, man."

Clear as day. Not a voice in his head or an afterimage ghost in his periphery. Sean. Blond and blue-eyed, no greasy hanks and pinprick pupils. That half grin that used to charm the girls curled the corner of his lips. They sat side by side, not in the limo another piece of Gale could somehow still feel rolling through New York City, toward New Haven. Savin Rock? Of course. Isn't that where it all began and ended?

"Hey, Sean."

"You did great today."

"I lost, but yeah."

"I'm happy for you."

"I'm happy for me too. I just feel so . . ." Tears didn't sting. Not in dreaming. Gale felt the warmth of them and smiled. "I feel lucky."

"You are lucky. I wasn't. You got to let it go at that."

"How?"

"You're getting there." Sean grinned that shit-eating grin of his.

"I don't want to forget you."

"But you should. Be happy. I told you a million times. You keep me around. I don't want to be haunting you. I don't want to stick around. I got places to be too, you know."

"What places?"

Sean laughed. The sound like tires on asphalt. Ocean waves. The wind coming in off the Sound.

"I miss you."

"Nah. You miss this me." Sean waved a hand from his head to his toes. "The me I was when we were kids, not the me I was when I died. We sucked, man. We really sucked. It's time to move on. Neither of us is that guy anymore."

The sway, in this nowhere, jostled them into each other. Somewhere far off, Gale heard Regina's voice, if not her words. They fluttered about in his brain, down to his chest.

"On to better things, man."

"Yeah." Gale leaned his head to Sean's shoulder that wasn't, after all, actually there. Only the leather seat underneath him. The limo. The road. The soft jazz barely audible through half dreams and exhausted slumber. Regina, no longer on the phone, in the seat opposite him, settled onto the bench seat. The top of her head didn't quite touch his, but he could feel the warmth of her. That long, dark hair streaked with white. In his half sleep already regrouping, he worked beside her in the soup kitchen that became the set on *Cut!*, that morphed into Bova that looked pretty much like the kitchen in the Rock Landing apartment she'd no longer live in, because it's all his brain could come up with but would know intimately soon enough.

Gale didn't look for Sean, or call him back, or even wish he knew what came after that "Yeah." He only dreamed.

44

Confit: Meat cooked slowly in fat.

1989

The apartment is a mess. Regina hasn't had a chance to clean up, and Marco is even more useless than she is at cleaning. Someday, when they have a restaurant or two of their own, they'll be able to afford a cleaning lady or something. Today, she'll meet the PBS people at the coffee shop down the street; they'll spring for coffee. Regina is pretty sure she doesn't have the three bucks in her wallet to buy her own.

"You sure you don't want me to come?" Marco is scrambling about, his chef coat open and in need of a wash. "I can call in."

"No, go to work. We can't afford for you to lose your job."

Kissing her, Marco grabs his keys from the bowl by the door. "You going to mention the name I came up with?"

"I don't even know if they're going to offer me the spot yet."

"Come on, baby. You're brilliant. Too big for local access."

"PBS isn't exactly network."

"It's not local access, either. You going to tell them?"

Regina rolls her eyes. "It's so stupid!"

"Regina Benuzzi is fine, but Queenie B has class."

"I think you mean kitsch."

"You could just mention it."

"Fine." She pulls him into another kiss. "I'll mention it. Now get the hell out of here."

Regina stands by the door to their two-room-plus-bathroom apartment, arms crossed over her chest, waiting until the door two flights down slams behind him. Only then letting go the long breath of relief. She doesn't have the heart to tell him she doesn't want him there, that he tends to take over. It is she PBS is coming to see and, much as she loves him, Marco will blow it for her if they think he's part of the package. Regina started her local access show on her own, attracting the biggest audience in Citizens Television history. Granted, the station is fairly new, but that's beside the point. It is this audience PBS wants to tap into, and Regina Benuzzi is young enough, talented enough, pretty enough, and charismatic enough to make it happen.

In the pitted mirror of their bathroom, Regina brushes her long hair into a ponytail, then decides against it. She's so used to tying it back, it always takes her by surprise to see how pretty it actually is. Sorting through the old lipsticks in her basket, she pulls out a bubblegum pink. Gross. She tosses it in the trash, wipes it from her lips. There's a brownish one that looks nice. Marco likes it, at least. Very early eighties. She tosses that one, too.

Digging into the bottom of the basket, she pulls out the tube of Bésame red lipstick she'd stolen from the makeup counter at Macy's a couple of years ago. She wore it the first time she went out with Marco, and hardly ever since. It makes her lips look too big, accentuates the slightly crooked bottom teeth foster care hadn't seen fit to give her braces for. Swiping it on, Regina studies herself in the mirror. She looks . . . glamorous.

Pulling her ankle boots on as she hops out the door, she doesn't think about how she looks or Marco or foster care. She keeps her mind focused on the future. On the food, the all, the everything, she lives for. If she gets this gig with PBS, she could have it all. She *would* have it all. And then the world would know Regina Benuzzi—Queenie B? Maybe it did have a ring to it—isn't just a chef.

She is a star.

ACKNOWLEDGMENTS

Thanks to my Ever-Magnificent Editor, Rachel Kahan. Her belief in and appreciation of my stories never fails to get my heart skipping. Agent Elaine Spencer, who hit the ground running and hasn't stopped. This is our first book-baby together. As always, the Knight Agency, that village raising their writers so well. I want to give special thanks to Janna Bonikowski, who read this book first, and who will always be in my corner. Special thanks to copyeditor Laurie McGee for her gift of catching all those things my eyes missed, and then some. Thank you to the whole William Morrow team, yet another village of support I can never do justice to. I am humbled by all the love, attention, and belief in these stories that trip out of my head and stumble about until we all manage to coax them into a book.

I owe my sincere gratitude to a lot of people I've never met, never will meet, and who will most likely never read these words of thanks; but you will, O reader of the acknowledgments page. Maybe you'll tell them for me, if you ever run into one.

I want to thank all the nonas, the yayas, the bubbes and abuelitas and daadis and every grandmother in every language who cooked the food of their people with love, wooden spoons, and secrecy. We are still trying to replicate the recipes you took to the grave. Thank you to the dads and uncles, brothers and sons who got past the "girliness" of cooking and took up spatula and rolling pin to charge into the breach. While the professional culinary world has traditionally been a place of men, the household kitchens are only now starting to be—and how does that work, anyway?

Thank you to every mom who got her recipes from ladies' magazines, served up their Jell-O molds and tuna-casserole masterpieces with pride-light in their eyes. Thank you to the babysitter who made fried bologna sandwiches, and the dad who thought Steak-umms were a delight. Thank you to every greasy spoon and every bad meal that sparked a kid into saying, "I can do better than this."

Thank you to the early stars—Julia Child, Graham Kerr, Jeff Smith, and Martin Yan who lit those first sparks in me on PBS, before the Food Network came along. Thank you, Wolfgang Puck and Alton Brown, Rachel Ray and Ina Garten, who came next in my obsession. Thank you, Gordon Ramsay for being a culinary/television juggernaut; not sure what I watch these days that doesn't involve you. Massive thanks to Nyesha Arrington and Alex Guarnaschelli, for taking absolutely no shit whatsoever; Queenie thanks you for that, too. Thank you to Richard Blais for growing from self-doubting hopeful to a superchef with magnificently earned confidence, right there in front of the cameras; you served as inspiration for what Gale could be. Thank you, Anthony Bourdain for your honest, public, and heartbreaking life.

Thank you, Food Network. MY WORD! Thank you.

Special thanks to *Chopped* and every amazing chef who has judged, played along, and guided the next generation of superchefs into the culinary world. I actually applied to be an amateur contestant, once upon a time. Maybe I will again.

Thank you to every cook, baker, and chef who ever competed on *Chopped, Top Chef, Master Chef, Hell's Kitchen, The Great British Baking Show, Iron Chef,* and every other cooking show I have or will come across, watch, love, and derive inspiration from, both culinarily and literarily.

Thank you to every foodie, famous or not.

Mostly, thank you to every line cook, every sous chef, every member of every brigade in every restaurant who sweats and bleeds and pours their hearts into this art that will probably never even get them a living wage, let alone stardom. You do it because you must, because food is your medium, because it is your all, your everything.

Though they got the dedication page, I have to also thank my sons,

Scott and Christofer, and my late husband, Brian. They're not just inspiration, they live and breathe on these pages in ways intended and unintended. Thanks, boys. I love you forever.

Special thanks to my Jamie, we grew up together; she taught me everything I know. And to my Grace, the ultimate embodiment of fortitude. Saying I'm proud doesn't even come close.

Last, as always, thanks to my Frankie D. He knows.

ABOUT THE AUTHOR

TERRI-LYNNE DEFINO was born and raised in New Jersey but escaped to the wilds of Connecticut, where she still lives with her husband and her cats. She is the author of the novels *Varina Palladino's Jersey Italian Love Story* and *The Bar Harbor Retirement Home for Famous Writers (and Their Muses)* as well as the Bitterly Suite romance series.